THINGS IN JARS

JESS KIDD

CANONGATE

First published in Great Britain in 2019 by Canongate Books Ltd,
14 High Street, Edinburgh EH1 1TE

canongate.co.uk

1

British Library Cataloguing-in-Publication Data
A catalogue record for this book is available on
request from the British Library

ISBN 978 1 78689 376 5
Export ISBN 978 1 78689 375 8

Typeset in Bembo by Palimpsest Book Production Ltd,
Falkirk, Stirlingshire

Printed and bound in Great Britain by Clays Ltd, Elcograf S.p.A.

MIX
Paper from
responsible sources
FSC
www.fsc.org   FSC® C018072

For my mother

Prologue

As pale as a grave grub she's an eyeful.

She looks up at him, startled, from the bed. Her pale eyes flitting fishy: intruder – lantern – door – intruder. As if she's trying to work out how they all connect, with her eyes cauled and clouded.

Is she blind?

No. She sees him all right; he knows that she sees him. Now her eyes are following him as he steals nearer.

She's pretty.

She's more than pretty. She's a church-yard angel, a marble carving, with her ivory curls and her pale, pale stony eyes. But not stone – brightening pearl, oh soft-hued!

He could touch her: stroke her cheek, hold the wee point of her chin, wind her white curls around his finger.

Her lips are beginning to move, pouting and posturing, as if she's working up to something, as if she's working up to *sound*.

Without further thought he puts his hand over her mouth, his skin dark against hers in the lantern-light. She frowns and her feet beat an angry tattoo despite the restraints and the coverlet is off. She has two legs, *like a girl*. Two thin white legs and two thin white arms and not much else in-between.

Then she stops and lies still, panting.

The touch of her: she is like nothing in nature. Skin waxy and damp, breath cold: an unnatural coldness, like a corpse living.

And that smell again, stronger now, the sharp salt of the open ocean, an inky seaweed tang.

She fixes him with her pearly eyes. He feels the slick nubs of her teeth and the quick, wet probe of her tongue on his hand.

The man fancies that his head is opening like an easy winkle, the child is tapping and probing, her fingers are inside his mind. Touching, teasing the quivering insides. She is dabbling and grabbing as with a jar of minnows, splashing and peering as with a rock-pool. She hooks a memory with her little finger and drags it out, and then another and another. One by one the child finds them, his memories. She cups them in her palm, shimmering, each a perfect tear.

A boy slips on wet cobbles, himself, following a cart with a potato in his hand.

A woman turns in a doorway with the sun on her hair, oh, his brother's wife!

A four-day-old foal stands in a green field, a pure white flash on its lovely nose.

The child tips her palm and watches the tears roll away.

Panic floods the man. Something swells in him – a pure and compelling disgust, a strong sudden urge to finish this creature off. To throttle her, stove in her face, snap her neck as cleanly as a young rabbit's.

A voice inside him, the lisping voice of a child, mocks him. Isn't he the most ruthless of bastards, wouldn't he smother his own mother without a care? Hasn't he done all things, terrible things, not stinted on the things he's done? And here he is frightened to grant the kindest of *mercies*.

The man looks at the child in dismay and the child looks back at him.

He loosens his grip on her and takes out his knife.

A lantern dips and flares in the doorway and here's the nurse. An ex-lag with a few years on her and a lame leg, clean of garb but not of mouth, used to bad business. Likes it, even. The others behind like her personal guard – two men, neck-erchiefs up around their faces. Odd birds; elbows tucked in, heads swivelling, light-stepping, listening, blinking. With every step they expect an ambush.

'Don't touch her,' the nurse says to him. 'Get away from her.'

The man, looking up, hesitates, and the child bites him, a nip of surprising sharpness. He pulls his hand away in surprise and sees a line of puncture holes, small but deep.

The nurse pushes past him to the side of the bed, glancing at his hand. 'You'll regret that, my tulip.'

She makes a show of pulling on fine chain-mail gloves and unhooks the restraints that hold the child to the bed, dressing her in a harness of strong material, one limb at a time, buckling the child's arms across her chest, lashing her legs together. The child lunges, open-mawed.

The man stands dazed, flexing his hand. Red lines track from palm to wrist to elbow, the teeth-marks turn mulberry, then black. He twists his forearm and presses his skin. Sweat beading on his forehead, his lip. What kind of child bites like this, like a rat? He imagines her venom – he feels it – coursing through him, from arm to heart, lungs to bowels, fingertips to feet. A blistering poison spreads, a sudden fire burning itself out as it travels. Then the lines fade and the marks dull to no more than pin-pricks.

All the time the creature watches him, her eyes darkening

– a trick of the lamp-light, surely! Two eyes of polished jet, their surfaces flat, so strangely flat.

The nurse is speaking low, standing back to direct. 'Roll her, bag her, make haste, watch her mouth.'

They wrap the child in canvas, a staysail to make a hammock of sorts.

The man, manipulating his arm, examining the pin-pricks, suddenly finds himself beyond words. He makes a sound, a vowel sound, followed by a string of gargled consonants. He drops to his knees, like one devotional, and falls backwards onto the hearthrug. He would scream if he could, but he can only reach out. He lies gasping like a landed catch.

From the floor he watches the two men lift the bundle between them. They move with deliberation, as if underwater.

The nurse limps over, lantern in hand, and looks down at the man. Her diagnosis: he is in a bad way, face as grey as his county-crop. Not old but already life-waned – and now this.

He begins to sob.

The nurse could sob too for the loss of a good thief, the kind who'd abstract the teeth from your head without the opening of your mouth.

She kneels with difficulty. 'Close your eyes, lad,' she whispers. 'It will help me no end.'

Trussed in a canvas hammock she's no weight. But the two men would carry a far heavier burden with greater ease. Of course they'd humoured the nurse, heard her stories in the tavern with a few inside them. But they see it now, in the child, as she said they would: all kinds of wrong.

What of the man fallen? They baulked to touch him after. The carrying of him would be worse than the leaving of him and they feel the leaving keenly. The child swings swaddled between them, big-eyed in the lantern dimmed;

oh, they see it now, in her. By the time they reach the landing the men are sweating with the effort of not dashing her head against the wall. One would shoot her through the eye in a heartbeat; the other would cut her throat in a blink. At the top of the stairs they are in danger of hurling her down.

The nurse keeps them in check. Giving whispered orders, steadying them with her strong fingers on arms and ribs.

Bringing them back to the job in hand, for the money.

'Don't think on it!' The nurse speaks urgent and low. 'Don't think on anything. Hoist her, aye, and we'll be gone.'

The big house is silent tonight, but for our intruders moving through corridors with their trussed burden and breath-held shuffle. Awake to loose floorboards and creaking doors and light-sleepers.

But the servants slumber on. The housekeeper, tidy-bedded, neat of nightcap and frill (like a spoon put away for best), inspects the linen cupboards of her dreams. Smiling at immaculate piles, heaven-fresh, as clean as clouds. The butler, proper, even in his nightshirted sleep, patrols an endless cellar. The bottles giggle in dark corners. They ease out their corks and call to him in honeyed voices. They sing songs of laden vines and sunny hillsides and duty forgotten – liquid bewitchment! He grips his lantern and will not stop. The housemaids, in their attic nests, are dreaming of omnibuses and panto-mimes. The cook snores fruity, unpeeled and well-soaked under warm sheets, as solid and brandy-scented as plum pudding. She dreams of matchless soufflés; she hunts them down as she sails in a saucepan over a gravy sea. All are senseless in the tucked-in, heavy-breathing, before-dawn quiet.

The big house is silent tonight, but for our intruders, hurrying out of the servants' door.

The dogs lie poisoned in the yard, their muzzles flecked

with spittle, a breeze ruffling their fur. This is the breeze that came over the sea, miles inland, past wood, fields and lane to whisk the gravel on the drive and dance around the rooftop chimney pots and whistle through the keyholes.

The mice are wakeful and so too is the mean-eyed kitchen cat who needles after their fat pelts, sly and silent. This snake-tailed curse of the larder watches the figures hasten across the cobbled courtyard, throwing moonlit shadows in their wake. The barn owl sees them as they round the house. She ghosts above on silent wings.

The lord of the manor. He, too, is awake.

A lamp burns in his study as he frets and puzzles, considers and adjusts. He bends over his writing, his handsome whiskers peppered with grey, his brow furrowed. He could be a fortune-teller, the way he's inventing the future, coaxing and muttering it into being.

The shadows pass outside, crossing the terrace.

Perhaps hearing their footsteps, the lord of the manor looks to the window, but, remarking no change in the night sky, returns to his plans.

The shadows move quickly over the lawn, towards the gate, two with swag slung between them, one following, limping.

The bundle is cradled over the ground. The child feels the grass whip under her canvas hammock. She feels the night air on her face and takes a breath of it and lets out a sigh you can't hear.

The sea rocked asleep, now wakes and answers, a refrain of waves and shale-song. The rain in the sky that is yet to fall, answers; a storm gathers. All the rivers and streams and bogs and lakes and fens and puddles and horse troughs and wishing wells wake and answer, adding their voices; faint and rushing, purling and gurgling, muddy and clear.

The child looks up. For the first time she can see the stars!

She smiles at them, and the stars look back at her and shiver.

Then they begin to burn brighter, with renewed fever, in the deep dark ocean of the sky.

September 1863

Chapter 1

The raven levels off into a glide, flight feathers fanned. Slick on the rolling level of rising currents and down-draughts, she turns her head, this way and that. To her black eye, as black as pooled tar, London is laid out – there is no veil of fog or mist or smoke-haze her gaze cannot pierce!

Below her, streets and lanes, factories and workhouses, parks and prisons, grand houses and tenements, roofs, chimneys and tree tops. And the winding, sometimes shining, Thames – the sky's own dirty mirror. The raven leaves the river behind and charts a path to a chapel on a hill with a spire and a clock tower. She circles the chapel and lands on the roof with a shuffling of wings. She pecks at brickwork, at lichen, at moth casts, at nothing. She sidles up to a gargoyle and runs her beak affectionately around his eyes, nudging, scooping.

The gargoyle is a creature designed to vomit rainwater from the gape of his mouth onto the porch. The parishioners (when there were parishioners) blamed the blocked gutters, but it was always the gargoyle, holding back only to let go a sudden flood upon the faithful below as they stood at God's threshold, looking up to the heavens, flinching.

The raven hops to the edge of the porch roof and peers down.

A woman is standing below: she looks up, but she doesn't flinch. Bridie Devine is not the flinching kind.

What kind is she then?

A small, round upright woman of around thirty, wearing a shade of deep purple that clashes (wonderfully and dreadfully) with the vivid red hair tucked (for the most part) inside her white widow's cap. She presents in half-mourning dress, well-cut but without flash or fashion. On top of her widow's cap roosts a black, feather-trimmed bonnet of a uniquely ugly design. Her black boots are polished to a shine and of stout make. The crinoline is no friend of hers; her skirts are not full and she's as loosely laced as respectability allows. Her cape, grey with purple trim, is short. This is a practical woman, or at least a woman who finds it practical to be able to fit through doorways, climb stairs and breathe. At her feet, a doctor's case, patched and antiquated, the leather buttery from handling.

She takes from her pocket a pipe. Here's a teaser: a *fast* habit in one so *seemly*? And isn't there is canniness to her smoking in the shelter of a deserted chapel (and not puffing down the Strand with a chinful of whiskers and a basket on her head?).

The raven eyes her with interest.

The woman winks at the bird. There is a world of devilment in her wink. The raven responds with a soft caw.

The bird gauges the gargoyle. No water falls; the gargoyle is dry-mouthed, the lips frame an empty grimace.

Reassured, the raven takes to the air.

Bridie Devine watches the raven fly out of sight. Now all that's moving in this chapel-yard are her thoughts, she thinks. The occasional cart or carriage passes the open gate. Otherwise there is a wall of a decent height between Bridie and world and that is enough.

Bridie breathes out, turning her face up to the sun: autumn warmth, fuller-bodied and lovelier than summer heat, with the mellow dying of the season in it. Bridie welcomes it on brow and cheek. That the sun has found a clear patch of air to shine through (in these days of smoke-haze and mist and fog) ought to be appreciated.

Bridie is alone with the sun and her thoughts and her pipe.

The pipe is unremarkable: clay-made, shaped to sit snug in the hand or in a tooth gap, of a cheap variety favoured by Irish market harpies. Short of stem and small of bowl so that the nose of a hag may overhang and keep the rain off the tobacco. The pipe may be unremarkable but the contents are anything but. To her usual twist of any mundungus Bridie has lately been adding a nugget of Prudhoe's *Bronchial Balsam Blend*. A crumbly, resinous substance which burns with a pleasant incense scent followed by a lancing chemical stink. This is less unpleasant than it sounds, being simultaneously bracing and dulling. You add lots of Prudhoe's *Blend* for colourful thoughts and triple that amount for no thoughts at all.

Prudhoe's *Bronchial Balsam Blend* is just one of the recreational creations of Rumold Fortitude Prudhoe, experimental chemist, toxicologist and expert in medical jurisprudence. Prudhoe's previous legendary blends, *Mystery Caravan* and *Fairground Riot*, proved either blissful or petrifying. As such, these blends continue to attract loyal followers among his more adventurous friends, Bridie being one of them.

But now Bridie's pipe is empty. She has smoked it all.

Bridie puts the bit of her empty pipe in her mouth, just while she's thinking. A drop more tobacco would be nice. It wouldn't have to obliterate her thoughts, just line her lungs.

She'll smoke anything; earthy and wholesome or treacly and nasty, costermonger's dust or gentleman's savour.

As if in answer, in the far corner of the chapel-yard, a wisp of smoke wends its way up into the air.

Bridie takes this as a sign.

Bridie looks down at the man sprawled by the showy tomb of a successful family butcher. Two things strike her as immediately wrong.

Firstly, the man is deficient of clothing (his wardrobe consisting, in its entirety, of: a top hat, boots and a pair of drawers).

Secondly, she can see *through* the man.

She is able, with perfect ease, to read the inscription on the tomb that should, by rights, be obscured by the body of the man. She can even see the angels on the decorative stone frieze.

This is an ingenious trick – like Pepper's ghost! There will be mirrors, screens certainly, black silk or some such, an illusionist's contraption, a phantasmagorical contrivance. A rudimentary search of nearby graves turns up nothing.

Bridie is baffled. If no *external* explanation for the presence of this transparent, partially clad man is evident, the cause must be *internal*. She cannot recollect transparent partially clad men being a symptom of the consumption of Prudhoe's *Bronchial Balsam Blend*. But the list is long and includes many adverse reactions, from sweating of the eyeballs to sensitivity to accordion music.

She resolves to inspect this apparition, systematically, from crown to toe.

A top hat is tipped down over the eyes of its owner. Like its owner the hat is transparent. Despite this, Bridie can see that the hat has known better days. It is dented of body and misshapen of rim. The transparent man is naked to the waist; below the waist he sports close-fitting white drawers, tight at the thighs, sagging at the knees. The boots on his feet are unlaced and his fists are sloppily bound with unravelling bandages, none too clean. He is massive of chest and bicep, strong-shouldered and thick-necked. And tattooed: stern to bow.

Below the tipped-down hat-rim: a nose that hasn't gone unbroken, a clean-shaven jaw and a shining black moustache (generous in proportions, expertly waxed, certainly rococo). In the mouth, a pipe lolls. A draw is taken from it, intermittently. The smoke has dwindled to a wisp now and has no discernible scent. On inhalation the tobacco in the pipe bowl glows blue.

Bridie wonders if the man has a pinch of tobacco to spare and, if so, whether that's likely to be transparent too.

The man, perhaps sensing her presence, pushes up his hat idly. His eyes open and meet hers. He springs to his feet in alarm, holding his fists up before him.

He is nothing short of miraculous.

The tattoos that adorn his body – how clearly Bridie sees them now – are, in fact, moving. She is put in mind of Monsieur Desvignes's Mimoscope. A device of cunning construction (a wonder amongst wonders at the Great Exhibition), pictures looped between spools, illuminated by a spark. Bridie, transfixed, saw animals, insects and machinery – static images – flickering to life, to bounce and flutter, slither and winch. Bridie watches this man with the same fascination as, in one continuous motion, an inked anchor drops the length of his bicep. High on his abdomen an empty-eyed skull, a grinning memento mori, chatters its jaw. A mermaid sits on his shoulder holding a looking-glass, combing her blue-black hair. On finding herself observed the mermaid takes fright and swims off under the man's armpit with a deft beat of her tail. On his left pectoral an ornate heart breaks and reforms over and over again.

He is a circus to the eye.

'Had a good look?' he asks.

Bridie reddens. 'Forgive me, sir, if I startled you. I was after borrowing a smoke.' She gestures to her empty pipe.

The man lowers his fists. 'Merciful Jesus, *it is you*. Is it not?' His expression turns to one of delight. He sweeps off his hat. 'Oh, darling, do you know me?'

Bridie stares at him. 'I do not.'

'Ah now . . .' He runs a hand over shorn hair, black velvet, dense as a mole's pelt, and wrinkles his strong square forehead. 'Your name is Bridget.'

'My name is Bridie.'

'It is.' The man nods. 'Your full appellation, if you would be so kind?'

Bridie hesitates. 'Mrs Bridie Devine.'

The man grins. 'What else would it be, with those eyes divine?' He pauses. 'And Devine would be your husband's name, madam?'

'*Late* husband, sir,' corrects Bridie.

The man bows. 'My sincere condolences, Mrs Devine.'

Bridie turns to go. 'If you'll excuse me, sir.'

'Won't you stay, Bridget? We could talk about the old times.'

Bridie stops. 'Sir, you are quite mistaken in your belief that you know me—'

'But I do know you: you are Gan Murphy's girl.'

Bridie's eyes widen. 'He was my gaffer.'

'I know that!' The man pauses, his expression amused. 'You don't remember me at all, do you?'

Bridie looks at him in desperation, sensing a game that could go on for all eternity. 'That is not the point, Mr—'

'Doyle.' He wanders to a grave across the way and gestures down at it. 'Not a bad spot, is it?'

Bridie follows him. She reads the headstone:

"THE DECORATED DOYLE"
Here lies RUBY DOYLE,
Tattooed SEAFARER and CHAMPION BOXER
Untimely taken, 21 March 1863
"He felled them with a bow"

'Do you know me now?' asks the dead man.

'Well, sir, you are a boxer by the name of Ruby Doyle. You have been deceased half a year, and still I do not know you.'

Ruby Doyle puts his hat back on. 'Throw your mind back, Bridget.' He taps his topper down at the crown. 'Think awhile. I'm in no hurry.'

'If this is some kind of trick, Mr Doyle—'

'Ruby, if you please,' he says, with a rakish tip of his hat rim. 'What trick?'

'You being dead.'

'Trick's on me.'

'I do not believe in ghosts, sir.'

'Neither do I – why do you not?'

'I have a scientific mind. Ghosts are a nonsense.'

'I agree.'

'A parlour trick.' Bridie looks at him hard. 'Smoke and mirrors.'

Ruby smiles disarmingly. 'A chance to pull one over?'

'A fashionable flimflam.'

'And what of table-tipping?' Ruby, who seems to be enjoying this, scans the heavens: '*Send me a sign, Winifred.*'

'Dark, overheated rooms and suggestible types.'

'Half of London is at it!'

'Half of London is duped. To believe in the existence of ghosts, spirits, phantoms – that one can see and converse with them – is deluded.'

'Are you deluded, Bridget?'

'I see you, sir, but I do not believe you exist.'

Ruby Doyle is crest-fallen.

Bridie frowns. 'If you will excuse me, I have work to do.'

'Church-yard work, is it?' He glances slyly at the bag in her hand. 'Is there a shovel in there? Let me guess: you're a resurrectioner, like your old gaffer, Gan?'

She rounds on him. 'And I look like a resurrectioner? I help the police.'

'Do you, now. In what way?'

'Working out how people died.'

'How did I die?'

'A heavy blow to the back of the neck.'

'Now that's clever. But you read about it in the *Hue and Cry*?'

'I did not.'

'*Boxer bested in tavern brawl.* I'd survived this fella trying to knock me to pieces, stepped in for a quick celebratory one and then—'

'Ruby, I'm wanted in the crypt. They have found a body there.'

'That'll be the place for it. Off you go, so. And my compliments to your gaffer – how is Gan?'

'Dead. In jail.'

Ruby stops smiling. 'Then I am sorry. Gan was one of those fellas that go on: a long, thin strip of gristle, everlasting. Do you not see him too?'

Bridie regards the man with desperation. 'Gan is dead.'

'Then am I the only dead fella you see?'

'Appears like it.'

'What about Mr Devine?'

Bridie looks puzzled.

'Your late husband,' Ruby prompts. 'You must see him?'

'Never.'

'Then I'm *peculiar* to you. Are you surprised, Bridget? Are you rattled?'

'Nothing surprises or rattles me.'

'Is that so?' He reflects on this a moment, then: 'Can I come with you, watch whatever it is that you're doing in the crypt?'

'You may not.'

Bridie walks through the gravestones. Ruby ambles alongside her. The boots, unlaced, lend a loose parry to his boxer's strut.

At the edge of the path she stops and turns to him. 'I am hallucinating. You are a waking dream.' She bites her lip. 'You see I smoked something a little stimulating earlier . . .'

Ruby nods sagely. 'The empty pipe – is it Kubla Khan you're visiting?'

Bridie is dumb-founded.

Ruby gestures at his bandages. 'Ringside doctor, recited while he patched.'

When they reach the chapel, Bridie holds out her hand. 'This is where we part company.'

Ruby smiles; it's a charming kind of a smile that gaily remakes the contours of his fabulous moustache. His eyes, in life, would have been a handsome dark-molasses brown. In death, they are still alive with mischievous intent.

'I would shake your hand, Bridget, but—'

Bridie withdraws her hand. 'Of course. Good day, Ruby Doyle.'

She heads into the chapel.

'I'll wait for you, Bridget,' calls the dead man. 'I'll just be having a smoke for meself.'

Ruby Doyle watches her walk away. God love her, she hasn't changed. She's still captain of herself, you can see that; chin up, shoulders back, a level green-eyed gaze. You'll look away before she does. She has done well for herself, with the voice and the clothes and the *bearing* of her.

If it were not for that irresistible scowl and that unmistakable hair, would he have recognised her? But then, the heart always knows those long ago loved, even when new liveries confuse the eye and new songs confound the ear. Does Ruby know the stories that surround her? That she was an Irish street-rat rescued from the rookery by a gentleman surgeon who held her to be (ah now, this is a stretcher!) as the orphaned daughter of a great Dublin doctor. That despite her respectable appearance (it is rumoured among *low* company) she wears a dagger strapped to her thigh and keeps poisonous darts in her boot heels. That she speaks as she finds, judges no woman or man better or worse than her, feels deeply the blows dealt to others and can hold both her drink and a tune. Ruby Doyle meanders back to his favourite spot, to muse on all he knows and all he doesn't know about Bridie Devine, lighting his pipe with the fierce blue flame of the afterlife.

The curate of Highgate Chapel is battling the locked door to the crypt with his collar pulled up and his hat pulled down. On seeing Bridie his face betrays surprise, which turns to displeasure when she reminds him of her business. The vicar is expecting her in relation to the delicate matter of the walled-up corpse. The curate fixes Bridie with a look of profound begrudgement and, managing to unlock the door, leads her into the crypt.

The corpse is propped in an alcove behind loose boards. Discovered by workmen clearing up after a flood, now abated. More than a few Highgate residents blame both the flood and the resurrected corpse on Bazalgette's subterranean rummagings. All well and good creating a sewerage system that will be the envy of the civilised world, but should one really delve into London's rancid belly? London is like a difficult surgical patient; however cautious the incision anything and everything is liable to burst out. Dig too deep and you're bound to raise floods and bodies, to say nothing of deadly miasmas and eyeless rats with foot-long teeth. The rational residents of Highgate defend Mr Bazalgette as a first-rate engineer and deny the existence of eyeless rats.

The corpse had been immured in an alcove; its shackles and wide-socketed expression of terror suggest foul play. This poor soul met their fate an age ago, lessening police interest in the case. This is a bygone crime in a city flooded with new crimes.

The coppers are up to the hub in it: London is awash with the freshly murdered. Bodies appear hourly, blooming in doorways with their throats cut, prone in alleyways with their heads knocked in. Half-burnt in hearths and garrotted in garrets. Folded into trunks or bobbing about in the Thames, great bloated shoals of them.

Bridie has a talent for the reading of corpses: the tale of life and death written on every body. Because of this talent Bridie's old friend, Inspector Valentine Rose of Scotland Yard, passes her the odd case – with the understanding that she stops short of a post-mortem, her unqualified status being a bar to this procedure. The cases usually have two things in common, other than having piqued Rose's interest: bizarre and inexplicable deaths, and victims drawn from society's flotsam (pimps, whores, vagrants, petty criminals and the insane). For her considered opinion Bridie receives a stipend (paid, unbeknownst to Bridie, from the pocket of Rose himself) and signs her report with an illegible signature. If anyone asks, her name is Montague Devine. In the event that she is called to give evidence, she'll give it in a frock coat and collar.

With the curate's help Bridie clears the remaining stones from the alcove. The crypt is a grim space, with a vaulted ceiling and flagstone floor. As with many subterranean, lightless places it has the climate of a year-round winter. The recent flood has left a rich, peaty smell not unlike a dug bog.

The corpse, a woman, Bridie judges, by size and apparel, is well preserved, allowing for her lengthy entombment. A macabre spectacle decked in finery. There is a cruel theatricality to her, costumed as if for a tableau vivant. A tragic heroine, a goddess – an unknown figure from history! Her gown, rotten now, could be Grecian, Roman. Her pale hair, shedding in clumps, falls onto withered shoulders. Bridie divines last moments spent shackled by the neck in the suffocating dark. It is there in the open mouth, stiffened around a howl.

The curate fusses with the lamp, swearing under his breath. He is a young man with an unfavourable look about him. Slight of stature and large of head, with light-brown hair that cleaves thinly to an ample cranium with bumps and contours enough to astound even a practised phrenologist. His complexion is as wan and floury as an overcooked potato and his mouth was made for sneering. Otherwise, Bridie notes, he is shabbily dressed for a curate and vaguely familiar.

'Sir, have we met?' she asks.

The curate regards her blankly. 'I think not, Miss—'

'Mrs Devine – I didn't catch your name, sir.'

'Cridge.'

Bridie resumes the examination. Trying to ignore Mr Cridge straining to see past her.

The corpse's injuries (bone-deep lacerations to her right arm, three broken fingers, shattered mandible, fractured orbital) tell a dark story. A shawl hides her left arm. Bridie carefully unwraps it.

'She has a child,' she says.

A baby, swaddled, no bigger than a turnip, lies in a sling beneath the folds of its mother's shawl. Bridie feels a flood of pity. There hadn't even been space to sit, pressed as they were into a shallow recess, so this woman had died standing and her baby had perished alongside her.

Mr Cridge leans in nearer and bites his lip, wearing an

expression of ghoulish excitement. Bridie is offended on the victims' behalf.

'If this is at all disturbing for you, Mr Cridge, I suggest you leave me to it.'

'I'm not in the least disturbed. How old is the infant?'

'At death: a few months old. It suckles still on its mother's finger.' Bridie peers closer. 'The baby isn't suckling the mother's finger, it's *gnawing* it.'

'Well, I'll be damned!' The curate raises his eyes to the ceiling. 'Apologies.'

Bridie frowns. 'The lantern, Mr Cridge, as near as you can, please.'

Bridie sees the baby's face, wizened now, its features vague and leathery. Bridie puts the tip of her finger into the infant's tiny mouth cavity, gently pushing past the mother's shrivelled digit.

'They are like pike's teeth,' she says, astonished. 'Irregular needles in the upper and lower jaw, sharp yet.'

'How about that . . .' murmurs Mr Cridge.

'I will need to remove the corpses for a thorough examination in decent light.'

'That will be impossible,' says Mr Cridge sourly. 'At least, not possible today.'

'It must be today; the police will expect my report.'

'The vicar is out.'

'Then I shall wait for him.'

'I will raise this matter with him directly he returns, Mrs Devine.'

'Please make sure that you do, Mr Cridge.'

The curate turns from the corpse to Bridie with a look of such concentrated enmity she is in no doubt: if he could, he'd shove her into the alcove and wall it up again.

Mr Cridge closes and locks the gate behind them and pockets the key.

'I would strongly advise you to keep the nature of this discovery to yourselves, Mr Cridge,' says Bridie. 'London has a taste for aberrations.'

'I can assure you that this matter will attract the utmost discretion on our part. Good day to you, Mrs Devine.' The curate puts his hat on, bows resentfully and heads off towards the vicarage.

Bridie surveys the chapel-yard: it is empty of partially clad, imaginary dead pugilists. Then she catches sight of it, bobbing into view above the top of the wall: a top hat. A hat that has known better days, dented of body, misshapen of rim and transparent. With a firm hold of her case Bridie takes flight, around the side of the chapel and out through the back gate. She continues along the street alone – once or twice glancing back over her shoulder, with a mixture of relief and something approaching disappointment.

Bridie, crypt-cold to the bone, is glad to be above ground. As she descends Highgate Hill, below her, in the acidulated smoke atmosphere, London glimmers. She follows the hidden Fleet townward, as the sky darkens and street-lamps are lit and the gas-lights are turned up in shops and public houses. Past St Giles, Little Ireland, where the tenements totter and the courts run vile with vice. New Oxford Street marches down the middle. The Irish hop over it and spread out to the north, forming new footholds. They have flooded this town, wave after wave of them, spilling out from their rookeries to perch in all places. On the south side the buildings turn their backs on the main road, leaning inwards, like gaunt conspirators. Change is always drawing near. Innovation waits like an offstage actor, primed and ready in the wings, biting its lip and grinning. Rag-plugged windows and crumbling bricks will give way to open landscapes of stone and sky.

The rats and the immigrants will be sent running.

But for now, the slums are as they have always been: as warm and lively as a blanket full of lice.

Bridie could find her way with her eyes shut and her nostrils open.

Try it now. Close your eyes (eyes that would be confused anyway by the labyrinthine alleys, twisting passages, knocked-up and tumbling-down houses).

Breathe in – but not too deeply.

Follow the fulsome fumes from the tanners and the reek from the brewery, butterscotch rotten, drifting across Seven Dials. Keep on past the mothballs at the cheap tailor's and turn left at the singed silk of the maddened hatter. Just beyond you'll detect the unwashed crotch of the overworked prostitute and the Christian sweat of the charwoman. On every inhale a shifting scale of onions and scalded milk, chrysanthemums and spiced apple, broiled meat and wet straw, and the sudden stench of the Thames as the wind changes direction and blows up the knotted backstreets. Above all, you may notice the rich and sickening chorus of shit.

The smell of shit is the primary olfactory emission from the multifarious inhabitants in Bridie Devine's part of town. Everyone contributes, the Russians, Polish, Germans, Scots and the especially the Irish. Everyone is at it. From Mrs Neary's newborn crapping in rags to Father Doucan squatting genteelly over his chamber pot. Their output is flung into cesspits, cellars and yards, where it contributes to London's *perilous* reek.

Bad air (as any man of science worth his monocle will tell you) sets up stall for the latest bands of travelling diseases. Cholera is the headlining act. When cholera comes to visit you'll find the lanes empty. Cholera keeps the women and the children from pump and square and the men inside scratching their arses. When cholera comes to visit, the streets are quiet. There is no bustling to and fro, no gossip and ribald laughter, only fervent prayer and the dread of an unholy bowel movement.

Mercifully there is no cholera today and so the streets are full.

Full as only London is full – and the din of it! Chanters, costers and traders, omnibuses thundering along thorough-fares, horse hooves at a clip and carriage wheels at a growl, carts and barrows at a rumble and all of London jostling in all directions at once.

Bridie heads home.

Chapter 2

Bridie Devine has, for some years, resided on Denmark Street in the rooms above the shop premises belonging to Mr Frederick Wilks, bell hanger. Mr Wilks is a very old man with the look of something that has been carefully varnished and then put away for a long time. His face is as benign as his clothes are severe. Above a stiff jet-buttoned frock coat, with the rigidity of something ossified, moons a round face with large bleary eyes and a larger man's pair of ears framing a white-haired head. Bridie suspects that the old man lives in the shop, tidying himself away into the tool cupboard at night. By day, he sits by the window fiddling with his tollers or polishing his clappers. Held upright by his coat, Mr Wilks rarely moves, but when he does it's with a sudden flapping flit, from stool to workbench and back again.

Bridie rents from Mr Wilks the two upper floors (comprising: parlour, kitchen and scullery, bedchamber and maid's attic room) and the use of a yard if she wants it. It is not the most salubrious of addresses, granted; the more genteel or less robust visitor may recoil at its proximity to slums notorious and their noxious emissions (criminal, moral and pestilential). But it's a convenient spot in a friendly street nestled between Herr Weiss, baker, and Mr Dryden, gunlock manufacturer. Bridie Devine is unquestionably the best tenant Mr Wilks has ever had. Deaf from decades of bell testing and milky-eyed with cataracts he is nevertheless able to both *hear* Mrs Devine (oh, a melodious brogue that carries!) and *see* her (oh, glorious fiery locks!).

Mrs Devine arrived at Mr Wilks's widowed. Details of the late Mr Devine's demise, previous standing in the world and other particulars of interest remain unforthcoming. Mrs Devine is held to live either *above* or *below* her station (depending on who you talk to) on account of being in possession of a 'mahogany' sideboard, a library of books and a giantess of a maid she has taught to *read* these books. This is untrue; Bridie's maid *only* reads penny-bloods (stories old and new, chiefly those featuring romances of exciting interest, highwaymen and hangings).

Then there is the fact of Mrs Devine's *occupation* further to that of a widow with a modest annuity. A plaque hangs next to Bridie's front door, which is beside Mr Wilks's front door (all cosy-like). This plaque might offer a clue as to the trade conducted upstairs:

Mrs Devine
Domestic Investigations
Minor Surgery (Esp. Boils, Warts, Extractions)
Discretion Assured

Look up. There is a locked-down, tight-lipped feel to Bridie's residence. Her front door is always closed and the windows are rarely open, the curtains are sometimes drawn and the shutters occasionally fastened. Neighbours are not encouraged to stop by for the cupeen of tea. Cora Butter, Bridie's housemaid, is impervious to the joys of gossip and will not be baited into conversation, even when she's out sweeping the front step.

Cora Butter is the only, and most terrifying, seven-foot-tall housemaid in London. The local children never tire of spying on Cora. On fair weather days she can be seen hanging out washing in the yard, singing hymns in her glorious baritone. Or else shaving in the kitchen, stropping her razor, taking time to work the soap into the bristles on her chin. And if she catches the children watching there's the joy of hearing her bass bellow lift the rooftops and scatter rats and pigeons.

If you are calling on business, then Cora will fix you with an unnerving glare and lead you into the parlour.

Cora greets her mistress at the top of the stairs. Bridie hands Cora her cape. Cora shakes it violently, wrings its neck and hangs it up.

'There's a man in your parlour,' Cora says, a testy look in her eyes.

'On business?'

Cora nods. 'He has the manner of a weasel about him. I wouldn't trust him as far as I could throw him.'

Bridie smiles up at her housemaid. Cora has never trusted a client. Cora doesn't trust anyone. And, depending on his size, she can throw a man surprisingly far.

'Does he have a name?'

'Didn't ask.'

Cora opens the door to the parlour a fraction and they look inside. The caller paces from the fireplace to the window and back again, suggestive of a state of nervous agitation.

To be fair, the room itself would do nothing to contribute to his ease. It is low-ceilinged and dreary. The lights burn dim and there is no welcoming fire in the grate, for Cora is frugal with both coal and gas. The furniture is ill-matched and includes a gentleman's writing bureau of an unfashionable design, cabinets crammed with glass bottles and bookcases stuffed with difficult reads. The sideboard is pretty and makes a stab at mahogany (but even in this light it's clearly counter-feit). The caller squints at the spines of a few books, raises his eyebrows at several and takes one from its shelf and opens it under the gas-light, only to hurriedly put it back again. He turns and notices, gathering dust on the mantelpiece, an object of mystery and interest. A large unfathomable mechanism wrought in dull metal with a rubber attachment ending in a sinister kind of nipple. A gauge of some kind, an instrument of some sort, but who can tell what?

The visitor draws nearer to this device. He puts out his finger and tentatively touches the rubber nipple, stepping back quickly as if expecting repercussions. When nothing happens he touches it again, stroking it lightly.

'See what I mean?' Cora whispers.

'He has an unpromising aspect to him.'

'It's his head,' observes Cora, 'as bald as a peeled bollock.'

Bridie frowns. 'What's his business?'

'He wouldn't say, but it'll be sneaky business.' Cora glances at her. 'Will I give him a clatter and hold him upside down until he admits to something?'

'We will try to find out what he wants without the clattering. By using our intelligence.'

Cora snorts and sails off to the kitchen. Bridie enters the room.

The caller turns and offers Bridie a rigid bow.

A man of middle age with luxuriant side-whiskers, the twin carpets of which cover his cheeks, as if to compensate for the smoothness of his pate. His chin is clean-shaven and the wire-framed spectacles he wears hooked high on the bridge of his nose are thick-lensed. This inauspicious head is set on a hotchpotch body composed of a long back, thin arms, downward-sloping shoulders and large womanly hips.

He has a pettish face, with a tense, red-lipped mouth and

tiny eyes that flicker restlessly under glass, like tadpoles. They travel over Bridie in a series of inky darts.

He expected rather more.

But then people are always disappointing in the flesh if you've heard brave things about them. And, of course, Bridie Devine would be diminished, what with the debacle of her last disastrous case.

The caller looks closely to see how diminished Bridie Devine might be.

She is small and sturdy and stalwart in appearance; she'd stand in a storm. Divested of her bonnet her hair, a riotous shade of auburn, escapes in wisps from her white widow's cap. Her eyes are prominent, muddy green and roguish, changeable in expression. The caller is instantly put in mind of harems and savages, high seas and vagabonds.

'You are here on business, sir?' asks Bridie.

'On a matter of great urgency and even greater delicacy, madam.'

'You represent yourself in this matter?'

He shakes his head. 'No, I represent a man of great social standing.'

'Good for him, and who are you that he's sent to me then? His valet?'

The smile becomes rigid. 'His friend and personal physician, William Harbin.'

'Are you now? Well, isn't that grand.'

Bridie motions him to sit and takes the seat opposite. Dr Harbin perches his backside on the edge. He's a man with business so pressing he hasn't time to sit down properly.

'And he's entrusted this matter, this delicate, urgent matter, to you?'

The smile stays fixed. Dr Harbin puts a hand up to stroke his whiskers, one side and then the next, gently, reassuringly, as if they are fretful pets about to jump off his face.

'I must say,' says Dr Harbin. 'I thought my employer was misguided in seeking out your services. I was certain that you had ceased to trade. Shut up shop, so to speak.'

'As you can see I am still here, Dr Harbin,' replies Bridie, grimly.

He throws her a sly glance. 'It shows an admirable fortitude, carrying on, all things considered. Your last case: a young boy, was it not, Mrs Devine?'

A young boy she could not find in time.

She had read the story of her failure on his body: curly-haired, web-toed, dead. Perfect but for three inconspicuous bruises, one each side of his nostrils and one under his chin. Burked. A pattern a one-time resurrection girl would recognise, even if the buyer of the corpse didn't.

'Dreadful business.' The doctor adopts a sympathetic expression. 'We heard all about it, even where we are. Miles from London.'

Yes, you peeled bollock, thinks Bridie. It was in all the bloody newspapers.

'The trouble is,' continues Dr Harbin, 'any amateur can call themselves an investigator. But is it not best to leave that sort of thing to the police?'

'The police were involved in the case you referred to, Dr Harbin. I was not the only person searching for the stolen child.'

The doctor makes a gesture with his hand, a wave of sorts, at once dismissive and conciliatory.

Bridie looks him square in his sliddery eyes. 'If you are of a mind that a police investigation is preferable, sir, then why are you here?'

Dr Harbin reddens, a deep flush inclusive of ears and nose-tip.

Bridie stands and walks to the door. She picks up the bell. 'Would you care to join me in a drop of Madeira, Dr Harbin? It could only help matters.'

Cora comes instantly into the room. She throws Bridie an impatient look. This is taking far longer than a good clatter would.

'Cora, would you bring the Madeira? The special vintage.'

Cora winks at Bridie, glowers at the guest and goes to fetch the decanter. Bridie has a plan. She'll get this arse-sponge drunk on whatever coaxing mix that is in that Madeira bottle and then he'll be rattling with news.

'To recapitulate once more, Dr Harbin: you are here on behalf of Sir Edmund Athelstan Berwick – a baronet, no less. His six-year-old daughter, Christabel, is missing and, by your reckoning, almost certainly kidnapped.'

'That is correct.'

'Sir Edmund is widely held to have no heir, that his marriage to the late Lady Berwick was without issue.'

Dr Harbin's eyes scurry behind glass; he nods.

'But now it transpires Sir Edmund had kept a small and secret daughter at his home, Maris House.'

'Yes.'

'Sir Edmund is adamant that only four people know about her existence.'

'That is correct.'

'And those people are yourself, the butler, the housekeeper and the child's nurse.'

'Yes.'

'That is, the nurse who is currently missing alongside the child?'

Dr Harbin is hesitant. 'Yes.'

'And Sir Edmund has never mentioned his daughter to anyone else: friends, relations, interested parties?'

Dr Harbin is beginning to sound weary. 'That is correct.'

'And Lady Berwick is deceased.'

'Yes.'

'When and how?'

'Is that relevant, Mrs Devine?'

'I haven't decided yet.'

Dr Harbin looks resentful. 'Lady Berwick had a tragic accident. A few days after Christabel's birth.'

'What sort of accident?'

'Drowned, unfortunately.'

'Where?'

'In the ornamental pond in the grounds of Sir Edmund's estate.'

'Lady Berwick drowned in a pond?'

Even Dr Harbin doesn't seem convinced. 'Yes.'

'So Sir Edmund's heir has passed all six years of her life motherless, hidden away?'

Dr Harbin nods.

Bridie palms her pipe. 'Do you object, sir?'

She reads the lift in his eyebrows as assent.

Bridie finds her tobacco, fills the bowl, tamps it down, lights it and raises a cloud. Then she remembers her resolve not to smoke, and instantly disremembers it.

Dr Harbin's shuffles; his long legs twitch, wanting to be gone.

'Have you a problem sitting, Dr Harbin?'

'I am anxious to return to Sir Edmund in his hour of need, madam.'

'Naturally.' Bridie smokes her pipe serenely.

Dr Harbin makes an effort to stay still.

'I am a little confused, Dr Harbin. Why would anyone hide a child away from sunlight and playmates, parties and Christmas? I'm assuming that, deprived of her liberty, the child has experienced none of these things.'

Dr Harbin looks to be studying his glass of Madeira, but it is hard to tell where his eyes are moving in the far-off depth behind his spectacles.

'The child wants for nothing,' he says. 'She has everything she needs. As for playmates, she has my own daughter, Myrtle.'

'Then there are *five* people who know about her existence?'

Dr Harbin's fingers tighten on the stem of his glass. 'Yes.'

'Is there anyone else you've neglected to tell me about, sir?'

'No, madam.'

'The chimney-sweep, or the cats' mèat man? Perhaps they have met Christabel too?'

He is riled. Bridie detects a tightening of the mouth and an increase of leg-twitching.

She smiles. 'You still haven't answered my question, Dr Harbin. Why was the child hidden away?'

'She is somewhat *unique*,' says Dr Harbin, his voice stilted with anger.

'What variety of unique?'

'Sir Edmund has not given me permission to disclose that.'

'Come, come, as the family physician you must have examined the child?' Bridie studies the doctor closely.

And there it is: the doctor winces.

'What can you disclose, Dr Harbin?' asks Bridie evenly.

Dr Harbin's hand goes up to his whiskers, for a soothing pat. 'I can disclose that the child has singular traits – I *will not* disclose what these are – which have prevented her from entering society.'

'So many mysteries! A missing girl hitherto kept a perfect secret from the world . . . that must have been difficult to contrive. But then again, six-year-old girls are usually small and quiet.'

Dr Harbin winces again. Again, Bridie notices.

'And the missing nurse, how long had she been with the child?'

'Nearly a month. Mrs Bibby came highly recommended.'

'Not very long, then – and before Mrs Bibby?'

'Sir Edmund's own childhood nurse.'

'Please elaborate.'

Dr Harbin pauses. 'She drowned, unluckily.'

'In the ornamental pond?'

'No, in a wash-tub,' says Harbin stiffly. 'She slipped and fell.'

'Dangerous place to live, Maris House.' Bridie takes a puff on her pipe. 'And you are telling me that the rest of the servants know nothing of Sir Edmund's secret child.'

'They know nothing of the child, madam.'

'Dr Harbin, you know as well as I do – having kept them and doubtlessly having read the advice pertaining to them – that servants never know nothing. They have eyes, ears, brains and an addiction to gossip. This equips them to flush out secrets like trail dogs.'

'Sir Edmund's servants are loyal and discreet.'

'You passed the child's nurse, Mrs Bibby, off as—'

'A seamstress, restoring the hangings in the west wing.'

'The west wing being where the child was kept hidden?'

'Yes.'

Bridie relights her pipe, thinking, smoking with relish. A movement in the corner of the room catches her eye. Behind the potted palm, next to the window, the dead man from the chapel-yard stands. He is rummaging down the front of his drawers. He glances up and, catching her eye, looks momentarily confused, then melts into the wall. Bridie waits, marking his point of departure, but there are no further emanations of a phantasmal nature.

'Mrs Devine, are you quite well?'

'I am, of course.' She waves her empty glass in the direction of the decanter Cora has left on the sideboard. 'Would you be so kind, Dr Harbin?'

Bridie is on her fifth glass and Dr Harbin has hardly tasted his first. He drinks Madeira like a maiden aunt, but it's of no matter; the investigation is loosening up nicely now.

'Have the police been informed, Dr Harbin?'

Dr Harbin looks cagey. 'They were called by a servant who thought that a robbery had occurred.'

'And it had, of course. But the police weren't told of the theft of the small and secret daughter?'

'No.'

Bridie nods; it's as she expected. 'The perpetrators have yet to make any demands?'

'As I left there had been no word. Sir Edmund is willing to pay any ransom.'

'Ransoming the child may not be the intention of her abductors.'

'Whatever their intention, my employer wants his daughter found as a matter of urgency,' Dr Harbin counters coldly. 'Sir Edmund will recompense you for your trouble and your utmost discretion. And hopes that you will accept a generous bonus on the safe return of the child.'

Bridie frowns. She has the bones of the case – a stolen secret heir, missing nurse – but not the meat of it.

'There's a great deal you're not telling me, Dr Harbin.'

'I've told you everything Sir Edmund entrusted me to tell you.'

'Even so, you're a bit light on the old observations, the facts as they stand, for a man of science. The doctors I know love to put their guinea's worth in.' On Bridie's face a notion of a smile. 'Are you sure you're not the valet, sir?'

Dr Harbin puts down his glass and stands abruptly. He steps forward, threat flickering darkly behind his spectacles. He reaches his hand into the pocket of his frock coat . . .

With a rush and a blur Ruby Doyle strides out from the wall and stands in front of Bridie, in a fighting stance. One hand is raised in a formidable fist, the other hitches up his spectral drawers.

Bridie stifles a laugh.

Dr Harbin, undeterred (seeing nothing but thin air between himself and Bridie Devine), pulls his hand out of his pocket.

In it sits nothing more dangerous than an envelope.

★

Bridie contemplates the envelope on the mantelpiece as she smokes her pipe distractedly, not altogether alone in her parlour.

Ruby has taken the chair opposite, having made a great act of kicking the departing doctor up his arse. He sits with his top hat between his knees, pulling on the side of his magnificent moustache; his gaze roams the room but mostly it falls on Bridie.

Cora comes in without knocking. 'What did the bollock want?'

'You heard, you were outside the door with your ears flapping.'

Ruby straightens up. 'Does this one see me? Ask her.'

'Cora,' says Bridie, pointing at Ruby in the chair, 'what's that?'

Cora glances over. 'A chair.'

'And on the chair?'

Cora steps forward and runs a large hand over the arm of the chair and the back of it. Ruby crouches in the seat.

'Lint, dust, fluff,' says Cora. 'Is this about my housekeeping?'

Bridie looks at Ruby. 'Not at all.'

Cora turns down the gas-lights. 'You took the case, then?'

'They want the child found.'

Cora studies her. 'And are you ready for that, after last time?'

'Am I to decline?' Bridie asks. 'Even mutton is no longer on the menu. I've no idea what meat you're serving but it's hard to get down.'

'It's even bloody harder to run down,' mutters Cora, mutinously. 'Well, it's up to you. If I can help, I will.'

Cora the loyal, since the day Bridie brought her home. A
decade has passed since Bridie first set eyes on Cora, huddled
in a bear cage.

It had been a rapid descent for Cora, from circus noblesse
to livestock. She had long changed hands, from her unwed
mother to the orphanage, the orphanage to a travelling circus.
Cora had toured the country as headlining act *Gertrude 'Tree-
Topping' Gigantes* and long-term mistress of Benny Whitlow, a
well-respected showman from the north of England. When
Benny died unexpectedly his nephew inherited the show and
Cora along with it. Benny's nephew devised new and sordid
variations of her act, to satisfy select audiences with infernal
tastes. The beatings started when Cora refused him. They
worsened when she tried to run away.

Bridie, visiting the circus to investigate the alleged theft
of an audience member's emerald-set brooch, heard tales of a
giantess held captive in a bear cage. She explored the camp
and found Cora.

Bridie threatened Benny's nephew with the law. When
that didn't work she threatened him with a pistol. In an act
of glorious defiance Bridie picked the lock of the bear cage,
liberated Cora, and the pair of them walked out of the circus
in broad daylight. Benny's nephew had no doubt, from the
look on Bridie's face, that she would shoot anyone who tried
to stop them. Thereafter, Cora appointed herself Bridie's
housemaid. Bridie hasn't had a decent meal since.

Cora lays a frugal fire. 'You leave tomorrow for the scene
of the crime?'

'Maris House, Polegate.'

'A proper nob?'

'Sir Edmund Athelstan Berwick, no less.'

Cora grunts. Nobs are one and the same to her. She gets

up, wiping her hands on her apron. At the door she turns back, nursing a question.

'I'll find her, Cora,' says Bridie.

'Else you know where she'll end up?'

Bridie nods grimly.

Cora gives her a stern, sad, splay-toothed smile and is gone, whistling down the corridor with the coal-scuttle clanking against her muscled calves.

Bridie settles back in her chair to smoke her pipe and watch the mean little fire in the grate.

'Where will the child end up? If you don't find her?' Ruby's voice is soft.

'You, sir, followed me home from Highgate Chapel, entered my home without invitation and eavesdropped on my confidential business.'

'I did, madam,' admits Ruby, his expression unrepentant.

Bridie studies him carefully. He is no less wondrous now than he was in the chapel-yard. She sees him in perfect detail, from the mud on his boots to the loose button on his drawers and unravelling bandages on his fists. Yet through his bare chest she can see a tapestried cushion and the antimacassar on the chair behind him.

'Why are you here, Ruby Doyle?'

'There's no life at all in that chapel-yard.'

Bridie ponders this. 'Why would you not be in a Catholic church-yard?'

'I am where my friends saw fit to put me.' His face falls. 'They drank the money.'

'Ah no, they put up that nice headstone for you,' says Bridie, kindly.

'So they did.'

Bridie rekindles her pipe, giving it a few rapid shochs. She squints at the dead man through the smoke. 'I'm not in the market for a haunting.'

Ruby opens his bandage-bound hands. 'I'm not haunting you. I just thought seeing as we're old friends—'

'You would follow me home and haunt me. As I told you before, I don't know you.'

Ruby leans forwards and lowers his voice. 'Now, what did the big fella in the dress mean about the stolen child? Where will she end up?'

'Don't digress. Cora is not a fella, she's a lady.'

The ghost looks incredulous.

'I'm not joking.'

The ghost looks sceptical.

'You heard what Dr Harbin had to say, you were there hiding in the wall.'

'Rum bloody cove.'

Bridie smiles wryly. 'Thank you for saving me from him.'

'In my experience, if a fella hops up and reaches into his pocket he's likely to produce something that will sting a bit.'

'I appreciate your solicitude, Ruby.'

A polite nod. 'You were saying, about the child.'

'The stolen child, as you yourself heard from Dr Harbin's testimony, was born different. What Cora was alluding to are the three reasons why a child who has been born different—'

'Like little Christabel Berwick.'

'Like Christabel Berwick, should have been taken. For the obtaining of a ransom, for the collection of a private anatomist, or for a life as a circus curiosity.'

'A private anatomist?'

'A loose term, Ruby, I use it to denote individuals of considerable means with an unhealthy interest in the darker aspects of nature's diverse bounties.'

'How is the child different?'

'Your guess is as good as mine, Ruby.'

Ruby sits quietly, lost in his ruminations, absently stroking the battered silk of his spectral hat. Then: 'I'm at liberty, if you'd like a bit of assistance with the finding of the child.'

'I work alone.'

'Would you not make an exception, for an old friend with time on their hands?'

'I wouldn't.'

Ruby points to the picture over the fireplace. 'That's Ireland there.'

'Wicklow.'

'It's a likeness: the mud and the hills and the rain.'

'I hardly remember it.'

'I knew it was you,' he says, 'as soon as I saw you standing in the chapel-yard with your red hair spilling out from under your wee cap. I said to myself, "Holy Mother of God, there goes Bridget. Green eyes and a biblical temper."'

'What do you know about my temper, or my eyes?' Bridie puts the bit of her pipe between her lips.

'I'm tormented watching you.' There's a gleaming smile on him now.

Bridie narrows her eyes. 'Meaning?'

'What I'd do for a smoke.'

'Then don't watch me.'

They sit before the fire.

When Bridie glances up she finds Ruby studying her. Feeling a sudden heat in her cheeks, Bridie moves her chair further from the hearth.

Ruby casts her an arch look. 'It was you that conjured me up out of the ground, Bridie. I heard your little feet trotting above me and up I came, running after you.'

The tenderness in his saying of her name is not lost on her. She runs a stern eye over him. 'You were already conjured up, Ruby, slumped against a tomb. Besides, how could I conjure someone I don't know?'

Ruby stands. He arranges himself in front of the fire, as if warming his backside. 'And you really don't know me?'

'Jesus, just tell me,' says Bridie, and immediately regrets the saying of it.

There in Bridie's words is her trust in the truth of it: that they have known each other. And there in her words is her wanting of an answer.

On Ruby's face: triumph. The anchor tattooed on his arm lowers itself gracefully. The mermaid smiles into her looking-glass.

'You're the investigator, you fathom it.'

And with that, he drifts through the wall with a wink.

Chapter 3

The nurse, Mrs Bibby, sits with her bad leg on an upturned bucket. Strong and square of body and delicate of wrist and neck, with long deft pickpocket's fingers, she gives the impression of heavy ballast combined with nimble grace. She is in midlife, but truth be told she has never looked young. In her physiognomy one can detect the vicissitudes of decades of hard and soft living. There is something predatory about her, a wild slyness to her eyes, which are very blue and very wide apart. She has a flattened nose and negligible eyebrows. A wide, generous mouth takes up the rest of her face, with several teeth to each side lost. This gives her the air of a raffish tomcat. As does the scar above her eyebrow, the deep nick to her ear lobe and the stump of her missing index finger. Her hair, a greying mouse, is moulded into a remarkable arrangement; a severe parting in the middle with two fluffed cones high on each side of her head. Her face is mesmerising, moving as it does from wide-eyed innocent to vinegary crone in a matter of seconds.

The child, it seems to the nurse, never tires of watching her, or of listening; but then Mrs Bibby's voice, like her face, changes constantly. Every kind of voice lives inside her, from prim to wheedling, high-stepping to raucously lewd. After the previous nurse, who lay face down sleeping off her gin habit for the best part of six years, Mrs Bibby is a spectacle.

The child is observing her now; her eye peeping through the door of the vestry cupboard left ajar. This is where the good doctor saw fit to lodge the mite. He has brought lanterns and set them about so she can be kept in sight.

Mrs Bibby winks; the eye disappears. She returns her attention, forthright but caring, to Dr Harbin.

'With all due respect,' she says smoothly, 'I would advise you to rein it in, sir.'

The doctor, who is pacing the length of the room, halts. 'We can't afford this delay, Mrs Bibby. What if the buyers renege? If they find out that *he* knows that he's been . . .'

'Rooked, sir?' completes Mrs Bibby.

The doctor grimaces.

'Well, *he* would have to find out at some junction, he's all eyes and frigging ears. But those Parisians, now they're at a distance. And I ain't about to tell them you've bubbled your rightful buyer.'

Dr Harbin stares hard at her.

Mrs Bibby throws a devoted look up to the ceiling. 'Before my light and saviour, ain't we in this together, Doctor?'

'What have I done?' he whispers. 'Of all the people to cross.'

The inky dabs of his eyes dart behind his spectacle lenses. There's a newly haggard aspect to the doctor's countenance, as befits a damned man.

'This whole enterprise is slipshod.' His eyes fall frostily upon the nurse. 'How could there be no carriage?'

'The jarvey was delayed, sir, wheel trouble, it can't be helped.'

'And when he arrives I know what I'll find: a drunken coachman with a team of glue nags and a superannuated carriage that I could outpace on foot.'

Mrs Bibby's expression remains unchanged but there is a note of irritation in her voice. 'Would you have it above-board, all traceable-like?'

The doctor doesn't answer.

'Still, we found this place to hole up in and ain't that a fountain of luck, sir?'

'Mrs Bibby, we are not even a mile from Maris House yet.'

'Dr Harbin, all plans have their hitches. I doubt if Sir Edmund will have the coppers out searching.'

'Bridie Devine, she'll be searching.'

'Then we're frigged, entirely!' she laughs. 'Doctor, take heart, soon we will be across the Channel.'

'What if—'

'And the French will be clamouring to buy your little oddity of nature.'

The doctor rubs his pate with the flat of his hand in a comforting, polishing motion. He turns to her and opens his mouth.

'It's all arranged, sir,' Mrs Bibby says quickly. 'Carriage, Dover, first light.'

Dr Harbin starts pacing again. 'It must be tomorrow – the road is long, the risks increasing—'

'You're right there, Doctor,' pipes up Mrs Bibby in a helpful tone. '*He* might catch up with us yet, to say nothing of the other collectors out there. With an eye and a nose for goods on the move that they can add to their *cabinets of curiosities*, their *wonder rooms*. Oh – you know about them collectors, do you?'

Dr Harbin's face says he might.

'Mercenary types, Doctor. Un-gentlemanly.'

'I'd rather not think about that.'

'Word gets around, don't it?' She gives him a contented smile. 'Risk of ambush. Or being stopped by coppers.'

'Coppers?'

Mrs Bibby nods, blithely. 'Sir Edmund may not alert them but they'll be out there all the same, meddling. In villages, along the lonely roads, suspecting, searching.' She points at the vestry cupboard. 'Try explaining that.'

Dr Harbin is harried. 'What should I do?'

Mrs Bibby picks up her book. 'Oh, staying sanguine is all you can do, Doctor.'

The doctor collapses into a chair. From time to time he shakes his head with something like disbelief.

Mrs Bibby feels for him. This is strong business for a weak man.

'And no more impromptu burials.' He gestures with disdain at the muddied knees of his trousers. 'Promise me that.'

Mrs Bibby merely looks at him, placidly, half-amused.

'Do you realise how hard it was to get that body out from under Mrs Puck's bloody nose?' The doctor seems unnerved at the thought.

'Our fallen comrade,' laments Mrs Bibby. 'As I said: all plans have their hitches, sir.'

She watches the doctor a moment, then returns to the book in her hand.

The child shuffles to sitting along the wall of the vestry cupboard. She wears a costume so that she will not bite herself or others. It is made of strong material and buckles. It is a job of work to get out of it; despite that, she has a foot loose. There is some slack in the ankle strap so she can shift along the cupboard floor.

'The Kraken is short-tongued tonight,' says Mrs Bibby from the chair.

The child nudges the cupboard door open a bit wider with her foot.

'Playing mum? You understand more than you let on.' Mrs Bibby puts down her book and reaches for the bottle on the table next to her. 'Because I am dosed to the gills on Mother Bibby's Quieting Syrup and enjoying this pleasant change of scenery, we shall have an instructive story.'

The child looks at her blankly.

'You are going out into the world, Christabel, and it is only right that I should prepare you. Impart some of my wisdom and experience, so to speak.'

Christabel is silent.

'Such as, people in polite company don't use their feet to eat snails.'

As if in defiance, Christabel delicately picks up a snail between her two toes and bends her face to her foot.

'It's not well-bred,' adds Mrs Bibby. 'At least use your fingers.'

The child, inspecting the snail, ignores her.

Mrs Bibby takes a nip, corks the bottle and lays it in her arm crook. 'All right, so. In the old days . . .'

There lived a witch. And how do you recognise a witch? They run orphanages in Wanstead and like eating babies. This witch ran an orphanage and was an expert in selecting the choicest of babies. She enjoyed the plump babies with savoury gravy and drop dumplings, the lean ones she'd spatchcock and griddle with onions. Above five years old children were stringy and barely edible. One day a girl came in who was thin and five and there was no eating on her. Let's call her Dorcas. Life at the witch's house was difficult for Dorcas. She was—

'What was Dorcas like?' muses Mrs Bibby. 'I'm frigged if I can remember.'

Dorcas was a plain girl with a limp to her left leg. This was on account of her mother trying to lose her down the privy when Dorcas was born. A policeman fished her out by the ankle – and shook her by the ankle to get her started up again. Her mother swung for it and Dorcas's leg was never the same. It wasn't the policeman's fault of course, you never can tell if a good act will turn bad, no more than if a bad one will turn good. At the witch's house there were beatings and starvings (in that respect it was the same as every other orphan house Dorcas had lived in). Now it came about that one day a new baby arrived. The baby was not more than six months old and a fine fat chap with smiling blue eyes and rosy-pink cheeks. Dorcas, knowing the baby's fate, for the other orphans had told her all about the witch's tastes, devised a bold plan which would free all of the orphans, including herself, from the witch's tyranny—

Mrs Bibby breaks off. 'Put that bloody snail down. I see what you're doing.'

Christabel stops licking the snail shell and eyes the nurse through the open cupboard door.

'You heard.' Mrs Bibby waits.

The empty shell is delicately dropped on the flagstones. The foot slowly retracts itself into the cupboard.

Mrs Bibby nods.

Dorcas already knew how to do for rodents. You got the poison from the store, put it in the mush the rats liked and then you waited. Sometimes the high stink said that the rats had crawled somewhere to die. Dorcas was the one to go after them. It was a job she liked because no one else had the stomach. Dorcas decided that if she grew up she would become a rat-catcher. In the meantime, she would poison the fat baby; the witch would eat the baby and thereby be poisoned too. It would be quick for the babe (if the rats were anything to go by), saving him a long roasting . . .

Mrs Bibby pauses, leans forward, biting her lip against the pain from her leg and peers into the cupboard. The child has her eyes closed, she has worked one of her hands lose from her restraints and holds it between her head and the cupboard wall, palm to cheek. The child, roused by Mrs Bibby's silence, shambles upright.

'You want the rest of the story?'

Christabel looks at her with unblinking pearl eyes.

'The relentless demands of it.' Mrs Bibby, wincing, takes another nip from her bottle.

Dorcas mixed up the poison in a milk jug, enough for a score of rats. Then she put the poison packet away at the back of the store. Dorcas knew that if the witch suspected anything she wouldn't eat the baby and it might be a while before another fine plump baby came to the orphanage. Then she set flour, suet and a mixing bowl in readiness for the dumplings and laid a place at the table and put the cruets ready. Her preparations complete, she lugged the fat baby boy up into her lap and fed him the rat medicine. He waved his fists with delight when he saw the spoon coming, but when he tasted it, his face crumpled and he spat out the mixture and began to cry. Dorcas, who had picked up babies all her life, swung him backwards over her knee to surprise him. Her trick worked, his mouth opened, Dorcas spooned the poison in. Fighting with the baby made her hot and cross. She didn't realise how hot and cross until his body went limp, his mouth bitter with poison, his face flushed and his curls damp on his head. How her arms ached. Dorcas was not much bigger than the baby after all. She put the baby in a roasting tin, tucked a napkin over him and waited.

★

The child wakes to a brightening morning. The vicar's vestments, his cassocks and surplices, hang above her. She touches the hem of a stole with her free hand, strokes it between her thumb and forefinger. A sudden scramble in the cupboard and the child snatches.

'Going fishing?' laughs Mrs Bibby, who has been watching her.

The nurse is even more tom–cattish than usual. The fluffed cones of her hair are lopsided and she has scratches across the bridge of her nose and on her cheeks. While Christabel has been sleeping Mrs Bibby has been fighting.

Christabel opens her fist, carefully, carefully.

'Oh, strong wriggler!' Mrs Bibby mimes feeding herself and the child mimics newt to mouth.

She kisses the newt.

'One of your subjects, Lady Berwick, like these ladies and gentlemen.' Mrs Bibby gestures at the snails that stud the vestry walls. More are making their way across the floor towards the cupboard. They puddle the flagstones; there will be a moat of them soon.

The child inspects the newt's spotty body and tail, its limbs and digits and the shiny disks of its eyes. She strokes its snout with its two neat nostrils, with the tip of her fingernail. It wiggles, and, holding it tighter, she puts it into her mouth, biting the head clean off. She looks down at the body in her hand. A twitch, a shudder and still.

'Poor little bleeder.' Mrs Bibby smiles.

The child strokes the newt's soft belly against her lip, watching the early sun slant across the flagstones, following the snails.

Chapter 4

Bridie Devine travels neat and light with her old leather case and short cape, her white widow's cap and ugly black bonnet. It is early yet, just after dawn. Below her, rats swarm along the ancient covered rivers, the lost tributaries, Styx-black and subterranean, under London's feet. Above her, gulls wheel through still air. She crosses over the bridge. Mud-larks wrapped in rags are coming down to the low-tide, fog-wound Thames. Clinging to their long staffs, they walk out from the bank. The mud accepts them, sucking their little limbs sore with possessive kisses. They wade out into freezing water, watched by the stately herons that survey all with an ornamental disdain. The herons listen too, to the thin high song of the mud-larks, a song of things lost and found, of spools and nails, bones and coins and copper wire.

It is early yet and the costermongers are rising tired. They have felt the weight of their barrows all night as they bucked and swore between the juggernauting omnibuses of their dreams. The factory workers, too, are climbing from the warm sour pits of their families to walk to work with a heel of bread in their pockets and their hair on end. Kitchenmaids wake into their bodies and find themselves already up and staring at the cold coals of the unlit breakfast fire. Above them, their mistresses turn on frilled pillows, dreaming of steaming teapots and pug dogs. The senior clerks are rising in the suburbs, fastening collars and finding their omnibus fares. The junior clerks are checking for cuff fray and putting their patched and polished best foot first. They join the legions wearing London Bridge's pavement smooth twice a day.

It is early yet, and here are the ladies of the town about to turn in after a supper of new hot rolls straight from the bakers. They loll, hatless and bare-armed, red-lipped and rouged, in early morning doorways. Smoking, laughing, calling, they smile at Bridie, some address her by name, the lone woman walking the waking city.

Or is she alone?

Bridie checks behind her. Still nothing.

Ahead is Victoria Station, with its smart new train shed roof to shield the distinguished residents of Pimlico and Belgravia from the offensive emissions of the train: smoke and steam and the clatter of passengers and the hallooing of guards and the screeching and hissing of engines. Bridie passes the wooden huts erected in lieu of brick-built buildings when the works' fund ran out due to the smart roofing.

She checks behind her. Nothing still.

And now she sees him: dim in the brightening morning, the dead man, sloping round a hut, walking towards her as if he's been waiting for ever. Ruby Doyle, his dark eyes glowing, wearing little more than a top hat, drawers and a smile.

Bridie looks out of the window of the London Brighton & South Coast Railway carriage, watching the landscape change before her eyes. River and road, village and farm, the world remade at every moment. Coal smuts fly past and the train ploughs forwards, fire-bellied and smoke-spitting, a mystery of steam pressure and pistons, a miracle of gauges. The engine is a painted comet, its tail rattling behind with every class of passenger hanging on. Many undertake this mode of transportation with nervous trepidation, as well they might; it is well known that regular rail travel contributes to the premature ageing of passengers. Unnatural speed and the rapid travelling of distances have a baleful effect on the organs. Hurrying can prove fatal, notably when combined with suet-based meals, improving spirits and fine tobaccos. The worst offender: the new-built, gas-lit, steam-hauled carriages of Hades which will convey a passenger between Paddington and Farringdon *under* the very ground of the metropolis. According to reports miscellaneous, the passenger (smoke-blinded, nerve-rattled, near-suffocated) will emerge from the experience variously six months to five years older.

On the *over* ground train: there is no portion of it wholly conducive to safety or comfort. First-class offers all the advantages of tasselled curtains but is apt to be stuffy. Third-class promises an atmospheric ride buffeted by the weather and a choking stream of smoke. Second-class passengers have a roof but worry about their proximity to third-class.

In second-class there is additional cause for concern today: a woman who talks to herself. Small and handsome, with fine eyes and an ugly bonnet, she has been whispering emphatically to the empty seat opposite her since the train left Victoria Station.

Now she is ignoring the empty seat and staring silently out of the window.

The other passengers glance sympathetically at each other and return to their books or their musings.

The peace doesn't last.

The small, handsome woman begins to eye the seat belligerently. 'That is not the point,' she announces, in a fierce whisper.

She listens awhile to the empty chair, chewing her lip. Then: 'You are not a help, you are a hindrance – following and haunting and heckling—'

She hits her forehead with the heel of her hand. More than one passenger jumps. 'If I remember, you will vanish?'

There's an audible tutting from several occupants of the carriage.

A red-faced gentleman seated in the corner intercedes waspishly. 'If you would kindly lower your voice, madam.'

Bridie turns to him, maintaining a haughty tilt to her nose. 'I beg your pardon, sir?'

'You do realise, madam, that this is a *second-class* compartment?'

'I am not here by *choice*, sir.'

The red-faced gentleman raises his eyebrows.

'I am here under the auspices of my employer,' Bridie continues. 'If I was situated in third-class I would no doubt be enjoying a song and a meat pie right now. In first-class, I would be partaking in cigar and some tip-top-gallant gossip.'

The red-faced gentleman opens his mouth to speak. Bridie holds up her hand.

'But, being as second-class is gloomier than a funeral carriage, I am forced to make my own entertainment, sir, which is talking to this . . . seat.'

The confounded red-faced gentleman closes his mouth.

Bridie extends a recalcitrant glare to the rest of the passengers, who shrink into their frock coats.

'Furthermore,' she hisses to the seat, 'I will in future be ignoring your lascivious grins, cryptic messages, baggy-arsed drawers and illuminated bloody muscles.' She narrows her eyes. 'What person, in full possession of their reason, would choose to swagger through eternity half-naked with their boots undone?'

The red-faced gentleman looks on helplessly.

'All the legions of the glorious dead,' she informs him, pointing to a patch of air, 'and I'm plagued by that.'

At Polegate Station Bridie finds Sir Edmund's carriage waiting to convey her to Maris House. The weather has turned and the rain lashes with no let-up. Although it is early afternoon the lanterns on the carriage are already lit and the rain runs from the waiting coachman's nose and cap-brim. It pours, too, from the tails and bridles of the horses.

The ride is bad: the brougham has poor suspension, and the roads are rough in parts. The interior has been made sombre with dark-coloured plush and has the faint smell of mice and straw. The upholstery is thick enough to offer some protection to the fundament, but the experience is like being shaken to death in a velvet-lined horsebox. With no outward view from the steamed-up windows Bridie has time to contemplate the Berwick crest on the opposite wall of the carriage: two rampant moles and a baffled griffin.

The horses, skittish, slide on the rain-washed road, their ears flat. The driver doesn't know what's got into them; they've been acting queerly since he picked up Sir Edmund's London visitor. He can't imagine why; it's only one lone woman in an ugly bonnet. He blames the weather and the dark road through the woods to Arlington. The horses brace their flanks against the lurching movement of the carriage as the iron-trimmed wheels slip into divots and potholes.

When the rain relents, Bridie puts down the window and looks out at a shabby inn and a muddy farm, a duck pond and a deserted village green. Then there are just trees again and a few fields. She sits back in her seat and bounces on.

And where is Ruby?

He has sculled up onto the roof of the carriage, where he lies smiling at the rain that falls through him. He blesses every mud-spun field that passes by and every cloud above him.

He grins. She hasn't changed a bit. God love her.

The light is dying when the driver pulls up at the gates of Maris House. A stiff breeze is blowing the weather over; the clouds are no more than tattered dishrags now. The driver helps the visitor down. She'll walk up to the house to get some air, she says, as she finds her pipe. A way up the drive she hears the sound she hasn't been listening for – a footfall with a loose-laced step to it.

She doesn't turn, but rather concentrates on her first impression of Maris House as she approaches.

Sir Edmund's home is an architectural grotesque, the ornate façade the unlikely union of a war-ship and a wedding cake. A riot of musket loops, carved shells, liquorice-twist chimneys, mock battlements, a first-floor prow and an exuberance of portholes. On the carved stone pediment above the wide front door Neptune cavorts with sea nymphs. The lower floor windows are festooned with theatrical swags of stone starfish and scallop shells.

For all this, the house looks unlived in.

Rounding the side of the building, Bridie sees that the servants' quarters give the best welcome; the lights there have been lit.

A new pack of dogs have been let loose in the grounds, in the stead of those poisoned the night of the abduction. They run to Bridie and press their noses into her hands briefly, to find that she is not made of hot panic like peasants and poachers. Nor is she made of woolly fear like the men of the road who wash up on lawns casting for alms. This woman is made of boot polish and pipe smoke, clean cloth and the north wind. And as for the dead man walking behind her, well, he means no harm. He smells only faintly of the afterlife, cold and mineral, like new snow. The dogs return to the business of scratching and sprawling in their kennels, for there are no intruders here.

Sir Edmund Athelstan Berwick is following a circuit that runs from the terrace to the rose garden, the rose garden to the dovecote, the dovecote to the pond, and the pond to the rhododendron vale. It is a vigil that pre-dates the theft of his daughter; Sir Edmund has long had an unquiet mind.

He has been ruminating on the curses of his bedevilled existence. Sir Edmund has been blessed with supernatural bad luck. As a consequence he is uncommonly superstitious for an engineer and amateur naturalist – a man of industry and science! He keeps a rabbit's foot always upon his person and banishes black cats from his estate. Otherwise he draws comfort and perturbation in equal measure from the invigorating ministries of Mr Darwin. So that when he is not considering his own eternal damnation, his head fairly clangs with questions apropos brave science, religious dogmatism and the length of a giraffe's neck.

Sir Edmund steals himself daily against forces which lie in wait to punish him for his dark and secret infatuation with unnatural nature. Sir Edmund is a collector, an insatiable, relentless collector, with an interest in anomalies and mutations, aberrations and malformations of life in or around the realm of water. If it swims or paddles or blows bubbles in any way oddly, then he'll have it killed, stuffed or put in a jar and brought to his private library. Sir Edmund has sold off half his ancestral estate to fund his passion and participated in schemes ruinous to his peace of mind. Like the oologists who destroy future chicks in their lust for the egg, so the forces of acquisition and preservation, discovery and destruction wage war in Sir Edmund as in every collector. Take John Hunter. On one side of the coin: anatomist, surgeon and distinguished scientist. Flip the coin over: sick-man stalker, coffin robber, rabid boiler of an Irish giant's bones.

Sir Edmund has done wrong in his collecting. He has been ruminating on his wrong-doing and on the punishments (legal and spiritual) he might reasonably expect. And so rounding the house in a heightened state of remorse and morbid dread, Sir Edmund readily mistakes Bridie Devine for a retributive being of the underworld. A banshee perhaps, or a malevolent imp; it is dusk and her bonnet has the air of a demonic presence perching mid-flight. It takes Bridie several minutes to coax the baronet out of an hydrangea.

Gazing at Bridie by firelight, Sir Edmund isn't so sure. She sits comfortably in his study with her pipe in one hand and a sherry in the other. Sir Edmund doesn't doubt that Bridie's the sort of person who makes the most of every soft blessing. She is a riveting figure; Sir Edmund is riveted. A pleasantly stout, good-looking woman dressed in a purplish travelling twill. An outfit too warm for the room so that her face shines with perspiration, which, combined with her plump wool-swaddled breast, gives her the appearance of a delicious moist pudding. Her spectacularly ugly bonnet is curled up before the fire, bristling with feathers. She refused to give it up into the hands of the butler. Not that the butler was over-eager to take it. If it comes alive, Sir Edmund thinks, he will do for it with the poker.

Bridie Devine is a fairer prospect without her bonnet.

The red hair that peeps out from under her widow's cap is rich in the firelight, is likely abundant. When she raises her dirty-green eyes to him his mind conjures images of fickle wood nymphs in dappled glades.

He wonders if he can trust her.

'You could be an apparition, Mrs Devine,' smiles Sir Edmund. 'There's something very other-worldly about you, *ethereal*.'

By a bookcase, Ruby stifles a laugh.

Bridie smoothes her skirts over her solid knees and throws Ruby a sharp glance. 'I can assure you that I'm not an apparition, Sir Edmund.'

Sir Edmund looks at her closely and she looks back at him. How far can she see with those sharp brigand's eyes: into his mind, yes, or into his soul?

God help him!

All Bridie sees is that Sir Edmund is a tall, shabbily elegant man with doleful eyes and stately whiskers. His study is as it should be: wood-panelled, leather-chaired, and cigar-scented, exuding grandeur and solidity. But the man who occupies it is unsteady. He's like a rare vase, one that's suffered a break, has been mended badly and now, near useless, has been relegated to an occasional table in the corner.

'Dr Harbin outlined the particulars,' Bridie begins. 'I have the bones of the case but not the meat, if you'll pardon the expression. A few questions for you, sir.'

Sir Edmund, who is usually pacing the herbaceous border at this time of the evening, wedges his hands under his knees to stop himself from rocking. 'Go ahead, Mrs Devine.'

'Do you have any enemies, sir?'

'None, madam.'

'Are you certain?'

'Yes, entirely certain,' says Sir Edmund, not looking at all certain.

'Is there anyone you know who could have taken Christabel?'

Sir Edmund shakes his head.

'And you're confident about that?'

Sir Edmund nods, looking not at all confident.

'Sir, I must ask you what Dr Harbin refused to tell me: why did you keep your daughter a secret?'

Sir Edmund rises slowly. He walks to the window. The

rose garden awaits him, and the folly, and the orchard, and the road beyond. He has many miles to walk tonight. Sleep will come at dawn, or not at all.

'I feared this would happen.'

'You feared that your daughter would be taken?'

'Yes.'

'Why, Sir Edmund? Why would you fear that?'

The man's face is bewildered.

'The doctor mentioned that your daughter has *singular traits*. Could you elaborate?'

'They are somewhat . . .' Sir Edmund looks evasive. 'Slippery.'

Bridie endeavours to remain patient. 'Sir Edmund, if these *singular traits* somehow led to Christabel being abducted, then you must enlighten me – it may help me find and restore your daughter to you.'

Sir Edmund sighs. 'On the subject of Christabel, madam, I cannot enlighten you.'

Bridie puts down her glass. She fixes the baronet with a flinty look. 'Then let's try this question, sir: why did you send for me, rather than seek the assistance of the local constabulary?'

The baronet reddens, opens his mouth and closes it again.

Bridie waits.

Finally: 'Christabel makes you *remember*.'

'*Remember*?'

'Yes, memories you hardly knew you had. Not unpleasant, but' – he falters, frowning – 'then she also makes you think *thoughts*.'

'*Thoughts*?'

'Unfitting. Not entirely your own,' he replies quietly.

Bridie glances at Ruby; he is tapping his temple with his finger.

'It is hard to explain.' Sir Edmund smiles a brief sardonic smile. 'She *looks* at you and the thoughts come.'

With a sigh he gets up and goes to his writing desk, opens a drawer and takes out a silver-framed picture. He hands it to Bridie.

A fair-haired child sits in a chair, wearing a white floor-length gown. She seems to glow, the child, as if with a cold light. Not in the other-worldly way of Ruby, but as if she's carved from bright marble. Bridie wonders if it is a photographer's trick.

But her eyes are pale, too pale.

'Is something the matter with her eyes?' asks Bridie.

Sir Edmund takes the chair opposite, sitting forwards in the seat with his head bowed and his hands on his long knees; it's a position of defeat. 'Oh no, Christabel can see all right. That's the problem. She can see *too* much.'

Bridie studies the picture carefully. 'But they're so pale.'

'They change, actually.'

'Change, in what way?'

'From alabaster, to slate, to polished jet: quite remarkable.'

Bridie goes to hand the photograph back. 'Eyes don't generally change colour, unless of course the child is newborn.'

'Christabel's eyes do.' Sir Edmund gestures at the photograph. 'Keep it, for your investigations.'

'These thoughts she makes you think. Can you explain them?'

Sir Edmund runs a hand across his forehead. 'Perhaps they are not thoughts, perhaps they are feelings.'

'Feelings, what sort of feelings?'

Sir Edmund considers. 'Anger, chiefly.'

'So that's it: your daughter stirs up memories and thoughts, makes you feel angry and has stony, changeable eyes?'

Sir Edmund nods. 'Yes.'

'And physically, does Christabel have any distinguishing marks or features?'

'White hair, strong teeth and she can hit shattering high

notes.' Sir Edmund regards Bridie somewhat defiantly. 'And she can't talk.'

'She can't talk?'

'She understands everything perfectly well, of course.'

'But she can sing, with the high notes?'

'After a fashion . . . If that's all?' A brisk tone strides into Sir Edmund's voice. 'You'll wish to question the servants, discreetly I trust, madam?'

Bridie, aware that the interview is over, assents. 'And, with your permission, sir, I intend look over the house and grounds, starting with the nursery.'

'Not the nursery.'

'I beg your pardon, sir?'

'The west wing is private, no one is to be admitted.'

'Sir Edmund—'

'My late wife objected to strangers in that part of the house. It was where she kept her quarters. I still uphold her wishes. Besides,' Sir Edmund adds, airily, 'there's nothing to see.'

'The nursery may give up valuable clues, sir, as to the identity of Christabel's abductors.'

'You believe several individuals were involved?'

'In my experience, that is usually the case. On the matter of the nursery—'

'There are no clues there. I've looked.'

Bridie frowns. 'But the practised eye can detect—'

'No, madam,' says Sir Edmund, with surprising firmness. 'You have permission to talk to my servants and to scrutinise the rest of my house and grounds as you wish, but you will not gain access to the west wing.'

Chapter 5

The servants' hall is as it should be: teapot on the table and gas-lights burning cosily. Mrs Puck, the housekeeper, joyless and trim with a halibut pout, eyes Bridie coldly. The staff will be available for questions but Mrs Puck will not. It is Mrs Puck's evening off and she will not cancel it, not even if Queen Victoria herself turned up for supper at Maris House. Mrs Puck finishes with an astringent downturn to her mouth and a withering stare, which communicates that she has better things to do than be interrogated by some fast and loose *lady inspector*. Mrs Puck takes it all in: the propriety of Mrs Devine's dress, her bold countenance, the steady step of a woman who can afford a well-made pair of boots. But then Mrs Puck knows an Irish accent when she hears one, however diminished, just as she knows the shape of a finger from an always-worn wedding band. She'd only have to look at her own wasted ring finger. This flame-haired widow may be a charlatan but she's also the master's guest, and as such, Mrs Puck can't aim her out the back door as she'd like to. Mrs Puck informs Mrs Devine that if she wants the guided tour she can make do with Agnes, the housemaid. And with that Mrs Puck departs with a caustic curtsey and much tut-tutting and clinking of keys.

Bridie makes herself comfortable at the table. Finding her pouch of tobacco and her pipe she sets about having a smoke for herself. Ruby takes off his hat and perches on a stool next to her.

They sit in companionable silence.

Bridie strikes a match. The tablecloth moves. She encourages her pipe alight and blows out the match. The tablecloth moves again, further now, the teapot and milk-jug travelling two inches to the right.

Bridie lifts the edge of the cloth. A child is sitting under the table with her legs crossed.

She's a plain child, even unappealing, around seven years old with a blunt upturned nose and a stodgy, well-scrubbed face. Her light-brown ringlets are scraped back into a ribbon and she wears a viciously laundered pinafore.

She is whispering angrily to a woebegone china doll that has lost an eye and most of its hair.

Bridie drops the tablecloth and waits.

The child emerges and takes the chair opposite. She squints at Bridie through chaff-coloured eyelashes.

'I like your doll,' ventures Bridie.

'I like your pipe.'

'What's your doll called?'

'Rosebud. She's a caution.'

'Is that right?'

'You are Mrs Devine and I am Myrtle Harbin.'

'Dr Harbin's girl?'

Myrtle Harbin shrugs, as if she's not bothered either way. 'He's upstairs.' She raises her eyes to the ceiling. 'Sir Edmund has nerves again.'

'Has he, now. Does Sir Edmund have nerves often?'

But Myrtle is engrossed, rolling her doll along the table.

Ruby drifts over to the window. Bridie watches the dead

man as he hitches up his drawers, adjusts the tilt of his topper and leans on the sill.

Myrtle follows her gaze. Then she eyes the window with an expression of mild curiosity.

Bridie lowers her voice. 'Can you see something, Myrtle? At the window?'

Myrtle regards her coolly. 'Not especially.'

Bridie waves the pipe in her hand. 'You don't smoke Prudhoe's *Bronchial Balsam Blend* by any chance, do you?'

Myrtle shakes her head.

Ruby, who is tightening the waistband of his drawers, glances over and smiles.

Bridie studies the child with interest. 'So, standing at the window is . . .'

Myrtle studies her back. '*Nobody.*' She turns her attention to Rosebud's booties, adjusting buckles.

'You're Christabel's playmate, aren't you?' Bridie's tone is light.

'I'm not allowed to talk about Christabel.' Myrtle kisses her doll's face gently, on the side that isn't broken.

'What's she like?'

Myrtle looks up at Bridie with eyes like dishwater. 'That's a secret.'

'Could you tell Rosebud what Christabel is like? You could whisper in her ear.'

Myrtle pouts. 'Why would I? Rosebud already knows her.'

Bridie continues with her pipe, watching the child out of the corner of her eye. Myrtle lifts her doll up, as if to throw her in the air in a game of catch. Rosebud glares down with her one good eye.

The girl's sleeves fall back to reveal line after line of scars: healed puncture wounds, like blackened cat bites. Myrtle catches Bridie noticing her arm. She drops her doll and pulls down her sleeves.

'You've been bitten, Myrtle.'

'I haven't.'

'What bit you?'

'Rosebud.' She passes Bridie her doll, poking her finger into its mouth to demonstrate the sharpness of Rosebud's china teeth.

'Then she's a fierce one.' Bridie touches the doll's dented head. 'And she's been fighting, here?'

'No. Christabel threw her against the wall.' Myrtle frowns and clamps her hand across her mouth.

'Don't worry, I'm even better at keeping secrets than Rosebud.'

Myrtle slumps in the chair, with the weight of the world on her small shoulders. 'I doubt it. Rosebud can't speak. She isn't real.'

'But she can bite?' Bridie neatens the tie on the doll's apron and hands her back to Myrtle. 'I don't suppose you know where Christabel has gone?'

Myrtle shakes her head, vehemently.

'Are you quite sure?'

'Quite sure.' Myrtle nods with emphasis.

'You must miss her. She's your friend, isn't she?'

Bridie smiles at the child: Myrtle wrinkles her nose.

'Are you going to bring her back?'

'I'll do my best,' says Bridie.

'Don't,' Myrtle whispers. 'Please don't bring her back.'

Agnes Molloy has a mess of curly brown hair, hardly contained by her mob cap, and a sharp, freckled face. She has large feet for her size and hands swollen as if they are waterlogged. Mrs Puck maintains that the girl is a hoyden, but grudgingly concedes that she is good at her work (if being good at your work means taking greater pride in a clean floor than in the state of your own filthy, dirty apron). Agnes been in England for five years and a servant for all of them. Agnes misses Ireland not at all, for here she has three good meals a day and a half-day off on Sundays.

Agnes is happy to conduct Mrs Devine around the house, despite having a few last grates to bright (Brunswick bloody Black to mix, which fair gets up the nose with the turpentine), beds to turn down, wash-stands to ready, the servants' hall to sweep and the breakfast table to set ready for the morning, else Mrs Puck will roast her.

Agnes leads Bridie into the drawing-room, turning up the gas-lights. Ruby follows.

Agnes points at the window. 'That was found open, Mrs Devine.' She measures the distance with her hands. 'This much. They said that's how the kidnappers got in.'

'Kidnappers?'

Agnes flushes. 'I mean the *robbers*, ma'am.'

'Say what you mean, Agnes,' Bridie says. 'Do you know why I am here?'

'Begging your pardon, ma'am, but Mrs Puck said it was not her job to question the master, but what she could gather was that you are a lady investigator.'

'Your master has asked me to find something very important to him. You know what has been taken, do you not? Please be candid, Agnes.'

Agnes looks at her shoes.

Bridie speaks kindly. 'This is a delicate matter, I know. Anything you tell me will be treated with confidence and could help your master.'

Agnes nods, avoiding Bridie's eyes.

'So, then, around the time of the theft of the child—'

Agnes's hands bunch her apron. 'Begging your pardon, ma'am, but Mrs Puck told me not to talk to anyone about the theft.'

'Did she now?'

'If asked I must refer the asker to Mrs Puck herself, who will answer on my behalf, ma'am.'

'I don't want Mrs Puck's answers; I want yours. Have you seen Sir Edmund's daughter?'

Agnes's reply is hushed and accompanied by much blushing. 'No, Mrs Devine, I have never laid eyes on her. But we all knew she was here, as we all knew she was taken.'

'"All" meaning the servants?'

'Yes, ma'am,' allows Agnes. She picks her words with care. 'It's ever so hard to not notice things.'

Bridie goes over to the window. 'You said the thieves got in this way?'

'Not at all, ma'am, unless they flew in.'

Agnes opens the window. The day is nearly lost to them now but Bridie can make out a sprawling rose bush below.

'Thorns on it, as long as your thumb, ma'am, and if they did come that way they left no footprints.'

'You looked?'

'Oh, yes, ma'am, I got in under the bushes there.'

Ruby nods over at Agnes. 'She's none too tardy, is she?'

'Someone in the house helped them, ma'am,' says Agnes, lowering her voice. 'I'm sure of it.'

'And then opened the window to make it look like a burglary?' poses Bridie.

'Yes, ma'am.'

'You think a member of the household was involved?'

'I have suspicions, Mrs Devine.'

'Go on, Agnes.'

'Now I'm not one to speak ill of a person, ma'am, but – the missing nurse.' Agnes closes the window. 'I've never trusted her. No sooner had the old nurse drowned – in a *wash-tub*, I ask you – then Mrs Bibby turns up. Hardly a day between! And there was this *air* about her.'

'What sort of air?'

Agnes's expression becomes troubled. 'Oh, forgive me, Mrs Devine, but she was a nasty old thing, with these rough manners on her. Not at all what you'd expect of a child's nurse. And this awful rotten leg.'

'Which leg?'

'Left, with a limp to it, ma'am.' Agnes mimics, stiffly swinging her leg before her. 'But at least she kept herself apart. Which Mrs Puck said was needful, given her position.'

'Her position?'

'Mending tapestries, ma'am.'

'She hasn't been here long, has she?'

'Less than a month, ma'am.'

'But the servants knew her real role?'

'They did, of course, ma'am. Only everyone had a different idea as to what the master was keeping in west wing . . .' Agnes falters.

'Go on, Agnes. Trust that this is in confidence.'

Agnes nods. 'Some said that the mistress had borne a monster, ma'am, at her late age. Then, maddened by the sight of it, she drowned herself. Others said the master had shipped it in from abroad.' She looks up at Bridie, her face suddenly harried. 'But everyone said – they still say – it was an abomination.'

'Why do people say that?'

Agnes blesses herself. 'Saints preserve us, ma'am, it was the snails.'

'Snails?'

'Buckets full of them every morning, ma'am,' recalls Agnes, with an awed disgust. 'Mrs Puck would send me to pick them off the walls and the doors and the steps. Then there were the newts and the frogs and the toads; any wretched thing that crawled in slime would be outside trying to get inside. And these great packs of gulls would come baying around the rooftops. Oh, and this mist, ma'am, rising through the house with every window closed. Turning the bread to soup and dampening the clothes on your back.' She pauses. 'So, you see I knew Mrs Bibby couldn't be respectable and God-fearing.'

'Why do you say that, Agnes?'

'She was willing to get mixed up in all of that, ma'am.'

Agnes closes the curtains against the darkening sky.

'The night of the theft, Agnes, can you tell me about that?'

'Begging your pardon but I slept through it, ma'am. I'm to bed at eleven and up at five, I'm dead to the world in-between.'

'Who raised the alarm?'

'Mr Puck, ma'am. It was him that found the door to the west wing open that morning. It was always kept locked and bolted.'

'Who had access to the west wing?'

'The master, the nurse and Dr Harbin.'

'And there were no other visitors?'

Agnes shook her head. 'No, only poor Myrtle, ma'am. Dr Harbin would often bring her with him when he visited and he was here most days. She'd go in pale and come out paler and not a word could be drawn from her about what she'd seen in there.'

'Did Mr and Mrs Puck ever go into the west wing?'

'No, ma'am, but Mr Puck keeps a key in the butler's sitting room. I saw him pass it to the doctor when I was in there doing out the fire.'

'Does he now?' Bridie is thoughtful. 'So, the following morning Mr Puck discovered the door to the west wing wide open. Then what happened?'

'After a quick discussion as to whether they ought to or no, Mr Puck and Mrs Puck went in through the door while Winnie and I waited in the hall, ma'am.'

'Winnie, being the kitchenmaid?'

Agnes nods. 'Then they came out all wooden-faced, and said, "Something has been taken," and asked us to rouse the footman, the groom and the gardener, and search the house and grounds, ma'am.'

'Did they tell you what had been taken, Agnes?'

'No, ma'am, they didn't. I asked Mrs Puck, begging her pardon, how I could search for something when I didn't know what it was I was searching for.'

'What did she say?'

'Mrs Puck told me to mind my own business and get on with the searching. We went all over the house, from chimney to cellar, excepting the west wing, ma'am, as Mr Puck and Mrs Puck had locked the door behind them. The groom and the gardener did the grounds and the out-houses.'

'And what did you find?'

'Winnie found that window open and everyone else found nothing, ma'am,' Agnes recollects. 'Mrs Puck sent the footman to find the constable and Mr Puck went in to see the master, who was furious, for he didn't want the police called at all.'

'Sir Edmund was angry?'

'We could hear him roaring from downstairs. Then Mrs Puck rounded us up and told us not to say *anything* to the police.'

'And then the police arrived?'

'Yes, ma'am, and Mr Puck told them that a robbery had been attempted but nothing had been taken.'

'He said that, how do you know?'

'I heard him, ma'am. Then the police went and Dr Harbin came, and him and the master walked up and down the terrace smoking. Then Dr Harbin rode off in the master's carriage.'

Bridie thinks for a while. 'I need to get into the west wing, Agnes.'

'Oh, no, ma'am, that would not be allowed.'

'The keys to the west wing are in the butler's sitting room – could you show me?'

Agnes looks anguished. 'Forgive me, Mrs Devine, but you're after *taking* the keys?'

'Borrowing them.'

'Oh, I couldn't, ma'am!'

'A child is missing, Agnes, and I am puzzled as to why this child was kept secret and why she was taken. Are you not puzzled too?'

'I am, of course, ma'am. But being puzzled is one thing and taking keys from the butler's sitting room is another. With all due respects.'

'As I said: it wouldn't be taking, Agnes, it would be borrowing.'

Agnes considers this, brows knitted, and then shakes her head. 'I am sorry, ma'am, but it wouldn't be right.'

'Secrets have their place,' says Bridie. 'Every household has its secrets. But when a child's very life might be at stake, a secret held may be fatal.'

A conflict seems to be raging in the housemaid. 'But if we're caught, ma'am?'

'We won't be caught. Isn't it Mrs Puck's night off?'

Agnes's countenance brightens. 'Then I will help you, ma'am, for I would not want the life of a child on my conscience if I can help to save her. And Lord forgive me, but I want that nurse to get her come-uppance. I don't know why she took the child, or what sort of child it is, but I'm certain Mrs Bibby is at the back of this.'

Bridie follows Agnes up the main staircase, a blue-carpeted, polished-wood thing of beauty, wide-stepped and rising augustly from the marble floor.

'Sir Edmund is a great one for the water, be it the sea, ponds, lakes, fountains, rivers, even a well.' Agnes gestures up at the stained-glass window that runs the height of the stair-case.

In daylight, with the sun shining through, it shows an aventurine sea swelling three storeys. A golden galleon sails over this sea and iridescent fish swim under. Above, opal arrows of sea-birds fly in cloud-buffeted skies. Being dark outside now, the window is diminished, but Bridie has the idea of it.

They climb the stairs: Ruby, carrying his hat, comes up after.

'Mr Bazalgette has been a guest at Maris House,' says Agnes. 'You know, ma'am, the fella with the drains.'

'The famous civil engineer, you mean?'

Agnes nods. 'He distrusts sandwiches and must sleep in a north-facing room. He came here to ask the master about water. How it moves: fast, slow, can it turn corners?'

'Who told you this?'

They cross a landing and head up a further flight of stairs.

'Mr Puck,' answers Agnes. 'He says that when Mr Bazalgette's sewers are completed they will be world-famous.'

'Very likely.'

'The master has taken inspiration from Mr Bazalgette. He has been making great plans for Maris House,' Agnes relates. 'Self-filling baths and basins, raindrop machines with water cold and hot, miles of pipes so that no servant need carry another bucket.'

'Indeed?'

'The master designed the fountain, ma'am. Beautiful, it was. People used to come for miles to see it, until the tragedy.' Agnes blesses herself deftly.

'You mean Lady Berwick's accident?'

'God rest her, ma'am, that fountain never worked again and Sir Edmund never had the heart to fix it.'

They stop on the turn of the stairs and Agnes points out the painting above them. 'Herself, Lady Berwick, ma'am, at Pevensey Bay.'

A young woman in a white dress sits on a rock brushing

her brown hair with a mournful expression. Around her naked feet starry shells lie scattered. In the background, an ominous sea: the wind is blowing up waves, foamy horses stampede to shore.

'Is it a likeness, Agnes?'

'When she was younger, maybe, as I heard Lady Berwick was a big-boned woman with a cast eye. Begging your pardon, ma'am.'

Ruby laughs.

'It's said that she still haunts the grounds, ma'am, watching the master outside his study window when he's at his papers and his planning. The gardener sees her footprints. He followed them once; all around the pond, out of the estate, into the woods to the chapel beyond. They ended at her tomb.'

'And do you believe that, Agnes?'

'I don't at all, Mrs Devine. There are no such things as ghosts.'

They take the corridor towards the west wing. Paintings line the walls.

'The master did these himself, ma'am.'

A leviathan hunts a fishing boat, its great head cresting the waves. In the next painting the brute closes its maw around the boat's splintering hull. A fisherman clings to a piece of driftwood, his face a mask of terror. One painting in particular catches Bridie's eye. A travesty of a mermaid looms in a rock pool with a looking-glass, a receding hairline and a pike's grin. Below the surface of the water a barbed tail curls.

'We call her Mrs Puck,' whispers Agnes with a grin.

Bridie laughs.

'Your master seems to dwell on these horrors of the deep?'

'He has a whole library of books about the things that swim in the water and the things that crawl out of it, ma'am.' Agnes wrinkles her nose. 'There are *things in jars*.'

Bridie raises her eyebrows. 'Things in jars?'

'There's this hidden door in the bookcase. I found it by accident one day when I was dusting.' The housemaid shivers. 'Heaven help me, but I pushed it opened and went through it into this room.'

'The jars were inside this room?'

Agnes blesses herself, twice. 'Mary Mother of God – the memory of them!'

'Can you tell me what was inside the jars, Agnes?'

'Oh, I couldn't, ma'am!'

'Go on, so.'

Agnes grimaces. 'Drowned worms and these fish with teeth on them.' She mimes the teeth with her fingers clawed.

'Can you show me?'

'I can't see how, ma'am. The master keeps the library locked when he's not in it, and Mr Puck fairly roosts in that part of the house, with the master's study being along there.'

And here is a heavy-looking wooden door with a good stout lock to it. Bridie pulls the keys they lifted from the butler's sitting room from her pocket and unlocks the door into a windowless passage. There's a lantern hanging on a hook on the wall and a shelf for matches. Bridie reaches down the lantern.

'Allow me, please, ma'am.' The housemaid glances up at Bridie as she lights the wick. 'Begging your pardon, Mrs Devine, but you won't be telling anyone I brought you here, will you?'

'Of course not, Agnes.'

'Especially Mrs Puck, ma'am.'

'Last of all Mrs Puck, she would roast you!'

Agnes smiles weakly and hands Bridie the lantern. 'She'd pickle me, ma'am. I'd be in a jar with the worms.'

★

The smell of damp is heavy in the air. Mould blossoms over the wallpaper, creating elaborate growths to rival even the winding botanicals in Mr William Morris's imagination.

They come to a riveted iron door. Bridie unlocks it and together they manage to push it open.

Bridie holds up the lantern.

The room is vivid green and running wet with condensation. Across the walls a pattern is repeated. Flat leaves with bulbous ulcers. Plants of the sea: bladder-wrack and sea-rod; not garden flowers.

Ruby stands in the corner grave-faced and flickering dimly. The skull tattooed on his abdomen is chattering its teeth. The mermaid on his shoulder swims wildly over his spectral skin; she seems to be looking for somewhere to hide, and dashes under his arm.

'This is some class of place,' the dead man says.

Agnes goes about lighting lamps, they splutter and catch under opaline hoods. The smell is overwhelming: salt water and iodine, rotten fish and stagnant silt. Bridie goes to open the window; it is nailed shut and barred.

She surveys the nursery. It's unlike any nursery she has seen before. Everything is of a marine shade; from the doll with green hair to the story-books all bound in blue leather. The white marble fireplace has a delicate scalloped design.

There is a cage of sorts built around a bed-frame, with a mechanism for lowering the sides and for folding back the top, and a catch to keep them securely closed.

Bridie finds rings welded onto the metal struts. 'These are for restraints.'

Agnes looks horrified. 'They kept her in this? Why would they do that?'

'I don't know,' answers Bridie in dismay. 'But it hardly seems humane.'

Bridie opens the door to an adjoining room, motioning

for Agnes to follow her. Ruby, shaken by the surroundings, stands guard in the nursery.

The nurse's room is simply furnished. It holds a chest of drawers, a bed and a desk.

'We need to ascertain if any of the nurse's things are missing, Agnes.'

Bridie pulls a trunk out from under the bed while Agnes searches the drawers.

'There is no sign of her travelling things,' notes Bridie. 'No shawl, or bonnet, or sturdy boots.'

'Then she was dressed and ready for the robbers, ma'am. They didn't drag her out of the house by the hem of her nightie.'

There is a single shelf of books. Mrs Bibby's personal reading consists of a Bible, a worn encyclopaedia and a novel from Mudie's Select Library: *The Mill on the Floss*, Volume 2, two weeks overdue.

Bridie studies a slip of paper used as a bookmark. 'Our nurse left a reservation ticket behind.' She pockets the novel.

Bridie returns to Christabel's room and, taking the lantern, shines it on the wallpaper. 'It's peculiar, like being underwater.'

'Look at it too long and your eyes start to go funny, ma'am,' says Agnes. 'The seaweed starts to dance.'

Bridie checks the door. 'The locks show no signs of being forced, which supports the idea that Mrs Bibby was part of the plan, the one who slipped the bolt, unlocked the doors to the west wing and the nursery.'

'Begging your pardon, Mrs Bibby was in the thick of it, ma'am.'

Bridie looks around her. 'There's no sign of a struggle, or of leaving in haste.'

She pushes a nightstand a fraction of an inch and examines the indentations on the Turkish carpet. 'The furniture has been moved, or else the rug is fresh down. Help me, Agnes.'

Together they move the furniture and roll back the rug. A smell rises, like sump water.

Agnes covers her face. 'Oh, suffering Jesus, the reek of it!'

On the floorboards there is a patch, a shape, an outline.

Bridie gets down on her hands and knees: the floorboards are sodden. 'It's sea-water, I think. It has left some kind of silt or residue, but it has behaved very strangely.'

Agnes draws forward. 'How do you mean, ma'am?'

Bridie traces along the edge of the darker patch. 'It hasn't spread like a puddle ought to, as it would if you spilt your mop bucket. The lines are sharply marked.' Then she sees it. 'It is the shape of a person, an exact print – lying down, arms to the side.'

'It is, ma'am!' exclaims Agnes.

'If a corpse lies undetected for long enough it could rot into the floor, leaving a stain of sorts,' muses Bridie. 'Had that happened in this case, we would have smelt it coming up the stairs.'

'Blessed Mother of Christ, let me get out of here,' says Ruby and paces through the wall into the passage outside, rubbing his temples.

The clock in the entrance-hall chimes. They hear it faintly.

'We haven't got long, ma'am,' urges Agnes. 'I need to return the keys. Mrs Puck will be home directly and then Mr Puck will do his rounds.'

'Let's get this furniture back.'

They straighten the room and extinguish the lights.

Bridie picks up the lantern and then she sees it: a large stoppered glass jar, nestling on a shelf among the story-books.

The heart in her turns crossways.

Chapter 6

Bridie locks the guest-room door and pushes a chest in front of it. She takes her pepper-box pistol, loads it and puts it under her pillow. Then she steps slowly around the room, tapping the walls and scrutinising the joins in the flock wallpaper.

Ruby watches her quizzically. 'What are you doing, Bridie?'

'Hidden doors,' she murmurs. 'We know the library has them.'

'Why the barricade?'

'A precaution.' Bridie glances over at him. 'This house feels full of wrong.'

Ruby sits down at the dressing table.

A cloth covers the jar that Bridie took from the bookcase in the nursery, and Ruby is thankful of this. For the contents have the ability to rearrange even a dead man's sense of reality. As with all terrible, wondrous sights, there is a jolt of shock, then a hypnotic fascination, then the uneasy queasiness, then the whole thing starts again; the desire to look and the desire never to have looked in the first place.

Bridie, satisfied that all the walls are solid, pulls a chair up next to Ruby. She unwraps the cloth.

And there it is. Reflected in the mirror of the dressing table, an assault on the mind and the eyes and the heart.

Bridie leans in closer, touching the cold glass with her fingertips.

A jarred baby, of all the things in the world!

A perfect newborn with furled fingers and tiny nails, a wee button of a nose and the sweetest, most delicate shell-like ears. The skin is perfectly preserved, with the look of carved marble, but there's a softness that describes something very human: the tender pods of the baby's closed eyes, the plump spot under its chin, its dimpled arms.

The infant is held suspended in the fluid by fine wires. Sound asleep in its glass womb.

Bridie turns the jar and the picture changes.

At the back of the head, just under the wispy curls at the nape of the baby's neck, there is a line of scales. Subtle at first, then swelling into a filmy dorsal fin, slight but proud, that follows the spine down to end in the sweep of a curled tail. A tail as muscular as a salmon's: small, yes, but strong and pliant-looking. There is something diabolic at play: here, just below the hipbone, where the soft white marble of the baby's chest and belly turns mottled green, deepening to a rich jade towards the caudal. The fins are tissue-thin, flesh-toned, touched at the tip with crimson.

Bridie turns the jar again and comes face to face with the creature, thankful that the eyes are sealed, the pupils inky shadows behind the lids. Cheekbones ridged, like the curve of a gill. And inside the open rosebud mouth, teeth, just barely visible, pointed, pike-like.

'It's called the Winter Mermaid.'

'Is it real?' whispers Ruby.

'No one could ever test it,' says Bridie. 'Legend has it that the preservation depends on a perfect seal.'

'Is it old?' asks Ruby.

'Perhaps a hundred years.'

The mermaid on Ruby's shoulder swims down to his

wrist, slipping past the inked anchor. She stares into the jar and then recoils, darting back up the length of his arm, retreating into his armpit.

'I've seen this specimen before.' Bridie smiles stiffly. 'It's one of a kind.'

'Tell me,' says Ruby.

She exhales. 'It used to belong to the anatomist and surgeon Dr John Eames. I saw it then.'

'You knew this John Eames?'

'I was his apprentice; I was sold to him as a child for a guinea.'

Ruby waits. Watching her. Knowing there's a story and knowing that Bridie is trying to find the words to tell it.

Her eyes are riveted to the jar. 'It's exactly the same as the first day I saw it, Ruby. It's as unbelievable now as it was then.' She looks up at him. 'It changed everything.'

May 1841

Chapter 7

The man uncovered the jar.

Bridie was too old to cry and too proud to scream and she wanted to do both.

Too old – how old was Bridie?

No older than ten, no younger than eight, her gaffer had said: small for her age either way.

Bridie drew a breath and stepped closer to the jar. Although her feet were telling her to run and her head was agreeing.

'Take a good look,' the man said. 'And tell me what you make of it, Bridget.'

Bridie felt the man watching her, his eyes on her. He wanted to see how she reacted to it, this jarred nightmare. And she knew, somehow, that her actions would determine her future, here, with him, in this house.

Bridie reached out to touch the glass, then, realising the filth of her hand, withdrew it and hid it in her skirts. Begrimed beyond belief, she was more out of place in this fine room than the abomination in the jar before her. Oh, and it was a fine room: with glass-fronted cabinets and a polished-wood desk and shelves of leather-coated books. And framed by the window, lawn as far as the eye could see, then the sails of boats in the distance. But Bridie was gazing at the jar, not at the view.

She took a sly peek at the man.

He had blue eyes, gingery whiskers and sandy hair touched grey at the temples. His face was long, with a habitual expression like that of a sad, dignified horse. There was a grave smile in his eyes, which, Bridie would soon realise, smiled more than his mouth. He was of fair height and even-featured, although somewhat sharp of nose and thin of lip. He was calmly spoken, polite to all people (addressing everyone in the same manner, irrespective of station) and dressed well, if sombrely.

His name was Dr John Eames and he had acquired Bridie for a guinea several hours ago. Now he was waiting to see what he had bought.

Bridie looked back at the jar and the unholy horror inside it.

What would her old gaffer, Gan Murphy, advise?

When in doubt, take it apart, girl.

Dead frogs, birds, rats, cats, and once a poor dog hung by street children. All carefully dissected. Bridie would pore over their secret workings for hours, admiring the mechanisms of limb and wing, blowing through a dead bird's windpipe, reviving its song.

Afterwards Bridie would gather up the scraps and give them a proper burial in a tobacco box or some such, never forgetting to pick a flower, or a leaf, or to say a prayer over the grave. In this she was respectful.

When in doubt, take it apart, girl.

Bridie glanced at the man. He was waiting.

She wiped her hands as best she could on her skirts (which were as filthy as her hands) and produced her pocket-knife.

The jar would have to be prised opened, the liquid sniffed, the creature pulled out like an ugly pickle, shaken off, landed on the table . . . Bridie applied her knife to the seal on the lid.

'No!' Dr Eames started up, a hint of amusement in his voice. 'The seal must stay intact. Put your knife away, child.'

Bridie pocketed her knife.

'Have you ever seen a specimen like this before, Bridget?'

Bridie thought of the late-night trips to the hospital with Gan to conduct business. Dissection tables, buckets of gore and dripping sacks; she'd seen a lot. Had she seen anything like this? Not in her life.

'I don't know as I have, sir.'

Dr Eames regarded the baby in the jar with a look of affection. 'Is it a miracle of nature or a marvellous trick?'

'It is a trick, sir. Babies don't have tails.' Then a terrible thought surfaced in Bridie's mind. 'Oh, sir, they killed it, the baby, to put it in the jar there.'

Dr Eames shook his head. 'No, Bridget, the specimen was already dead. They put it in this glass jar to preserve it in special fluid, to keep it for all time. They felt it was too important to lose.'

'How do you know it was dead?'

'I am a doctor.' Dr Eames smiled.

Bridie looked unconvinced.

'So, Bridget,' he said. 'What are we calling this specimen?'

Bridie had no bloody idea. 'A fish *baby*?' she hazarded.

'It's called the Winter Mermaid.'

It was a lovely name and here was a lovely word:

Mermaid, mermaid, mermaid.

Bridie said it again and again softly to herself as she inspected the Winter Mermaid from every side, walking around the table.

When Bridie looked up again she saw that a young woman was standing by the door.

'Eliza is our housekeeper, she will help you settle in,' said Dr Eames.

Eliza bobbed to Dr Eames and nodded at Bridie. She barely noted the mermaid in the jar. Bridie wasn't to know it yet, but Eliza took everything with a pinch, for she had seen it all, working for Dr Eames.

Eliza was lovely. She had kind hazel eyes and glossy brown hair and a neat clean dress.

Bridie felt the full shame of the filth of herself. She was a shocker. Not just with London grime, but with blood. Although it had dulled to a dirty brown now, up her arms, caked to black under her fingernails. There was blood, too, all down the front of her dress, dried to rust, her skirts stiff with it. And her boots were thick with the worst of London's mire. Bridie's cheeks burned scarlet. It was as if her body was suddenly shouting out in that room that smelt of soap and polish, candle wax and cut flowers: Here I am, it roared, all sour armpits and sweaty arse, caked neck and greasy hair, rotten feet and pestilential breath.

'Miss Bridget valiantly attempted to save a man's life today, Eliza,' said Dr Eames, as if by way of an explanation for the state of her. 'I consider that very brave, don't you?'

'Yes, sir, Miss Bridget has a very brave countenance.'

Eliza smiled at an incredulous Bridie, sending her heart swooping.

Dr Eames rounded the desk. He went to pat Bridie's head but, thinking better of it, he put his hand on her shoulder and smiled sadly into her eyes.

'You go with Eliza now, she will show you around the house.'

Bridie glanced once more at the jar.

'The Winter Mermaid will be here when you return, Bridget.'

Eliza offered Bridie her hand. Bridie hesitated but then she took it, wondering how Eliza could see past the dirt.

★

The housemaids boiled up the copper and peeled Bridie's clothes off. With each garment there were low murmurs of awe. The tin bath was emptied three times and soap of a most stringent preparation applied. Bridie's hair was dowsed and brushed and the worst tangles cut out; she watched them through her watering eyes as they fell onto the laundry-room floor, hairy red spiders. She was scrubbed dry and given a beautiful thing to eat, which was a sugared almond, and promised another when she was dressed.

Then she was put into clothes that had belonged to Miss Lydia before she died.

There were layers and layers of clothes. For every layer Bridie was accustomed to wearing there were two more. A shift, lace-trimmed pantalettes, petticoats, a boned corset, a maroon dress made of shiny stuff, a little cape, a pair of stockings, buckled shoes stuffed with paper to fit. With each layer Bridie shrunk further. With each layer Bridie felt stranger and stiffer. So that now when she moved she felt like a puppet discovering its limbs for the first time. Then the maids led Bridie upstairs to the nursery and showed her Dead Miss Lydia's toys.

'What happened to Miss Lydia?' Bridie asked. 'That I'm wearing her clothes?'

But the maids looked puzzled and shook their heads.

Bridie tried again, much slower and with an English accent.

The maids gave Bridie another sugared almond and called for Eliza, and Eliza told Bridie that Miss Lydia had died falling out of a window when she was not much older than Bridie.

'She had been leaning out to feed a nesting blackbird,' said Eliza. 'So said Gideon.'

The maids who were folding linen in the corner of the room exchanged glances.

'Who is Gideon?'

'The young master, Dr Eames's son. Gideon is away at school.' Eliza patted Bridie's arm. 'Which is just as well, for Gideon isn't always very kind, but he is very handsome and clever and one day he will be a great doctor like his father.'

'Will he push me out of the window too?' asked Bridie. 'Like Lydia?'

In the corner of the room, one maid let out a cry and the other dropped a pile of petticoats.

Eliza looked at them coolly and then turned to Bridie. 'Gideon won't harm a hair on your head, for I will be looking out for you. You will be my second child.'

'You have a first child?'

'I do. He's quite small yet and his name is Edgar Kempton Jones.'

'He sounds just like a gentleman!' said Bridie.

One of the maids in the corner smirked. The other nudged her.

Eliza frowned at the maid. 'Are you finished, Dorcas?'

The bigger of the two maids scowled and bobbed.

'Then see to Mrs Eames's linen,' said Eliza sternly. 'Mary, you help her.'

Eliza watched the maids file out of the room. She turned to Bridie. 'They are silly gooses.'

Bridie laughed.

Eliza lowered her voice. 'The big one with the limp is called Bad Dorcas. Dr Eames got her from the reformatory.'

Bridie widened her eyes.

'But I am the housekeeper, so they have to listen to me.' Eliza showed Bridie the big hoop of keys she carried at her waist so she that could lock everything away so Bad Dorcas didn't steal it.

'Why did Dr Eames bring Bad Dorcas here?'

'Dr Eames likes to help *unfortunates.*'

'Were you in the reformatory, too?'

'Not at all,' Eliza laughed. 'I met Dr Eames at the hospital and he offered me a job. I had been a housemaid before I was married, you see.' Her expression became troubled. 'But then I found myself alone and sick and poor.'

'And unfortunate?'

'In a way.'

'But then you came here.'

Eliza's face brightened. 'Edgar was born here.'

'And you became the housekeeper.'

'Not at first. I was a maid, but I worked hard and learnt what I could.'

Bridie nodded. Eliza was a widow and a mother and a housekeeper and young for all of that. Bridie could tell by the sorrow and the steel behind Eliza's soft looks that she had experienced far worse in life than the scorn of housemaids.

'All's well though, Bridget.' Eliza squeezed her arm. 'And you'll meet my little boy Edgar tomorrow and we'll show you around the house. It's a lovely house, with orchards and a stable and right near the river. You can almost see Windsor Castle!'

'Can you see the Queen?'

Eliza laughed. 'You can! Strolling up and down eating ice cream on the battlements with the little princesses and princes.' She smiled at Bridie kindly. 'You are not all that far from London, although it is different, isn't it?'

'It is too quiet,' said Bridie very seriously.

Eliza laughed again and then, because she had work to do, she left Bridie with a story-book that had belonged to Dead Miss Lydia.

When it grew dark, one of the silly gooses brought

candles in. When it grew darker, the other silly goose came in, the one that was Bad Dorcas, and took Bridie's clothes off her and put different clothes on her and put Bridie into the bed.

Then Eliza came in to kiss her goodnight and told her she looked like an Irish princess with her red hair and buttermilk skin, and she blew out the candles because she knew Bridie wasn't afraid of the dark.

And Bridie wasn't, of course. But she was afraid of the idea of Gideon, because she didn't want to be dead like Lydia.

Bridie lay in the bed open-eyed, tracing the squares thrown across the ceiling from the moonlit window.

She didn't cry, for after all, wasn't this better than what she was used to?

A world away, in London, her old gaffer Gan would be having a pint for himself. If she were there now she would be under the table with the tavern cat, or traipsing up the road to buy tobacco, or fighting with the local boys.

When it was time to sleep they would go up to the room they had above the ship-chandlery shop and Gan would pull out two straw pallets, one for himself and one for herself.

Then Gan would have a good cough and a spit and lie down and smoke. Bridie would say her prayers:

'God bless Gan and myself and the tavern cat.

'God grant eternal rest to Mammy, Daddy, James, John, Theresa, Margaret, Ellen and little baby Owen.

'God grant that bastard Paddy Fadden a kick up his hole and severe death to him and his gang, of a slow and a terrible variety.

'God also wash us up a few more dead fellas so that Gan can earn a coin. And may they not be too far gone and have a head and two arms and two legs and be the kind the doctors like to play with. But only if they are dead anyway, not so's they would have to die, unless you've a mind for them to be

Paddy Fadden and his gang. For then that would be like killing the two birds with the one stone and would be much appreciated, dear Lord, who is above.'

Then Bridie would lie on her straw pallet listening to the ebb and flow of Gan's breath, the guttering and the grunting, the rasp and the hack.

Tonight, in the big house, Bridie said her prayers in the same way she always did. Only she added Eliza and Edgar and Dead Lydia to her prayer list. She might add Dr Eames, too, once she knew him better, and Mrs Eames, if she was nice. Bridie definitely wouldn't add Gideon or Bad Dorcas, but might rather ask God to smite them a bit.

She listened to the unfamiliar sounds of Albery Hall, inside and outside. The owls hunting and the wind through the trees and the floorboards settling. Somewhere in the house a door closed, then another, then all was like the grave.

Bridie turned over in the bed as best she could, for Eliza had tucked her in with fierce efficiency. There were layers of sheets and quilts and counterpanes, a barrage of pillows and bolsters. Maybe Eliza knew that Bridie might cut her lucky. Maybe Bridie would have bolted that first night if she could have got out of the bed. And if she knew where her old boots were: she wouldn't get far in Dead Miss Lydia's shoes, they were velvet and not for tramping.

Then there was the Winter Mermaid, and all the other wondrous things Dr Eames might show her: sights she did and did not want to see.

Bridie closed her eyes and tried to ignore the powerful smell rising from the bed: soap and pressed linen, clean wool and sun-aired feather mattresses. Bridie doubted she would get used to that.

★

Bridie had seen Dr Eames a few times before the day he bought her for a guinea. She had seen him at the Fortune of War public house. Dr Eames was a surgeon at St Bartholomew's Hospital. He was making a name for himself, popular with his students, steady, not too much the showman and well known to her gaffer.

Gan was an old hand: he persisted, although the work of the London Burkers – Bishop, Williams and May (do not say their names within the four walls of the Fortune of War. Do not think them!) – nearly did for the trade. Their ghosts have grown as stale as the beer. How many years hanged? Decades now – Christ! A constable still called at the pub, although not in earnest. Since the Act, the anatomists had a better supply of cadavers, with the unclaimed poor from the hospitals, the prisons and the workhouses (although there was, of course, the woeful drop in hangings). There was less of a need to engage a friend-less visitor to London in conversation. After the Act, work was slack for the resurrectionist unless there was an order to fill, something specialist. It still went on although the surgeons denied it, even as they buried their families in fortified coffins and set week-long guards at the church-yard.

Gan liked Dr John Eames because he never bargained. He just glanced at the corpse and paid full price, or else he took up his hat and walked away. If he bought it he would shake Gan's hand and call him Mr Murphy.

Most often Dr Eames sent the junior doctors, but some-times he conducted his own business; risking a lungful of feculent Fleet river air, he would take the short walk from the hospital, tipping his hat to the Golden Boy mounted in the wall above the pub, to make the needful exchange with his agent in a private corner.

On the day in question (the day Dr Eames acquired a small girl into the bargain) the corpse was laid out in the cellar, as always. It had shiny brown skin, a big round gut and one shoe. Gan said it was a Spaniard and Bridie liked the sound of the word.

Spaniard, Spaniard, Spaniard.

She said it again and again softly to herself as she inspected the Spaniard from every side, walking around the table.

Then they got its clothes off and Bridie rinsed them and hung them out the back to dry. It would be her job to press and fold them and wrap them in a neat bundle to bring them down to Monmouth Street and get a good price for them. Then Gan wiped the corpse down with a rag and covered up its Articles with an old sheet. Then, whistling, Gan took out his comb. He would do just about everything to make a cadaver presentable. The landlord put his head round the door and asked if Gan wasn't going to give the deceased a shave.

The deceased had been spotted down-river, an easy catch, and fresh. Gan and Bridie had reeled it to the side of the rowing boat, roped it onto a plank, towed it behind them and then hauled it up the river-bank.

Gan, as always, was first to arrive. As soon as the Spaniard was seen, a hunched shape in the water.

Gan was eyes, nose and ears, attached to a long coughing gristle of a man.

If anyone died, Gan Murphy knew about it.

If someone fell in the river at Chelsea, Gan would hear it in Vauxhall.

If someone keeled over friendless in Holywell Street (possibly striking his head on the way down), Gan would hear it in Chancery Lane.

He'd hear it with those great cockleshell ears he had, like dinner plates.

And what about Gan's eyes?

He could spy a fresh-dug grave at a hundred paces and a failing man at fifty. If Gan Murphy followed you home you knew you were doomed.

And what about Gan's nose?

One sniff and he would tell you the age on a corpse and why it had expired. Gan would get right up close and take a deep breath. He knew the workings, he didn't need to take anything apart. Not any more.

'This one,' Gan took a slow inhale, 'is less than a day old, fell in the river, flathered.' Gan pressed the dead man's gut, hard and low, and it let out a soft fart. 'He left on a good feed of drink. Good man himself.'

Bridie thought the corpse looked ashamed, so she smoothed down its eyebrows and patted its arm.

Gan rested the bit of his pipe in the slot of a missing tooth. He lit it and pulled on it and spoke through the smoke, hardly moving his lips.

'Leave that alone. Get out front, girl,' he said. 'Watch for the doctor.'

Then Gan sat down and stretched out his long legs and started to concentrate on bringing up a good deep cough.

It was common knowledge that Gan skipped Dublin after being apprehended near Kilmainham Gaol with a pocketful of human teeth. It was less well known that Gan had been a gentleman, a man of science and a renowned surgeon, before the drink and the loss of his inheritance at the gambling table. All or none of this might have been true, Gan wasn't saying anything; it suited him to keep his past a mystery. But Bridie had her suspicions. For one, Gan could play piano so beautifully it would make you weep. For two, Gan would spend a month's wages on the best bottle of wine to be had in London and drink it, slowly, whilst wearing the shoes he had pulled from a dead vagrant's feet.

On the day John Eames bought Bridie Devine for a guinea she was out the front of the pub throwing stones into the gutter. She could hear that a fight had broken out. It had been fermenting for days, the landlord later said, two lads head to head, over a girl, a debt, a slight, a slur. Insults were traded and then punches. There was a push, a shove, a knife appeared, and then it was all over.

Bridie heard the shouting, the jeering and then the silence.

It was the silence that did it. Silence always spelt trouble.

She ran back inside in time to see the fella slide along the wall, his face baffled.

The other fella was looking at the knife in his hand, then at the fallen man, then back at the knife again. As if he was trying to solve a puzzle, as if he was trying to work out how the two were connected.

Bridie shouted for rags and strong drink. Someone was sent into the cellar for Gan, although they knew full well Gan wouldn't come if he was smoking and having a cough for himself.

The child knelt down next to the fallen man. It was a fatal wound and the fella knew it. Bridie could see it in his eyes.

'Keep still, fella, keep still,' she said. The dying man showed the whites of his eyes like an animal trapped; he snorted like an animal trapped.

'Keep still,' she said. 'All right, so?'

The man nodded.

She had her two hands in his chest, as if she was holding him together, but she couldn't stem the bleeding and soon she was dressed in his blood. She fed whiskey into his mouth for the pain, holding the glass in one hand and his chin in the other. His teeth chattered, he choked and swallowed, whiskey and blood mixed. He held his lips pursed like the beak of a baby bird and looked for the glass again, until blood frothed up from his mouth.

When he died he fell sideways with his legs fidgeting and Bridie held his head lest he brain himself on the flags.

She stroked his hair. 'There,' she said. 'There now.'

When he was finally still she got up, wiped the bottle on her skirt and put it back on the bar.

The men bowed their heads. The murderer started to cry.

Dr John Eames sat in the corner with his hat in his hands, astonished. Not by the sudden savage loss of life, for he saw that every day at St Bartholomew's, but by the sight of this small girl, elbow-deep in gore, her face a picture of furious compassion.

When Gan Murphy sold Bridie Devine it was the first and only time anyone had ever seen him cry, for the wee girl was like family to him.

Gan had, of course, made great and preposterous claims for her. He solemnly informed Dr Eames that Bridie could amputate a leg by the time she was five years old (with a little help with the saw) and draw a clean gall-stone at seven. For wasn't Bridie the last in a long line of illustrious Dublin surgeons? Celebrated men who once lived on Merrion Square and owned carriages and paintings but who had fallen on hard times through no fault of their own. When Bridie's entire family died of poverty (and the sicknesses and the calamities attendant) Gan, who considered himself the family's last friend, had brought her to England, seeking to make a living for them both in London. He had cared for the child ever since, at his own expense. Dr Eames nodded but he hardly listened. He couldn't take his eyes off Bridie. She sat in the corner with her hands on her lap and her dress turned red.

Money changed hands and then there was a handshake. The body of the knifed man lay on the floor, his eyes fixed on a point somewhere behind the bar and his top lip pulled back, like a horse smelling the air. A few of the men carried him downstairs and laid him next to the Spanish bloater. By the time the constable called there would be one body in the cellar. The pot-boy brought sawdust and swept the floor, so that the room smelt like a butcher's shop.

Gan, with his eyes brim-full, told her to go with Dr Eames.

'You're no longer a resurrection girl, Bridie,' he said, wiping his face with his sleeve. 'From this day forwards you're a gentleman surgeon's apprentice.'

September 1863

Chapter 8

The day will change to night before the wheel is fixed. The rig is off the Dover Road, mud-sunk five miles out of Battle, the driver frantic. Thankfully the doctor is not with them, else he'd be hopping and whinging.

'We're deep in the mire,' says Mrs Bibby, dragging out the letters of the word, *mire*. 'All the trouble we go to for you, chick.'

Soldiers on a manoeuvre pass by and stop. They help with ropes and horses and planks.

Mrs Bibby watches them from inside the carriage, with her pale blue eyes narrowed and her wide tomcat mouth a taut line. Christabel is in a wicker trunk found in the vestry. Under her shawl Mrs Bibby keeps an Adams revolver ready. The gun goes by the name of Betty Reckoner.

The child pushes her finger through a gap.

'Knock that off,' Mrs Bibby hisses.

The child pulls her finger in again.

Mrs Bibby leans close to the trunk. 'No tricks,' she says, low and harsh, 'or this will go very fucking bad for you. Do you understand?'

The child runs her teeth along the wicker. It would take her no time to get out but for her restraining suit.

Mrs Bibby is still angry with her and she, perhaps, is still angry with Mrs Bibby.

Earlier, Mrs Bibby, demonic from the pain in her leg and the effort of feeding the child (wedged as the big woman was in the vestry cupboard), had snatched the headless newt the child was playing with. She had thrown it away, and called Christabel a godless little heathen.

Christabel screamed. It was a scream loud enough to shatter the church windows and loosen the roof tiles and crumble the font and melt the candles on the altar. Then Mrs Bibby hit her until the child was silent with shock − steering clear of the mouth end.

Mrs Bibby won't be bit again.

Three days in, green to the job, the child got the teeth in. In a way Mrs Bibby had been tickled, the child hanging from her toe like a tide-pool crab. The leg was already frigged: she'd long had a limp like a timber-toed sailor. The bite would make no difference; she'd known worse poisons. But it did, the bite; it did make a difference. But Mrs Bibby apportioned no blame and believed that the child felt no remorse. She fancies they are alike in understanding the law of bite, or be bitten.

A rasping sound as Christabel goes at the wicker. Mrs Bibby lets her.

The carriage straightens, then pitches and lurches. A horse whinnies and a rope gives way with a singing scream. The sound of swearing and curses and new plans being made. More ropes are brought and a dray-horse.

It starts to rain; it patters on the roof of the carriage and spits slantways in at the open window. Mrs Bibby watches as the child pushes her finger through the hole and waits and waits. A raindrop falls on her fingertip.

The finger is drawn back inside the trunk, carefully, carefully. But the raindrop has already rolled away.

★

When the child wakes they are moving and the light has all but faded.

'The Kraken stirs,' says Mrs Bibby. 'It's a long way yet to Dover and the white cliffs and a bad stew and a passable beer. The Walmer Castle suit you?'

She uncorks her medicine bottle, a pop in the dim of the carriage.

'Well, now, will we have another story?' There's a conciliatory tone to Mrs Bibby's voice, a rough good humour in it.

Christabel creaks the lid of the trunk in answer.

'If you learn to speak between here and the Walmer Castle the next story is on you.'

The carriage slows to a stop.

'What's this jarvey up to?' moans Mrs Bibby. 'Have we not had the high commotions today?'

The child scuffles in the trunk to get a better view.

'Listen.'

Mrs Bibby's ear is out beyond the jarg of the carriage and the shuffle of waiting horses. Harking for a coachman on the turn, a constable, an ambush by a collector betrayed—

The sound of pissing.

The coachman clears his throat and climbs back up into the cab. The horses walk on.

'False alarm.' Mrs Bibby is surprised at the relief in her own voice. 'All right, so. In the old days . . .'

There was this reformatory school, a stern, cheerless building, designed by learned, well-respected men for the containment of friendless, errant girls. It had heavy doors and an abundance of locks and wrought-iron staircases. The girls worked in the laundry, which steamed and hissed and was as hot as Satan's own wash-tub. Dorcas knew that she was lucky to be here, considering she'd poisoned a poor dear babe. She hadn't been hanged, nor had she been sent overseas to the Lord Only

Knows What Hole to die of fevers miscellaneous. The reform-
atory school was run by—

Mrs Bibby stops. 'How old are you supposed to be, Kraken?
Six, isn't it?'

Christabel makes no sound.

'*Bears*, the reformatory school was run by bears,' she declares
with grim glee. 'Should make it more palatable if you are a
child.'

*Bears ran the place. Big Warden Bear, Bigger Warden Bear
and Even Biggest Warden Bear. Big Warden Bear had arms
like a stevedore and a chain. Bigger Warden Bear had no
teeth and a cat-o'-nine-tails. Biggest Warden Bear had a
wall-eye she used to see around corners. She didn't need a
weapon; she just used her massive paws. Dorcas, who was
famous for the crime of poisoning a poor dear babe, had felt
the chain, the cat-o'-nine-tails and the paws. The skin on
Dorcas's arse was as hard as foot-skin and she had no feeling
in her fingertips.*

*Dorcas planned her escape. Only this time she would
take a friend.*

*Dorcas would only ever have one friend – let's call Dorcas's
friend Della. Della had big grey eyes and soft brown curls.
She was kind beyond kindness to everyone and everything.*

*Dorcas planned their escape carefully. Out through the
main gates, hidden in the cart that came to drop off the dirty
laundry and collect the clean laundry all washed and pressed
by the inmates. On a Friday with the workaday week all
but over, the bears would send out for refreshments. The next
Friday, Dorcas and Della watched the cart being loaded.
When the pot-boy came across from the Bell, Dorcas pushed
Della into the cart and under the tarpaulin and climbed in
behind her. In a while the cart began to move.*

Della was scared but Dorcas whispered in her ear until she became calm and fell asleep. Dorcas told her that she would find a home for them and become a rat-catcher. She would make a warm coat for Della with the pelts of the loveliest rats she'd caught. A patch-worked coat with a tabby-cat collar! Dorcas would become wildly successful at the rat-catching. Della would have a parlour and Dorcas would have a pocket-watch.

Della woke when the carriage stopped. When the men took off the tarpaulin Dorcas grabbed Della by the hand and they ran.

As bad luck would have it, the men decided to give chase.

As good luck would have it, night was falling and a fog was unfolding and Dorcas ran towards it, pulling Della behind her.

Dorcas didn't know where they were, only that there were warehouses and factories, narrow streets and tumbledown houses, jumbled in a row like snaggled teeth. She kept running, towards where the fog was thickest, holding fast to Della's hand.

Perhaps the god of errant friendless girls was looking down on them that day, but soon Dorcas and Della were not alone. Dashing beside them: a pair of magical creatures – formed of no more than the fog. Two dancing fog otters! With dog-like heads and lithe twisting bodies.

Della slowed to watch, Dorcas tugged at her, urging her to run. And then, from everywhere it seemed, came the sound of shouting. The fog otters startled and swam away. Dorcas, Della's hand still in hers, plunged after them, her eyes wide open but seeing nothing, hardly knowing where they were running—

The carriage slows and stops.

'Oh, frigging hell, what next?' says Mrs Bibby.

The carriage rocks a little as the driver climbs down. The

horses stamp and humph. Mrs Bibby frowns in the dark; if this is an adjustment of harness, or a fiddling with the lanterns, fine. But here are footsteps, rounding the carriage, stopping outside the door.

There is a rustling; it is Mrs Bibby rummaging in her skirts, under her shawl, followed by a sharp, metallic click.

Then her voice calling out into the pitchy-black, all sweet and calm-like.

'Is there a *problem*, driver?'

Chapter 9

All manner of spirits might be knocking about in a grand old pile like Maris House, or indeed any place with a bit of history to it. Some spectres rattle doorknobs and throw cats and fog looking-glasses. Others are satisfied with causing cold patches on the landing. Some sit up at the breakfast table with their elbows in your kedgeree while you read the obituaries. Others dwell, provokingly, just out of eyeshot. Our business is not with these. It is with but one manifestation: the constant Ruby Doyle, who, flickering with the lustrous light of the afterlife, keeps watch by Bridie's bedside during the hours of the night.

A vision; lost in his own grave-defying thoughts.

The inked heart on his chest shrinks to a peach kernel, then opens, petal by petal – a lotus flower! – only to close again. The mermaid on his shoulder bites her nails, her tail-fin rippling absently. The skull grinds its teeth in a slow, sad, deliberate way.

And Ruby gazes down upon Bridie.

Pale-lipped and lovely in the moonlight, the contours of her face gentle in her sleep. The mad foam of her hair, nightcap forgotten, spills over the pillows.

Towards dawn, when she begins to mutter in her sleep,

Ruby is there. When she calls out, her brow furrowed, Ruby is there. He speaks low and kind to her through her troubled dreams. And he wonders about these dreams; for there is much that Bridie hasn't told him about her life – a child bought for a guinea, a woman alone with her back to the past – and much that he will not ask. Stories, particularly the bad ones, are told in their own time. And so, for now, it is enough that she turns her face to him, like a flower to the sun, and that she sleeps.

For the first time in a long time Bridie will not rise from her bed in the early hours, hot and cold with remembered demons, to see the dawn in with a pipe and swollen eyes. Instead, she sleeps right through, and when she wakes she will blame her good night's rest on a plump feather bed, country air and a dinner of digestible meat.

Just before she wakes, before she starts to stir, Ruby Doyle will sink into the wall with his hat in his hand and a new liquid brilliance to his dark eyes.

Bridie squints into the sunlight. With no sign of Ruby at breakfast she takes to the terrace for the morning air and a rousing shoch on her pipe. And there, after a few moments, he is. Standing along from her with his boots unlaced and his topper jaunty, looking out over the grounds and rubbing his great broad chest. Bridie realises that London murk becomes Ruby; the clear country morning only makes him seem dimmer. As Bridie walks over to him the tattoos on his body wake up. The mermaid on his shoulder unfurls her tail and stretches. She catches sight of Bridie and shakes her hair out with a sleepy pout and nudges Ruby with her inked elbow. He turns and nods at Bridie, a gladdening smile beneath his glorious black moustache.

Bridie sets off across the lawn, which glitters this morning with spilled diamonds of dew. The spiders' webs, too, are made precious; crystalline lacework draped over bushes, strung between branches.

Ruby falls in next to her. He takes his hat off and rubs where the deathblow landed.

'How's the head?'

'Destroyed. Is this for eternity?'

'The spiritualist crowd would encourage you to depart for your home on high.'

Ruby grins, wickedly. 'What if my home's not on high?'

Bridie tightens her bonnet ribbons to hide a smile.

'Did you sleep, Bridie?'

'Like the dead.'

'You don't know the half of it.'

'Ruby—'

'Ah, no, it's grand, no need to open doors.'

'Where did you spend the night?'

'Moaning up and down the passages. Rattling my chains.'

Their eyes meet. His shine. Bridie frowns.

'So where are we headed?' Ruby asks.

'Agnes said that the servants searched the grounds and the lane beyond the gates and found nothing. It would be well to search again.'

'But if they've searched—'

'They'll have missed something, they always do.'

They turn down towards the orchard.

'We'll concentrate on the back route into Maris House.' Bridie points to a gate at the bottom of a track. 'This was the perpetrators' way in most likely.'

'You think so?'

'That's too high.' She gestures towards the boundary wall. 'It runs around the whole estate.'

'And the main gate?'

'Too noisy: gravel all the way down the drive. Besides, if Mrs Bibby colluded with them they would have known it was overlooked: the Pucks have rooms facing out over the front of the house.'

The morning is peaceful yet; they walk, listening to bird-song in the clear early air.

Ruby is the first to speak. 'She's sticking her neck out, Agnes.'

'She has reason enough to dislike Mrs Bibby.'

'With the nurse's rough manners.'

'Agnes has greater reason than that. Didn't you hear what Winnie the kitchenmaid told me?'

'All that whispering in the scullery? I took it to be affairs of the heart.'

Bridie laughs. 'You drifted off? And I thought you would be there with your ear through the wall. Well, affairs of the heart it was. Winnie told me that the footman is sweet on Agnes.'

'Is that right?'

'Only Mrs Puck got to hear about it and put an end to it, of course. Agnes vowed that Mrs Bibby was behind it. The nurse saw the lovers steal a kiss in the orchard. Poor Agnes cried for a week.'

Ruby pulls a disdainful face. 'I wouldn't have thought Agnes the crying kind.'

'And you've never cried yourself, Ruby? When your best dreams were thwarted? When you lost a fight?'

'I always won my fights.'

'Or when your love left you?'

'I've had no love, Bridie.'

'Or when you were a sailor and your ship hit squalls?'

'There were no squalls, only good driving winds in the right direction. I was a lucky sailor.'

'I should say. Didn't you cry when your ship set sail from the coconut beaches?'

'From the sapphire waters and golden sand?'

'The same.'

'You're right of course, that was when I cried.' He grins and the tattooed mermaid on his shoulder shakes her head and turns back to her mirror.

Bridie laughs.

'It's a terrible thing, a heart torn asunder. I should know.' Ruby looks at her slyly. 'A broken pledge; that would do it.'

A smile still dances on Bridie's lips. 'Are you here to torment me, Ruby Doyle?'

Ruby's eyes are bright.

'I don't believe you knew me at all,' Bridie says with conviction, for she has frisked every corner of her mind for a memory of Ruby and found none. 'You are having a lark.'

'I knew your name when we met at the chapel-yard! I'll prove it – wait until I remember.' Ruby closes his eyes and puts his palms together. '*God grant eternal rest to Mammy, Daddy, James, John, Theresa, Margaret, Ellen and little baby Owen.*'

Bridie is overcome at hearing the names of her long-gone family. 'Ruby, how do you know me?'

'If I tell, you'll expect me to go.'

Bridie frowns. 'I don't understand.'

'Our agreement on the train; have you forgotten? I promised to leave you in peace if you solved this great mystery.'

'You *telling* isn't me *solving*.'

Ruby shrugs. 'You'd uphold it anyway, I'd be banished to the church-yard.'

Bridie studies him closely. 'Did we not get on, then?'

'As I said . . .' Ruby grins. 'You're the investigator. You fathom it.'

Past the orchard they follow the track that leads to the gate; it's a churned mess of wheel ruts and footprints.

'It shows some traffic. I'll not be able to read much here.'

The back gates are open. They pass through them and follow the road round, with the high wall bordering Sir Edmund's estate to their left and the woods to the right. The autumn colours are rich in the early sun, with golden tones and deep reds and startling oranges against a rinsed blue sky. The wood is rowdy with bird-song.

'Clean air: a tonic to the lungs,' says Ruby. 'What does it smell like, Bridie?'

'Leaf mould, cow shit and this fella's feet.'

The man sitting by the side of the path tips the brim of his hat and hugs his knees. 'Alms, miss. For a gentleman of the road.'

He is well wrinkled, with the look of a turkey about him; a gizzardy string of neck rising from a bulked-out breast, achieved by the layering of many weather-stained clothes upon his body. The toecaps of his boots are splitting open like ripe peel to reveal blackened feet.

'Is herself in, the formidable Mother Puck?'

'She is. You'll get short shrift up there.' Bridie rummages in her pocket for some coins. 'Here, Father Road, buy yourself a new pair of boots.'

The old man stretches his turkey neck and looks at the money. He takes it and nods. 'Ingratiated to you, I am.'

'Not at all.'

'This house has a cursed aspect.'

'Go on, Father Road.'

'A fell spirit stalks the lord of the manor. She stands outside his window, all night sometimes. She trails him on his constitutionals.' The old man ruminates. 'She sobs in the bushes and washes her face in the pond.'

Bridie bites back a groan. 'A ghost, is it, you're after seeing? Lady Berwick who drowned?'

The old man scratches his head. 'Ah, no, Lady Berwick was a big auld woman, and this one is a young slip of a spirit. A blue-eyed waif, hair like sun-spun corn.' He stops scratching and scrutinises his fingernail. Then he bites it. 'Livestock.'

'There are no such things as ghosts, Father Road,' says Bridie, careful to avoid Ruby's eye.

'Now I didn't say the fell spirit was a ghost, did I?' He pouts. 'Although, granted, she haunts the place.' He ponders this, then adds, darkly, 'She has cause to return.'

'Tell me — what cause?'

'That's the mystery, right there.' The old man picks his ear reflectively.

'I'm looking for something, Father Road, not long stolen from the house. Would you have any wisdoms?'

The old man perks up. 'Let me guess: a pretty parlour maid, a golden spoon, a crown?'

'None of those things,' admits Bridie. 'Do you know the servants, up at the house?'

'I have had my dealings.'

'Mrs Bibby, would you have come across her?'

The old man sucks air in with a sudden hiss.

'Rough manners, bad leg?'

He winds his neck back into his over-stuffed body and pulls his hat down over his eyes.

'Father Road?'

Not a peep.

She puts another coin in the old man's open palm. 'Obliged, Father Road,' she says.

He tips his hat.

Bridie walks a while. If she were to keep going straight ahead, in a few days she'd reach London. She can't help but feel that this is where the thieves headed, where she would head, with a stolen child to hide or trade. Woods run parallel to Sir Edmund's estate. Ruby stands at the edge, watching, shimmering. He takes off his hat and runs his hand over his shorn black hair.

'Look at those lines there!' Bridie points at the churned-up mud. 'That deep arc, that swerve, then the wheels going backwards. The width, the depth of the wheel tread, it was a gig, Ruby. I can see it.'

'You can?' Ruby draws nearer, pulling at the side of his moustache. He glances at her doubtfully.

'The rest of the marks are wagons, carts, see?' Bridie walks a few paces. 'But these are different, these tell us something.'

'They do?'

Bridie crosses back and forth over the road, careful not to step on the prints.

'They tell us that a gig in a hurry turned out from these gates . . . further down it stopped – suddenly; it was ambushed. No, that doesn't seem right.'

She goes over to the trees. 'There are three sets of footprints leading off into the woods.'

The dead man marvels at her.

'Broken branches, they stumbled there.' She's in the undergrowth, touching plants, leaves. 'They were carrying something awkward, a foot sunk here, and here.'

Bridie casts around, forging forwards, head down. Wading into drifts of leaves, pushing past brambles. Ruby, beside her, strides through tree trunks and fallen logs. They reach a clearing, where stands a mouldering chapel with a mossy roof and an awkward tower.

Yews, full of the squabble of crows, stand in solemn groups. They cast a solid shade. On the path that surrounds the chapel, Bridie's boot heels skitter on shattered glass; she stoops to examine and then looks up in surprise.

'The windows have been broken. This glass is fresh on the ground.'

Bridie walks to the porch. The door is ajar; she goes inside.

The chapel is an unwelcoming place. Bridie shivers to think of time spent here, in the hug of cold stone and damp air. Among sagging Bibles and mildewing kneelers, coughing through *Thy kingdom come, Thy will be done* on hard pews. That the chapel has been abandoned for some while is clear, Sir Edmund's household preferring the village church no doubt, if not for the sermons then for the gossip.

Ruby strays up the aisle with his hat under his arm, stopping to examine the broken font and the candles melted on the altar, or to peer up at the blown windows.

'It's all been happening here, Bridie.'

She's already heading into the vestry.

The room is bare but for a shelf with several smashed lanterns. There are signs of recent habitation: an apple core and a half-eaten meat pie on the windowsill, a chair dragged across the unswept floor, finger marks on dusty surfaces.

But it's the vestry cupboard that Bridie is looking at intently.

Ruby follows her into the room.

'In there, Ruby, at the bottom, beneath the vestments.'

Ruby frowns. 'What is that?'

'Snail shells, hundreds of them. Remember what Agnes said, about the buckets full of snails every morning up at the house?'

'What does it mean?'

'I've no idea, unless Christabel is somehow drawing this to her.'

'You think they brought the child here?' Ruby deliberates. 'Surely they'd have wanted to get her as far away as possible?'

'You'd assume so.' Bridie touches the walls. 'They're running wet.'

'Like in the west wing.'

Bridie kicks the snail shells out of the way and climbs inside the cupboard. 'They kept her in here.'

'What makes you think that?'

Bridie holds up a bent nail. She gestures at the back of the cupboard, a pattern of bumps, wavy lines and circles scratched into the surface of the wood.

'Do you see what she's drawn, Ruby? It's her nursery wallpaper at Maris House.'

Bridie walks between the headstones, the crosses, the covered urns, the plump marble pillows inviting everlasting slumber. At the apex of two walkways is Lady Berwick's tomb. Stone angels perch on all four corners of her tomb: wings folded and faces impassive, they are giving nothing away.

Beyond the main pathways the memorials are older: cracked and mossed, worn and pitted, tangled with briars and carpeted with last years' leaves. Bridie clears away the foliage to read names, dates.

'Bridie.'

Bridie glances up and looks at Ruby. He is pointing beyond a rusted railing. Between two graves, a body lies face down.

The dead woman is lodged between the final resting places of Winifred Godsalve and Robert Swann, obscured by the kerbstones and hidden by brambles. It would be easy enough to pass this corpse by.

Bridie draws nearer. Ruby stays rooted, hat in hand and horrified.

'On first sight she doesn't appear to be our missing nurse,' Bridie remarks. 'But let's see what we have here.'

A young woman; small in stature and clearly underfed, so that Bridie is able to turn her, after taking careful note of the surrounding area. Beetles run across the corpse's muddied bodice. She has lost her bonnet and her fair hair is tangled in the thorns. Her lips are pale. Her blue eyes are wide open.

★

The body is laid out on a trestle table in the vestry of the chapel. The local sergeant has visited at the site of discovery and supervised the removal of the corpse inside, pending the arrival of the undertaker. The district inspector and the doctor have been sent for and a police officer stands guard outside the chapel door.

Mr Puck is in shock. He sits with the young officer in the porch. They drink the tea brought down by Agnes, who has taken the news back to Maris House that Mr Puck has identified the body as a perfect stranger.

For some of the servants this discovery will be the last straw; they have already put up with so much. The locked doors and the snails and the mists and the rumours of Sir Edmund's abomination in the west wing.

Mr Puck stares into his teacup. He has barely said a word since viewing the body. He is beset by the anxious thought that he *has*, in fact, seen the poor young woman before. At dusk, flitting between the roses in her dark cape and bonnet. He rather imagined that she was the presence of the late Lady Berwick, in younger, happier times. Mr Puck reasons with his teacup: even if the poor dead woman is not, in fact, the presence of the late Lady Berwick she is still, nonetheless, a stranger. With that part of his testimony ship-shapely, Mr Puck resolves to think no more about it and immediately feels better.

Bridie works quickly in the vestry. Although Dr Harbin is nowhere to be found, the inspector is on his way and the undertaker will come thereafter. This may be her only opportunity to examine the body.

She opens her leather case, puts on an apron and tucks her hair carefully inside a clean scarf. Then she turns to the table, pulling down the sheet, making an initial assessment of the condition of the corpse. Ruby faces the wall, for the sake of decorum, he says.

'The cause of death is strangulation,' deduces Bridie. 'The

bruises on the victim's neck are compatible with the span of an average-sized man's hand, I'd say.'

'The bastard.'

'On first inspection, there is no evidence that the deceased was defiled.'

Ruby shuffles in the corner. Bridie suspects he's blessing himself.

'Her clothes are weather-stained.' Bridie bends over the corpse. 'Her feet are calloused, showing that this young woman tramped. She's very undernourished. She's been living hard lately.'

'Poor little soul.'

'A blue-eyed waif, hair like spun gold . . .'

'Old Father Road!' exclaims Ruby. 'You think she's the young woman he's seen around the grounds?'

'She matches his description.' Bridie examines the corpse's hand. 'Her nails are broken and there is damage to her wrists, forearms, indicative of a violent struggle. I would say that she put up a fight. Her attacker may be injured, scratched, possibly to the face.'

'That might help us identify them.'

'They'll be miles away now. But this is curious: her hands are cleaner than I would expect, much cleaner than the rest of her. It's possible that the assailant wiped them over, wishing to remove any clues as to their identity.'

'What sort of clues?'

'Hair, snagged strands of cloth, perhaps.' Bridie inspects under the remaining fingernails. 'There's nothing left here.'

Bridie searches down the length of the skirts. 'I thought so. She's a stuff-pocket sown here. It's empty now, though, but for a couple of coins.'

'A stuff-pocket?'

'An old pickpocket's trick, I use it too, to hide things in my petticoats.'

'Of course you do, Mrs Devine. So there's a few clues on her?'

'If I can find them before the inspector arrives and throws me out.'

'And you here on Sir Edmund's invitation.'

'Sir Edmund's not likely to tell the police why I'm here.' Bridie pauses. 'Besides, some people have notions about fitting conduct for ladies – scrutinising dead bodies isn't seen to be seemly.'

'Some people are awful bloody ignorant,' says Ruby, with feeling.

Bridie glances up at him, not much more than an arm's length from her. Noticing how, in this moderate, even light, against the whitewashed wall of the vestry, he shimmers and is marvellous. She can see the vestry wall through him, but she can also see his drawers, his bandaged hands and his boots. All in perfect detail. His back is massive and muscular, in the centre a tattooed gunship bobs over blue-inked waves, full-rigged, her insignia flying. On the nape of his neck a tattooed moon glows as she moves through all her phases.

Above, at the base of his skull, the site of the stunning blow that dispatched him; blood coagulating.

Bridie frowns.

He shifts on the spot, turning his head a little, as if aware of her gaze. She sees the side of his face; dark lashes and clean-shaved jaw.

How can a dead man be so alive?

Bridie can almost smell this fighter: the sweat and the liniment, the smoke and the violence and the heat. His skin glistens. She could trace the beads of sweat with her fingers, down the curve of his spine. Then lightly, her fingers could dance across his back, along his sides – and, oh, turning him to face her, touching the broad chest of him, his shoulders, his arms. Unwrapping his bandages, kissing his palms, his blasted knuckles. Meeting his dark eyes holding hers, so that it's hard to ever look away.

Ruby sways and flickers. The moon on his neck wanes; a perfect bright crescent. He coughs and hitches up his drawers.

'Any more clues there, Bridie?' he says. 'With the inspector on his way to throw you out?'

A flush steals into Bridie's face. She turns her attention to the body on the trestle table, unbuttoning the corpse's clothes with careful fingers. She finds further bruising to her hips and ribs.

'She was carried. Dragged maybe.'

Ruby stands silent, his head bowed.

'What's it like, Ruby? You know . . . being dead.'

'Not much different really.'

'You can walk through closed doors.'

'That's different.'

'Can you feel things?'

'What like?'

'The wind on your face, or the rain . . .'

Ruby's voice, when it comes, is soft. 'I can't say that I can.'

There is silence for a while: Ruby examining the wall, Bridie examining the body.

'When did she die, Bridie?'

'It's not exact. Taking into account weather, location, the natural processes of the corpse – skin colour, extent of rigor mortis—'

'Do you have to?'

'I would say this corpse is a day or so old, Ruby. No more than two, perhaps.'

'So she may have had something to do with our stolen child?'

'Possibly, or perhaps she chanced upon the thieves hiding in the chapel. Whatever her reason was for haunting Maris House' – Bridie carefully rearranges the dead woman's garments – 'it could have made her an accidental witness.'

'Surely Sir Edmund will tell the police about his daughter now.'

'He'll be even less likely to tell them, Ruby.'

'You'd expect him to want the police out looking for her.'

'Not if he has a good reason to keep her secret.'

'She wasn't born to his wife,' poses Ruby. 'Or the servants were right and she's some class of abomination.'

'Or because Sir Edmund acquired the child illegally himself.'

'You think he stole Christabel?'

'Stole, bought, it would fit.'

Muffled voices in the chapel, footsteps ringing nearer, and Bridie just has time to pull the sheet back over the corpse and push her case under the table before the vestry door opens. The district inspector accompanied by Mr Puck. The inspector is a large man with a round face easily reddened by exertion and the bearing of someone who has been around for a while and knows everything.

'Have you reason to be bothering that corpse, madam?'

Bridie glances at Mr Puck; the butler shakes his head.

'I was just straightening things out, Inspector,' she says.

'Is that right?' And what would your name happen to be, madam?'

'Mrs Devine.'

'*Mrs Devine*, is it?' The inspector nods. 'Well, Mrs Devine, there will be no altering or concealing of evidence, no pilfering of pockets and snipping bits off on my watch.'

'He's a sharp one,' mutters Ruby.

'There has been no altering, concealing, pilfering here, Inspector.' Bridie meets the policeman's eye squarely.

The inspector grunts and escorts Mr Puck to the side of the table. 'Right, sir. Can you confirm for me that this poor unfortunate is a stranger to Maris House?' The inspector pulls back the sheet.

Mr Puck looks down. 'Yes, Inspector. I can confirm that this is a perfect stranger.'

The baronet, in his study, sits behind his desk wearing a surprisingly stern expression.

Bridie, undaunted, continues. 'So, what you are saying, sir, is that the murder of the young woman found in the chapel-yard is in no way linked to Christabel being taken?'

'A mere coincidence.'

'Even knowing, as we do, sir, that the perpetrators hid Christabel in the vestry before moving on again?'

Catching a hint of Bridie's suspicion, he frowns. 'As I said, madam, a mere coincidence.'

'Sir Edmund, I'm sorry, but I'm not convinced.' Bridie takes a careful breath. 'Tell me, is there one good reason for me not to tell the police that this young woman's death may have been a consequence of the abduction of your daughter?'

'His jaw is going! The clench to it!' says Ruby, who is sitting on the corner of Sir Edmund's desk, scrutinising the baronet's responses. 'You've got him riled now.'

Sir Edmund scowls. 'I thought you were an expert in these matters, Mrs Devine. If the police are involved it will make it harder to find Christabel. Those people will run to ground or take her out of the country.' He looks at Bridie pointedly. 'Or a worse fate might befall her, if her abductors panic.'

Bridie decides to ignore this provocation. 'And what of the young woman lying dead in the vestry of your chapel?'

'As Mr Puck says, she's a perfect stranger.'

'And yet she fits the description of a young woman who has been seen around the grounds, Sir Edmund.'

'Who has seen this young woman? I haven't.'

'Perhaps she was an ex-servant, or one-time beneficiary of the estate. She'd plainly had a difficult time of things; walking distances, probably without abode, half-starved—'

'Hedge-creepers and vagabonds are not tolerated here.' Sir Edmund seethes. 'My servants are not out tramping the roads, madam, they are all accounted for.'

'Apart from your child's nurse, sir. I wouldn't say Mrs Bibby is accounted for.'

'See him flinch!' says Ruby. 'That's a sore point right there, Bridie!'

'How did Mrs Bibby come to work here, sir? And what do you know about her character?'

'Impeccable references. Highly recommended.'

'Recommended by whom?'

'William Harbin. He'd come across her in a professional capacity, working for another family. He was greatly impressed by her diligence and discretion. Her situation was ending and we were suddenly in need—'

'Why had Mrs Bibby's previous situation ended, sir?'

Sir Edmund looks impatient. 'The child had grown.'

'This other family, Sir Edmund, they provided references?'

'Naturally.'

'Would you happen to have their names, sir?'

Sir Edmund rears. 'Harbin organised it.'

'I see – and where is Dr Harbin now, sir? He could not be found to attend the chapel-yard corpse. The inspector had to send to Polegate for a doctor.'

'How would I bloody know—'

'Of course,' Bridie counters calmly. 'Just to be clear, there have been no other incidents in the time – not quite a month, is it? – that Mrs Bibby has been in your employ?'

'No.'

Bridie waits. With nothing forthcoming, she changes tack.

'You're a collector, Sir Edmund, are you not? With a specialism: a profound interest in water, how it behaves and what organisms, particularly those of an anomalous nature, might live in and around it.'

Ruby leans over the desk, observing Sir Edmund with deep scrutiny. 'The Winter Horror, don't deny it, man.'

'I fail to see your point, madam,' says Sir Edmund, coldly.

'I wish to ask you a candid question, sir. I would welcome an equally candid answer.'

'Careful,' warns Ruby. 'He's about to hop.'

'Is it possible, Sir Edmund, that Christabel is not your natural daughter, but rather you acquired her on the premise of some unique properties she may, or may not, have?'

Sir Edmund is rigid with rage, his eyes are locked on Bridie's, his hands grasp the backs of his thighs. 'How dare—'

'I propose,' she continues grimly, thinking of the restraints in the nursery, 'that Christabel was kept secret as a result of having been removed from her original friends, who would wish her returned, sir.'

Sir Edmund's face is an apoplectic red.

'He's scarlet, oh Jesus, he'll burst, Bridie—' whispers Ruby.

'Sir Edmund, did you acquire Christabel by means nefarious?'

'You, madam, are asking the wrong questions to the wrong person,' replies Sir Edmund, with choked-back fury.

'I require the truth, sir.'

Sir Edmund looks Bridie dead in the eye. 'Christabel is my daughter and I want her safe return, that's all there is to it. I'm not a suspect, Mrs Devine. I'm your damned client.'

Chapter 10

Sir Edmund's carriage waits on the drive to convey Mrs Devine back to Polegate Station. Bridie is ready to return to London, for Maris House has offered questions rather than answers, dissembling rather than truth-telling. And isn't the metropolis just the place to hide a remarkable child? And if she is remarkable, well, there will be interested parties in London, too.

But Bridie has one last stop along the way.

She calls out to the footman as she takes her seat. 'Tell the driver I want to visit Dr Harbin on the way to the station, if you please.'

A dead boxer climbs into the carriage. Bridie watches him settle beside her. He takes off his top hat and lays it on his transparent knees.

'The doctor's next, is it?' he asks.

'He's been lying low since we got here. Where was he when it came to examining the chapel-yard corpse? We'll give him a jounce and see if any clues fall out. Not least, where he fetched this Mrs Bibby from.'

The footman extracts a pocket-watch fussily.

'We've time,' shouts Bridie. 'If the driver gets on with it.'

The footman winces, folds up the steps and shuts the carriage door with an air of good riddance.

The carriage pulls away from Maris House. They ride in silence for a while.

'I'll not miss this place,' says Bridie.

'It's been a treat, what with the snails and the thing in the jar and the kidnapped child and the corpse. And everyone hiding something, it seems.'

'That's usually the way of it, Ruby. The snails, I must say, aren't usual.'

The carriage takes the gate at a decent clip and is a way down the stretch of the road by the wood before it abruptly loses speed.

'Ah, now, what's going on?' Bridie lowers the window and leans out.

Ahead, in the middle of the road, a man stands facing the coach. His hand held up, palm outward. Behind him stands a hired gig.

In the gesture of this man's outstretched palm is the conviction that a team of carriage horses, a ton of metal and painted wood, a resentful driver and a guest already late for the London train will stop at his command.

The coachman curses him to hell and brings his horses to a jolting halt.

The man rounds the side of the coach and nods up at the passenger leaning out of the window.

'My, my, Mrs Devine, is it? Are you well?'

Here is a man with an inscrutable face. Only, see here now the beginnings of a smile behind the immaculate sandy beard. And surely, a quickening brightness in the grey eyes that look into the carriage.

This man appears possessed, above all else, of considerable intelligence and alertness. He would never be ambushed, surprised, duped or hoodwinked in any way. Alongside this, a natural authority and none of the deference expected from his class. Though dressed in well-tailored clothes, his accent marks him as the product of a ragged part of London and he makes no attempt to hide his origin. *I was a street orphan*, states the steel in his jaw and his eyes, and isn't the strongest backbone found in those who fight to survive?

There is only one incongruous note to this man: the fine blousy flower in his buttonhole, a thing of real beauty, of the palest apricot.

'Inspector Rose,' says Bridie. 'Always a pleasure.'

'You are making haste from the scene of a robbery and murder, madam – what are you hiding in there?'

'Who's to say I'm hiding anything, Inspector?'

His face shows mild amusement. 'There's a furtive turn to you.'

'That's habitual.'

He laughs. The horses shift, the carriage rolls. 'What's going on up at the house?'

'Ask Sir Edmund, or the red-faced inspector. They'll enlighten you.'

'And that's all?'

'From me, it is.'

'This is a long way to come for a specialist like you.' He glances around him, at the empty country lane.

'Likewise, all the way from London for an unidentified corpse?'

'I am hunting a master criminal.'

'What's his name?' asks Bridie.

'Her names are too many to mention.' Rose smiles. 'Hard to pin down, like her, but I'm working on it.'

'One of the servants had a limp and rough manners,' remarks Bridie, attentive to the inspector's expression.

His smile doesn't waver. 'Did she now?'

'It's delightful to converse with you, Rose. But I have a train to catch.'

'Then you must go. We should work together again, Bridie. Remember Monsieur Pilule? Whenever you're ready for something livelier than bygone crypt bodies.'

Bridie frowns. 'You are forgetting my recent failure, Inspector.'

'And you are forgetting your many successes,' replies Rose, smiling into her eyes.

Ruby watches them closely, pulling his moustache sullenly.

Rose tips the rim of his hat. 'Well, look me up in London, Bridie. I say it every time—'

'It's always better to live in hope.'

Rose grins. 'And love to our uncle Prudhoe – you'll see him before I do, no doubt.' He taps the side of the carriage. 'Take her away, driver.'

The carriage moves forward. As they pass the gig Rose jumps into the driver's seat and salutes.

'Is this cove family to you, Bridie?'

'I've no family living; he refers to our shared friend, the chemist Rumold Fortitude Prudhoe.'

'Uncle Prudhoe?'

'Rose was a street orphan, Prudhoe gave him a home.' Bridie leans out of the window, watching the inspector go off in his gig at great shake. 'Prudhoe took me in for a while, too. Rose and I were play-fellows, I suppose.'

'You've known him a while, then, this Rose?'

Bridie sits back in her seat. 'Woman and girl.'

'Isn't that grand.'

Bridie glances at him.

Ruby makes an effort. 'He's done well for himself,' he adds, begrudgingly.

Bridie nods. 'Prudhoe was a good mentor. We'll visit him on our return to London. He knows collectors, good and bad; he may have heard something about Christabel.'

'And then he'll tell his adopted nephew what you are up to?'

Bridie shakes her head. 'Prudhoe would never betray a confidence.'

'You've worked with Rose before?'

'Ever heard of Monsieur Pilule's Roast House?'

'Can't say I have.'

'Just as well. The proprietor, Charlie Pill, was running the establishment while he worked on the sly in the body trade. His old man had done well in the resurrection business before the Anatomy Act.'

Ruby looks confused.

'The Act gave the medical men a better supply of cadavers to play with – the bodies of the destitute at their disposal if no one laid claim to them. Before that, a fresh-dug corpse from a night-time grave-yard was more welcome than a clutch of new potatoes.'

'Ah, no!'

'Of course, it was only a matter of time before Charlie brought his two interests together: fine dining and corpses.'

'Bridie, don't—'

'He powdered human bone for the French rolls. Brought 'em up nice and white, Charlie said, far better than chalk and alum.'

'Blessed Apostles!'

'Then he began to serve more unusual cuts of meat. You know, for the connoisseur. Highly spiced. Difficult to digest.'

Ruby takes off his hat and rubs his forehead. 'Jesus, Bridie, wouldn't you ever have had a normal sort of life? Poking and nosing after stolen children and murders and bits of bodies, heaven knows what you have in your case there.'

'And what if no one wanted to poke or nose around, Ruby?' Bridie's voice is barbed. 'Wrong-doers would get away with whatever they like.'

'That's not what I'm saying.'

'Is it because I'm a woman that you object to it?'

'Would you hear yourself? I object to it because it turns my insides. Now tell me about this Charlie Pill but without all the grisly details.'

'We helped prepare a case against him – Rose and I. Charlie swung for it, but his wealthier customers' – Bridie's eyes are lit – 'they were the worst off, especially if they'd opted for the fricassee.'

Ruby groans.

The carriage draws up outside a new brick house on the outskirts of a village.

Bridie checks her pocket-watch. 'There's still time to have a few words with the doctor before we catch the train. Find out why he's a lie-low.'

On Bridie's arrival at Dr Harbin's house she immediately establishes two things. First, the doctor is nowhere to be found and, second, his laundry woman doesn't know if she's on her ear or her arse. Mrs Swann came to collect the wash and found the whole house turned over. Bridie feels for her, the large, baffled and vaguely hostile woman who stands in the hall still in bonnet and shawl. Mrs Swann becomes more amenable when Bridie mentions her acquaintance with the doctor and Sir Edmund.

'This bodes bad indeed, Mrs Devine,' says Mrs Swann. 'See here – the doctor's hat and coat – the doctor, wherever he is, hatless and coatless! I have never known him to go out thus.'

Bridie follows Mrs Swann into the parlour.

Ruby goes ahead. 'I'll take a look around.' He melts into the wall.

Anything that can be broken is broken. The potted parlour palms have been seized and dragged across the carpet. Chairs lie slashed and books torn to pieces.

'They've gone through like a dose, ma'am.' Mrs Swann points at the leather case up-ended on the floor. 'The doctor's medical bag is there. He would no sooner leave the house without his medical bag than fly up into the sky.'

Bridie follows Mrs Swann into the surgery. The room has been ripped apart with an even greater ferocity. Panelling has been prised from the walls, seats knocked from chairs and every last drawer smashed like driftwood.

Cabinets have been wrecked, boxes of vials and bottles shattered, their contents drip still on shelves. Bandages and dressings have been thrown like streamers around the room.

On the floor, under the desk, a cigar butt. Bridie picks it up.

Ruby returns, by way of an open door this time. 'The rest of the house is ransacked, there's nobody else here.' He glances at the object in her hand. 'What is it?'

She rolls the butt between her two fingers and sniffs it. '*Hussar Blend*, sold in a cheap tobacconist's near Bart's. A favourite of medical students, but an uncommon choice for a fully fledged doctor.'

'Why is that?'

'It's like smoking cat shit and straw, Ruby.'

Bridie turns to Mrs Swann, who is standing nearby tutting at the carnage. 'Did Dr Harbin smoke these cigars?'

Mrs Swann peers at her. 'Is it *me* you're talking to now, ma'am?'

'It is, Mrs Swann.'

'Then, no, ma'am, I've never known the doctor to smoke in his life or countenance it in others. He disagrees with it wholesomely.'

Bridie picks through the contents of Dr Harbin's writing bureau, tumbled and torn-up papers and pamphlets and letters.

'The child,' says Ruby. 'What about Dr Harbin's child?'

Bridie turns to Mrs Swann. 'Where's Myrtle?'

'She's in the garden, ma'am, but I can't get no sense from her.'

'Can you show me?'

Mrs Swann leads Bridie into a kitchen strewn with smashed crockery and dented pans. They slip on spilt semolina and scattered tea. The pantry door is off its hinge.

Bridie surveys the damage. 'The question is: were they simply destruction-bent, or wild to find something?'

Mrs Swann looks dismayed. 'If they did take anything, ma'am, how would we ever know with all this ruination?'

Myrtle sits on a wooden bench set into the hedge in the vegetable garden. Bridie can only see her hand; it is rocking a doll's wicker crib.

When Bridie approaches, Myrtle stops and holds a finger in front of her mouth. 'Shh, Rosebud is sleeping.' She rolls her eyes. 'Finally.'

Myrtle's hair is burnished to a rich brown in a shaft of autumn sun that falls in this sheltered pocket of the garden. But the child's face is pale and her eyes dull.

Bridie takes a seat next to her. 'Rosebud is a world of trouble.'

Myrtle nods wearily. 'She is, Mrs Devine, she really is.'

From the house comes the sound of Mrs Swann doing battle with dust-pan, mop and bucket. It's a modest spot, but comfortable, for a doctor and his young daughter (the doctor's wife having expired introducing Myrtle to the world and the doctor showing no fancy towards remarrying, as far as Mrs Swann can see). In the garden the last leggy beans wigwam and dusty cabbages sprawl. Around them the hives are busy, the bees dance in the sweet-apple air of the orchard. Ruby reaches up to the fruit, as if he'd like to pick one. Remembering, he retracts his hand, folds his arms and wanders on.

Bridie turns to the child. 'Where's your papa, Myrtle?'

'Don't know really, Mrs Devine.'

'Did your papa turn the house topsy-turvy?'

'No, someone came.'

'Did you see them?'

'No, I heard them. Bang, bang, crash. So I hid, like this.' She stops rocking the crib and presses herself into the hedge.

Bridie nods. 'Was your papa here when they came?'

Myrtle thinks for a while. 'Maybe he was, maybe he wasn't. Papa slips in and out.' She makes a shape with her hand. 'Like a grass snake.'

Myrtle stands and pulls Rosebud from the crib. Holding the doll by the ankle, she pulls a scrap-book out from under the mattress and hands it to Bridie.

'You mean for me to look at your scrap-book?' says Bridie.

Myrtle sidles up to her elbow and leans over to turn the pages for her.

'What's this?' Bridie points at a drawing of a stout woman with blue lines streaming from her mouth and nose and hands.

'That's the old nurse before the new nurse.'

Ruby moves closer to look.

'What are these blue lines, Myrtle?' asks Bridie.

Myrtle rubs her nose. 'Water. She's drowning.'

'Drowning? So that's a wash-tub she's in?'

Myrtle laughs. 'That's not a wash-tub. She's sitting on a chair and that's the fireplace.'

'I don't understand, Myrtle. Where would the water be for her to drown in?'

'Christabel makes the water come.' Myrtle takes the scrap-book from Bridie's hands and closes it. She puts it back under the crib's mattress, drops Rosebud in on top and covers all with a quilt, patting down vigorously.

'You didn't see this happen, did you?'

Myrtle shakes her head. 'No, Mrs Bibby told me about it.'

'People don't drown in armchairs,' Bridie says kindly. 'Do you think Mrs Bibby meant to scare you with that story?'

'She's worse stories than that,' sniffs Myrtle. 'She killed a gentleman and a lady and chopped them up. She put the lady in a picnic hamper.'

'Mrs Bibby told you this?' asks Bridie, incredulous.

'Oh, yes,' says Myrtle, mildly. 'And she was nearly caught, once when she was Lil, once when she was some other name. But she's no fruit of the gibbet.'

Myrtle sits down and rests her head against her hands with a deep sigh, gazing around with tired eyes at the bees and the cabbages, the windfalls and the dying leaves.

'Mrs Swann said I can stay with her until Papa comes home, for as long as that takes. I told her that Papa will never be back.' Myrtle pauses. 'Then Mrs Swann said I could only stay until next Tuesday.'

'Why won't your papa be back?'

'Because he stole Christabel.'

Chapter 11

In the parlour above Wilks's of Denmark Street, Cora Butter is swaddling a specimen jar. The contents of this jar are disturbing to Cora's peace of mind. She moves it carefully, so as not to drop it, or joggle it unduly. Heaven forbid that the contents would find some egress. The creature is attached to its home by a web of wire and the glass seems strong and the stopper well made. But this doesn't reassure Cora. She has studied the thing in the jar for the longest while, unnerving herself in the process. Sometimes she's certain she sees its fist twitch, or a bubble escape from the nubbin of its nose. But she is mistaken: the beast is beyond dead, its features frozen, its little barrel chest still. Knowing from Bridie what collectors do and what they are capable of, Cora has looked for the connection, the tell-tale splice where flesh meets scale, the crinkled ridge. But if there is one, Cora can't see it. She carries the jar downstairs and lays it in the borrowed perambulator alongside a comprehensive box of pastry delights from Frau Weiss's bakery and a few bottles of adulterated Madeira (for it's never nice to go visiting empty-handed).

Cora ambles back up the stairs to the parlour. 'The infant abomination is tucked up tight and ready for its outing. You ought to leave it with Dr Prudhoe,' she says, peevishly. 'Let him find a home for it among all the nasty articles he has in his workshop.'

'It worries you, Cora?' asks Bridie.

'It gives me bloody nightmares. Who would create something like that?'

Ruby Doyle, who is standing by the parlour window, casts Cora a sympathetic glance. Having no answers for her (at least none that she could hear), he turns his attention outside again. The street is hopping: the living swarm before Ruby's dead eyes – costermongers doing the go-around with trays of oranges and nuts; street performers limbering; kitchenmaids sallying forth with market baskets, eyeing the ribbon vendors and eluding the coalmen. Tribes of pickpockets, fleet-footed miscreants, thread through the traffic. Here trots a dapper wag, high collar and resplendent whiskers. There steps a blue-eyed beauty in a fetching bonnet. Ruby wishes himself a frock coat and a new top hat, a hot shave and a good breakfast, a scarlet cravat, a pair of kid gloves and a pocket-watch. He would give the world just to saunter out onto the streets as a living man again, to look and be looked at.

'I miss being seen,' he announces. 'I was a spectacle.'

'You still are,' mutters Bridie.

She folds the note she has just dashed into an envelope. It is addressed to the Reverend Edward Gale, Highgate Chapel. The subject of the note: Mrs Devine craves an audience with the vicar at his earliest convenience. For Bridie's mind keeps returning – via the Winter Mermaid and the puncture bites on Myrtle Harbin's arm – to the walled-up infant in the crypt with teeth like a pike. She needs to examine the corpses again, in decent light and preferably without the curate Cridge leering over her shoulder.

'Will you get this across to Highgate today, Cora? I can't understand why the vicar hasn't responded to the letter I sent before I left for Maris House. You say there's been nothing from him?'

'Not a word.' Cora takes the letter.

'I'll have to go back.'

'Tramping all over, spending shoe leather. You should entreat Dr Prudhoe to come here to Denmark Street. Dragging that awful jarful miles out of town and into the country.'

'I need the walk; I want to think, Cora. And besides, it will be no effort with the perambulator.'

Cora concedes to that. The contraption handles beautifully and is spacious enough for three babies sardined. And it's sturdy. Six of Mrs Ackers' offspring can be simultaneously borne by it: on top, inside and in the parcel rack beneath. Mr Ackers, a master coachbuilder, has put his expertise into this vehicle. The suspension is without equal and the lines as pleasing as a barouche.

The Winter Mermaid will be conveyed in style and safety.

Cora nods. 'Well, the thing is intact yet and it's already come all the way from Polegate.'

'That's the spirit.'

'I knew it would be offensive when I read *handle with care* on that crate.' Cora wrinkles her nose. 'Fancy sending that item to me.'

'How else would I have got it past Mrs Puck? I put it in a box and told Mr Puck it was my microscope and there would be hell to pay if it arrived broken.'

'Won't they miss it?'

'With Sir Edmund's present worries?' Bridie catches Cora's disapproving expression. 'I'll return it, of course. Once I work out its bearing on the investigation.'

'You might have packed the family silver.'

'You're right, Cora. But this jar is worth much more.'

★

Bridie finds the walk to Brixton pleasant, for the day is fine yet. Over Waterloo Bridge: carriages and carts and horses and humans, moving in and out of the maw of the great metropolis. She heads past St John's and Waterloo Station, the breweries and printers and tanneries, towards clearer air and Kennington Road. Mrs Ackers' perambulator glides ahead, now and again people stop Bridie to pry and coo, only to be disappointed of an eyeful of a fine fat baby.

Ruby walks alongside her with the awkward, deferential air of a new father, pointing out divots and holes in the road, scowling at carriages and carts that swerve too near as on they go, leaving behind Kennington Park and St Mark's. Bridie steals a look at Ruby. He catches her and smiles back, his brown eyes full and kind and hot on hers. She feels the sudden keen pain of something like sadness. If he wasn't dead and she was inclined – she *is* inclined. She could just imagine a life beginning and ending with him. Ruby drunk home with his boots on in bed – oh, the rows and the making up! Having a rabble of dark-eyed children to him. Growing old and the familiarity of his touch, his thoughts, his breath, his fingertips smoothing a lose hair, his lips bent to her neck. And she's awash with sorrow, because she can't have a dead man. The sudden watery lustre to her eyes she blames on the freshening air.

The walk does her good, the early afternoon fair and breezy. Bridie pushing a baby carriage with an incredible cargo down onto the Brixton Road, towards St Matthew's and the Hill. And there is the White Horse tavern and the pleasingly untidy run of villas. A mill's sail turns into view above the trees. Just beyond lies the women's prison, further in the distance the water works.

Ruby steals a look at Bridie. She catches him and smiles back, her eyes full of devilment and who knows what thoughts and oh, he could kiss her for that. She walks fast, her widow's cap and black bonnet slipping back, her cape discarded and bundled under the perambulator, so that Ruby sees the contours of her fine, strong body in motion, the open, easy grace of her. For all the world like a proud mother. Ah, now, another smile glimpsed and caught, green eyes shining, and does she feel herself liquid and would she pour herself into his arms and abandon reason and cleave to him? A life ending and beginning with her – her roaring, him drunk home, in the bed with his boots on, brawling and loving, serenading. Their raucous children, green-eyed, please God. A babe on the knee before the hearth and his *London Illustrated* self, pinned on the wall. Bridie. Growing old together and the familiarity of her touch, her voice, his fingertips threading foxy autumn hair. Ruby wipes his eyes briskly on the back of his hand, a fault of the freshening air, and notes a rough bit of road coming up.

Prudhoe's windmill is the second one along. The first is functioning: full-rigged with burr-stone and bed-stone, gears and brake-wheel, quant and moving sails. As a youngster Bridie would follow Valentine Rose to the top of that windmill, creeping up the ladders past the miller, to make-believe they were in the crow's nest of a ship. They would lie on the floor listening to the wash of the sails and the creak of the ropes. The fields below were the sea, the wind through the grasses the changing tide. The Surrey House of Correction (as they knew it then) was another ship approaching. *Ahoy!* The inmates were fearsome pirates all! Or sometimes the prison was just a moored hulk, lying heavy in the water with its cargo of doomed souls.

Prudhoe's windmill once looked like its tidy neighbour but the sails stopped long ago, and as far back as Bridie could remember the roof has been promised a lick of bitumen. Windows have been opened haphazardly in the body of the building and there's a ring of them at the top with a balcony under. This gives something of a lighthouse feel and floods Prudhoe's workroom, located on high, with beneficial light and air.

There is no sign of Prudhoe at his windows today. Although he could be looking out, for his eyeglass is trained often on the landscape. Prudhoe surveys all of London from his panopticon on Brixton Hill. From the north-east window: the Thames framed, and at its curve Bentham's Penitentiary. From Barry's Parliament Prudhoe's eye follows the bend of the river on to Covent Garden, then to Denmark Street, through to Bloomsbury and his enemies at the Pharmaceutical Society. A tilt of his head right, there's the old Roman Road eastward.

Several large ravens patrol the balcony belligerently, keeping a gimlet eye on proceedings, stopping only to stretch a claw, or peck under a wing. Intermittently there is bickering among the guards, conducted with much flapping and posturing and dark cawing. A system of buckets and winches runs down the outside of the building. Everything from specimens to babies, bread rolls to nitrous oxide, has been hauled up the side of this windmill. The original workings, the millstones and the wheeled gears, lie discarded in the garden. Prudhoe claims he dismantled the works in protest at Cubitt's confounded prison treadmill – nothing should have to spin, grind and labour at the behest of another. Besides, his sails were sweeping up all his neighbour's wind and Prudhoe was no miller. And without the machinery, perfectly round rooms could be cramped with every comfort to accommodate Mrs Prudhoe, Prudhoe and the orphans.

The orphans, a great tribe of children of all ages, shapes and sizes, run backwards and forwards across the garden screaming. Mrs Prudhoe, a short, plump delight of a woman in a wide felt hat, is hoeing carrots with a baby on her hip. She raises her hand to Bridie in greeting.

Nothing grows in the Prudhoe's garden but foundlings, washing and gritty long-tailed carrots.

Mrs Prudhoe points to the perambulator with a grin. 'You've brought me a new charge, Bridie?'

'Haven't you enough?' laughs Bridie.

'Never.' Mrs Prudhoe jiggles the baby on her hip until it giggles.

She calls over two children from a savage crew chasing the life out of a chicken. They come directly, each the spit of the other, with pale green eyes and fierce red hair on end.

'Here are the twins.' She nudges the nearest. 'Say hello to Bridie who brought you here, remember?'

The children drone a greeting with one eye on the chicken, which is getting away.

Bridie nods at them. 'You've grown. Don't you remember me?'

They frown, unsure. A year in the life of a five-year-old is an eternity after all.

'Prudhoe's inside,' says Mrs Prudhoe. 'He'll be glad to see you, he's had no visitors he likes recently.'

'Does he ever have any visitors he likes?'

'Yes: you.' Mrs Prudhoe regards Bridie craftily, her eyes full of mischief. 'And Valentine.'

'Will you not start?'

Mrs Prudhoe laughs and squeezes the baby's chin and the baby laughs and dribbles the more.

She gestures at the perambulator. 'If you and the lad stir yourselves, you could fill that and give me some more delicious babies to eat.' She nibbles the baby's hands ferociously until it hiccups with joy.

Bridie glances at Ruby. He looks away.

Because Prudhoe's workshop is at the top of the building he can pull the ladder up when he's had enough of the world.

However, today he must be in a cordial mood for the ladder is down. This is the only region of the windmill where chaos is not allowed to reign and orphans gain no admittance. Unless they can write in a neat hand, step silently and read Latin.

Bridie doesn't suppose that Prudhoe ever lies on the floor and fancies himself in a crow's nest. Every moment of the chemist's waking day (and sleeping night, for this is when he dreams up his best inventions) is spent on his work. Ask him what he does for a living and he will only admit to the following: testing the stomach contents of the deceased. These arrive daily from all corners of the country in the jars that Mrs Prudhoe winches up to him. Prudhoe also gives evidence at inquests, compiles broadsides, writes scathing letters to medical journals, and enjoys being written about scathingly in medical journals. He holds certain truths dear to his heart. Namely, that most members of the medical profession are inordinately stupid. Moreover, women should have the uncontested right to enter the medical profession, being, as a general rule, notably less stupid than men. Further, that a rural doctor will take, on average, three months to realise that his patient has been poisoned, whilst a town doctor is four times more likely to poison his own patient in the first place. Testing the stomach of a relatively fresh corpse is one thing. Testing a three-month-old smear of rot is another. Based on his experience in the arena of criminal behaviour, law and justice Prudhoe has also developed several unwavering beliefs. These being: that lawyers (both for the prosecution and for the defence) are the devil's own horned bastards, the accused are always guilty and there are more efficacious tests for arsenic than Marsh's but none are as beautiful.

He comes from a long line of apothecaries. Raised at the back of a chemist's shop, his baby days were spent bathed in the jewelled red and blue light thrown down by the glass carboys in the window. Behind the counter his father stood, as his forefathers had before him, guardians of walls of drawers, cabinets of stoppered bottles, rows of jars. Gatekeepers to an esoteric world of unguents and potions and powders. They sold opiate dreams for fractious babies to exhausted mothers, or ointments to unfaithful husbands with the itch. They poisoned and cured in equal measure and everything they dispensed came with a good old-fashioned bracing purgative.

As a young man, Rumold Fortitude Prudhoe decided to tip his boom and strike out alone, across waters uncharted. Not for him a life behind the till. He hated the bowing and whispering, the constant interruption of customers, with their hopes and distresses and bodily functions. Prudhoe wanted to expand the fabric of science, medicine and his own mind. His full-steam experimental nature has not changed since the day, as a medical student, he licked a stain on a bed sheet to determine the tincture that put a rich widow to death. Neither has his burning curiosity waned. Mesmerism, spiritualism, vegetarianism, time-travel using magnets and the therapeutic potential of hallucinatory substances are recent areas of interest.

Prudhoe's shelves, curved of course, are packed with periodicals, pamphlets and books, ranged in deliberate disorder, for the doctor likes juxtapositions.

Several well-scrubbed workbenches are set up with the equipment of Prudhoe's various trades. Bearing stills and spirit-lamps, mortars and pestles, beakers and flasks, evaporating dishes and crucibles, tripods and funnels, clamps, stands and test-tubes.

Presently Prudhoe is at one of his workbenches staring with rooted concentration at a substance in a small round dish. Prudhoe is the opposite in stature to his wife; an elegant whipcord against her soft, round, fruity plumpness. Of average height, Prudhoe is lithe with a sinewy strength and graceful of posture and limb. Only his hair betrays his age: it is white, but thick withal, and kept long, plaited and fastened with a black velvet ribbon. His face is steep of forehead, straight of nose, firm of chin and trim of whiskers. His clothes are as finely made as him, although cut on the austere side. His chief adornment is a single pearl drop ear-ring, which he wears unselfconsciously and slightly in the manner of a high-seas privateer. His eyes, amber-toned, kind by default, and given to peering, squinting and periods of sustained observation, are capable of great warmth and that rebellious glint which always indicates an unfettered mind. In Dr Prudhoe's countenance, refinement meets rogue.

'Bridie . . .' Prudhoe holds a slim hand up, his eyes on the dish. 'Indulge me, two more minutes.'

The sound of a bell from below alerts Bridie to a delivery. She opens the window onto the balcony and retrieves the swaddled jar from a hoisted bucket. A raven takes the opportunity to follow her inside, greeting Bridie with a low threatening chuckle.

Ruby has settled on a chair next to a bureau, with his hat on his knee. There's a despondent look to him Bridie hasn't seen before.

The raven flutters up beside him. She edges sideways along the top of the bureau, claws slipping on polished wood, and fixes Ruby with one barbarous eye.

'The bird sees me!' exclaims Ruby, brightening.

'She's a raven,' whispers Bridie. 'She sees everything.'

The raven, unruffled, begins to preen her feathers.

Prudhoe studies the photograph. 'First principles, let's reconsider the evidence: Christabel is special, how?'

'She stirs memories, provokes angry thoughts, has colour-changing eyes, bites like a pike, attracts gastropods, raises dampening mists and drowns people by manifesting water.'

Prudhoe nods. 'To substantiate this, we have the scars on the arm of the doctor's daughter, a pile of empty snail shells and a sodden patch under the rug in the nursery which forms the shape of a person, possibly a body laid out?'

'More or less.'

'The eyes of this child are pale, it is true, and oddly fogged, but the art of photography can accomplish many extraordinary effects.' He hands the photograph back to Bridie. 'And Sir Edmund Berwick claims to be her father?'

'A dubious claim. I think he might have collected her. Do you know him?'

'Only by correspondence. He has a broad interest in marine life, some freshwater, nothing land-based. No birds, with the exception of wading birds.'

The raven hops down from the bureau and up onto the back of Prudhoe's chair. With a tender croak she rubs her beak in his hair. He puts his hand up to pet her and she nips him.

'Nasty, darling.' He turns to the jar on his desk. 'What I'd like to know is how Sir Edmund acquired the Winter Mermaid. On Mrs Eames's death her late husband's collection would have passed to Gideon, but with the son dead—' He hesitates, continuing slowly. 'The Eames estate went unoccupied whilst lawyers rumbled and distant relatives laid claim. The Winter Mermaid sank without a trace . . . It's not impossible it was stolen and sold by some dishonest servant.'

Prudhoe has opened the door and let a spectre of the past in. It whistles through the room; stale fear, bitter hurt. Bridie remembers to breathe, to calm her kicking heart.

'As to the Highgate remains, you see a link between the walled-in infant and this preserved mermaid here?'

Bridie nods. 'They are somehow connected, Prudhoe.'

'The formation of the teeth?'

'Yes, primarily.'

'You know, of course, the story of the Feejee Mermaid?'

'That turned out to be part capuchin monkey, part salmon. Are you saying that Christabel is a Feejee Mermaid?'

'I'm saying, Bridie, that people can be tricked, or they can trick themselves. There are children with all sorts of strangenesses running around this windmill. Some are a little unusual, granted, but all of them are *human*.'

'I know, but this case is different somehow.'

'The Winter Mermaid is a marvel, it is true.' Prudhoe smiles dryly. 'I'm not sure that I would have had the audacity to abstract her from under Sir Edmund's nose.' He chooses his words carefully. 'But she's not real; whoever put her together was a genius. Likewise, the child you seek, however *unique*, will be just human.'

'And the snails and the fog and the changing eyes . . .'

'Such stories have a potency, Bridie. And a further thought, perhaps: the theft of Christabel could only raise interest among collectors.'

Bridie reflects on this. 'You think that her abduction is a hoax set up by Sir Edmund and Dr Harbin?'

'Isn't it a possibility?'

'And the dead young woman, is she a hoax too, Prudhoe?'

'The best-laid plans go wrong. She may have been involved, or just an innocent bystander. The vagrant said she had been haunting the grounds.'

'So, the baronet and the doctor, intending on selling the child, staged the whole thing to drum up intrigue and raise her price?'

'It's happened, I recollect another case—'

'Then they chose me as the person least likely to find her,' says Bridie, quietly.

Prudhoe frowns. 'I don't know where you are heading with this.'

'My last case.'

'You did everything you could to rescue that child, Bridie. Valentine told me you couldn't have done more. You made yourself sick over it.'

'I didn't find the child, though. I mean, not in time.'

'Neither did the police.'

'A boy lost his life because of me, Prudhoe.'

Prudhoe shakes his head. 'You know that's not true. Have you forgotten the people you have found? And saved? I haven't. There's a fair few of them chasing my bloody chickens.'

Bridie looks to the windows. She sees nothing but sky from where she's sitting. She wishes for an eyrie and a ladder to pull up.

'Cora, for one, would be the first to put you straight.' His voice softens. 'You help individuals the police wouldn't help, couldn't help. You barely make a living and sometimes you take great personal risks. It worries Mrs Prudhoe.'

'You're one to talk, with the bedsheet-licking test.'

Prudhoe laughs. 'Have you considered what you will do with the child when you find her?'

'Of course.'

'Let me guess: you'll return her to Sir Edmund and claim the reward?'

'I rather thought I would bring her here to chase chickens.'

'You'll never be a rich woman.' He glances at her. 'You've stopped attending lectures these last months.'

'I've been spending my money on Madeira.'

'Will you be back? Garrett Anderson is making news, you know.'

'Good for her.'

Prudhoe's expression turns triumphant. 'The Worshipful Society of Apothecaries is still reeling. Garrett was in, out and got her credentials while they were there, scratching their arses. Blackwell, Garrett, women with gumption, claiming their rightful—'

'Yes, Prudhoe, I know. Garrett will make a doctor yet,' says Bridie, leadenly.

'If the other students stop petitioning against her, the pismires.'

'She has her supporters, too.'

'Medical women—' begins Prudhoe.

'Are precisely what the world needs,' Bridie adds, before he does. If they move swiftly on to Seacole and Nightingale he might exhaust his favourite topic by nightfall.

Prudhoe, catching a note of flatness in her voice, studies her intently. She is downcast; he can see that. She is watching the raven worry the hem of an ottoman, only she is not really seeing anything.

'Are you sleeping, Bridie?'

'Of course.'

'Are you eating, well and regularly?'

'These are Mrs Prudhoe's questions.'

He points at the jar and the Winter Mermaid in it. 'Lester Lufkin would buy that. If you could teach it to juggle.'

'Lester Lufkin is a toad.'

'Ringmaster Lufkin is the Grand Panjandrum now.' Prudhoe leans forward. 'His circus is invading Chelsea in a fortnight's time. He is planning an *extravaganza* with a nautical flavour. The Cremorne Gardens will be reborn as Neptune's watery paradise.'

'He's taking over Cremorne Gardens?' asks Bridie, surprised. 'Why didn't I know this?'

Prudhoe looks at her kindly. 'You've been otherwise absorbed.'

'Then a child with fantastic maritime properties would fit the bill with Lufkin,' speculates Bridie.

'She would sell more tickets than a two-headed dogfish.'

'Where's Lufkin now?' says Bridie.

'He's camped out in the wilderness, Hounslow Heath, planning his incursion. You will be paying him a visit to see if he's got wind of your stolen child?'

'I will, of course.'

'It's a tonic to see you working again, Bridie.'

Bridie attempts a smile.

'And Valentine?' Prudhoe asks genially. 'Have you seen my boy recently?'

Bridie steals a glimpse at Ruby. He is following, with fascination, the raven's bid to open a decanter of port wine.

'He gives me work sometimes.'

'He does, of course. Valentine holds you in the highest regard, in every sense.'

There is the sound of cut glass ringing as the raven raps the decanter with her beak.

'Quite right too, my evil love.' Prudhoe turns to Bridie. 'Elodia suggests a glass of something, now that we've discussed the matters in hand.'

'Elodia? Are you naming your ravens again?'

'Only the most gorgeously villainous. I've enough to keep up with the names of my human flock. It appears that Mrs Prudhoe can never have enough nestlings.'

Bridie laughs.

Prudhoe gets up and bustles around finding glasses. 'And we shall have a smoke. What's in your pipe today?'

'Your *Bronchial Balsam Blend*.'

Prudhoe grimaces. 'A concoction not without side effects.'

'Your concoctions never are.'

'My latest and my greatest' – he casts a look at the raven – 'was inspired by my corvid muses; Prudhoe's *Arial Excursion*. Will you partake, madam?'

'Ah, Prudhoe, the case—'

'On account of today being the day that it is?'

'What day is today?'

'September equinox, reason enough to celebrate.'

Bridie laughs. 'You old Druid!'

Prudhoe grins.

★

Night has long fallen by the time Bridie bumps Mrs Ackers' perambulator over the threshold of her Denmark Street abode. What with the distance walked and with Bridie's protracted negotiations with Hackney cab drivers diverse, who, on seeing the proportions of Mrs Ackers' perambulator and the condition of the intended passenger (pipe in mouth, widow's cap crooked, tendency to converse with thin air), were apt to pass by and leave the fare uncollected.

Ruby follows Bridie inside. She closes the door and turns to him.

He's all out, even for a dead man. His face pale in the gas-light Cora leaves on in the hallway when Bridie is likely to be late home.

The tattooed mermaid on his shoulder is sulkily plaiting her hair. An inky rope bumps the anchor up his bicep.

'Ruby Doyle, about Valentine Rose . . .' Bridie stops.

The effects of Prudhoe's latest creation have turned her mind to something glutinous, so that it's hard to find a right-angled thought.

She takes a deep breath and strings easy, difficult words together. 'He's a friend, Ruby. A good friend, an old friend, just a very good old friend.'

'Right you are,' Ruby replies, his eyes liquid-black and brilliant. 'I'll say goodnight, then.'

Bridie could kiss his eyes, his moustache, oh, his glorious mouth—

'Ruby—' She reaches out to touch him, but he's already gone.

She stumbles and turns to the perambulator. And, lifting the swaddled jar, dances the specimen up the stairs to a rousing rendition of 'Listen to the Mockingbird'.

With effort, Bridie unlocks the cabinet in the parlour, unwraps the Winter Mermaid and pushes her onto a shelf. Now there are three specimens in a row, all very different. To the left of the mermaid, a common dormouse with the look of something a cat had good sport with: Bridie's own apprentice piece. To the right of the mermaid, a human heart, its intricate workings splayed and open to the eye, prepared by Dr John Eames. Each of these specimens speaks of moments long gone, when these perishable scraps were examined, chosen and meticulously preserved.

They disturb the natural order of things: life − death − dust.

Here is time held in suspension.

Yesterday pickled.

Eternity in a jar.

May 1841

Chapter 12

Bridie's new home was complicated. First there were names to learn: Bill, William, Will, Kate, Maggie, Mr Greaves, Mrs Donsie, Eliza-you-know, the silly gooses: Bad Dorcas and Tiny Mary. And those were just the servants. Then there was the family. Apart from Dr John Eames there was Mrs Maria Eames, his wife, and their children, Master Gideon and Dead Miss Lydia.

If Dr Eames resembled a long-faced, sad-eyed, courteous horse, then Maria Eames showed as a huffish thoroughbred. She was long of limb and thin of hair, which was tawny in colour and dressed fuller by the artifice of her lady's maid. Her nostrils flared permanently with some perceived slight, her blue eyes were prone to flashing, rolling, gleaming and glittering (like all individuals with a splenetic temper). She had two speeds, depending on the time of day (and, it was reported, her consumption of laudanum): supine or stampeding. Her voice held affected vowel sounds she uniquely developed as a girl for her presentation at court. She laughed chiefly through her nose, had a wealthy industrialist father (innovations in ball bearings) and loved nothing as completely and devotedly as her son, Gideon. It was a tragedy that Gideon did not return his mother's fondness. As the ever-wise Mrs Donsie observed: both of them were the worse for it.

As for Dead Lydia: she was a fair, plump, pensive child in a blue dress in a painting in the hall.

Dead Lydia.

Bridie slept in her bed and touched her things: the china dolls and the picture books, the dapple-grey rocking horse and the toy theatre.

Bridie wore Dead Lydia's clothes.

Sometimes Bridie fancied she heard the deceased girl complaining, coming back to enquire as to why a hoyden was wearing her dress. Bridie imagined that the rustle of her petticoats was Dead Lydia's whispered disapproval.

Sometimes Bridie would catch Mrs Eames watching her closely and frowning. It struck Bridie that it might be upsetting for a mother to see her late daughter's clothes on a slum-child.

Bridie gathered the courage to raise her concern at Mrs Donsie's range-side one evening. The cook told her that whilst Mrs Eames worshipped her son, she had been indifferent to her daughter. At best she had viewed poor Lydia as a dress-up doll, at worst an inconvenience, like February or indigestion. Bridie should take heart: the mistress had nothing *personal* against her. She wouldn't know Bridie from a door-stop and would not recognise her dead daughter's gowns and much less care if she did. The mistress was most likely ruffled at having to accommodate another of her husband's fancies. At this point Mrs Donsie glanced over at Eliza, who was darning a sock in unheeding reverie.

After all, Bridie was no more than a pet. Legend had it that Eames's Irish street rat could whip out a gall-stone in a minute and saw a leg off in five. Eames's friends were intrigued, until they encountered Bridie with her pinched orphan face and wild red hair.

Eames had been sold down the river – only – wait; wasn't there a modest competence in the child's manner and an intelligence of expression about the eyes?

Dressed in Dead Lydia's clothes Bridie looked near enough one of them. Soon, under Dr Eames's instruction, she began to sound and act like one of them too. And it was remembered that Bridie was a luckless descendent of a talented but tragic Dublin medical family (who had lived in Merrion Square). So Dr Eames's pet began to accompany him to the hospital, where she made friends with doctors and surgeons, matrons and ward-sisters, almoners and officers and even the apothecary and his assistants (who were not renowned for their amicability). She was, on numerous occasions, mistaken for Dr Eames's own daughter as she trotted beside him on his ward rounds.

When news of Bridie's popularity (and her mistaken identity) reached Mrs Eames, she was incensed. Any pet, even a favoured one, ought to have boundaries. These were quickly laid down by Mrs Eames and were a condition of her husband being allowed to keep his waif (and secure a sizable donation from his father-in-law for improvements to his beloved St Bartholomew's Hospital). Bridie would no longer accompany Dr Eames to the hospital, neither would she eat with the family, be demonstrated to visiting guests, or share the Eames's pew at church. Mrs Eames did, however, consent to Bridie continuing to assist her husband in his home laboratory, for she was loathe to return to her (neglected) wifely duty of pasting labels on jars of gristle.

Now Bridie ate her meals with the servants, and sat with Eliza and little Edgar and Mrs Donsie at church, helping them clack through a quantity of humbugs. And although she mourned the loss of the hospital visits, Bridie would have found herself content enough if she wasn't brim-full of dread.

★

Bridie had never been afraid of anything, not really. Not of the slum boys who ran after her with broken bottles, or the affectionate drunks in the tavern, or a night spent in a church-yard with Gan Murphy, a pick, a shovel and a sack. Bridie had never felt fear, although she understood well and good how it worked in others.

All the servants at Albery Hall were afraid of Gideon Eames, in their own way, from the scullery-maids to the butler and everyone in-between.

'He's a lying, cheating snake of a boy and you'd better beware if he gets a notion to toy with you,' said Mrs Donsie, who knew about all things.

Gideon destroyed servants on no more than a whim. Mrs Donsie shook her jowls and went watery-eyed at the thought of it. Gardeners lamed in fishy accidents, grooms framed for stealing, housemaids led sobbing out of the gate with their bags packed and their reputations in rags.

'He is shot through with rotten,' Mrs Donsie said. 'Unhinged, like the mother.'

They were sitting together in front of the kitchen fire. Bridie, Mrs Donsie and Eliza. Little Edgar played on the hearthrug before them.

Little Edgar wiggled a piece of string over Mrs Donsie's foot and made hissing noises. She shrieked and laughed. 'Oh, my heavenly days, it's a snake!'

Edgar laughed too.

As did Eliza, watching her boy, her face lit with love.

Edgar was an unfavourable-looking child: wan of complexion, with a large, oddly-shaped head. It was a puzzle as to how a beauty like Eliza could produce a child so unap-pealing. There was much speculation as to the physiognomy of the father and it was decided that he would have been a definite creature. But then, two of the handsomest parents could create a horror. Mr and Mrs Eames were a prime example

– but then Gideon was only ugly on the inside, which was better, if you were to be ugly at all.

Eliza ruffled Edgar's hair. Her smile ebbed, the shadow of a bitter thought settling on her lovely face. 'He's back from school this weekend.'

Mrs Donsie groaned. 'So soon, and the doctor away?'

'The son and the mother; together, unchecked.' Eliza turned to Bridie. 'You must try to stay away from Gideon and Mrs Eames, do you understand? You must work out where they are at all times and then avoid them.'

Bridie nodded, a little startled.

'If you see them, mizzle! Hide, if you have to, child,' said Mrs Donsie, gravely.

Bridie looked at Eliza, who just lugged Edgar onto her lap, to sit for the longest while, abstracted in thought.

Gideon, like his mother, was tall and well-formed and imperious, with clear blue eyes. Only his tawny hair was thick, and unlike Mrs Eames he was perceptive and quick-witted. Gideon had soft beginning-whiskers, a full mouth, beautiful hands and a supercilious stare that could ruffle even Mrs Donsie.

It wasn't long before Bridie heard tell of the cruelties of the son and of the mother. When Mrs Eames spiked the palm of her lady's maid with her embroidery needle, Gideon smiled. When Gideon kicked a spaniel up and down the breakfast room, Mrs Eames laughed. When Mrs Eames pulled the chambermaid's hair out by the roots, Gideon went one better, whipping the stable lad until the boy was insensible.

Then there were the rumours. That Gideon, now a young man of seventeen, had begun to pursue in earnest every housemaid, milkmaid and barmaid in the local area. Running them down with a kind of joyless determination, to inflict bruises and babies. It was whispered that Gideon Eames maimed livestock in dark and terrible ways.

Mrs Donsie shook her head. 'He's a charming boy with such wicked coldness inside him. Have no doubt: he would smile into your eyes while he knifed you in the heart.'

Mrs Donsie should know. She had been with the family since Dr Eames was an infant in his crib. But when Gideon was home it was impossible to speak openly. He had the vexing habit of appearing in the servants' quarters without warning. Pulling up a chair in front of Mrs Donsie's range of an evening, watching Eliza and Edgar closely with a half-smile, sending everyone scuttling off to bed early. When Gideon was home Mrs Donsie had to disguise her warnings as cautionary tales in case he was eavesdropping. The kitchen would be tense with talk of vipers and foxes, wolves and innocent young girls being dragged from sunlit paths to the infamy and disgrace of shady walkways.

Some days Bridie wished herself back with Gan Murphy and the tavern cat. She continued to curse Paddy Fadden and his gang with a raft of gruesome deaths. Once, in the early months, Bridie's old gaffer came visiting and was cordially welcomed by Eliza and Mrs Donsie (Gan saw fit not to trouble the master of the house). He blew in on a south-westerly from London, smelling of coal smoke and fog, so that Bridie felt homesick for the city. Gan took Bridie by the ears, pointed her towards the light. Then he nodded and sat down to start work on a cough while Mrs Donsie poured them a glass and began a slanderous story. When Gan left, Bridie watched him all the way down the drive. Afterwards she remembered you must never watch a leaving friend out of sight, else you'll not see them return. And she found this, to the pain of her heart, to be true.

But now Bridie had a new gaffer, Dr Eames, who, to Bridie's surprise, never stopped holding her in high regard. He told her that he expected great things of her. She wondered what these great things might be and whether Dr

Eames gave credence to Gan's tall stories about her surgical talents.

He didn't of course, but he almost could have, because Bridie in the big house was different to Bridie alone with Eliza, laughing and playing. Around Dr Eames, Bridie was hush-stepped and soft-voiced and steady-handed. When Dr Eames was home she was always by his side, as she had been by Gan's side. But now she was in an anatomist's laboratory, not sculling up and down the Thames looking for a ghastly variety of catch or running up and down back alleys with a sack and a wheelbarrow.

Now Bridie had her own little gauntlets and apron and a set of wheeled steps Dr Eames had made for her so that she could reach the worktops. She was careful to lift things without dropping them and careful to set them down without making a noise. She learnt quickly: predicting, preparing and innovating.

Dr Eames was surprised to find that Bridie could read and write. Gan had taught her from a young age using the Newgate Calendar and the Bible – the only sources of written information he thought worth reading. Bridie had got her numbers from a costermonger's son who lived across the passage above the old ship-chandler's shop.

Sometimes Dr Eames would stop what he was doing and observe Bridie going about her tasks. Cleaning equipment, recording figures, measuring liquids, assisting with the specimens. He was never less than impressed by her. Dr Eames, with his perfect, spoilt, unhinged offspring Gideon, had forgotten that children younger than Bridie supported whole families. And if he had little patience with his dissolute son before, he had less now that he had a comparison in the diligent Bridie.

Bridie worked hard. But this wasn't her only asset. She was also stout-hearted and inquisitive, rigorous and intuitive.

Soon Dr Eames could almost believe Gan Murphy's tales. If she had been a boy a future in medicine would have been assured, but Dr Eames felt sanguine that he could create a skilled laboratory assistant out of Bridie. She would make the perfect wife for a young doctor. When the time was right he would oversee her marriage (a solid match, from a good family, who may be encouraged to let pass Bridie's beginnings).

Dr Eames started to look forward to going home, in a way he hadn't done for a long time. He looked forward to Bridie's serious smile, her questions and the rustle of her moving calmly around the room. He began to see his own work through her eyes, reviving his excitement, his curiosity. He began to whistle, and sing, on occasion. He grew happier, less guarded. Then Dr Eames made a terrible mistake.

He told his wife about his growing affection for the steadfast little girl. He wondered, out loud, how he ever did without her.

He would give her one of Swift's puppies, he said. 'Not a lap-dog for Bridget, a gun-dog.'

Mrs Eames was incensed. 'Is that wise, John, darling?' she asked. And there was frost in her blue eyes, and her words were as brittle and sweet as acid drops.

Bridie was alone in Dr Eames's laboratory when Gideon visited. It was the room she loved best in the house. The laboratory was reached through the study, where Bridie had first stood in front of Dr Eames dressed in rags and a dead man's blood. The window seat was Bridie's spot. This was where she read or drew specimens whilst Dr Eames worked at his desk. Her notebooks were ranged there on the ledge.

From the study, double doors opened onto the laboratory. South-facing and bright, too, with polished wood and sparkling glass. There was a scrubbed bench and cabinets full of supplies and specimens – including Bridie's dormouse, curled in fluid, marked up by Dr Eames and displayed next to his own jars, which contained things disturbing and compelling.

For Dr Eames was a magician. He specimenised the commonplace and the exceptional, applying the same subtlety of technique to both. His wife called it his charnel house – oh, she shuddered to think of what went on behind that closed door! – but Bridie knew that what was in Dr Eames's jars was not death – but life.

There was the human heart. Laid open to the eye, the size of a fist, a miracle of muscle and ventricle, artery and vein, splayed with precision. One perishable human heart, preserved and presented, saved from corruption, for ever! It hadn't really stopped beating, at least not for Bridie, who with Dr Eames's help traced the flow of blood and imagined the rhythmic contracting pulses and felt the genius of nature.

There was a lung. Country-clean and pink, it had drawn millions of breaths before Dr Eames pickled it. The dewy air of a rustic dawn, or harvest air, heat and dust, and the wholesome smells of a market town; cattle and pigs, good beer and hot pies. There was a London lung, blackened by coal-dust, palsied by smoke, stunted with gin and tarred with factory vapours.

Bridie was so absorbed, with her ordering and dusting, arranging and sorting, she didn't notice him. When she did notice him, watching her from the doorway, you could have raked her off the ceiling.

At first, she could hardly understand what he was saying. At first, she was fixed rigid by his eyes, the amphibian coldness of them. Gideon Eames had never really looked at her before, or at least not directly. His eye had tended to sweep over her, as if she were a workaday object, a coal-scuttle or a footstool. Bridie found herself trembling, her breath catching, her blood roaring and her heart rataplanning a warning.

Her mind responded. Hadn't she dealt undaunted with a

world of rough customers in London, real nasty pieces? Yet here she stood before some boy with all the trepidation of a lame mouse under a cat's lifted paw.

Her heart said *fear him* and her mind followed.

Even in her state of terror she could tell that Gideon's face had all the beauty of a young god's. His features were perfect, regular; straight nose, strong chin and long eyelashes. His brown-gold hair was brushed back: a bright corona. When he smiled his teeth were dazzling and when he frowned his features were fine still.

He asked Bridie two questions and he repeated them until she understood. Until the sounds he made with his lovely hard mouth became words: *where had she come from and when was she going back?*

For the rest of it, Gideon told her a story.

'In the old days,' he began . . .

There was a thief's apprentice. She was a scrap of a creature with tangled red hair and a thick brogue that came out with words so corrupted to the civilised ear that no one knew what she was saying. One day the thief sold his apprentice to a gullible surgeon, along with a story. It was a story about talent and tragedy — the cataclysmic changes in one family's fortune: the sort of story that everyone adores! The thief's apprentice was no less than the daughter of a gentleman, some great medical man fallen on hard times.

And so, the little imposter came to live with the surgeon and his family. The guttersnipe, as you would expect, was only there to rob the gullible surgeon. Stealing time, knowledge and portable possessions, that sort of thing. Luckily the surgeon had a dashing son of a mind to study medicine, if only he could apply himself and stop battering the stable boy, chasing the girls about the village and having terrible murderous fun with ewes at midnight.

The son, knowing full well the guttersnipe's game, knocked her down and cut off her two thieving hands and her two sneaking feet. He would pickle them in a jar. When the guttersnipe came to, her hands and her feet were gone. She looked up and there they were on the counter. In a sealed glass jar, newly preserved, palms waving, toes turned prettily outwards. She tried to wobble to the door on the two points of her ankles but the surgeon's son knocked her down again. When the guttersnipe came to, her legs were gone. She saw her legs from where she lay: neatly severed at the hip, standing nicely together, pickled. In the jar next to her hands and feet! She tried to drag herself to the door by means of her elbows. She didn't get very far before the surgeon's son knocked her down. This time she found her arms were gone (folded neatly – in a jar, of course!) and she had been skinned. The surgeon's son had made a pocketbook from her; he sat calmly at his father's desk writing in it.

The guttersnipe lay there, a bloody lump howling through her missing lips, staring at the surgeon's son with the lidless horrors of her two eyeballs. Until the surgeon's son finally put her out of her misery with a pistol applied to her temple.

'So, you see,' said Gideon, 'it didn't end at all well for the guttersnipe.'

Bridie, who had been raised on worse stories than that growing up under the table with the tavern cat, would have laughed in Gideon's face, if it were not for the look in his eyes.

The look in his eyes said that he meant every last word. That if he could, he would gut her on the spot. His hands yearned to draw a knife all over her body and his eyes were aching to see inside her, the organs and hot gore and gristle of her. His nose was itching to smell the skin and hair and blood of her.

He leant very close to her ear and breathed softly the words.

'Get out of my fucking house.'

Bridie called the puppy Willow. He was all bright-eyes and black velvet, soft nose and tiny nipping teeth. For two weeks she neglected her duties while Dr Eames watched her romp up and down the lawn, laughing at her shining-faced joy. Here was Bridie as he had never seen her: as a child.

Then Willow disappeared.

Two days later, when Dr Eames was away, Willow came back.

A wet sack on the nursery floor.

Bridie knew, as soon as she opened the door. It was the smell.

She opened the sack. Skinned and jointed, like a rabbit for the pot, was the little dog. With his eyes cloudy-blind, set in a pared-back skull. His milk teeth revealed in a final snarl.

Eliza helped Bridie bury Willow under a rose bush. Then she held Bridie and stroked her hair as Bridie recounted the story that Gideon had told her, about the thief's apprentice and the surgeon's son. When Bridie looked up, Eliza's hazel eyes were burning and her face was very pale.

'Keep away from him,' Eliza said. 'And I'll do what I can to keep you safe.'

September 1863

Chapter 13

Bridie, wrapped in a shawl, sits in her night-time parlour; her eyes are dark in the low light and her hair tumbles loose. The house is quiet, apart from the bass rumble of Cora snoring in her attic room. That hardly bothers Bridie, for her mind is miles away. Denmark Street is quiet, too, tonight. Flaxman's Eclectic Theatre has long discharged its playgoers and amateurs. The residents are sleeping now: the engraver, the tassel-mould maker, the knob-turner, dyer and weaver. Bridie's landlord Mr Frederick Wilks, bell-hanger, is sleeping too, in the stiff embrace of his ancient coat. As rigid as a rasp, as straight as a chisel, propped in the tool cupboard till morning. But the rooftop cats and the basement mice are awake, of course. As is Frau Weiss, the baker's wife, always the last to bed and the first out of it. Dredged with flour, rocked rhythmical by kneading, and rendered poetic by Riesling wine, she can be heard (as she can be on all clear nights) composing odes to the moon.

And beyond Denmark Street?

A raven hop will land you in the wild black sea of the Rookery, where the inebriated lilt and pitch all the hours of the night, reciting words less lyrical than those of Frau Weiss. Where draughts come cutting through paper-patched windows and every cellar, attic, room and corridor holds a family, or three. Listen: there's the clattering of dropped bottles, a tumble on a broken staircase, a catcall, a slap. A curse scatters the rats. There's the thin cry of a drugged infant. Perhaps there is sleep too, tonight, among the slop buckets and wet sheets and the stinking drain, between the late-night squabbles and early-morning fights.

And beyond?

The metropolis isn't sleeping, not really. For every Londoner in bed there are ten awake and up to no good – on the fly, on the loose, on the tiles!

The moon knows; she sees all. Tonight, she's our guide, for it's late and every self-respecting raven will be perched in her own black-feathered embrace. Let the corvid sleep!

The moon sees the beauty and cruelty of London: her whores and drunks, saints and murderers, thieves and lovers and fighters.

The moon sees every back alley and yard, scrubland and marsh. Where the rowdy gather, to shout and swear and spectate, as dogs with gory muzzles rip each other's barks out. Where fighting cocks pounce and slash each other to red shreds of feathers. Where men with bare fists keep on coming, spitting: teeth, snot, blood and tears.

These men are a far cry from the professionals, those who fight with design, sidestepping maiming blows; those who do more than just batter each other to numb meat. Fighters who give a show – the crowd is in awe of their speed and skill.

But it is in the back alleys and muddied fields that the fast-burning stars of the ring are born. Where men with gleaming skin step forward, shake hands, wink or glare. Where Ruby Doyle's name is spoken still and his skill and his wondrous tattoos remembered. *The Decorated Doyle!* A nowhere-to-knockout sailor who sparred with glorious fighters galore and thrashed them in style. As great as Tom King even, or Jem

Belcher! A lion-hearted life cut short in the meanest of tavern brawls.

But the dead boxer hears none of this as he sits watching the living red-haired woman drowning in thought in the gas-lit gloom of her night-time parlour. He would hold her hand, small in his own, if he could. He leans forward and the movement is enough; she looks up.

'What is it, Bridie?' he says softly.

'The Winter Mermaid.'

'Go on.'

'I told you about Dr Eames, the original owner? I was his apprentice.'

'You did.'

'Well, I lived with him and his family for a while, as a ward of sorts.'

Ruby waits for the story Bridie has been unable to tell him.

'I was all right there, for a while,' Bridie says, avoiding his eyes. 'Until I came up against his son, Gideon.'

'What happened, Bridie?'

'Gideon Eames committed a terrible crime against a young woman, a servant in his household. He protested his innocence, despite evidence to the contrary.' She pauses. 'I found that evidence.'

Bridie sits. Gaze sunk. Body taut against the memory. Ruby wills her to breathe.

'He was a young man of bad character from a good family. There was hope that with the right influences he could reform.' Bridie exhales. 'So, the matter was dealt with discreetly. Gideon was sent overseas with his reputation intact and given every incentive to stay away and every deterrent not to return. He was an adventurer, it seems, dying a hundred deaths.' She shakes her head. 'God help me, but I prayed for every story to be true. Then finally, an obituary in *The Times*, a reputable eyewitness, a captain, confirmed that Gideon Eames drowned off the coast of Western Australia.'

'So he was dead?'

'Yes.'

'And that was the end of his story, right there?'

'Yes.'

Bridie stares into the fire. 'It was just the shock of seeing the Winter Mermaid in that peculiar room, not expecting it.'

'It was a shock all right,' smiles Ruby, weakly.

'And why wouldn't it be there, with Sir Edmund a collector? Didn't Agnes mention the specimens?'

'She did.'

'As Prudhoe said, after the death of Mrs Eames and the wranglings over the estate, the doctor's collection could have ended up anywhere.'

'There you are then. You've no cause for fretting. Past is past, for good or ill. It can't bother you in the present.' Ruby sits back with a nod, apparently pleased with his dead man's wisdom.

Bridie, saying nothing, refills her pipe and lights it.

Chapter 14

Not a bad place to hole up. Where is it? Hougham Without, on the fringe of the village. Which is just as well, if things get unordinary.

Only a short hop to Dover, says the doctor.

The jarvey lies buried in the garden out the back of the cottage.

Mrs Bibby had known him from a baby, strapping, brutal, London-reared, so when he had cried she had cried with him. With Betty Reckoner's snout pressed between his ribs.

It had been stop-start on the high road, with the driver expressing an interest in throttling her young charge. But Mrs Bibby had persuaded him from that course of action.

On arrival, the driver had carried the trunk into the cottage without a bother on him (Mrs Bibby, gun cocked, ready for any kind of debate).

Then he reared up, with the burning urge to carve the child's throat out and stamp on her curly head. The long and the short: the child put her teeth on the lad and then it was over.

He had stood, grown man that he was, with his bitten hand clamped under his armpit, sobbing, like a boy with a bee-sting.

'Close your eyes, son,' Mrs Bibby had said as she took aim. 'It will help me no end.'

The child watches her from inside the wicker trunk; Mrs Bibby sees her face framed by the hole she's gradually gnawing bigger. The child's eyes track the doctor as he paces across the room and back again. He crosses the floor in three steps with his long legs but the child keeps up with him, captivated, it seems, by movement.

'I am undone,' moans the doctor, just in the door with his hat and coat on. 'There is no buyer in Paris. There is no sailing from Dover. He has found out and warned them off.'

'You don't know that, sir.'

'For what other reason would the Parisians renege on a deal previously so entreated for?' He lets out a sharp sigh. 'The agent informed me that no French circus or collector would have any further dealings with me or my merchandise.'

'We ought to count our blessings, Dr Harbin,' says Mrs Bibby. 'We still have the child. We can try the London market.'

'What makes you think we can find a buyer in London? If the French are not prepared to buy a stolen child, *his* stolen child—'

'Isn't it worth a try, sir?' she says crisply. 'From what I understand London collectors are most wanton and competitive. They take risks, sir, and rarely question the provenance of their acquisitions.'

Dr Harbin shakes his head. 'I'm done with this business: if some criminal or other doesn't ambush us, then we'll be found out by the police—'

'Of course, if *he* catches up with you, then you really will be in shit straits.'

The doctor may be weeping. It's hard to tell, given the thickness of the glass in his gig lamps.

Mrs Bibby smiles her cattish smile, her voice pleasant, fond even. 'Don't lose heart, dear doctor.'

Dr Harbin takes off his spectacles and searches for a hand-kerchief. 'I'm as good as in the ground.'

'You are, sir, but accept my counsel; be stout of spirit and we'll strike for the city. If we're fortunate we'll make the vend. Then you can buy yourself a little sea passage to the dim distance.'

'What choice do I have?'

'Then it is decided. London is the place.'

★

'She is changing,' says the doctor, taking off the chain-mail gauntlets. 'She's cutting her adult teeth.'

Christabel draws her legs up and turns her face towards the wall. She regards the doctor down the scythe of her cheekbone, her eye darkening to black.

Dr Harbin walks to the window. 'She needs to be in water. Her limbs will atrophy.'

Mrs Bibby has her revolver trained on him, although the doctor never lunges, cries or gets carried away, no matter that his mind is in tatters. It's the last shred of his professional pride that he can hold himself at a remove from the patient, even a patient like Christabel.

'Has there been hair loss?' he asks the nurse.

'Mine or hers?' She points to the hairballs in the corners of the room.

'She'll start sloughing soon.'

'Sloughing?'

'Shedding her skin.'

'Christ. What will be underneath it?'

'More of the same; Christabel, only bigger.' The doctor pauses. 'It's what they do, according to the late Reverend Winter.'

'An' he was the expert,' murmurs Mrs Bibby.

'Then there are nature's portents.'

'The seagulls breaking their necks to get in the windows, the snails and the frigging newts, you mean? And that . . .' She points at the walls already running wet.

'Soon she will attract a lot more than a few snails and seagulls,' warns the doctor.

Mrs Bibby swabs the floor, for the doctor has told her to leave no trail. She collects fallen curls, wispy and white, empty snail shells and needle teeth. Christabel lies readied in the hall, safe inside a plain rectangular wooden box. A casket, not unlike a coffin, only the doctor won't hear of it. Lined with blankets and with air holes set inconspicuously under the rim. Made by the local carpenter, to the doctor's design, it's an improvement on the wicker trunk. The hired carriage will be here directly. Mrs Bibby will leave the windows open. Try as she might she can't get the smell out of the room; like a hot day at Billingsgate fish market.

Rain like this will turn the roads to soup and add hours to the journey to Gravesend. The hired driver is uneasy, why wouldn't he be? This one with the leg, the breadth of her shoulders, her leering eyes and her pickpocket's hands. And this other one: the doctor, a twitching, shifty type of customer. To say nothing of that box: he was convinced he felt something move inside it when he lifted it into the carriage (for they would have it in there with them for all the space inside) – a sudden pitch and slump. They paid three times over, up front. That buys hush and that alone would make a man uneasy. Then there are the gulls. He's never seen such a gaggle. Covering the roof of the cottage and the garden and the fields all about. The horses shy and worry and snort, eyes wide under their blinkers; he has sent it down the reins to them, his disquiet. He considers upending the lot of them from the carriage and riding on, but he's spent the money in his mind a hundred times over. This will be bad business, of that he is sure.

Mrs Bibby sits with Betty Reckoner up under her shawl, liking the cool feel of the gun in her palm. The doctor is asleep next to her, his head lolling with the motion of the carriage, his mouth open, his spectacles fogged. The walls of the carriage are already running wet. Mrs Bibby hears the accompaniment of gulls, screaming overhead. Thank Christ the carriage hasn't stopped for long enough for the snails to climb on board.

The doctor snores in his sleep. This is all the conversation Mrs Bibby wants from him. She'd given him a draught before leaving the cottage. A calming tonic, she said, thus ensuring a peaceful ride for herself and the Kraken. More fool him, a doctor, for taking it, but nowadays he's hardly making good judgements.

Mrs Bibby's mind runs on cutting the dead weight, sharpening up this venture. She studies the doctor. He has proved a poor thief and a nervous dealmaker: he hasn't the mettle. Unlike herself. She was born for bad business. If not the legs, she's the tooth and the claws and the backbone for it.

There is a tapping sound from inside the casket at Mrs Bibby's feet. She extends her good foot and kicks it.

'Stop that and go to bloody sleep.'

Silence. Then the tapping again on the side of the casket, a sharp, repeating rhythm.

'Once for yes, twice for no, do you understand?'

Silence, then twelve taps. Silence, another five.

Mrs Bibby smiles. 'All right, so. Because the doctor is dosed off his shiny pate here's a story, just for you, Kraken. In the old days . . .'

Dorcas and Della were fished out from the silty bottom of the Thames – for this is where the fog otters had led them, of course. They were landed on the bank blinking and spluttering and gulping, and, found to be delirious, taken to St Bartholomew's Hospital. The doctor on duty listened carefully to Dorcas's account of life at the reformatory, as to the chain, the cat-o'-nine-tails and the laying on of paws. He proposed a plan. He would offer the girls gainful employment; they would live in his house and learn to be servants, and there would be no corporal punishment. On their arrival at the doctor's house, a lovely spot by the river, their hopes were sunk. The doctor's wife agreed to take plain limping Dorcas but refused lovely Della. She well knew that a pretty orphan is likely to grow into a pretty housemaid and pretty house-maids only brought vexation to their mistresses. Della was found a position with another respectable family in a nearby village.

Dorcas was ill-suited to domestic servitude. She hated working hard and taking orders and being separated from Della. One day the nurse took sick and Dorcas was charged with caring for the daughter of the house, a flouncing little nit. The doctor's wife, when she wasn't baffled on laudanum, would dress the child exactly like her and the pair of them would simper and pout around the drawing-room all day: the mother, being the queen, the daughter, the princess.

The princess, like the queen, was an insufferable idiot. She would talk at length about her silks and her chiffons, her ribbons and her baubles, all the while coveting what was in her mama's grown-up jewellery box.

Dorcas began to attend to what the princess was saying.

The queen, it transpired, had sapphires the size of greengages and rubies the size of plums.

Dorcas began to think of a way to get her thieving reformatory-school hands on the queen's jewellery box.

It just so happened that the princess's favourite toy was a golden ball; she would throw it in the air and catch it, giggling, a thousand times a day. One day the princess was playing by the river when she tripped over her own satin-shod foot and dropped her ball; her ball went rolling into the water.

The princess was beside herself with grief!

Dorcas seized her chance. Noticing that the ball had, in fact, become lodged in the mud of the bank, she told the princess that she would go into the water and retrieve the golden ball. On one condition – that the princess brought her mama's jewellery box to her. The princess, desperate, promised. Dorcas told her to shut her eyes for she must change into an eel in order to swim down into water, with eyes to see in the murk and teeth to hook up the ball. The princess stood with her eyes closed and Dorcas picked up the ball from the bank, spat on it and placed it in the princess's outstretched hand. The princess was delighted, of course, and she skipped and spun in a nauseating fashion.

Unbeknownst to Dorcas, the princess's brother, the young prince, had been watching from a nearby tree, laughing heartily to see his detested sister tricked. He also knew what Dorcas was yet to find out – that the princess would renege on the deal and refuse to bring Dorcas the jewellery box.

Dorcas went walking with a riding crop, whipping the head off every flower she met in fury. Until she ran into the young master of the house.

And a deal was made between them.

If Dorcas helped him get rid of his hated little sister he would steal Mama's jewellery box for her. Although, he admitted, everything in it was paste.

But Dorcas had decided on a different reward now.

She'd heard that the young master was gifted with learning, although lazy. She asked him to teach her to read *and write. This way she could communicate with her dear Della, who had learnt her letters well.*

The young master was taken aback, but he agreed.

Dorcas returned to the house. She would transform herself into an eel, not outside, but inside. She needed the traits of that fish. Its ability to sense danger, its ancient malice and, most important of all, its slippery ability to evade capture.

It was surprisingly easy to dispatch the princess.

Dorcas simply told her all about the darling bird's nest she'd seen. Oh, full of the dearest fluff-topped babies, miss! Like itty grey powder-puffs, miss! Where, miss? Why, miss, just outside the nursery window, miss! On the ledge there, miss! Put your head out and you can see them, miss! A little more, miss—

The driver knocks on the side of the carriage. 'Gravesend. Sir, madam,' he calls and not without relief.

Mrs Bibby locks Betty Reckoner and puts her away. She opens the window to the smell of the Thames and the quarrels of water-birds and the river alive with steam packets and barges and watermen. The light is dwindling and a bed at the Three Daws awaits, and another calming draught for the doctor. Then early to the pier with their cargo.

Chapter 15

The pigeons started it. Taking flight as one cooing cloud like the whole thing had long been arranged. The crows watched them leave and then followed, covering the sun with a sudden sweep of night. Then the ravens, the rooks and the jackdaws went too (so that Prudhoe's flock are the only black birds left in the whole of London, for they would never leave the chemist's side). Then went the jenny wrens and starlings, sparrows and song thrushes, robins and tits. All gone – scrabbling up into the air, their eyes bright with panic. But the waterbirds remain: swans, ducks, herons and cranes, moorhens and cormorants and grebes. Only now they are joined by great marauding flocks of seagulls. And not just gulls, but also storm petrels, oystercatchers and frigate birds, crakes by the dozen, plovers and lapwings. Puffins perch on Nelson's Column and guillemots prabble over the Houses of Parliament. Kittiwakes roost on rooftops and gannets descend on Covent Garden.

Maybe the water-birds bring with them wetland winds and marine breezes, for the haze begins to dissipate and the sun, very briefly, shines. And the air is lit up visible and is beautiful – soot glitter, smoke dew and the delicate mist of unborn raindrops shine above every Londoner.

Even the omnibus drivers rein in their horses and look up.

Which is just as well really.

For under London, beneath pavement and cobble, garden and yard, the cesspits and the sewers are beginning to churn and boil. Culverts are inundated as water levels rise. Generations of subterranean toshers are swept away in an eye-blink, their lanterns put out and their staffs torn from their hands. They turn and bob in the dark, their mouths and ears and eyes plugged with the unimaginable.

The tributaries of London are waking!

The Walbrook, the dour-hearted Tyburn, the Fleet and the Effra – abused, re-routed, dammed and buried. Some no more than a silty dribble; some great, disease-spreading, far-roaming blackguards. All are beginning to swell and course. Outside every tenement the water butts resonate, in every puddle and pond, bucket and trough there is a quickening.

Fill a teacup, watch it rock.

Now that the rain has abated, the sky above Hounslow Heath is washday-blue and flurrying with gulls. They turn and curse above Bridie Devine as she makes her way across the wilderness. The gibbets and the highwaymen may be gone now, but Bridie sees that the land still has a villainous tinge, although new villages are starting to nibble away its peripheries.

Walking at Bridie's side, Cora Butter, conspicuous in her travelling cloak and bonnet as only a seven-foot-tall housemaid can be. There is a stalwart set to her jaw and a stern bristling of her eyebrows. Cora the reticent warrior: not looking for battle but resigned to it.

Bridie would not mess with Cora.

She is relieved to have Cora the redoubtable by her side.

For Lester Lufkin is known to be lawless and will not welcome questions as to the provenance of his acts. And Bridie is grateful to her friend, for a visit to the circus can only stir up memories of Cora's painful past.

On Bridie's other side, a dead man strides, a glimmering sheen to him in the watery air. His topper worn to the back of the head and his face tipped up to the sun, he feels nothing.

Behind them straggles the man who has been following them since they left Denmark Street. In London, among the crowds, he blended in, but on the open heath it's a different matter.

'We're being followed,' says Bridie. 'Don't make it obvious.'

Cora and Ruby look round.

'Now there's a man at full trot,' observes Ruby.

'A man of questionable intent,' Cora decides.

Bridie glances behind; she would tend to agree with both of them. The pursuer is a stocky pear of a man with a wideness of the arse, who, to his credit, is keeping up with them, for anyone who walks with Cora will necessarily move at speed given the length of her legs. He lifts his bowler hat to wipe his forehead, revealing a receding hairline with a sparse fair froth to the front. A muculent man, of the type who tends to snort, his nose having the bulbous quality of a seasoned imbiber of strong spirits, various.

'Will I pounce on him and give him a shake?'

Bridie smiles. 'We'll wait and see what he does yet, Cora.'

'He'll be one of Inspector Rose's men. That's a plainclothes bobby.'

Ruby nods. 'Tell her she's right, Bridie. He's a bobby all right, with those shambly feet on him. No ways nimble.'

Cora prods Bridie's shoulder. 'He's sent him to protect you. Your investigations could lead you into peril and Inspector Rose is looking out for you. He has *affections*.'

'It's more likely he suspects I'm holding something back

from him.' Bridie frowns. 'And we'll have no more talk about Rose and his affections.'

Lester Lufkin's banners are flying. His tents have the medieval style and a glisten to them from the fresh rainfall. Everywhere Lufkin's ensign, his initials intertwined in gold on crimson. It's a sight, Lufkin's nomadic circus city. Were it not for the glamour, you would swear he was camped for war; the burley guards on patrol would give that impression.

Bridie and Cora are stopped immediately. They state their business: they are here to visit the circus king. Their names mean nothing. The guard cranes his neck back and takes a long lour up at Cora, who takes a long lour down at him, her eyebrows lowering and her fists clenching. He thinks better of it and beckons them to follow.

They negotiate wooden walkways between structures of flapping canvas. Ruby follows, enthralled.

'Holy Mother of God,' he says under his breath.

A caged lion with paws the size of tea trays lies on straw, his coat pale golden-brown in the sun, his mane darker and wildly resplendent.

Ruby is transfixed. 'I've never seen the like.' He looks as if he might cry. 'All my life I've wanted to see one of them.'

The lion curls his lip at Ruby in a lazy snarl.

'He sees me,' whispers Ruby.

'He's a lion,' whispers Bridie. 'He sees what he wants to see.'

The lion, indifferent, begins to clean his paw, biting between claws as big as steak knives.

'I might hang around here for a bit, you know, make friends,' says Ruby. 'I'll be right there if you need me, Bridie.'

'I'll be sure to roar.'

Bridie and Cora follow the guard deeper into the camp, past circus folk talking and smoking on the steps of painted caravans. Babies are cradled in the dipped hammocks of skirts and potatoes are peeled into buckets. There is the chink of put-away china and the song of caged birds out to air. A macaque dances in a fluted skirt to the tune of a man with an accordion, a child does cartwheels while a dog watches. A contortionist waves up at them from a mat, his head between his legs.

Cora keeps her bonnet pulled down, focusing straight ahead. Bridie nudges her and is relieved to see Cora's lovely, sad, splay-toothed smile in return.

Painters are working on signs under an awning. Neptune, with a trident, a ginger beard and a ringmaster's hat, stands with his arms outstretched; it's a gesture that introduces all of the wondrous chaos behind him. Trapeze artists dive from on high into white-peaked waves. Penguins run in formations. Clowns with lobster claws for hands grin from every corner.

Over the top of a two-headed dogfish the artist is painting a new design.

A mermaid with white curls and a coy smile leans over the side of an aquarium. Her tail dips into the water below.

Cora raises her eyebrows. 'There's a likeness to that photograph of Christabel, surely?'

Bridie nods.

Across the top of the sign golden letters proclaim the wondrous news:

Lester T. Lufkin's Circus and Travelling Menagerie Presents:
NEPTUNE'S PLEASURE GARDEN
Now with an ASTONISHING MYTHICAL
SURPRISE (to be unveiled)
Marine Curiosities, Magical Sea Creatures,
Daring Aquatic Acts, Etc., Etc.
An OCEAN-FLOODED amphitheatre!
MILLIONS of GALLONS of genuine water!
(The Management will not accept liability for seasickness, drowning,
or miscellaneous water-damage to the audience.)

The guards conduct Bridie and Cora to an imposing tent with canvas turrets and bunting flags fluttering above. This, announces their escort, is Mr Lufkin's feasting hall, within which the man himself is holding court in a space rich with courtiers and tapestries, furs and gold platters.

Mr Lufkin is a gentleman who likes a drop of history.

As a child he dreamt of building a formidable circus empire and looked around for inspiration. He identified King Henry VIII as the best possible exemplar of the qualities requisite for a man intent on making his way in the world.

When Lufkin was younger he wore padding to achieve the right bulk in chest, bicep and codpiece. Now, aside from the codpiece, Lufkin is no longer in need of padding. His portrayal of a monarch past his prime is unfeigned; unfettered indulgence has given Lufkin the wide-bellied, jaded-eyed sprawl of a true gourmand. Lufkin also has a historically accurate case of gout, a beard of improbable red, a steel-trap strategist's mind and a tendency to cry over haughty women.

The most significant difference between the historical monarch and the circus king is height. Lufkin does not have the statuesque proportions of Old Coppernose, he compensates with a plumed Tudor bonnet and high-heeled boots.

His fourth wife, Euryale, *Queen of Snakes*, an East End beauty with black hair and a brass corset, stands dejectedly behind him, holding a royal python. The snake, too, is gloomy as it hangs about her neck, its tongue flickering listlessly. Cora, moved by the boundless sadness in Euryale's kohled eyes, throws her a sympathetic smile. Euryale blushes.

Lester Lufkin shades his eyes with a goose leg. 'Heavens, is that Bridie Devine?' His voice is as rich as over-spiced gravy. 'I'd recognise that horrible bonnet anywhere.'

He waves the visitors to seats. His minions shut the tent flaps and light a few more candles. The paste stones in Lufkin's tunic twinkle. He gnaws thoughtfully with one eye on Cora.

'Would you join my circus, big handsome woman?' he says.

Cora drags her eyes away from Euryale. 'Not on your life.'

Lufkin laughs. 'No matter, there's taller than you, with beards to their knees. Although I'd wager none of them would match you in an arm wrestle.'

Cora glowers.

Lufkin's eyes meet Bridie's. 'Sincere condolences on the failure of your last case.' He turns to his court. 'Is everyone here present acquainted with Mrs Devine's last case?'

His courtiers are nonplussed, unsure if the little king requires a reaction.

'For those of you who *haven't* been paying attention: little boy stolen, ransomed and dead. The kidnappers,' continues Lufkin, 'given time enough to consider the net closing in upon them, concluded that a *preserved* child would be easier to trade than a *living* one. Heard of this case, courtiers?'

There is emphatic nodding.

'Of that I'm doubtful,' he says starchily. 'Pleasantries over: why are you here, Devine?'

'You've increased your guard,' notes Bridie.

'We've always looked after our acts. Ever since John Hunter ran the Irish giant to ground we've been at war.' He jabs the air with his goose leg for emphasis. 'The show folk and the anatomists – natural enemies.'

'So it seems,' says Bridie. 'When you're not trading stolen, dug-up or contraband curiosities between yourselves.'

Lufkin draws a sharp intake of breath; he is outraged. He puts down his goose leg and holds up his plump be-ringed hands. 'What are you even saying to me, Mrs Devine?'

'You have connections, Lufkin; don't deny it. I've heard that nothing comes in or out of this country these days, on two legs, four, or carried in a jar, without you knowing about it.'

'You think I parlay with the enemy?'

'I think you're a businessman.'

Lufkin narrows his eyes. 'You've pitched up at my court, Mrs Devine, in the ugliest bonnet in Christendom, to tell me about my moral failings?'

Bridie takes out the photograph of Christabel and pushes it across the table. 'This child was kidnapped from her home in East Sussex. I need to find her.'

Lufkin wipes his fingers on the tablecloth, extracts a monocle from the pocket of his tunic and makes a performance of putting it in.

Euryale rolls her eyes and Cora hazards another smile. Euryale smiles back, showing charming dimples in her cheeks. The python unravels a little.

Lufkin angles the photograph towards the light and makes a big point of looking surprised. 'Pretty Polly,' he says.

'Bears a resemblance to the headlining act on your sign, wouldn't you agree, Lufkin?'

'Coincidence, Mrs Devine.'

'She's bad business; one corpse already in her wake.'

'Then I should be frightened, madam?' Lufkin hands back the photograph.

Bridie draws herself up in her chair. 'Remember that spot of bother you had a few years back, with the constabulary, specifically with Inspector Valentine Rose?'

Lufkin polishes his monocle on his slashed leg-of-mutton sleeve. 'I'll thank you not to speak that name in my great hall, madam.'

'The evidence I unearthed let you off the hook, Lufkin. Would you like me to remind you of the particulars of the case?'

'I wouldn't. What you're saying is: *remember you owe me a favour, Lester, dear.*'

'I'm asking for your cooperation, Lufkin. The last thing

you need right now is a police raid scuppering your Cremorne plans.' She pauses for effect. 'Inspector Rose is showing interest in this case.'

Lufkin flinches. 'He knows the ins and outs?'

'If he doesn't he will soon, and you're not exactly his favourite ringmaster.'

Lufkin grunts and slips his monocle into his pocket. 'I shall keep my eyes peeled for your missing poppet.'

'Do you know a nurse called Mrs Bibby Bad leg, rough ways?'

'I don't. Has she been stolen too?'

'Disappeared alongside the child, likely involved.'

'As I said, eyes peeled.'

'Don't even think about trying to put one over on me, Lufkin.' There's a quarrelsome set to Bridie's chin and steel in her brigand's eyes.

The effect is thrilling. Lufkin is thrilled, preferring, as he does, a woman of fiery temper and contemptuous demeanour beyond any other. He could adore a woman who would treat him with such unbridled scorn. Lufkin's heart begins to soar with the growing realisation that Bridie could well be the Anne Boleyn he's been hoping for.

He selects a halved pomegranate from a golden platter on the table and takes a bite with as much virility as he can muster, chewing pips and gazing at Bridie with passionate intent.

He considers growling, but instead he asks, 'Have you plans for dinner tonight, Mrs Devine?'

Under Bridie's scathing glare his heart goes pit-a-pat.

'I'd rather eat my own eyes, Lufkin,' she says.

Euryale, *Queen of Snakes*, is beckoning to Cora from behind the tent with a grass snake around each lovely ankle.

Cora nods politely and scratches her whiskers.

Euryale winks. Cora giggles.

Bridie looks to the heavens. 'Go and see what she wants.'

Cora returns directly, bright-eyed. 'She wants us to go to her caravan, she has dirt on Lufkin.'

They all sit together in Euryale's cramped caravan, Cora with her legs out of the door, Bridie with her ugly bonnet on her knees.

Cages of snakes line the walls and there is the musty smell. Now and again Bridie catches sight of forked tongues darting between the bars. Or hears the dry rasp of scales on scales as the snakes shuffle themselves, like reptilian decks of cards. Several grass snakes are coiled around a broom handle and several more lie stretched out along shelves. Chicks hop in the bucket at Bridie's feet. In a cage by the doorway white mice wait for a fairy godmother to turn them into footmen and carriage horses, happily unaware of their real fate.

The *Queen of Snakes* boils a kettle on a tiny stove with a python draped over her shoulder. 'Lufkin has a big deal on, that much I know, ma'am. It has cost him dearly; everyone is saying that he's calling in his debts,' Euryale says, in her soft, hissy, lispy voice.

Bridie wonders if she spends too much time talking to snakes.

Euryale busies herself setting the tea things; Cora watches her every move, a growing flush of colour on her face. She smoothes down her whiskers and straightens the ribbons on her cape. Bridie catches her eye. Cora's blush deepens.

'This will be the biggest show he's brought to London and he's found the biggest spectacle to match.'

'Is that what Lufkin is saying?' asks Bridie.

'Lufkin says nothing, ma'am. He's a close-lipped little bastard when he wants to be.'

'So, these are just rumours?'

'Oh, they are more than rumours, ma'am. His guard told

me that Lufkin intends to unveil the new act at Cremorne Gardens, at the grand opening.'

'Two weeks from now,' adds Cora.

'Has Lufkin received any visitors beyond his usual circle, perhaps in secrecy?'

The snake bumps its muzzle along Euryale's arm. She strokes its head with absent-minded affection. 'About a week ago, Mrs Devine, this cove came.'

The water comes to boil. Euryale takes the kettle off the stove.

'Do you know the name of the cove?'

She glances out of the door and draws nearer. 'I don't, Mrs Devine. I heard Lufkin call him "my old friend".'

'Can you describe him?'

'Funny-shaped head. Bit of a sneer.'

'Smoking a cigar?'

'Don't know, ma'am. I only saw him for a moment and then Lester sent us all away, even his bodyguards. Which I was surprised about.' Euryale swirls hot water round the pot and throws it out of the door. The python slips and she pushes it back onto her shoulder.

'Why did that surprise you?'

Euryale shrugs, measuring tea-leaves into the pot. 'Lester Lufkin is never alone. Too many people have it in for him.'

'He imagines.'

'Oh, there's no imagining in it, Mrs Devine.' Euryale glances at Bridie. 'I can't think of one good reason why someone *wouldn't* want to kill the man,' she says, coolly.

Cora laughs.

Euryale's venom lessens slightly. 'He keeps his guards near him always, even when he's asleep or in the shitter. Even when he's having his maritals.'

The python recoils. Cora looks distressed.

'Which isn't often,' Euryale adds. 'Because of the little

king's gout an' all.' She draws a full gut in front of her with a quick swing of her hand.

'Go on,' says Bridie.

'I hid and tried to earwig and if it wasn't for that bloody snake I would have heard the whole thing. It spotted a rat, you see, and went after it. Giving me away.' Euryale taps one of the cages. 'Bad, Clarissa, bad girl.'

A snout bumps along the bars. Glittering eyes unblinking.

'When Lester discovered I was listening he got angry and threw me out of his tent. I've been living in this caravan ever since, although he allows me back for the feasts. Appearances' sake.' She wrinkles her nose. 'I much prefer it here to his royal bloody court.'

Euryale pours the tea and Cora watches her with admiration.

'He's threatening to annul me, or chop my head off. I'm too Anne of Cleves, he says,' Euryale admits. 'I'm the reason he can't get a – *you know*.'

The snake on Euryale's shoulder droops. Cora examines her boots.

'Well, any sign of trouble: get out. Come to us and we will help you get on your feet.'

'Thank you, Mrs Devine, and if there's any sign of your stolen girl I'll let you know.'

'If she falls into Lufkin's hands we stand a chance of saving her.'

Cora scowls. 'They'd be treacherous hands to be in.'

'Oh, there's worse,' says Bridie. 'Believe me.'

'I will send for you,' Euryale assures. 'I promise.'

The snake drops down from her shoulder and furtively slips under the bunk in the corner.

Ruby is where Bridie left him. Only now he's sitting cross-legged inside the lion's cage with his top hat on his knee. The big cat is wearing an expression of grave sympathy. From time to time it nods in agreement. When Ruby sees Bridie, he stops talking and colours a deep red, the like of which she wouldn't expect to see on a dead man. The lion regards her with momentary interest then yawns, stretches and lies down, resuming his habitual air of bored savagery.

Ruby frowns at Cora. 'What's wrong with her?'

Cora has lost her glower and found the trace of a smile.

'She's love-struck. Lufkin's wife.' Bridie mimes big-eyed rapture.

Ruby raises his eyebrows. 'I wouldn't have thought you would notice those sorts of things.'

'What sorts of things?'

'Oh, you know.' Ruby lowers his voice, his moustache twitches with effort. 'Romance.'

Bridie snorts.

Ruby looks away. The lion glances at him sympathetically.

Chapter 16

A lull in the rain and the river's a mirror: a breath-held still-
ness to the Thames. Every vessel it seems, from Gravesend to
Deptford, is in the direst of doldrums. There's no wind for
the sail and no thrust for the engine and a dipped oar won't
make a difference. No one can make headway today. It's as
if the river is conspiring against them, flatly checking any
progress.

One vessel is moving, and above it, a maelstrom of crying
water-birds.

The crew are not paid to wonder, but even so. All sailors
are superstitious and there's a cursed aspect to this voyage. The
hired Thames barge goes at a pace that bears no correspondence to the sails, which hang limp. It is as if unseen forces are
under the hull, directing it, lifting it, for the boat sits high in
the water.

The cargo: a woman, a fella and a casket, nothing to
speak of.

The captain won't speak of this business. Not of the gleam
in the woman's eyes, her very blue, wide-apart eyes, nor of her
cat-cream smile. He will not talk of the haunted look of the
man, unshaven, eyes alarmable behind smeared spectacles. And

he knows his crew will not utter a word about the scuffling sound that came from inside the casket as they loaded it.

The passengers have paid three times over, that buys hush.

The cargo is in the hold. The casket secured and the woman passenger seated on a sturdy chair with her leg up. Her eyes are closed, but there's alertness to her and a sense of something held ready under her shawl.

The gentleman passenger, green to the gills with boat motion, sits up on deck, crumpled in on himself.

Christabel sniffs at the air holes, her face as pale as a marble carving, still a church-yard angel, only now she is changing daily, in Mrs Bibby's opinion. Mrs Bibby takes note of these changes to pass them on to the doctor – for his accurate records. Aren't the child's eyes more sunken today, her pupils a little flatter? Her cheekbones are sharper, surely, with a harder edge, a skeletal hollowness? Her curls are falling out; they are making way for hair thicker, straighter, with the slippery texture of sea-thong. There is an uncanny speed to her movements now, oh, predatory. And her new teeth are cutting; gums distinctly damson, dog-like. Lord help the next poor bastard bitten.

Christabel taps on the casket, a rapid pattern.

Mrs Bibby bangs on the lid. 'Stove it. I've not a drop of medicine and a stay in bloody Deptford because of you.'

The noise stops.

Mrs Bibby takes in her surroundings. It is nice below deck, in the dim timber belly of the hull, sitting in the light let in by a few scattered portholes. The smell of past cargos lingering, spice, cloves, not unpleasant, mixed with Thames reek.

She could fancy herself a free-trader. Smuggling a bit of contraband. Or a river-pirate! She has the frigging leg for that.

A gentle scraping.

'Would a story keep you quiet?'

The sound ceases immediately.

Mrs Bibby settles back in her chair and breathes deeply. Becalmed by the boat's sway she begins. 'All right, so. In the old days . . .'

A maid was the property of her master and mistress, like a horse, or a teacup, then as now, it has not changed. In return for swollen knees and the bent back of a beast of burden – the housemaid is rewarded with pay, shelter and, on leaving, a first-rate 'character'.

Dorcas's friend, Della, sadly found no such security.

As Dorcas was learning to read and write, Della was fending off her master's attentions. The mistress, although near-sighted about her husband's behaviour, was hawk-eyed when it came to the silverware. Della was expelled into the world, without her character, after five years of faultless service due to a mislaid mustard spoon.

Della found a tumbledown cottage two days' walk away and, with the farmer's leave, scratched about on the land. With comings and goings, she made a living discreetly and dishonourably. Della's shame and her fear of tainting her friend's position by association prevented her from finding her Dorcas. And by the time Dorcas found out about Della—

Mrs Bibby leaves off. She runs her hand over her face and looks up to the wooden heavens.

The wooden heavens creak in answer but offer nothing more profound than the sound of the boat ploutering through water. In the sweet, spice-smelling dim Mrs Bibby hears the softest tap.

'No more, Kraken,' she says, her voice hollow. 'That story ended badly. Even you cannot make me remember it.'

She closes her eyes, her brows draw together as she lapses back into some bitter stream of memory, and the child in the casket, fallen silent, lets her.

And so the barge drives onwards, through the river din, for the river is wakening, quickening, as they pass. Sounds carried over water: church bells, watermen's oaths, thrumming steam-engines, children playing and the ever-present sound of the water-birds that fly overhead. Onwards drives the barge. Past quays and boatyards, warehouses and landing stages, houses and spires. Past old crooked-beamed public houses that teeter down to the water. Onwards drives the barge. Amid mail boats and passenger boats, paddle and screw steamers, rowing boats and skiffs, steam-yachts, steam-ferries and tugs. Watercraft of every size negotiating the beneficent, polluted, bottomless, shallow, fast-rushing, mud-slickened, under-towed Thames. The world enters London by river – vessels are converging from all corners and heading out to all corners. India, America, seas Baltic, Black and Mediterranean. The river a confusion of spars and rigging, flags and sails, masts and smoke-smudged funnels. For Millwall: marble and timber; for St Katharine: tobacco and wine; for Limehouse: coal; for Surrey: corn – and for Butler's Wharf: tea, of course!

The barge approaches Deptford, past the steam-boat piers and the gas works. Driven through the water like something controlled by fate.

On the banks dogs howl and cats raise hackles. Babies and drunken men bawl, falling into some strange spontaneous fear which wanes as the barge passes.

Chapter 17

Bridie moves between the stalls at Seven Dials market. Ruby, offended by the jostle of the crowd and the propensity of people to inadvertently walk through him, has gone to find a peaceful spot for a smoke. But Bridie is not alone; she can see her muculent copper in tow. Today he has added to his pocket a natty yellow handkerchief, which he uses to wipe the sweat from his red face. And he needs it, for Bridie is moving twice as fast as usual, just for the fun of seeing the man flustering behind her. What information this spy is taking back to Rose is beyond her, she gives him the slip so often. He'll be left with her breakfast habits and what the grocer's boy delivers.

The other idea, that Rose sent this buffoon to *protect* her, is less palatable. Either Rose knows of some kind of undisclosed threat to her person, or he thinks Bridie is unable to defend herself. Neither proposition is welcome.

The market is hopping today. Everything is on sale, from songbirds to tooth powders, crockery to corn-salves, rabbits to broom-handles. There are cobblers, sheet-music sellers and portrait painters. Coffee stalls, lemonade stands and sellers of quack remedies. Buyers come; dithering and eyeing, lifting and bartering, poking and pawing. Sellers call out, entreat, cajole. Trade, when it happens, is brisk; goods are bought, wrapped and handed over in an eye-blink.

Bridie finds what she's looking for: Dr Rumold Fortitude Prudhoe, wedged between a button seller and a knife-sharpening stand. The respected toxicologist is hawking his wares from a trunk, his produce being: radical broadsides and experimental smokables. Consumption of which could be made separately or together; individually they are illuminating, together quite transformative.

The raven perched on the shop awning above him fixes Bridie with the bright black bead of her eye and lets out a chuckle, low and morbid. Prudhoe glances up and smiles.

In the snug at the Clock House, Prudhoe raises a glass.

'To your good health, Bridie.'

'And to yours, Prudhoe. Commerce is swift?'

'I make nothing on my broadsides. The blends go down better than my ideas. Now they earn more than an autopsy. This afternoon I may sing my ideas, it works for the chanters.'

'It's worth a try.'

Prudhoe looks weary. 'I'm done with poisoning, Bridie. There's just no *innovation*. It's just arsenic, arsenic and more bloody arsenic.'

'It's a popular choice, Prudhoe.'

'Cheaper than sugar.'

'A Bradford humbug for you, sir?'

'A spoonful of murderers' relish, madam?'

'That famous condiment of killers!'

'So why is death by poisoning always such a bloody mystery?' Prudhoe despairs. 'Six months the last corpse I tested was in the ground. It took that long for her neighbours to realise that old Mrs Kittiwake, or whatever her name was, was done in.'

'Remarkable,' agrees Bridie.

'I can think of better ways to spend my days than searching for arsenical residue in a broth of suppurating stomach lining. But then, it's a living.' Prudhoe drains his glass. 'And the investigation?'

'Coming along.'

Prudhoe's expression is uncertain.

'What is it, Prudhoe?'

'I have some news.'

'About Christabel?'

'It's not pertaining to the stolen child.'

'Go on.'

'You're not going to like it, Bridie.'

'Go on.'

'Guess who is back from the dead?'

Bridie looks at the empty glass on the table before her. It is real. As are her hands, palms down, either side of it. The table is real, too: heavy, dark wood. Prudhoe, sitting before her, is undeniably real and so is the bar and the drinkers, the lead-lighted windows and, very likely, the landlord. Only nothing feels real; it's as if something has altered, some basic rule of the universe so that she doubts the substance of everything.

'And it's definitely him?'

Prudhoe nods.

'Not drowned, in Fremantle?'

'He's a doctor, Bridie; a surgeon, like his father.'

Bridie shakes her head. 'How?'

'He's been working on the continent, outlying places, making quiet contributions. He's returned to London to take up a surgical post at Bart's. His father has influential friends yet, but it appears that Eames the younger has done a good job in promoting his own interests. He's made money on his travels, Bridie, a great deal of it.'

'But he fell out of the world, for all those years?'

'I'd say he was strengthening his position against his return. He had his detractors when he left, those who worried at the reason for his going. After all, it smacked of banishment.'

'I told no one. Dr Eames swore me to secrecy.'

'Just me and Mrs Prudhoe?'

Bridie can't answer.

'People speculate, it's human nature.' Prudhoe frowns. 'Well, now he's back, and by all accounts he has some swash.'

'How can it be,' Bridie shakes her head, 'that the General Medical Council baulk at a woman practising but that killer—'

'Gideon Eames is not a killer in their eyes,' says Prudhoe, gently. 'He's taken a house at Cavendish Square.'

'Oh, Jesus, I'll be bumping into him in Oxford Street.'

'You are forewarned now.'

A thought occurs to Bridie. 'He's a collector?'

'If he follows his father, very possibly.'

'Prudhoe, what can I do?' asks Bridie, her face stricken.

Prudhoe takes her hands in his. 'Keep wide awake, that's all you can do.'

They sit in silence for a while. Prudhoe holds up Bridie's empty glass; when the pot-boy comes he takes the bottle and pours her another.

Then: 'Did you ever hear about Ruby Doyle, the boxer?'

Prudhoe, sensing a shift in her, replies with relief. '*The Decorated Doyle*, you mean?'

Bridie nods. 'You knew him?'

'I saw him fight. The man was thrilling in the ring, that great illustrated body of his. A glorious violent spirit!'

'But you never knew him, personally?'

'No. Why do you ask?'

'Oh, I don't know. He seems familiar,' says Bridie, vaguely.

Prudhoe is reflective. 'It was a waste: a man with his talent cut down in his prime.' He glances at her with a half-smile. 'Is that your next case? Who killed Ruby Doyle?'

Bridie knocks back her whiskey and pours herself another. 'Jesus, I hope not.'

A bird hops over the threshold of the pub and skitters across the floor.

'You're a mystery, Bridie, a wild dark tornado of a mind – just like my corvids.'

The raven sets a course for Prudhoe and flaps up on the table. She dips nearer and closes her beak affectionately around his thumb.

'My horrible love!'

The landlord eyes Prudhoe from behind the bar; he holds a rag ready. The doctor is his best and worst customer, what with the liberal ordering of fine victuals on the one hand and the bird crap on the other.

'We shall watch out for your stolen child, won't we?' Prudhoe gestures towards his raven. 'You see, Bridie, I have eyes all over London.'

The raven lets out a jagged caw, startling more than a few of the Clock House regulars.

'So you do, Prudhoe. But God forbid she'll be lost to the circus or worse.'

Prudhoe nods in sad earnest. 'It happens . . .'

'Not if I can help it,' says Bridie grimly.

Tonight, Bridie undresses without Cora's assistance. She never needs it, but Cora insists, for she enjoys pretending disgrace at the slackness of Bridie's corset and the challenge of untangling her hair. At this moment, Cora is occupied elsewhere. She is in the Horse and Dolphin, gazing into the kohled eyes of Euryale, *Queen of Snakes*. They are sharing a jemmy and a few while Euryale tells Cora about her childhood in a fishmonger's shop in Bermondsey. It was simple, Euryale explains, the move from eels to snakes. Cora glances with consternation at the royal python wound around the table leg. Euryale opens another bottle with her teeth and smiles, unleashing her dimples. Cora is smitten.

Bridie is glad of the time alone in the privacy of her own room; she is in an irritable mood. After leaving Prudhoe, she took a hackney to Highgate Chapel to make another request, in person, to examine the walled-up corpses. She found the vicarage closed, with a note pasted to the front door. The note suggested the imminent return of the vicar. After waiting some considerable time, Bridie left, with a distinct sensation of being watched to the gate by the vicar and, like as not, his unsavoury curate Cridge.

Bridie unties her petticoats and steps out of them and sits down at her dressing table. She unpins her hair and begins to brush it out. Without the distraction of Cora's gossip, Bridie studies her reflection. Her chemise is undone and her auburn hair falls about her face in rich waves. Her hair makes her look paler, older. Her eyes are fine, she can see that, and her shoulders are lovely, smooth and well formed. She wonders if she should have taken a lover, she wonders if there's still time for one, she wonders if she wants one at all or if she ever did.

What of the late, fictive Mr Devine? Bridie took his name but never fleshed him out. Although sometimes she fancied he was an ill-fated young doctor who died serving the poor; a fever contracted at a sour bedside.

Otherwise: *spinster, governess – old maid! Alone? Unchaperoned? Heavens!*

Hear the rattling of her womb, a pea! Bosoms, blossoms withering; lips, untasted; legs, unparted. Roll up! Roll up! Still some life in her, some plumpness, some heat! Those haunches! Check her teeth. Who will take her? Who will take her?

Perhaps a widower, a clerk, with ten children and a pianoforte, a model of application and perseverance – of self-help!

He reads Samuel Smiles aloud to his family daily. No? Then a gentleman of letters, triple her age with a stoop – she can read to him aloud while she tucks him into bed! Or, perhaps a love-match with a well-turned rogue, who will woo her, wed her and make her coffee *just right*. Nothing is too much trouble, my dove! Prudhoe will receive her stomach lining in due course.

And all at once Bridie is filled with the hot rage that comes over any sane woman who rails against her market price, or the damnable fact that there is a market price in the first place. She glares into the mirror.

What about a lover?

Her glare softens.

She tries to see herself through their eyes: lips open, a blush of pleasure on her cheeks, hair wild to tangle around fingers and kiss.

There's a polite cough outside her door.

Bridie slips on her nightgown, wraps a shawl around her shoulders and pushes her hair haphazardly under a nightcap.

At the door she listens; she can hear him shuffling on the other side. He'll be pulling up his drawers, his feet loose in his boots. His tattoos will be roaming over his glistening skin. Over the swell of his back and his wide shoulders, the gun-brig's cannon smokily blasts an inky, circumnavigating blot. The mermaid circles the anchor on his bicep in surprise and curls up in his arm crook.

Bridie touches the door. This is where his chest would be. She closes her eyes and imagines the path of her fingers along his chest, his neck – him taking her hand in his and kissing her palm. His other hand pressing, softly, so softly, into the small of her back as he pulls her towards him, as he bends his face to hers.

'Are you decent, Bridie?'

She steps back from the door.

★

They sit together before the fireplace, as is their way now of an evening, Bridie smoking and watching the fire, Ruby watching Bridie.

Bridie tells him Prudhoe's news, her face expressionless. She stumbles only once when she names Gideon Eames. Ruby notices how she holds her pipe a little tighter and talks a little slower than usual, with careful deliberation. He listens without interruption until she is finished.

He smiles at her, but the smile is forced, so no smile at all.

'You are a fine, fierce grown woman,' he says. 'This Eames fellow will have a hard job bullying you nowadays.'

Bridie doesn't answer.

'What do you think he'll do, Bridie, with him just returned and the eyes of London on him?'

'You don't know him, Ruby.'

May 1843

Chapter 18

Bridie sat alone in the hay barn at Albery Hall. It had been a miserable morning. Last night Gideon had arrived unexpectedly, weeks before the end of term. It was the worst possible time. Dr Eames would be away for days, having been called to give evidence at a trial as a medical witness. What's more, Mrs Eames was in a powerfully spiteful mood. This was a cursed combination; mother and son having full freedom to exercise their whims, unchecked, for a whole week.

But in twelve months Bridie had learnt a lot. She was no older than twelve, no younger than ten now, and she knew the lay of things. She could all but disappear when she had to.

With Gideon home Albery Hall was deserted. A house tended by invisible hands, shadow servants. No one loitered in the yard, or joined Mrs Donsie by the range, or had even the briefest of exchanges on the stairwell. Those who could, found excuses to have business elsewhere, volunteering for errands in town.

The potting shed was Bridie's regular refuge, or the laundry when it wasn't washday, but the barn cat had not long delivered of kittens and Bridie was in the habit of feeding her breakfast kipper to the new mother. Being anywhere near the stables was risky; Gideon liked to ride and would have a whip with him. But Bridie daren't move the cat, for the gardener said it would confuse her and she would eat her babies. Instead, Bridie had pledged to visit every day, for the cat looked haggardly, her black and white fur dulled. Her young fell over themselves, tumbling and mewing, the tiny pink cuts of their mouths opening and closing. Bridie had found a box with high sides and filled it with clean straw. She had put the family in it so that the kittens didn't have so far to wander before the queen had to scruff them and carry them back to the nest.

The cat licked Bridie's hand and Bridie stroked her head, carefully and with great respect.

The stable door opened and slammed closed. The cat blinked.

Footsteps down to the last stall, adjacent to the hay barn, and the creak of the gate.

'You agreed. I have the money—'

'And I thank you, but the terms have changed.'

The horses snorted and shuffled in their stalls.

The cat went wide-eyed and the kittens stopped mewing. Bridie crouched to peer through a crack in the wood slats and saw only the twitch of the tail of the roan foal.

'All I'm saying—'

'I know what you're saying, Gideon.'

The foal's hooves rustled the straw; she was unsettled by the intrusion.

'You've lain with others, what's the difference?'

A pause. Then: 'I'll have it.'

'When I can help you?'

Bridie couldn't see Gideon's face but she knew the expression it wore from the sound of his voice: blue-eyed sincerity.

'Mother won't tolerate another of father's bastards in the house,' he said, quietly.

There was silence but for the soft snuffling noises of the foal.

'Come now, I'll make it quick. You'll hardly feel a thing.'

Eliza, for it was Eliza there in the stable with Gideon, said something low that Bridie couldn't catch. Then there was a muffled cry and the sound of something thrown against the wall.

The foal took fright and ran around the stall.

Hardly knowing what she was doing Bridie picked up a hayfork. She hit the wall with it as hard as she could.

The mother cat startled and fled, leaving her kittens behind.

Next door: scrabbling, hastening from the stall, the stable door flung open, boot-heels striking the cobbles all across the yard.

Bridie gripped the hayfork.

She could hear the foal quieting by degrees. Nothing else. And Bridie began to think there had been two sets of boot-heels. That Gideon had given chase.

She kneeled to look. The foal passed by, calmer now.

A sudden darkness.

Then a blue eye, widening.

September 1863

Chapter 19

In London, rumours are carried upriver. Something's happening to the Thames: it's not just rising, it's becoming clearer, sweeter and calmer. Gone are the vicious undertows, the spiteful currents. The watermen are mystified. The mud-larks, too, are confused. They stand on the bank with their long poles and their little blue feet, eyes widening as the Thames softens and deepens by the day.

Something miraculous is happening.

Everything that has ever drowned has begun to surface again. Not the dead dogs and broken bottles, but the priceless beautiful things. Roman coins and pagan brooches turn and twinkle under the surface of the water. Viking swords rise up majestically. It's just a case of rowing out and seizing them. But try as they might, no one can catch this ravishing treasure; as they draw nearer, the river gifts shimmer and vanish. Many lose their lives in pursuit, plunging in after the sinking riches.

Some Londoners report hearing music, late at night, emanating from the river. Consensus has it that it is choral and either sung backwards or in a foreign language, Greek or Italian, who knows? Soon it can be heard all the way from Blackfriars to Barnes.

Coming up from beneath London's streets, another new sound: a tumultuous rushing. The ancient rivers of London, newly awoken and gathering force, now erupt. Flooding lane and street, drowning basement-dwelling families and over-whelming cesspits.

Then there is the rain. Great drops of the stuff, a constant patter on every window and shutter, tin can and bucket.

And the Thames keeps rising.

Bridie is watching the rain from the parlour window above Wilks's of Denmark Street. Specifically, Bridie is watching the passage of the rain across the glass. Today the raindrops are meandering upwards, as well as downwards, sometimes changing direction mid-path. She frowns, certain that this is not the way rain usually moves. Maybe she can attribute this aberration of nature to Prudhoe's *Bronchial Balsam Blend*, along with the dead man picking at his bandages in the corner of the room. Her musings are interrupted by a letter, brought into the room by a triumphant Cora.

'It's from Highgate Chapel.'

Reverend Edward Gale appears at the door of the vicarage with a lop-eared rabbit under each arm. Bridie, who is well-versed in the eccentricities of the clerical classes, maintains a neutral expression. She follows the vicar into the vestry, where he puts down one rabbit; the other he holds, nuzzled against his cheek.

Reverend Gale is a thin, wild-haired man with the burning eyes of a prophet. His beard is kept long, sometimes to his knees, and is often studded with twigs. The vicar is known to frequent hedgerows.

Reverend Gale, reluctant French master of the Cholmeley School and the superannuated vicar of the school chapel, is living out his doddering years in charge of his assembled menagerie. His current flock consists not of pupils (free or pay-boys) or miscellaneous parishioners (they have decamped to St Michael's for the benefit of newer facilities and under-standable sermons) but of God's much more worthy creatures.

The chapel is full of them.

A one-eyed badger sleeps in the choir stalls, a vole family nest in the vestry, mice run riot, shredding hymnbooks. A broken-winged duckling swims in the font and hedgehogs snuffle under the pews.

This is Reverend Gale's preferred congregation.

Several years ago, the vicar came to the realisation that human animals were beyond his ministries. Being, as they are, block-headed and irredeemably fallen. Oh, the most eloquent of sermons – wasted! Reverend Gale thus resolved to avoid human animals, or if the necessity arose, be more economical in his dealings with them.

He frowns at Bridie. 'Well?'

'You summoned me, sir.'

'Remind.'

'The matter of the corpses found in the wall of the crypt, Reverend Gale. I wanted to re-examine—'

'Gone.'

'Gone, sir?'

The vicar shrugs.

Bridie is surprised to find that she is hardly surprised. 'Your curate, Reverend, is he about by any chance?'

Reverend Gale holds up one finger, goes to the door of the vestry and calls. 'Widmerpole.'

They wait.

Reverend Gale rolls his eyes. 'Widmerpole.'

A neat, grey-haired man comes in carrying a ciborium full of birdseed. He has frayed cuffs, a round honest face and a mild-eyed expression that speaks of either inborn placidity or hard-won resignation.

'You're not Cridge,' observes Bridie. She turns to the vicar. 'You had another curate, Reverend? A young man named Cridge?'

Reverend Gale taps Widmerpole on the forehead. 'This one: twenty years.'

Widmerpole bows. 'What Reverend is saying is that I've been curate here these last two decades. There has been no other curate in recent times, madam.'

Bridie inhales. 'A young gentleman by the name of Cridge showed me into the crypt on my previous visit; slight stature, large head and a tendency to sneer?'

Reverend Gale and Widmerpole glance at each other.

'Do you know the gentleman I speak of?'

Reverend Gale reddens and shakes his head.

'No,' says Widmerpole, to his shoes. 'Sorry.'

'This matter of the corpses in the crypt, Reverend—'

'Translate.' Reverend Gale points a long finger at Widmerpole.

Widmerpole looks closely at the vicar's face as if reading some complex communication there. Then he turns to Bridie. 'Reverend has no idea where the remains of the deceased are. Upon entering the crypt the day after your visit he found them gone. Vanished!'

'Is that so?' asks Bridie.

Widmerpole bites his lip. 'Assuredly, probably, conceivably, *yes*.'

'So, you didn't sell the bodies? Perhaps to the young man with the unfavourable aspect masquerading as your curate?'

Reverend Gale hides his face in the plush of his rabbit.

'Undoubtedly, most possibly, plausibly, *no*,' Widmerpole translates.

'Then I've had a wasted journey,' Bridie says. 'I'm investigating the case of a stolen child, whose father is a gentleman of some standing. Peculiar as it seems, I thought that the bodies in your crypt would cast light on the matter.'

'Sorry, we can't help you,' says Widmerpole, not without remorse.

A hedgehog bumbles against Bridie's foot and makes a big to-do of rolling over.

Bridie smiles with delight and bends down to it, all snout and spines and wicked little eyes. 'Ah, this wee fella.'

Reverend Gale nudges Widmerpole and nods.

'Would you care for a cup of tea, Mrs Devine?' asks Widmerpole.

Bridie ignores the interrogative stare of the elderly donkey stabled between a cabinet and an aquarium in Reverend Gale's library. The tank is full of crustaceans that have been liberated from seafood emporiums. The donkey, finding no response from Bridie, turns to Ruby and fixes him with a baleful eye.

'It can see me.'

'It's a donkey, Ruby, it sees nothing; it's short-sighted.'

The donkey turns its long ears, following their conversation.

'It can hear me too.'

'It can of course, it has the ears for that.'

Reverend Gale takes a seat opposite, next to the donkey, and they wait in companionable silence for Widmerpole and the tea, with no more sounds than the ticking of the clock and the scuffle and patter of the vicar's various charges.

Widmerpole returns with a tray and sets it down. Reverend Gale leans forward, gently removes a dormouse from the sugar bowl and pops it into his pocket.

After the tea is poured, the curate and the vicar look at the photograph of Christabel. Widmerpole makes sympathetic noises and Reverend Gale makes none.

Halfway through his second cup of tea the vicar has an epiphany. He sits bolt upright on his chair, with his eyes wide, and points to the bookcase.

'Winter!' he exclaims. 'Winter!'

Widmerpole follows his gaze with dawning comprehension. 'What Reverend is saying is that he may not have the curious *remains* that you wished to view again—'

'Briefly!' Reverend Gale barks.

Widmerpole flinches. 'Reverend would, however, like to share with you his scholarly findings and speculations on the matter as to the *identity* of said bodies.'

Bridie leans forward. 'You know who they were?'

'We think we do. If this could, in a way not presently clear to us, assist you in the finding of the child—'

The vicar groans. 'Book.'

Widmerpole sighs and rises and goes over to the bookcase. Moving a bird's nest, he chooses a book and, blowing a downy feather from the top of it, hands it to Bridie.

The book is leather-bound and mottled with age. Bridie turns to the frontispiece.

On the Manifold Wonders of Fresh and Salt-water Creatures:
A Scientific Observation
By Rev. Thomas Winter
1771

'Winter – like the *Winter Mermaid*,' Ruby remarks.

Bridie nods.

'Get on.' Reverend Gale waves at Widmerpole.

'Reverend would like to put forward his potted findings. The book, as you see, has an indifferent title but was written by a great naturalist.'

Reverend Gale grunts in agreement.

Widmerpole continues. 'Reverend Winter was the vicar of Highgate Chapel and master of Natural Philosophy and Latin at Sir Roger Cholmeley's School, the latter end of last century. He was also the foremost authority on the merrow.'

'The merrow?'

'A mythical sea creature said to be found in the waters of your own native Ireland, Mrs Devine. A marine nightmare and the stuff of legends, something like a violent mermaid, I dare say.'

Ruby widens his eyes.

'Winter had a tragic and turbulent life,' Widmerpole recounts. 'He was a driven man, a self-appointed taxonomist of the fantastic, gulled by any seafarer's tale of a siren, obsessed with finding and cataloguing creatures that only he believed existed. This passion took him from his rightful work and inflamed him with an irresistible urge to uncover marine anomalies—'

'Yea,' proclaims Reverend Gale, his eyes lit. 'Slimy things did crawl with legs. Upon the slimy sea.'

Widmerpole smiles at him indulgently. 'Quite right, Reverend!'

'Coleridge,' notes Bridie.

'Vault,' volunteers the vicar.

Bridie looks at Widmerpole.

'Reverend Gale would like you to know, madam, that the great poet and his family are interred in the crypt here.'

'Fascinating.'

The vicar seems pleased. 'Pugilist,' he suggests. 'Irish.'

'Yes, indeed.' Widmerpole carries on, taking up the subject. 'Our most recent burial was the fighter Ruby Doyle. Reverend Gale is a great boxing aficionado.'

The vicar holds up two scrawny fists in a threatening manner.

Ruby, on the age of his seat, claps his hands. 'Good man!' He turns to Bridie. 'How about that? The vicar likes a fight!'

The vicar, oblivious, drops his fists and picks up his teacup.

'Reverend Gale was at Mr Doyle's last fight and when he heard about his unfortunate demise—'

'Tragedy,' interrupts the vicar. 'Vast.'

'When Reverend heard about Mr Doyle's vastly tragic demise following a tavern brawl, he arranged for the remains to be buried in our chapel-yard,' Widmerpole explains.

Ruby regards the vicar with astonishment. 'So that's why my bones are all the way out here.'

'Mr Doyle, being a feckless sort, had made no provision for his funeral. Fortunately, his friends pitched together for the memorial.'

Bridie takes a furtive peek at Ruby. He hangs his head, examining his bandaged fists.

'To return to the Reverend Winter,' Bridie prompts, 'you were saying, Mr Widmerpole, that he had become consumed by his work, searching for and cataloguing marine anomalies?'

'It happens, occasionally, even to the best of clerics. One falls away and seeks greater mysteries, greater even than the mystery of faith. This may lead one to pursue uncharted paths.'

'I'm not sure I understand, sir,' says Bridie.

'Winter was following another route, one of his own devising, unmapped at that time, of course.' Widmerpole pauses, his face brightens. 'Now, Mr Darwin's recent scientific—'

'Flannel,' coughs the Reverend. 'Digression.'

Widmerpole stops and takes a calming breath. 'It is not documented as to when Winter had first heard about the merrow, but by degrees he exclusively applied himself to their discovery.'

The donkey, which has been dozing as it stands, harrumphs, surprising everyone.

Widmerpole takes a moment to regain his composure. 'Of course, the scientific community knew Winter was as mad as a spoon, but his research on the merrow had coincidentally turned up many important discoveries about the natural world. Wouldn't you say, Reverend?'

Reverend Gale rummages in his beard. He pulls out a leaf, inspects it and puts it back again.

Widmerpole resumes: 'But every valuable contribution Winter made was undermined by his insistence that the merrow were real: he was mocked and ostracised. He carried on working alone and shared no further findings. Soon stories were circulated about him, some very dark indeed.'

'What sort of stories?' Bridie asks.

Widmerpole looks to Reverend Gale, who purses his lips and nods.

'That he kidnapped a young woman and her child from an Irish fishing village,' says Widmerpole.

Bridie frowns. 'When was this?'

'The summer of 1770, we think. The young woman in question was from a well-respected family who lived in a remote spot along Bantry Bay. She had recently been delivered of issue. Mother and child were kept apart from the other villagers and there was much speculation about the father of the baby . . .' Widmerpole colours.

'Go on, please, Mr Widmerpole,' encourages Bridie.

'The young woman was unwed.' Widmerpole's cheeks bloom a deeper red. 'She insisted that she had never had relations with any local man. But as none of the villagers had laid eyes on the baby no one could reach a verdict about this. One day, when Winter was out walking on a beach near the village, he came across the mother and child.'

'What happened?'

'He hid and watched as the mother took the newborn from its wrappings and dropped it into the sea. Reverend Winter saw that the child was not formed like other infants and that it changed on contact with the water.'

'Changed how?' asks Bridie.

'Grew a tail and so forth, as a merrow is wont to do in sea-water. Winter approached the mother, who took fright. Later he went to visit with the girl's family. He informed them that he was a man of science and asked if he could meet the mother and child. He was refused. Winter tried every entreaty, bribe and threat until the villagers ran him out of town. But obsession made Winter canny and daring and he stole the mother and child and brought them here to Highgate with a view to making further studies of them.'

'But this is not in Winter's book?'

'Not at all, Mrs Devine. This story, for the most part, was told by the young woman's family, specifically her father, who followed Winter to London to try and find his daughter. He wrote a letter documenting these events towards the end of his life. This letter was found in the bindings of this very book, dated, and sent some years after Winter's death.'

'Would it be possible to view this letter, Mr Widmerpole?'

'It wouldn't, I'm afraid.' Widmerpole glances at the donkey. 'Hodges ate it.'

The donkey pulls back its upper lip, baring a set of long yellow teeth. It makes a snapping sound, its eyes still riveted to Ruby.

The vicar snorts.

'And the young woman was never found?'

Widmerpole shakes his head. 'Her father visited the vicarage demanding the return of the abductees. Winter finally relented. He told the man to return the next day and he would return his daughter and her child to him.

'The man left and returned the next day, when Winter denied all knowledge. In the skirmish that followed the man was arrested. When he relayed his story the vicarage and chapel were searched, but nothing was found.'

'So it's possible that the walled-up corpses lately in your crypt were this young woman and her child?'

Widmerpole nods. 'Her name was Margaret Kelly. The child's name was unrecorded.'

'Why did you not tell me this before, sir, Reverend?

Knowing that Inspector Rose had sent me to learn more about this find?'

The curate looks mildly embarrassed. 'Reverend feared that a macabre case like this would bring *droves* to the chapel.'

Reverend Gale shudders. He points at the book, then at Bridie. 'Take. Read.'

'Reverend says that you are welcome to borrow the book. You may find it useful.'

Reverend Gale turns to Widmerpole. 'Blue eyes.'

'Some time ago, oh, at least—'

'Five. Curate.'

'Thank you, Reverend. Around five years ago a young woman came to speak to us. She was from Bantry Bay, it transpired, and claimed to be a descendent of Margaret Kelly's.'

'Did she give a name?'

'Ellen Kelly.'

'Can you describe her?'

'A little anxious and somewhat underfed, but extremely polite. Pale hair, bonnet, shawl, that sort of thing,' ventures Widmerpole.

'The body in the church-yard?' Ruby murmurs.

Bridie nods. She turns to Widmerpole. 'So presumably Ellen Kelly knew about Reverend Winter and Margaret?'

'She had heard family fables, but only learnt the story as we know it when Dr Harbin tracked her down.'

Ruby lets out a whistle.

'You know Dr Harbin?' Bridie asks, taken aback.

'Dr Harbin prompted our enquiry into Winter's work,' explains Widmerpole. 'He came across his name while researching the legend of the merrow.'

'Berwick,' adds Reverend Gale.

Bridie needs no translation. 'Research conducted in conjunction with Sir Edmund Berwick?'

Widmerpole looks delighted. 'Yes, you know them: the baronet, the doctor?'

'We're acquainted. When did they visit the chapel?'

'Oh, some years ago now—'

'Seven,' mutters Reverend Gale.

'Do they know about the discovery in the crypt?'

'We wrote to them straight away,' says Widmerpole, 'given their interest in Winter and his work. But we've had no response.'

'And now Margaret Kelly and her infant have disappeared again. You have no idea where they could be?'

'As I said, it's a mystery, Mrs Devine,' says Widmerpole.

The donkey draws air in through its teeth.

Bridie sits with her back against a tomb in a quiet corner of the chapel-yard, a pleasant place with wild flowers yet, and sunny too. Although the shadow thrown down by the chapel is wending round, lengthening over the weedy paths. She strikes a flame and holds it to the bowl of her pipe, a few deft puffs to get the tobacco going, then turns to the book on her lap.

Ruby sits beside her. 'So, Curate Cridge took the bodies?'

'Whether he bought or stole them is not clear, but I suspect Reverend Gale entered into some sort of a deal with him.'

'And Ellen Kelly – she'd be the poor soul we found strangled?'

'Seems so. I'll put forward her name to Rose.'

'And the reason she was there, haunting Maris House?' Ruby lays his hat on the ground. 'You'll tell Rose about the stolen child?'

'He'll know by now, Ruby. A lightning fella like that.'

Ruby looks off into the distance, a muscle working in his fine, firm, dead jaw. 'So the baronet and the doctor, hearing the stories about the mad Reverend Winter, went to Bantry Bay to find their own special Kelly infant.'

'Only they just wanted the child and not the mother too, it seems. But Ellen had, of course, learnt about her ancestor from them.'

'And that's why she came here.'

'Perhaps she thought that Margaret's life could somehow shed light on her own.'

'What, having a child with pike's teeth and it being taken?'

Bridie stifles a smile. 'In a nutshell, Detective.'

'You're a wagon.'

'Go away, I'm reading,' she says, and laughs.

'You think you're very clever.'

'I do, of course. Now let me read.'

Ruby lies back and closes his eyes.

As Bridie turns the pages of Reverend Winter's book she finds two stories. Under a composed, objective surface a darker, wilder current flows. Bridie becomes immersed in the habits of manatees and molluscs, frogfish and sea cucumbers. And then she becomes beguiled by the lore about them. Soon fact and fiction are delightfully mixed. But by the middle of the book she finds herself in murkier waters as she begins to read about Reverend Winter and the merrow: a story that started in Holland and ended walled-up in the crypt at Highgate Chapel.

★

In 1600 a remarkable creature was found in Holland after a great storm. Part woman, part fish, she had swum inland, become lost and trapped in a dyke. She was found, mud-bedraggled and weeping, by a farmer, who put her in a canvas sack and carried her home. They fell in love and she converted to Catholicism and learnt to sew. By all accounts they were very happy and she bore him five children, all with legs not tails. Winter travelled to Holland and spoke to the descendants of the farmer and the part fish, part woman. They were proud of their ancestor, as they were of the webs of fine skin, like onion membrane, between their toes, and their ability to catch eels bare-handed. Next, Winter went to the island of Mersea, where in 1680 a gaggle of superstitious villagers had killed a baby of unholy design. The infant had washed up on the shore, barely alive, with the tail of a salmon, the face of an angel and the teeth of a pike. Believing that throwing it back in the sea would somehow attract its parents' wrath (and them, like as not, sea-demons) the villagers stoned the child to death and buried it at a crossroads in a box.

Winter heard about an intriguing creature in the Camargue region of France. Monsieur Espadon had a prominent spine, no navel and large webbed feet. His legs were fused together with an expanse of corrugated skin. M. Espadon's entire epidermis dried out if he wasn't regularly basted in mud. He had fathered a whole succession of children; all girls, all named Delphine, and all of them had tails. Sadly, every one of M. Espadon's incredible issue had died in infancy. M. Espadon proved elusive; Winter arrived in France and waited in a nearby village for some weeks, hoping for an audience with him, to be eventually told by locals that M. Espadon had shrivelled up and died after a nap in the noonday sun.

But it was the merrow, more than any other creature, that began to claim Winter's attention. He had read about the merrow in the fairy legends of Thomas Crofton Croker, of course, but delving deeper into the lore behind the stories, he began to hear rumours. Tales told about a certain Kelly family, of Bantry Bay, who, every few generations, would produce the most extraordinary girl child. These children were conceived with no recourse to the usual relations and were hidden from the neighbours at birth. But glimpses had been seen of these oddest of offspring – pale beauties with white hair, flat corneas that changed colour, from pearl to jet in an instant. Winter's prose sheered between scepticism, objectivity and enchantment.

From Irish lore he had gleaned that the merrow were killers by design, taking human form in the upper body and, when in water, the form of a strong-tailed salmon in the lower. The females were beautiful, although pike-toothed, but the males were horrific. This had led to interbreeding between the merrow and humans, for a young merrow female was apt to fall in love with any fisherman of average physiognomy. A merrow would dwell on land, but if her beloved wanted to keep her there, he must take the caul she was born with – her *cochallin dratochta*, her little magic hood – and hide it from her. This would bind her to a land-based existence, for without her caul she was unable to manifest her merrow self. The caul must be hidden well – up the chimney, in the thatch, dug deep beneath the rosebushes – and her mate must refuse to give it back (even when those fierce fits of longing for the sea came over her). Without it, she could live out her days peaceably on land, in her house, with her man and her children. Or else she would become bored, find her hidden caul, burn down her house, murder her children and drag her man screaming into the sea. Winter doubted the existence of the caul – that a creature equipped for purpose by nature could be hampered so – and wisely attributed this notion to folklore.

The merrow were fully grown at twelve and lived to be no more than twenty, when they would dash themselves to death against the sea cliffs. They were said to control the weather, tides, sea-birds and all marine and damp-loving life. The merrow could save lives and take them: foretell disasters and cause disasters in the first place. Floods, storms and shipwrecks would be the fault of the merrow. Their kisses could heal wounds but their bites burnt. A merrow bite, while painful for the human female, was fatal for the male, producing a death so infernal that the merrow were bound by some ancient rule to use their teeth only in defence.

Indeed, a man had much to fear from a merrow. Even if she never laid a harmful mouth on him she could peer into his mind, if she felt so inclined. As clear as any tide-pool it would be to her. She could stir and fish and hook any thought or memory that swilled in a man's head. And if that wasn't enough, she could drown him on dry land.

Over the page there's a picture. Bridie touches it.

On a rock, she sits. Her tail, delicately scaled, dipped into a fine calm sea. She is fair; skin like carved marble, pearl-pale eyes, hair bright, she winds a strand of it around her finger.

Bridie turns the page and the picture changes. She stares at it.

Bridie meets the merrow.

Horned spine raised like cat-hackles. Contorted fingers, uncanny, as if set backwards. A tail made for thrashing. Her hair comes out in handfuls. She rips it out.

The sea is whipped to high peaks by the coming storm.

The merrow: with fury in her flat black eyes and teeth like a pike's.

She is all wrath and power.

Muirgeilt: the sea-lunatic.

No wonder. Her man lured her onto land, hiding her magic caul for long years while she took human form and craved daily her element. Yearning to return, to dissolve back into the seething beautiful sea.

Bridie sees the terrible triumph in the creature's face. Beside her, on the rocks, lies her man, blanched and withered. He has suffered a thousand love bites. Rows of puncture wounds on his bare arms, his face and his neck. Water streams from his nose, mouth and eyes, from his fingertips, back into the sea.

The merrow had changed before him – as he confessed where he hid her caul when he tricked her into loving him. She had pulled the trinket box from beneath their home's stone flags, levering them with her teeth. And the rain had lashed and the tide had turned and in all this water she had turned too.

Leaving their newborn keening in its crib, she had slithered down to the beach to meet the rising sea, pulling her man with her, like a dog with a rabbit. She moved by spasms, strong contractions along the length of her tail, crawling over rock and sand.

Her house burns, her child cries, her man lies lifeless.

In a moment she will be born, with a gasp of bliss, into the waves. One deep breath of ocean and her lungs will fill with water. One beat of her tail and she'll be gone.

★

Bridie closes the book and stands, looking for Ruby.

He's wandered across the chapel-yard and is standing, hat in hand, at his own grave. He bends down and tries to clear the leaves lodged against his headstone. He can't, of course.

Then, perhaps hearing Bridie's footsteps, he turns around. His face is sadder than she's ever seen it.

'I don't believe that the merrow exist,' Bridie says, halfway down Highgate Hill. 'Despite the best efforts of Reverend Winter.'

'Or ghosts?' smiles Ruby. 'You don't believe they exist either, do you?'

Bridie looks mutinous. 'To believe merrow exist, and that Christabel is one of them, is to believe she can dabble in a man's mind, kill him with a fatal bite and drown him standing.'

'She'll be able to rescue herself, by the sound of it.'

'That's still my job, Ruby. Only I won't be returning her to Sir Edmund. Nor will I be leaving her in Dr Harbin's hands, if he still has her.'

'Do you think they were involved in Ellen Kelly's murder?'

'I don't know. But they were the reason Ellen was at Maris House. She was trying to get her child back, or perhaps just be near her. With her hiding in the grounds we know she wasn't a welcome visitor.'

'God rest her,' Ruby says. 'Cut down at no age, left for dead.'

They walk in silence for a while.

'Will we have a tidy-up around your memorial there?' she asks gently. 'A few autumn blooms?'

'Why bother, when I'm hardly there?' There's a note to his voice, a mild offence.

Bridie glances up at him. But all she can see is Highgate, overcast now.

Chapter 20

London will turn Atlantis. If the rain keeps falling and the river keeps rising. In some parts the omnibus horses swish pastern-deep in water. The conductors wear galoshes and measure the floods with great officiousness using long sticks (two-foot-deep near Victoria Station, three inches at Walthamstow). In Covent Garden cabbages are yesterday's news and sea kale is all the rage. For asparagus there's samphire, for turnips there's kelp. Before the rain came, the fish had all but vacated the Thames and those that remained were slime-coated, dull of gill and gritty of flesh. Now nets teem and lines hop with the delicious: crayfish and crabs, salmon and trout. Fresh, clear-eyed and succulent!

Some people, of a morbid, catastrophising sort of disposition, say the floods, which will only worsen, are divine punishment for the orgies of sin that Londoners enjoy. Which is true: there's plenty of sin to be had in London. The river will keep rising, they say, London will be washed away.

Mediums report an increase of communications from the drowned. They rise up squelching and inundate séances, imparting wet footprints and the faint smell of sump-water. Incidents of piracy increase tenfold. The London underworld swaps knives for cutlasses and fighting dogs for parrots. Even those with a full complement of eyes take to wearing patches.

Bridie Devine takes most of this – especially when it's out of the mouth of Cora Butter – with a barrel full of salt. Knowing London's propensity for historionics at the slightest change in the weather, she sidesteps the worst of the puddles and concentrates on the task in hand. Which is lurking about Butcher's Lane, stalking down Paternoster Row and loitering about Amen Corner and Ave Maria Lane. Above her, St Paul's Cathedral rises – oh, godly high – or at least above the city haze a bit. Immune to Bridie's street-level plots: a building immutable to the fluctuations of people and weather. Wren's master-stroke: dome glittering in the watery sunlight that sends the soot particles dancing.

Now and again Bridie hails a stranger, or coughs fatally, or makes some sudden startling exclamations, then scrutinises the faces of passers-by.

She is testing her disguise.

Today, Bridie has traded her skirts for trousers, bodice for a frock coat, bonnet for a top hat. Cora has pinned up her hair and fashioned her a pair of Piccadilly weepers out of an old fur tippet, attaching them to Bridie's cheeks by means of specially prepared glue.

The effect is, surprisingly, moderately convincing. But this may have more to do with Bridie's mannerisms than with the costume itself.

Ruby, leaning up against a shop doorway, watches her progress with amusement.

It has been some years since Bridie has donned her gentleman's disguise. She takes an unpractised turn around a knot of narrow streets, coming back along Little Britain. Soon enough she's met with blank looks rather than startlement and Bridie remembers how proficient she is. Adept not just with hat, cane and pocket-watch but also with whistling (cheerful, spreeish) and winking (flower sellers, shop girls and coster-mongers' mules). She remembers her old walk: a purposeful clip. To this she adds something of Ruby's swagger, commensurate with her age and experience. And she rejoices again in this old freedom of movement, of legs unencumbered by petticoats and skirts, to stride, hop or long-leap. And those other freedoms – the male's license to roam – why, he has the key to the city! And with the free-roaming comes the eye unfettered, for (smart new mutton-chop whiskers aside) isn't it a gentleman's primary occupation to *look* rather than be *looked at*?

Bridie tips her hat to Ruby and blows a kiss at a char-woman, and grasping the head of her cane sets a course to the viewing gallery in the main operating theatre of Bart's. She has a front-row ticket.

Or not quite, for Bridie decided it might be more propitious to stand at the back of the upper tier, knowing, as she does, two things. Firstly, that the hallowed halls of medical learning are open only to men. Secondly, that she could soon come face-to-face with the biggest Antichrist that ever walked the earth. And if she does, she doesn't want Gideon Eames to recognise her.

The audience jostle and fidget and exchange medical slanders. They speak in low tones, so that the accumulation of noise in the high-ceilinged, sky-lighted room is that of a buzz, interspersed with coughing and foot shuffling. There is a mordant air of anticipation, an atmosphere of grim excitement. The room is warming up and with it the smell of hair preparation and stale smoke and last night's alcohol rises. With the increased heat Bridie finds it harder to keep her whiskers on. She presses them to the side of her face, mops her forehead and hopes for the best.

She sees no one she knows, which is a blessing. If she

does, she'll keep her head down. For now, she is a medical gentleman, like all the rest.

The patient is laid out and anaesthetised, a process overseen by a doctor with an immaculate apron and rolled-up sleeves. He fastidiously checks and modifies glass bottle, rubber tubing, dials and pumps. Thanks to this blessed giver of sleep the scene before Bridie is a very different one to the first operation she witnessed here.

September 1846. Standing between Prudhoe and Valentine Rose, same hospital, different theatre. She was no older than fifteen and no younger than . . . who knows. Prudhoe had disguised her as a boy and smuggled her in, no doubt with a bribe or two. Rose joked that she was his new little miscreant brother and she had left a button undone on her waistcoat in a disaffected way. She'd watched as the burly attendants dragged the patient into the room. He was putting up a good fight, the patient, but the audience could see his heart wasn't in it. To his credit, he was still screaming, but by then it was hoarse and surprisingly rhythmic.

Prudhoe had turned to her. 'He has a compound fracture in his right leg. He is buggered entirely.'

The patient was strapped, sobbing now, to a long wooden bench. The dressers cut off his trousers.

The surgeon, dour in a stained apron, stalked into the room and was met with a deep hush.

'Compound fracture,' he demanded. 'What do we do with a compound fracture?'

'Saw it off, sir,' a medical gentleman called out.

'Bravo.' The surgeon selected a straight-backed amputation knife from the table nearby.

Prudhoe nudged Bridie. 'He'll use the *tour d'mastre*, the knife brought up under the knee and round. Then swiftly through the bone with the surgical saw. Not the time to lose heart.'

'Stuck saw, panic sets in,' parroted Bridie.

Prudhoe smiled. 'Surgeon's panic, not the patient's. What next?'

'Tie off the arteries and tether the skin flap?' suggested Rose.

Prudhoe nodded. 'All in four minutes, well, three minutes thirty-eight seconds is the best I've seen with this fella.'

'There's a newer method, sir,' Rose said.

'There are newer surgeons. Wait, though, he'll go like the clappers . . .'

The patient thrashed on the table, his eyes protuberating and spittle flying. The assistants, one either side, struggled to keep the man's shoulders down.

The surgeon glanced up at an assistant standing next to him with a pocket-watch in his hand. 'Ready, set, off we bloody well go then.'

The surgeon's hands closed around the man's shattered leg and the patient screamed. Hitting a note of such shrill terror Bridie wanted to run. Instead she put her fingers in her ears. The surgeon felt all along the length of the leg with movements brisk, commonplace and practised.

The knife was positioned. Bridie and the audience leant forward.

It was a mercy when the patient passed out.

'He's a brilliant bugger,' says the man on Bridie's left.

He is a tall, thin fella with prominent teeth, so close that Bridie can feel his breath on her cheek.

The man on Bridie's right, red-cheeked, stout and smelling of meat, answers. 'He's a genuine genius bastard.'

The man on her right cocks an eye at Bridie. 'Don't know you. First time?'

'In London, it is,' answers Bridie, in a deeper voice than she meant to use.

The men glance at each other. Toothy grins. Meaty frowns.

'Irish?' proposes Meaty.

'You've heard of Dr Gideon Eames, Irish?' enquires Toothy.

'Remind me.'

'Long time gone,' answers Meaty. 'Presumed dead, jaunting about the colonies, Europe, so forth and so on. Learnt trade, inventions and the rest—'

'Gadgets,' interjects Toothy. 'Gim-gams.'

'Innovative surgical techniques and apparatus,' corrects Meaty. 'World travel, such and such, acquiring knowledge—'

'*Paris!*' sniggers Toothy. 'You'd acquire some knowledge there, eh?'

Meaty gives Toothy a disparaging glance. 'Eames has been to every corner of the world.'

Toothy looks surprised. 'Has he? I knew he'd visited Copenhagen.'

'Why is he back?' asks Bridie.

'You missed that part, Irish?' asks Meaty.

'Must have.'

'He's finished sowing his oats, simple as that,' says Toothy.

'There were no oats about it,' Meaty retorts. 'Eames was a hunter, a gatherer of medical knowledge.'

'He died a hundred deaths for science!' exclaims Toothy. 'Garrotted in the antipodes. Shot by gendarmes in Rouen. Aced in a duel in Vienna.'

'Succumbed to surgeon's sepsis in Edinburgh,' adds Meaty, begrudgingly.

'Under the likes of Liston.'

'Lucky to come out of it with a full complement of bollocks, then,' says Meaty.

The door opens and a hush immediately falls over the collected gentlemen.

Dr Gideon Eames walks into the operating theatre.

★

Bridie fights the wave of sickness that rises in her.

He is like the boy she knew and unlike him.

Tall in stature, wider of waist now and with the broad shoulders of an athlete. His hair, tawny still, is worn unfashionably long, his beard, gold, threaded with grey, is worn fashionably full. He would compete with Ruby for size and swagger. Unlike Ruby, he claims all the space; he takes all the air. Bridie is struggling to find any left to breathe.

The murmuring voices quieten.

He looks around the theatre with blue sardonic eyes. Bridie wills him not to see her. Up to the back, passing her by. She keeps her breath held yet.

He has his sleeves rolled up and a clean apron on.

'Settle down now, piglets.' His voice is rich, strident. 'Hands up who wants to watch me spatchcock this patient?'

The anaesthetist frowns.

'The miracle of anaesthesia, demonstrated by Mr Blake-James here, is such that we can now attempt complicated procedures' – he whispers, confidentially – '*involving intestines.*'

The audience laughs.

His dresser moves the trolley of instruments nearer.

In the close heat of the room Bridie is dizzy.

A memory overwhelms.

As if no time has passed.

A bright, narrow room in a tottered old cottage, Bridie, small again, holds a bowl of blood and water as big as herself. Her arms will give out, with the fear and with the effort. Gideon, young again, running with sweat, fighting to close the woman he has opened . . .

'Today,' announces Dr Gideon Eames, 'we have an inconvenient obstruction; bladder, nothing fancy, but I'm partial to an obstruction.'

Dr Eames glances at his dresser. 'If you would kindly lift the patient's scrotum, Mr Hindle, we shall proceed.'

As Gideon works he recites medical anecdotes, addressing the room as if they are guests at a dinner party. His tone is warm and comfortable and the medical gentlemen crane their heads, riveted. Gideon alternates between the delicate touch of an artist and the workaday deftness of a blacksmith shoeing a horse.

Bridie watches with the rest of them, enraptured. Only one member of the audience looks away, the dead pugilist in the back row. He could handle blood in the burn of a fight, of course, but it's a different matter in the cold light of the operating theatre. Instead, he inspects the benches and pulleys, the instrument cases and the audience, in their tiered rows. Ruby contemplates their various appearances. Some are unkempt and some are ordinary and some fair smudge in dress.

These are gentlemen who have benefited from every advantage education, application or money can bring. Gentlemen of varying ability and intellect, with forthright, stalwart or just passable characters. Gentlemen eminently fitted to their profession, or here under duress. Gentlemen who have gathered to observe an operation performed by another gentleman and who don't have to disguise themselves to do so. Ruby turns to Bridie. Her whiskers are crooked, her waistcoat's too tight and the cut of her trousers is wrong. But then there's that level green-eyed gaze, chin up, shoulders back, captain of herself. Taking note, calmly, despite the turmoil that must rage inside her, seeing that monstrous bastard again.

Of this Ruby is sure: nobody belongs here more than Bridie.

Bridie hangs back as the medical gentlemen file out and the dressers collect the surgical instruments and an assistant mops the floor. She pulls the collar of her coat up and pushes her hat low on her head.

And then she spots him, over by the operating table, in animated discussion: Curate Cridge from Highgate Chapel. As shabbily dressed today as he was when he was a clergyman, only now Bridie recognises him for what he is: a medical gentleman. He's not sneering, but he's still slight, large of head and generally unfavourable-looking. The spurious curate stands with a group of other young reprobates, smoking and gabbing. The burly assistant draws forward to have words. Cridge drops his cigar in a mop bucket, dons his hat and is off out the door.

Bridie makes haste to follow, pushing through the ambling, babbling rabble. Stopping to stoop to the mop bucket to hook out Cridge's extinguished cigar. A cheap kind, favoured by medical students: *Hussar Blend*.

She hurries out of the theatre; there is no sight of Cridge. She spies him again, in the hall, near the wide oak stairs. In a crush of people, she stops.

At the open doorway stands Gideon Eames.

Bridie goes as near as she dares, pressing herself against the wall.

Gideon is waiting for his carriage to be brought round. A crowd surrounds him, men shaking his hand, laughing at his jokes. A young doctor presents his wife; Gideon turns to her with a smile. He kisses her hand, his fingers moving above the cuff of her glove, her face colours and he smiles all the wider.

Perhaps sensing that he's being watched, Gideon turns.

Bridie feels the blood halt in her as their eyes meet, just for an instant. He touches the brim of his hat – and then, distracted by a man's hand on his arm, he looks away. It is Cridge, there beside him. Gideon pats Cridge on the shoulder with a gesture both dismissive and not without affection.

People push by, momentarily obscuring Bridie's view. When the crowds clear again, the men are gone.

Chapter 21

The old ship-chandlery shop is the place to go to find something lost and to lose something found under questionable circumstances. The shop slumps in a state of elderly decline along Deptford creek, its windows cobwebbed and dust-crazed. Peer inside and you will see a world of haphazard riches! Ropes so old that Noah himself used them to moor the Ark – they are no more than twists of dust!

Cracked nautical floats, rowlocks and boathooks, axes and pitch, storm lanterns, moth-mauled mop heads, monkey paws and a thousand other items of net, metal, string and twine. Arcane nautical objects hang from hooks in the ceiling; dusty treasures are stacked in ever-upward-growing piles. The sign on the door is cryptic:

> *Open every second TUESDAY of the month*
> *Excepting when shop is open every third THURSDAY*
> *Excepting when shop is open alternate MONDAYS*
> *For board and lodgings enquire within*
> *For mooring and caulking apply without*
> *By order of Mr. W. Tackett*

When the door to the shop is open the river breeze (which otherwise prowls the creek aimlessly) takes its chance, rushing in alongside the unwitting customer. The breeze delights most in ringing the bell inside the door – the same bell that rang on board the *Flying Dutchman*. It resounds morosely, a funereal greeting for the hapless customer. The breeze then turns its attention to the rest of the shop, setting diverse what-nots swinging and rattling, shaking and clanking, toppling and rolling. So that it seems as if the shop itself is suddenly out at sea. Above the shop are the lodging rooms, tenantless now. In the halcyon days when trade was swift, the rooms could be filled ten times over. They took all sorts, saints and sinners; a blind sea captain and a one-armed stevedore, gentleman-paupers by the score and an Irish corpse collector. On fair weather days the inmates would line up outside the shop. Scowling at the sun, spitting at the passers-by.

Bill Tackett, shopkeeper, assumes, during hours of commerce, his post behind the counter. Under which the cash-box lives (which nowadays is empty of needful but full of other things: smooth pebbles, gull-feathers and a green glass marble). A clawed knuckle of a man, as one preserved by curses and salt-water, much like an ancient mariner himself. He wears a waxed sou'wester pulled down around his ears and rope to keep his trousers pulled high. He has a pursed corrugated mussel of a mouth and glancy black eyes that would not be unfitting on a crab. Bill's mouth and eyes are currently expressing a heightened pursing and glancing. His wife has been away for years and he wasn't best pleased to see her returned. Nor was he best pleased that she had some ramshackle cove in tow (a doctor, it is alleged), along with a waterman needing paying and a casket containing goods mysterious.

The doctor, faint on arrival and with violent gurgulations of the stomach, was shown to an abandoned guest-room. Bill's wife attended him immediately with preparations and a drop of calf's-foot broth, and not a peep from him since. The casket, however, has been nothing but noisy, what with the scraping and the tapping. At the behest of his wife, Bill moved the casket into the repair-room just off the main shop. Too dark to work in and too damp to use as a store, it offers a barred window set at floor level, too low for light, a bench, a chair and naught else. His wife called for a wash-tub and a bucket of market fish of whatever variety. These provisions being delivered for the comfort of the new occupant, Bill was banished from the room whilst his wife opened the casket. This done, she came out, locked the door and hung the key about her neck on a strong cord.

Now Bill sits one end of a table in the back room of the old ship-chandlery shop. At the other end sits his wife with her bad leg on a footstool.

'So, there it is,' she says. 'That's the story of it.'

'Of all the twisted things you've done in your life, wife,' Bill says, 'this takes the frigging biscuit.'

She laughs across the debris of their meal, three empty gin bottles and a dish of cold slink veal.

'You pretended to be a child's nurse at a country house . . .' Bill is incredulous. 'What are you even calling yourself now?'

'Mrs Bibby,' she grins.

Bill groans. 'My own mother's maiden name!'

'I've no shame.'

'You go on to steal this child, under the nose of a bleeding lord—'

'A baronet.'

Bill narrows his tiny eyes. 'And transport the poor wretch about the country in a coffin.'

'A casket, for her own good.'

'You truly are a nasty old bitch,' Bill replies. He picks up a knife from the table. 'Release her. Return her to her friends,' he orders, heroically.

'Put the knife down, you'll cause yourself a calamity.' His wife adjusts her bad leg on a footstool with a stream of emphatic curses. 'That child represents an investment of trouble on my part. I am expecting a return on that investment.'

Bill puts the knife down. 'And the doctor? He'll want his share and if this goes arseways he'll be the first to direct you to the gallows.'

'What doctor?'

'Ah, no—' Bill looks up at the ceiling. 'You didn't do that *here*?'

'Why must you think the worst of me?'

Bill gets up from his chair, lists around the table and takes a seat next to her.

He chooses his words carefully and delivers them with great sincerity in his eyes. 'Here I sit, wife, next to this stinking bleeding leg of yours, to implore you, nay, to beg you: give up that child. Do what is right and fitting and proper.'

'Husband, you are a blunt tool and you always have been.'

'Your leg is bad, wife, that big swollen foot on you and them toes just pus bags, rotten soft.'

'You're right.'

'I hope they drop off, them toes, one after another. I hope that blight spreads and claims you. After all, it's only the rot you've always had at the heart of you.'

Bill's wife laughs like water draining.

A man calls in at the old ship-chandlery shop, a stranger; large, but agile, scarred face and hands, close-cropped hair and a grown-out beard in the Crimean fashion. He has a quiet, hostile way about him. Bill knows enough about the world to know that this fella is not only used to bad business, he excels in it. Bill says nothing, but keeps a weather-eye open below the brim of his sou'wester. His wife leads the stranger through the cobwebbed clutter and into the back room and closes the door behind them. Tightening the rope on his trousers and pulling down his hat against probable squalls, Bill loiters near the door. He hears words – *package, Polegate, delivery* – then footsteps heading towards the door. Bill scuttles back behind the counter, his old thumper yammering its complaint against the hull of his rib-racks. As the stranger leaves he tips his hat and sends Bill a look of such dedicated malice that the ancient mariner would run away to sea in a bucket if he had one sound enough to paddle.

The child doesn't notice Mrs Bibby come into the repair-room because she is standing at the window.

The lid has been pushed off the casket. The restraints lie tangled in the bottom. Mrs Bibby blames herself, for hadn't she, in a fit of kindness, left the lid open for a bit of air and loosened the straps on the growing child?

And there she is: Christabel Berwick.

Standing in the light from the low, barred window. Pale of limb, white of nightie, like any plain, thin, two-a-penny child.

Mrs Bibby finds herself touched with something that could be pity – that might be pity. How would she know, with a callused heel of a heart inside her? But there it is: a sudden urge to weep at the sight of those arms and legs and feet, pigeon-toed. Or, at the child's uncertain shrug and bob as she steps forward, chary chick. Add her too-thin garment, the peculiar curve of her spine and the frail knots of her wrists. Yes, Mrs Bibby could be set weeping forevermore, if she wasn't a flint-souled old hex.

Outside: voices, high-noted, piping.

Inside: Christabel, cautious, sniffs and peers.

A small hand comes in through the barred window. The hand opens slowly. In the palm: a pebble.

Christabel lowers her face the better to see. The hand

moves; she recoils. The hand is urging her to take the pebble. She takes the pebble, carefully, carefully, between her finger and thumb. She presses it to her mouth. It is a kiss.

Mrs Bibby limps closer.

Christabel startles and scrambles to the corner, forgetting to walk in her alarm – forgetting she can stand and walk like a plain, thin, two-a-penny child.

Mrs Bibby ignores her. Her tomcat smile widens as she draws nearer the window. She bends down.

Three small faces look in at her from outside.

'Would you like to join us for tea?' She addresses the largest girl, the one in the middle, in a voice sweet and easy. 'We have cakes: seed, pound, tipsy and fruit. And apple hat, I do believe!'

There is a brief exchange, then the largest girl turns, nudging the others, and trudges towards the doorway of the old ship-chandlery shop.

Chapter 22

Cora clatters around the bedroom collecting the appurtenances of Bridie's gentleman disguise: ineffables, tippet-fur whiskers, waistcoat and hat. Bridie is late to rise, for she was late to bed and barely slept when she was in it.

She drinks coffee and turns to the letters Cora has presented her with. When Cora leaves the room, she'll light her pipe, still in the bed. A shameless vice Cora heartily disapproves of. But Bridie deserves it, having survived the first sighting of Gideon Eames since he was sent away. That he has the power to unnerve her, after all this time, she isn't surprised. That he is a different man now than when he was young, Bridie has her doubts.

Bridie opens the first letter. It is written in a plodding hand with some pooling of ink (suggesting lengthy consultations of dictionaries and suchlike).

Maris House
Polegate
East Sussex
—September 1863

Dear Mrs Devine,

Gone about as asked. Here is the NEWS. Mrs Swann closed the house. Myrtle away with London uncle. But <u>HEAR THIS</u>. Mrs Swann says doctor is gone to BATH if you please. I pray Myrtle finds a good spot in London PLEASE GOD. Having no mother but what one expired in bringing the POOR CHILD into the world and now no father of any use. HAVE YOU SEEN HER?

The tramping woman as you found was put in the parish church-yard. GOD REST HER SOUL. She wants a name and the police reckon they have found one. Master grows thin and walks as one HAG RIDDEN. Mr Puck says Master has not shut his eyes since the child was taken.

<u>MAY GOD BLESS AND KEEP YOU</u> and believe me most sincerely yours,

Miss Agnes Molloy

Bridie turns to the second letter, written in shaky copperplate, as befitting a hag-ridden baronet.

Maris House
Polegate
East Sussex
—September 1863

Mrs Devine,

What news? Address to MR PUCK. Earliest convenience.

I remain, etc. etc.

(*Unintelligible)

Bridie puts down the letters, lights her pipe and sinks back into her pillows to watch the smoke curl.

The residents of Denmark Street have been up for hours. She can hear them outside going about their every-days: hawking, scrubbing doorsteps and complaining about the low, thick fog that has descended upon the city like an unwashed bedsheet. Oh, the unwholesome colour! Like sinus rot, and dense, like only a London Particular can be. You could scoop it into a tankard and it would mug there. Only today the fog is behaving even more queerly than usual. For one thing, it has been seen moving *against* the wind. In Richmond, where the air is more refined, the fog is as needle lace, drifting by in delicate patterns. Under Waterloo Bridge it takes the form of gambolling otters. In Southwark it undulates like eels. The day is already dark and it has hardly begun. Omnibus lanterns are lit and progress is at walking pace, with the drear rattle of harnesses and the slow growl of wheels. People and buildings emerge and disappear, as does your own hand when it's not half an inch before your eye.

Bridie sees neither otters nor eels at her window, just a touch of dirty weather: reason enough not to get up. Soon Cora will be back to nag her out of the bed and into a corset. They'll argue about the plan for the day while she threatens Bridie's hair with a brush. Then Bridie will sit down to breakfast. Ruby will be there, in the corner of the room, waiting. Re-tying the bandages on his fists, or stroking his magnificent moustache, or hitching up his drawers absent-mindedly.

But for now Bridie smokes her pipe and lets everything she knows, and doesn't know, and thinks she knows, wash over her. The cast of this pantomime present themselves in the playhouse of her mind.

Bridie watches them file on stage.

Christabel Berwick, white-haired and pearl-eyed, is the first to arrive. She skips on human legs and bobs a perfect curtsey. She smiles, pike-toothed and terrifying. Sir Edmund and his servants, Dr Harbin and Myrtle, follow. The little circus king Lester Lufkin dressed as a ringmaster makes an entrance. Ellen Kelly floats by, with her fair hair wet and her lips blue and beetles in her corset. Mrs Bibby is there too: a limp and a space where her face would be (if Bridie knew what it looked like). Reverend Gale and Widmerpole join the group, and here is the spurious Cridge, cigar in hand, sneering. There is a whispering and shuffling and a parting of the crowd – everyone steps aside for a latecomer. Smiling and golden, Gideon Eames claims centre stage and takes a bow.

★

The post room at Mudie's Select Library is a grand place to have a sit and a wait for yourself. The bustle of New Oxford Street and Museum Road seems far away here. The only sounds to be heard are the slump and sway of Ruby Doyle pacing in his unlaced boots and the clock in the corner ticking. Out in the main hall, the library clerks move behind their desks with polite precision, issuing a baffling number of books with a sleight-of-hand deftness. Footmen wait to carry out bundles while gentlemen and ladies peruse the catalogues. Carriages draw up outside, bringing illustrious readers. Bridie leafs through the neat piles of books waiting to be wrapped and dispatched to Mudie's postal subscribers. One book catches her eye.

The Psychic Way
By Madam Volkov
A discourse on HAUNTINGS,
Poltergeists, Spectres, Lost and Stubborn Entities
Keep your home FREE from GHOSTS
OR
ENCOURAGE them into your home.
Séances for EDIFICATION and PLEASURE

· 253 ·

Ruby throws her a curious glance. 'What is it?'

'Novel.'

'You'll get nowhere reading them,' advises Ruby and continues pacing, hat in hand. 'They shrink the mind.'

Bridie snorts.

The clerk returns, a thin young man with a sickly pallor and long fingers that pat and dab with prim reverence on book and paper.

He looks at Bridie with anxious eyes. 'If I give you this information, Mrs Devine—'

'I'll be as silent as the grave,' Bridie reassures. 'You have my word.'

The clerk, Willie, is the son of William Whitaker, Denmark Street, tassel-mould maker. She'll do nothing to jeopardise a neighbour's position.

Willie nods. 'This is the client's reading list, all fiction.'

'What sort of fiction?'

'Popular. Likes a bit of sensation.'

'Who doesn't? Kidnapped heiresses, Gothic houses, heinous crimes – that sort of thing?'

'*The Woman in White* has been requested several times. Lady Audley, she's been in and out on this ticket.'

'Rattling tales, Willie. You have an address for this reader?'

'A residence in Somers Town, only the name on the account is different from the one you gave me. I double-checked the docket.'

He hands a neatly written card to Bridie.

Fanny Squeers.

'Something tells me we have a fan of Mr Dickens,' she says.

Ruby ambles back and looks over her shoulder at the card. He's none the wiser.

'It's the name of a fictional character,' Bridie explains to him.

'I'm aware of that, Mrs Devine,' Willie responds. 'But there's a real reader behind the name, all right.'

Bridie glances at him with curiosity. 'You know them?'

'No, madam,' frowns Willie. 'But they send their maid to collect the books – I wouldn't forget her in a hurry.'

'Can you describe this maid?'

'Rough-mannered, limp.' Willie's frown deepens. 'She has *language*.'

Bridie produces from the pocket of her skirt the book she found in the nurse's room at Maris House. 'One of Fanny Squeers's. Overdue, I think.'

'It would be.'

Ruby, sensing the interview is nearly concluded, sculls to the door and watches the librarians go about their work.

Bridie points to the book on the table. 'I'll borrow that,' she whispers. 'Can you add it to my ticket?'

Willie picks up the book. 'I wouldn't have put you down for this kind of thing, Mrs Devine. Ghosts and ghouls.'

Ruby glances over his shoulder.

'If you could just issue the thing.'

Willie turns the pages and lets out a chuckle. 'Oh, sublime! *Spectral Love: When Your Beau Is Deceased.*'

Bridie snatches the book and pushes it into her pocket, ignoring Ruby's delighted expression.

A deluge of rain and the roads have become a slippery quagmire; mud, in prodigious quantities, keeps the crossing-sweepers busy on every corner and the pedestrians busy staying upright. Bridie makes her way down New Oxford Street towards the British Museum. Ruby is at her side of course, drawers hoisted, topper tipped back, walking with his rolling prize-fighter gait. They pass Russell Square and Woburn Square, all laid out in gardens. Gordon Square with University Hall and knots of students. Euston and beyond; the grandeur of the squares behind them. Ahead, Somers Town and the once-fine houses overrun with ragbag families.

Fanny Squeers's residence in Sidney Street is a thin, tired, loveless house, wedged between two large, encroaching houses with the look of dowagers elbowing their way onto an omnibus. By the door is a sign: *Mrs Peach's Guest-House.*

On gaining admission, by way of Mrs Peach's maid, a nervous girl of no more than twelve, Bridie soon realises that the care-worn façade of the house belies the extreme vivacity of the interior. Mrs Peach's narrow parlour is decorated as exuberantly as Mrs Peach's person. A gaudy old parrot, her avian counterpart, lolls on a perch in the corner. Its plush is a little frayed and its beak is a little flaked, but its beady eye is unfaded.

Apart from a parrot there is a comprehensive collection of knick-knacks and trinkets, many of which are placed high out of reach of Mrs Peach's crinoline, an expansive structure demonstrating a bewildering range of swags, ruffles, pleats and bows.

Bridie takes a seat while Mrs Peach battles her crinoline into an armchair. Ruby stands out of the way in the chimney-breast, amid shelves bearing silver-framed photographs, china animals, samplers, ormolu clocks and embroidered bunting. Mrs Peach shows a full leg length of flounced pantalette before managing to beat her hooped cage into submission.

Ruby politely averts his eyes.

The narrow proportions of Mrs Peach's parlour and the extraordinary wealth of possessions crammed into it mean that Bridie is seated in close proximity to the landlady herself. From this intimate distance, of no more than two feet, Bridie can marvel at the artistry and invention behind Mrs Peach's radiant complexion.

From a distance, the average-sighted could be forgiven for mistaking Mrs Peach to be in the first flush of wide-eyed, pink-cheeked, white-toothed youth. Mrs Peach is, in fact, somewhat beyond flowering age. Her freshness has been retained – the years rewound, even – by sheer artifice. Face creams, powders and paints – all applied with an unstinting hand. This cosmetic artistry is supplemented with the pinning of wigs and postiches and the donning of false dental bridges.

Close up the effect is disturbing; Bridie is disturbed.

The parrot shakes its ancient wings and lets out a series of low-throated croaks as it watches Bridie from its perch. Mrs Peach takes the lending library docket and looks at it for a while, sucking at her unsteady teeth.

'Well, Mrs Devine,' she says, in the polite voice reserved for company (whereby every syllable is stressed and the vowels are elongated, all refined-like), 'I can confirm that no such persons as *Miss Fanny Squeers* took rooms here.'

There is a slow batting of her cerulean eyelids and a general shaking of her powdered jowls. 'And I can't for the life of me think why someone should give out my little address if they ain't boarding here.'

'It's a fictional name, Mrs Peach,' says Bridie. 'A character in a popular novel by Mr Dickens.'

'Popular novels and fictional names are all very well, but I never take them, Mrs Devine.'

'You let rooms to lodgers?'

Mrs Peach is affronted. '*Lady guests*, if you please, of which I'm down to three and one of those is on an occasional basis.'

'*Occasional friends*,' screams the parrot, with a sudden resentful shriek. '*Occ-asion-al friends!*'

Mrs Peach ignores it. 'And then only respectable ladies, like myself.'

'*Up your nose*,' assents the parrot, looking Bridie dead in the eye. '*With a rubber hose.*'

In the chimney-breast, Ruby laughs.

'Have you, or have you ever had, a respectable lady guest who also goes by the name of Mrs Bibby?'

Mrs Peach purses her lips. 'I'm not sure as I can tell you. With all due respects, Mrs Devine, I don't know you from Eve.'

'Mrs Peach.' Bridie smiles. 'I am conducting an important investigation: crimes have been committed, of a serious nature.'

The parrot ducks its head and whistles low.

'Whilst I can't divulge the particulars of my investigation,' Bridie continues, 'I can assure you, madam, that your assistance would be greatly valued.'

Bridie gives this a moment to sink in. Mrs Peach remains impassive, the mask of her face set solid. The parrot shuffles up and down its perch muttering mutinously.

'Would you prefer I sent a member of the constabulary to converse with you on this matter, Mrs Peach? I am very good friends with Inspector Valentine Rose. You've heard of him?'

'*Hide the candlesticks!*' answers the parrot.

Mrs Peach's expression doesn't change, only her nose-tip starts to redden, despite its thorough dusting.

'That won't be necessary, Mrs Devine.' The landlady smoothes down her skirts pettishly. 'My two permanent ladies, Miss Figgs and Miss Flash, are clergyman's daughters, govern-esses currently between positions.'

'*I should cocoa—*'

'And my occasional lady, Miss Windsor—'

'*Hop-along pirate!*'

Mrs Peach's nose burns brighter. 'Is a very respectable lady, clean and most pleasant.'

The parrot cackles derisively.

'Would Miss Windsor happen to have a limp and colourful language?' suggests Bridie.

Mrs Peach gives an imperceptible nod.

'*DIRTY PUZZLE! CRUSTY TWIST!*' shouts the bird. '*RUDE JUDY!*'

Mrs Peach subdues the parrot with a gorgonising glare. It drops its head and rocks from claw to claw.

'When did you last see Miss Windsor, madam?' asks Bridie.

'Some weeks,' says Mrs Peach, tartly. 'Or months.'

'Would you happen to know Miss Windsor's whereabouts?'

Mrs Peach nearly swallows her teeth. 'Miss Windsor's whereabouts are none of my concern, madam!'

Bridie waits for Mrs Peach's jowls to settle. Then: 'Did Miss Windsor receive any visitors?'

'*Muck snipe.*' The parrot coos. '*Fruited bun!*'

The pencilled arcs of Mrs Peach's eyebrows reconfigure into an expression of offended astonishment. 'I run a decent house, Mrs Devine!'

'*Show us your drawers!*' whistles the parrot.

'With every propriety observed, of course,' adds Bridie.

Mrs Peach rearranges her face to display supreme disapproval. 'I really could not say. Will there be anything else, Mrs Devine?'

'I'd like to see Miss Windsor's room, if you don't mind.'

The parrot shuffles sideways along its perch and cocks its head. '*You're 'aving a laugh, ain't ya?*'

'Miss Windsor may not be agreeable to that—'

Bridie looks the landlady in the eye. 'Madam, Miss Windsor may not be back.'

'*In the clinker,*' whoops the parrot. '*Lock 'er up!*'

The landlady's lips draw a hard line. Her painted brows shutter down.

'*Bye bye, Naughty Nancy!*' sings the bird, with glee.

Mrs Peach's maid escorts Bridie to the attic room where Miss Windsor stayed on an occasional basis. When Bridie tries to talk to her, the girl flees downstairs.

Miss Windsor's attic room is sparsely furnished. The smell of breakfast kippers haunts the painted rafters.

When searched, it yields nothing but a meat pie (not fresh), a pot of mustard and a skeleton key. Bridie pockets the key.

'So, this room hasn't been turned over. But then what's to turn, once you've made it past Mrs Peach?'

'Where are they?' Ruby stands at the window watching two cats chase each other on the jumbled rooftops below.

'Who?'

'Mrs Bibby and the doctor; they're in this together, up to their oxters.'

'It appears so.'

'They may yet have the child?'

'Possibly.' Bridie inspects some likely-looking floorboards but they are nailed down. 'I think they've gone to ground, waiting for a buyer. Or else they're running scared.'

'Of being caught? The police aren't after them.'

'Someone in the business, perhaps.' Bridie turns to the fireplace, checking up the chimney, poking in the grate. She pulls out a half-burnt object.

In her palm: a cigar butt.

'*Hussar Blend*?' asks Ruby.

Bridie nods. 'Curate Cridge really gets around.'

May 1843

Chapter 23

Bridie had her head all but in a hedgerow watching the nesting bird. It was a wren and she was fond of these tiny birds. Only she wasn't really watching the bird, she was thinking. And apart from the thinking, she was letting the errand she was running for Mrs Donsie keep her out for hours. It was a relief to be away from the house. The atmosphere in the servants' quarters was bleak. Gideon had been sent down for some misdemeanour and would not be returning to college this time. Talk ran to leaving Albery Hall and of finding new positions. Even Mrs Donsie had her eye on an inn along the coast there, where she could serve beer and stews and be queen of her own little kingdom.

Bridie, with her head in the hedgerow and the wren long gone, wasn't ruminating on this news about Gideon as much as her friend's reaction to it. Eliza barely seemed to care.

She had changed since her meeting with Gideon in the stable. She was sullen, distracted, and often nowhere to be found. Edgar toddled behind her, as he always did, his arms outstretched, pulling on her skirts. But Eliza just stared down at the child, as if trying to place him, before lifting him wearily to her hip.

If Eliza knew it had been Bridie hiding in the hay barn that day, she didn't say. And neither did Bridie, although a few times she had wanted to, not least because of her fear of Gideon's retribution. But then, Bridie reasoned, how could Eliza defend her against Gideon if she couldn't defend herself? Bridie was not certain about what had transpired between the two of them that day, but she knew Eliza had been afraid. It was there in her voice and in the sound of her fleeing foot-steps.

And so Bridie was considering the root of all this evil – Gideon – when she heard a gig come down the road. With her head still in the hedgerow she heard it before she saw it.

Had Bridie realised who was approaching, she would have thrown herself into the hedge. She ought to have heeded old Gan Murphy's advice: *Don't bring the bad to mind else you set it galloping towards you.*

Gideon brought the gig to a halt. 'Get in. I need a helper with strong nerves.'

Bridie hesitated. There was no one on the lane, before or after her. She thought of running. She was fast. She could be through the hedge and across the field before he climbed down.

'Hurry, Bridget, someone is gravely ill.'

Maybe it was the way that Gideon said her name, plainly and without sarcasm, or his open expression. But to her eternal regret Bridie came out from the hedge and climbed up into the gig.

The cottage was beyond the village of Cranbourne. When the road ran out they abandoned the gig and continued on foot across fields. Gideon carried the case he'd brought with him, leather, not unlike the one his father took to the hospital. Bridie carried the parcel Gideon had handed to her, something soft wrapped in brown paper. Their journey took them along overgrown tracks tangled with weeds and briars. Bridie knew not where she was. Finally, they reached a dwelling, a tottered old cottage.

A woman was sitting alone on the porch with a bowl on her lap and a shawl around her shoulders. When she saw them approach, she tried to stand and the shawl slipped and she let it. Bridie had never seen someone so exhausted.

'She is going to have a baby,' said Bridie, who knew this from the shape of her belly, for Gan had told her about such things.

Gideon shook his head. 'No, she isn't. She has an ovarian tumour.' He glanced at Bridie. 'I'm here to remove it.'

Bridie stared at him. 'Should we not take her to a hospital, sir?'

Gideon flushed red. 'We'll give her the choice, shall we?'

'But you're not a surgeon, sir.'

'I will be.'

'How would you even know how to begin?'

Gideon looked aggravated. 'I've read about it and practised on a pig.'

'A woman is one thing and a pig is another.'

'Have you heard of Ephraim McDowell?'

'No, sir.'

'American physician, vastly successful removal of ovarian tumours: his patients survived post-operatively.'

'Sir?'

'They didn't succumb to peritonitis.' He spoke with barely concealed excitement. 'His first attempt, the removal of a mass from one Jane Todd Crawford, was in 1809. She was back on a horse in a month and lived to be seventy-eight.'

Bridie frowned. 'Should you not ask your father to help this poor woman, sir?'

'No. I am here to operate on this poor woman.'

Bridie stared at Gideon with horror. 'Ah, no, please—'

'If McDowell did it, Bridget, it can be done.'

'I urge you, sir—'

'You are here because I need a pair of steady hands, not for your fucking opinion,' he said. 'Stifle it.'

Her name was Della Webb and she lived alone in the cottage and tended her plot and kept herself apart. Della was sallow of complexion, white-lipped and drawn ragged with pain and fever, so that it was hard to tell how old she was. Her eyes were large, grey and baffled. Gideon was her young forest buck, she said. He was her gentleman visitor. Bridie knew it was best not to ask, even if she were allowed to speak. Della told Bridie this, between retching into the bowl and trying to get up to offer them wine, whilst Gideon watched from his chair on the veranda.

She turned to him. 'Your best advice, sir.'

'We've been over this, Della: you are less likely to die under my hands than in the hospital.' There was a note of irritation in Gideon's voice.

'And you can get this out of me, sir?'

'Yes,' said Gideon.

Della nodded grimly.

The cottage had two rooms and neither was ideal. The first was light but too narrow, the second was bigger but dark. Gideon opted for the brighter space and, with Bridie's help, cleared the room and dragged a sturdy table into it. He unwrapped the parcel, unpacking a notebook and clean sheets. He spread the brown paper down on the mantelpiece and laid out surgical instruments.

Between them Bridie and Gideon helped Della onto the table. She shook with pain, and cursed and apologised. When Bridie stepped forward to help her with her clothes she began to cry very softly.

Gideon showed Bridie the notebook. 'We follow my notes to the letter. Read this while I am readying the patient.'

Bridie tried hard to concentrate on Gideon's clear and perfect copperplate. The words were difficult but she knew that you could read anything if you went slowly enough. It instructed: *midline incision, wash intestines, evacuate blood from abdominal cavity.*

Gideon fastened strong bands of his own design about Della's legs and torso, then he checked the bands, then he drew a cross with chalk on the wall. He told Della to turn her head and keep her eyes on the cross. He would be finished, he said, in less than half an hour.

Gideon came close and spoke low in Bridie's ear. 'You do everything I ask quickly and calmly, no matter what. Do you understand?'

Bridie was too frightened to nod.

★

Bridie waited for Gideon on the veranda, heart-mauled, fear-dulled. She could hardly say what had just happened in the room, whether it had been quick or slow or in what order. She saw it as if through a series of pictures, each with its own vivid, awful detail. Della Webb with her face turned to the chalked cross on the wall. A pulse of blood as Gideon worked to tie a ligature. The bowl of warm water Bridie held ready and then Della's insides half in it and the weight of them and how in God's name could the woman still be alive staring at the wall with her eyes demented and her mouth moving and some unhearable sound coming out. A broken howl.

If the sight of such lavish gore disconcerted Gideon, he didn't show it. Nor did he show uncertainty. As he fought to close the wound. As he wrestled Della closed. As he bandaged her, sealing the wound tightly against the air. As he dosed her, still as she was, with laudanum. Bridie wiped Della's face; she was already cooling to the touch. Bridie bent near and felt no breath. Then Bridie rolled blankets either side of her, following Gideon's directions. They would leave her on the table. She could not be moved yet.

Bridie left Gideon stripping off his shirt. Wiping his face and neck and arms with it, bundling it up with the worst of the blood-soaked sheets. She heard him come outside and splash at the butt of rainwater along from the door.

Bridie waited, sitting on her hands on the veranda.

Gideon came round the side of the house. He had on a clean shirt, open at the neck. His fair hair was dark with water, plastered to his head.

'She has every chance. I followed McDowell's account and my own notes to the letter.'

'She is not breathing,' Bridie said.

Gideon ignored her, finding tobacco, setting to smoke. 'You did well, surgeon's little helper.'

Bridie surveyed Della's garden, the wigwams of climbing plants, the flowers and the shell-decorated path. The few chickens picking around and a tortoiseshell cat stretched out in the spring sun.

'Tell no one what we did here today, Bridget.'

Bridie said nothing.

'You are complicit. Do you know what that means? You were involved: you assisted me. There would be consequences for you, too.'

Bridie looked at him.

'Ask it,' said Gideon. 'The question you have on your mind.'

'Why didn't you ask your father to help her?'

'Do you know what she is? What she does?'

'She lives alone and tends her garden.'

Gideon laughed. 'She was a barmaid at the Fleur de Lys

– before she was dismissed for entertaining the customers. She isn't someone a man of good character would know.'

Bridie watched the cat in the sunshine and fought the urge to cry.

'The truth is: I wanted to see inside her,' Gideon said.

'She belonged in the hospital.'

'They would have turned her away, even if she had survived the journey.'

Bridie knew this was a lie.

'I'll take you back.' Gideon stood and held out his hand. 'They won't miss me but they'll send out a search party for an Irish street stray.'

Bridie ignored his hand. 'What about Della?'

'I'll return, stay with her. See her out of the woods.' He folded his arms.

They walked back to the gig in silence and drove back through the lanes in silence too, as the day began to dwindle.

As Bridie turned to dismount Gideon laid his hand on her arm.

'You are thick with Eliza. I see you always together, whispering.'

'Not lately,' said Bridie. 'She has been busy,' she added quickly.

'Does she ever talk of me?' he asked.

Bridie caught something behind the carefully careless tone. She met his eyes. 'No, why would she?'

Gideon studied her with interest, then suddenly smiled.

September 1863

Chapter 24

Cora Butter peers out into the road. There is no sign of the person who has just banged on the front door so frantically, bringing her running, be-floured, down the stairs. On the doorstep is a parcel the shape and size of a gentleman's hatbox. Cora takes a look around: just Denmark Street going about its usual. Even so, Cora has the distinct feeling she's being watched as she stoops to pick up the parcel, which is surprisingly heavy for its size.

Cora sets the parcel on the table in the parlour where her mistress is dining on tobacco, coffee and Frau Weiss's leftover pastries. Cora cuts the string and unwraps the brown paper.

Inside is a hatbox and inside the hatbox is a head.

'Bloody hell,' says Cora.

Bridie drains her coffee.

'Well, I'd hazard a guess at decapitation,' says Cora. 'For the cause of death.'

Bridie checks the cut. It's neat, surgical. 'The head was taken after he died.'

Cora looks impressed. 'So what did he die of?'

'I'd probably need the rest of Dr Harbin to tell you that.'

'When did he die? This head's been knocking about a bit, hasn't it?'

'Two or three days, I'd say. The head has been stored cold, but is significantly gnawed; missing earlobes, part of a cheek, the tip of its nose—'

'That would be rats?'

'It would, Cora.'

'Ah, Jesus, no,' moans Ruby, who is through the fireplace at a flinch, agitable since the head arrived.

Dr Harbin, with eyes veiled and sunken behind broken spectacles that sit crookedly now. Unshaven, with side-whiskers untrimmed. A head hairless and puckered: a peeled, dead bollock.

'It's a shame really, the state of him,' says Cora. 'He was a man who took pride in his mutton cutlets.'

Bridie catches sight of something protruding from between Dr Harbin's lips. 'We'll move him over by the window, Cora, better light.'

Cora, with the greatest of decorum, slips her fingertips into the doctor's ears. Moving cautiously, as if Dr Harbin was a full soup tureen, she sets him on a card table.

Bridie pushes tweezers between the late doctor's lips and eases out a flattened lump of paper. She inspects the mouth cavity; as far as she can see it is empty now. She lays the ball of paper on the table and begins to smooth it out.

'It's written in registrar's ink,' notes Bridie, 'so it's waterproof. Can you read it?'

Cora bends closer.

With a comb of pearl I would comb my hair;
And still as I comb'd I would sing and say,
'Who is it loves me? who loves not me?'

Cora contemplates Dr Harbin's pate. 'I don't understand. What would he be combing? He doesn't have a bit of hair on his head.'

'It's Tennyson,' says Bridie. 'From a poem called "The Mermaid".'

'Someone is telling you that they have Christabel.'

Bridie is thoughtful. 'Possibly.'

'Well and good luck to them: they've bargained for a mermaid and caught themselves a merrow. A memory-reading, dry-land-drowning, man-biting sea lunatic.'

Bridie momentarily regrets letting Cora read Reverend Winter's book, but she was encouraged by her interest in anything other than a penny-blood.

'Christabel is a child, Cora. She is not a merrow because they are legendary beasts that do not exist in real life, only in fables.'

Cora looks mutinous. 'And the evidence?'

'What evidence? Wet walls and a few snails.'

Cora, deep in thought, scratches a side-whisker. 'And the Thames misbehaving and the flood and the rain — what do you think is causing that?'

'Not a six-year-old child.'

'The Reverend Winter made room for fables and he was right to, because there's a lot of truth in a fable,' opines Cora majestically.

Bridie squints at her. 'Is that a new dress?'

Cora is wearing a red velvet gown that seems to have been sewn from the stage curtains at Flaxman's Theatre. It is tied at the waist by a cord as thick as Bridie's wrist. A pair of foot-long tassels trail at her side. Her chin is freshly shaven and she is wearing a dab of rouge.

'Are you *courting*, Cora?' asks Bridie.

'None of yours,' Cora growls. 'If that's all, it is my afternoon off.' And she gathers her monumental skirts and flounces out of the door.

Chapter 25

He has his orders and the job is in hand. He heads to the Coach and Horses, Greek Street, for a swift one. A little livener for Mr Boyd, he takes a pew, then has a spit and a snort for himself, for he is a muculant man of prodigious phlegm and these present London conditions, what with the raining and the flooding, are of no assistance to him. The job in hand requires stealth and quietude, not spitting and snorting.

The shopkeeper below, the batty bellman, will be asleep now, propped in his tool cupboard, ready to flap into action in the morning. The Big Housemaid is out (a tryst with the Snake Queen, he'd stake a bet on that). The Redhead will be in bed soon, but then she's in, out, pipe alight, talking to herself at the window half the night. He'll need to time it so she's abed. Besides this, he'd be well to remember that too early and the last watch will be swinging by, too late and Frau-up-at-the-frigging-crack will be baking. Mr Boyd knows every habit of the street and of the house and of the Redhead. He's followed her for days. For a woman, a tiddy one at that, she has locomotion in her. Up and down, down and up, flights of stairs and taking the long way and never a bloody cab or an omnibus.

Mr Boyd checks his reflection in the mirror behind the bar.

He has lately gone in for a bowler-hat: he finds it becomes him. Tonight he's added a fancy scarf, blue and red to match his eyes. He likes nice apparel and now that he's earning the needful he can look the part; every day in full fig. He takes off his hat and frowns at his hairline, artfully arranging the sparse fair froth at the front.

Long may his association with his current, generous employer continue – and with that thought he reminds himself:

Tonight, he is to conduct a robbery *not* a dispatchment.

Inventory. One item:

Jar containing specimen of a little baby with a tail.

(*By the nightgown of Christ, how did he get into this occupation?*)

Robbery, Mr Boyd, he reminds himself. *Not* a dispatchment. Sometimes the two go hand in hand.

Sometimes you arrive at a job calling for the cessation of an individual. Accomplished. You have a prowl and there are a few nice bits and it would be rude not to. But you can't always vend what you rob. Instead you bury it under the floorboards. Then there's an unexpected decampment by moonlight. This is the way it goes.

Sometimes you arrive at a job for the purposes of robbing. Accomplished. Family wakes and contests the situation with you and you stifle them with a touch too much fervour. This is another way it goes.

Mr Boyd leaves the pub and heads to the house. He'll approach to the rear. The front of the house is no way in.

A tradesman passes, paying no note to his person or his phiz (he always sets his face pure, smooth of brow, like a clergyman). Mr Boyd praises himself for having the sense to come smart-attired.

The back gate is locked. With effort he's over the fence, mopping his forehead and adjusting his hat.

(By the dugs of Mary Mother, how did he get into this line of work?)

Not so many years ago Mr Boyd was a roof dancer at the top of his profession; four burglaries a day and six on a Saturday, but never – God forbid! – on a Sunday. But you need a lightness of feet and arse for that game.

In through the pantry and here Mr Boyd takes a moment . . .

Oh, the thrill! Breathing someone else's private, out-of-bounds air!

This is why he does the job.

He moves with stealth, careful not to snort, spit or swear. Occasional tables, lose floorboards and rugs don't trouble him. He's after a likely lockable. And here it is. Rows of jars, as they said there would be. Glass cold to the touch.

He strikes a Lucifer and holds up the lit match.

(By the beard of Saint Peter, his fucking heart won't stand this.)

He sacks the thing with a shudder and is done, with no waking on the Redhead's part.

As Mr Boyd makes his exit he feels a trifle despondent. He finds himself reluctant to return to his solitary lodgings, or repair to a tavern for a lonesome drink. He'd like a bit of company, some admiration first. Doesn't he look the part tonight?

Mr Boyd saunters to the bedroom.

Bridie is asleep in the bed. A light burns still and the book she was reading is open beside her. If she hears a noise at all – the discreet opening and shutting of a door, the soft tread on the stairs – she decides that it's Cora retuning home late and stays asleep. Then she remembers that Cora has never treaded softly or closed a door without testing its hinges.

She sits up with a scream into a man's hand.

He kneels on the bed, one leg either side of her.

Oh God, the horror of his body on hers—

He's a neckerchief wrapped around his mouth but she recognises him instantly as the copper who's been trailing her.

If Ruby is here she can't see him—

Hatless, balding, rheumy blue eyes, sweating with effort. He's saying something to her that she doesn't understand.

And how can a dead man defend her—

The same question over and over, he asks, muffled by the neckerchief.

She twists free and lunges for the nightstand.

Understanding her intention, the man lands Bridie a blow, half punch, half slap. Like he'd changed his mind partway through.

This is not Valentine Rose's man.

He has his hand over her mouth and is doing something with the bedsheet. His face against her neck; snorting, breathing. She goes cold with disgust and with anger. Bridie gets her arm free and catches him hard in the mouth.

He replies with a fist this time.

August 1843

Chapter 26

They talked about it around Mrs Donsie's kitchen range in hushed voices.

Eliza: half-strangled, beaten and worse. They glanced at each other with expressions of shocked meaning on their faces.

Bridie pretended to be asleep on the couch in the corner. She watched through narrowed eyes. What could be worse than a beating?

'And the child looking on, bless his heart. He was sitting next to her when they found her. His eyes wide and his little hand on her poor broken face.'

Mrs Donsie started to cry. A quick, angry-sounding sob that was over before it started and made Bridie's heart stop in a way the words had not.

'Ah, now, Mrs Donsie.' The servants pressed forward with handkerchiefs. Mrs Donsie found her own and mopped her face with it.

The servants sat in disbelief: what next?

The laundrymaid piped up. 'And the baby—'

Mrs Donsie shook her head and gestured over at the couch.

The laundrymaid tried again. 'On our doorstep, that isn't right.'

There was mumbled assent.

But the police had made an arrest, there had been a fella hanging around.

'There's some justice there then,' said the laundrymaid.

The servants pursed their lips. Mrs Donsie said nothing.

The man protested his innocence but he had been seen the afternoon of the attack in the field where Eliza and Edgar were found.

Mrs Eames had witnessed the accused trespassing in the field with a furtive demeanour as she headed back towards the house subsequent to her stroll along the river. The servants raised their eyebrows. In the afternoon Mrs Eames took laudanum and planned a fictional ball. There was never strolling and particularly never in the afternoon.

The alleged attacker was an itinerant of no fixed abode who had turned up in Windsor in search of work, a meal and a bed. Previously accused of robbing a quantity of building materials and sleeping under hedges, he'd a wife in Portsmouth and had been a coalman. He had a weakness for drink and a weakness to his right arm as a result of an argument with a dray-horse. His left arm fared no better, having been wrecked by a fall through a cellar hatch whilst in his cups.

Could this man have knocked Eliza insensible, delivering the shocking severity of injury that she sustained to her face and body. At the trial, his defence had him clench a fist and then lift, with each of his weakened arms, a series of weights. But Mrs Eames knew what she had seen: the man was in the field shortly before Eliza was found unconscious. What's more, Mrs Eames now recollected that the accused had blood on him. The prosecution called for a thorough medical examination of the accused, which showed he was playing up his infirmities. This was substantiated when the man was allegedly discovered arm-wrestling in a pub in Datchet.

Eliza's injuries were hard to accept. Not just the look of her, her lovely smile remade into a grimace, her glossy hair gone in handfuls, her jawline destroyed. It was hard to accept what was taken from her that day in that field. Now her speech was slurred, her rage quick to flash, her humour lost. She found no pleasure, unless sometimes in her meals, and had recollection of few faces and never names. She had no tolerance of her child, who clung to her like a little ugly limpet until in her unheeding fury she threw him off and tried in earnest to hurt him. After that, Mrs Donsie kept the two apart. Edgar played with his string, laughed not at all and was liable to bite anyone who came near him.

Mrs Donsie gave charge of the boy to the Bad Dorcas, the rough-mannered housemaid. She controlled him well, it had to be said. And it got the pair of them out from under Mrs Donsie's feet. After the attack Dorcas was seen often with Gideon, laughing and walking, with Edgar sulking behind. Even Mrs Donsie wondered about this state of affairs.

Bridie watched Gideon closely at this time; she no longer hid from him. In fact, she began to realise that it was Gideon who was taking pains to stay clear of her. Before, it was as if she were an inanimate object, unworthy of his consideration. But now, if their paths crossed, he avoided her eyes. She made him uncomfortable. Bridie thought about what would happen if she walked up to him and said a name, out loud, to his face. *Della Webb.*

Late one night by Mrs Donsie's range, when there was just the two of them, Bridie asked the cook, who knew everything about everything, a careful question. Had she heard tell of a woman who lived alone just outside Cranbourne who might have fallen into difficulties? Within days, Mrs Donsie returned a story to Bridie, of a young woman, a barmaid of questionable character, who had perished, not long ago, in a house fire. Rumour had it that the fire was deliberate. That the young woman had poured lamp oil around the house, setting a blaze so fierce there was hardly anything left of her, or of the room she had been lying in.

To set a fire and go and lie down in it, who would do that?

Mrs Donsie had looked hard at Bridie for the longest while. Bridie felt that, as she stared into the range.

Bridie knew about evidence. How small, unnoticed things could tell a story, maybe a story someone didn't want told. It was possible that Eliza's attacker had left evidence behind and if she searched hard enough she would find it.

Bridie searched, and was rewarded.

She found the boots in a sack hidden in the boathouse. They were Gideon's. She found the signet ring pressed into the mud in the field where Eliza was found. It was Gideon's. And after some persuasion, the footman gave her the jacket Gideon was wearing on the day of Eliza's attack.

The boots, under Dr Eames's microscope, showed threads that matched Eliza's shawl. The ring, beneath the mud, had traces of dried blood within its engraving. The jacket had burrs, embedded in the seam of the cuff, missed by the ministrations of the footman and his clothes-brush. These corresponded to the sticky willow that grew where Eliza had lain.

Gideon had attacked Eliza; the evidence told a story and this story was indisputable.

October 1863

Chapter 27

Bridie has two swollen eyes and bruising that ranges in colour from the faintest pollen-kissed yellow to the deepest deep-blue-black-green. Her nose came out of the attack unbroken, but her central and lateral incisors didn't fare so well. Where her teeth should be, she now has soft gum and a gap odd to the stab of her tongue and flavoured with iron. The torn inside of her mouth is mending well; Prudhoe felt confident that her lips would heal without undue scarring. Later, alone with a mirror, Bridie agreed with his prognosis, then cried a few quick, hot tears of self-pity and was done with it. Bridie's attacker took nothing but the Winter Mermaid. Leaving the cabinet door ajar and a vacancy between the gnawed dormouse and the wide-open heart.

Deciding one day is ample to be abed, Bridie is up and about this morning, moving stiffly and ignoring Cora's fussing concern. It takes Bridie a while to get into her gentleman's clothes. Joking that she'll be out the door by nightfall, she lets Cora help with the buttons and tippet-fur whiskers. And Cora makes sure to keep her huge hands gentle, and her words as light as her touch.

If Bridie looked shabby before, she looks derelict now. She

hails a cab and heads to Bart's. There is no easy amble today, no cane twirling and no winking, whether flower seller, shop girl or costermonger's mule.

Ruby walks close beside her. He hides his pity as well as he can but it's her smile that gets him. Bridie's wide tooth-showing smile has been replaced by an uncertain pressed-lip affair as if she doesn't understand the joke.

Bridie will start with the porters at Bart's, on account of them knowing more about the hospital than anyone else. Their offices are just inside the entrance, or at the Rising Sun, if it's that time of day. Bridie tries the offices first. An off-duty porter is carving up a game pie. His colleague dozes in a nearby chair. The room is bedecked with homely comforts; Bridie spies a bottle of port and a pipe rack. These are bribes from patients. Make friends with a porter and you will get supplementary benefits to the basic hospital provisions: it will ease your stay no end.

'Sir: a young fellow who may go by the name of Cridge, do you know where I could find him?'

The porter glances over at her. 'You didn't win then, sir?'

Bridie shakes her head. 'Not this time.'

'Let's hope you got a few blows in?'

'Not as many as I'd have liked,' says Bridie.

'Cridge, you say? There's no Cridge.'

Bridie isn't surprised. 'Do you know a young man of unfavourable aspect: slight, big head and a tendency to sneer?'

'An unfavourable aspect?'

Bridie nods.

The porter thinks a moment. 'Sir, are you aware of the proportions and general character of this hospital?'

'I am.'

'Then you will know it to be a veritable maze of winding

passageways where no bleeder stays put and no one is ever where they are supposed to be.' He pauses. 'Is this Cridge a patient, sir?'

'He's likely a medical man.'

'Then you have a better chance of finding him alive.' He gently scratches his nose with the point of his knife. 'We're full to the brim of the groaning and the suppurating, the roaring and the gurgling.' He allows himself a chuckle. 'And that's just the surgeons.'

His colleague, the chair-dozer, snores loudly, as if on cue.

'We have it all here: sepsis, consumption, nose-rot, stump-rot, flute-rot, maniacs and pus, beneficial and not-so-beneficial, by the bucketful.' He lowers his voice. 'And on occasion: cholera.'

'But not today?'

'No, not today,' he admits. 'Still, it is the last place I would come if I were sick, sir. I would as soon lie in the grave-yard ready. Or put my head under the wheel of an omnibus. Or find a friendly rope—'

'This man, sir—'

The porter returns from his musings. 'A medical man, you say, sir?'

'He attended Dr Gideon Eames's obstruction.'

'Good show, I heard.' The porter counts up the segments of pie and puts down the knife, satisfied. 'And we have had some rollicking shows.'

Chair-dozer wheezes happily in his sleep.

'But it's not like the old days. Great doctors, oh, the speed of them, no more than a flash of knives. Liston needed no tourniquet,' he recalls, starry-eyed. 'He used his left *arm*, oh, the strength of the man! Tying off arteries with his knife between his teeth and the patient bucking beneath him. There's just not the same *entertainment* when a patient sleeps through.' He licks his fingers. 'Big head, you say?'

'Yes, sir.'

The porter ponders awhile.

'He smokes *Hussar Blend*,' adds Bridie.

'So does half the hospital. Now, has he the look of someone who might keep body parts in his pocket, shifty-like?'

'You could say that.'

'Kemp, the dead-house assistant,' replies the porter assuredly. 'He would fit the bill. Otherwise there's a senior phlebotomist called Whispers but he's eighty if he's a day.'

The porter nudges a sliver of pie out from the whole and hands it to Bridie. 'God loves a loser. Next time, go in tight and fast and get out quickly. Use your size to your advantage. You're nippy on your feet, I dare say.'

Bridie tips her hat. 'Much obliged to you, sir.'

He is barrelling out of the mortuary door as she approaches – Mr Cridge turned Mr Kemp – moving at speed. Bridie flattens herself against the wall as he passes. Then turns and follows as fast as her injuries allow. Ruby quicksteps along with her. She heads towards the entrance, past the porters' office, where her advisor, awaiting his next instruction, salutes her with a pie-crust.

Striking off down the road, Kemp stops an omnibus and takes a seat on the top deck. The omnibus is delayed by two ladies climbing on board with a whole world of parcels long enough for Bridie to hobble to it. She hesitates on the ladder.

'Make up your mind, sir,' says the conductor.

Bridie has lost her tippet-fur whiskers giving chase. With or without them Kemp would certainly see through her disguise if she were to follow him up onto the open top deck and perch herself on the knifeboard. Instead she steps inside, after the ladies and the parcels, braving the crush and the odour of wet umbrellas and dirty straw. At each stop along the route Bridie ignores the glances of interested passengers and watches for Kemp's descent.

Kemp dismounts along Oxford Street and Bridie follows. He cuts into Cavendish Square, runs up a flight of steps and raps on the door. Bridie heads into the gardens opposite the house. Clambering in among the bushes, she watches through the railings as the door of the house opens to receive Kemp.

Ruby draws near. 'Whose house is this − not his surely?'

'I can hazard a guess,' says Bridie, grimly.

She calls out through the railings to a crossing-sweeper, who trots over and peers into the foliage.

'Who lives in that house, Master Broom?'

'Damned if I know . . . *miss*?'

'*Sir* would do for now,' corrects Bridie.

'Sir,' grins the boy.

Bridie finds a coin and holds it out.

The boy pockets the coin. 'A doctor, *sir*.'

'Is his name Eames, by any chance?'

The boy demonstrates an intense effort of recollection, with much frowning and looking skyward for divine assistance. He's a brown-eyed boy of great filthiness of face, the type with business everywhere, who knows everyone else's business. He sports a bright neckerchief showing his allegiance to one or other pugilist and a felt wide-awake. The once-broad hat-brim has been trimmed to allow its wearer greater all-round vantage, as befitting his occupation. The outfit is completed with the addition of a grubby silk flower in the buttonhole of the boy's too-short jacket.

Bridie finds another coin. 'Would this assist your memory?'

'It would, sir.' The boy pockets it. 'Eames. That's the fella.'

'Is this your patch?'

'Here and abouts, sir.'

'I need an agent. Someone to keep an eye on local proceedings.'

'Jem,' says the boy, catching her meaning. He straightens
his wide-awake and gives her a firm nod. 'At your service.'

Chapter 28

Ruby Doyle is throwing punches, his jaw tightened and his eyes flashing and his tattoos darting about his transparent body. Since Bridie's attack he is often to be found sparring with a parlour palm, or threatening thin air. Noticing Bridie's eyes upon him, Ruby lowers his fists and shakes out his arms.

Bridie sets about opening the post, sipping coffee. Halfway through the second letter she puts down her cup and curses under her breath.

'What is it?' asks Ruby.

'News from Maris House; in this letter, Mr Puck thanks me on Sir Edmund's behalf for my latest report regarding the confidential matter in hand and states that all is as usual in his master's estate.' Bridie turns to the second letter. 'Agnes Molloy, the housemaid, tells a very different story: the headless corpse of Dr Harbin has been found at Maris House. In Sir Edmund's study.'

Ruby widens his eyes. 'Jesus, Mary and Joseph.'

'Mr Puck will never recover, according to Agnes. He discovered the body sitting on the chair by the fire.'

'That would be a shocker.'

'Mrs Puck sent for the police. While they awaited the local

constabulary, Berwick absconded. They caught up with him on the road to London.'

'I've no sense that the baronet could kill a man and have the head from off him, Bridie.'

'Then set the corpse before his own fireplace there, when he had previously entrusted his most private affairs to the victim.'

'Didn't the victim betray him? If Dr Harbin kidnapped the child, that is?'

'There is that,' grants Bridie.

'But why would Sir Edmund send the poor bugger's head to you?'

'I've no idea, Ruby.'

★

Inspector Valentine Rose's office at Scotland Yard is a picture of order and gentility, apart from the plaster copies of Newgate death masks above the picture rail. It's an identity parade of the murderous, old and new. Bridie recognises the face of Charlie Pill just over the door. Sandwiched between James Mullins and a strong-jawed smirker unknown to her. In death, Charlie Pill looks remorseful, as well he might. Bridie is not convinced that Monsieur Pilule didn't harvest some of the ingredients for his infamous roasts to order. After all, people go missing every day in London, many with a good lay of meat on their bones, or a nice bit of padding (and isn't the crackling the best part?). Every sausage – your humble 'bag o' mystery' – should earn its name.

Ruby strides into the room with a little more front about him than usual. Perhaps he is riled, finding himself inside a hive of coppers. He's had his dealings.

Ruby saunters up to Inspector Rose and walks around him, slowly, eyes trained on his face. He holds his great fists loose and low.

Bridie throws Ruby a sharp look.

The boxer leans forward and flicks Rose's cheek, as he would an opponent in the ring. Rose, intuition heightened by the best and worst of London's criminal society, glances around the room as to locate a draught. He sees nothing, of course.

Ruby sees a contender.

In the Red Corner:

Ruby Doyle. *Heavyweight*. Clearing six-foot. Left-handed. Stunning technique. Devastating brown eyes. Moustache, waxed, black. Favours drawers, tangled bandages, unlaced boots. Nose: broken on occasion, but always set with careful hands. Square of head like a dependable dog, broad of shoulder and passionate of temper. *Dead*.

In the Blue Corner:

Valentine Rose. *Middleweight*. Just shy of average height. Right-handed. Will fight dirty. Grey eyes, sandy beard, well-trimmed. Dapper dresser. Rose (currently pink) in his buttonhole. Nose: unbroken. Unremarkable of head, slim of shoulder and resolute of temper. *Living*.

★

'Short arse,' Ruby utters, in Rose's uncomprehending face. He strolls over to the inspector's desk, where he sits down on his chair, rolls his gleaming shoulders and puts his boots up on his blotter.

Rose frowns into thin air.

They sit side-by-side on the window seat, Mrs Bridie Devine and Inspector Valentine Rose. Ruby watches them from the corner of his eye, while pretending to nose at the papers spread over the desk.

A young policeman in his stiff serge suit and new leather belt brings in tea and arranges it on the table deferentially.

'We'll take it from here, son.' Rose waits for the door to close. 'So?'

'Developments at Maris House.'

'You've heard already?'

'What can you tell me?'

'Nothing you don't already know. The headless body was found by the butler. Dr Harbin was identified by his collar studs.' Rose pours the tea. 'The doctor's head has washed up at Bart's in a hatbox. A porter saw an unfeasibly large woman departing the scene pushing a perambulator.'

'Fancy that,' says Bridie.

The policeman's face is impassive but for a slight curve to his lips. 'Sir Edmund made a run for it, we picked him up a few miles from Maris House on the London road.'

Tea is drunk. Bridie looks out of the window, Rose looks at Bridie, Ruby looks at the pair of them.

'You're still searching for his missing child?'

Bridie wrinkles her nose.

'Oh, come on, I had to find out. Any luck?'

'A few leads. And you? Is Mrs Bibby your master criminal?'

Rose sips his tea, glancing over the rim of his cup with a sharp grey eye. 'It seems that way.'

'Mrs Bibby told the doctor's daughter something macabre.'

'Oh yes?'

'That she killed a lady and a gentleman.'

Rose puts down his cup and goes over to his desk and leafs through some papers. Finding a clipping, he hands it to Bridie and sits down again.

'Eight years ago: two murders back-to-back in that many days, one a wealthy spinster, the other a retired schoolmaster. Perpetrator was never found, labelled the Brentford Butcher.'

Bridie scans the article. 'They were strangled. Dis-membered.'

Rose nods. 'The spinster turned up jugged in a picnic hamper, the schoolmaster was found cradling his own severed leg. Remind you of anyone?'

'You think this Mrs Bibby is responsible?'

'I think you should be cautious.'

'What about Sir Edmund? You are still holding him.'

'He made a run for it and resisted arrest. He could be in league with her.'

'I doubt it: she stole his child.'

Bridie thinks a moment. 'Mrs Bibby met with a man called Kemp at Mrs Peach's guest-house in Somers Town.'

'You went there?'

'I found Mrs Bibby's library book, that was the address given.'

'Bridie, did you not think it could be a trap?' Rose rubs his forehead. 'She'll have a good idea who's chasing her now. Peach is an ex-Judy. A lag for hire.'

Bridie bites her lip.

'The man she met?' asks Rose, less sharply. 'You've suspicions?'

'Kemp: he works in the mortuary at Bart's. He posed as the curate of Highgate Chapel when I visited. He bought or stole the walled-up corpses from Reverend Gale.'

'You've proof?'

'Not exactly, Reverend Gale is not likely to be forthcoming on that. But Kemp is one to watch, Rose.'

'Kemp: noted.'

'He was at Dr Harbin's the day his surgery was wrecked.'

'He gets around, this Kemp.'

Ruby nods in begrudging agreement.

'He knows Gideon Eames,' says Bridie. 'I saw them together, at Bart's, and then I followed Kemp to his house.'

'Bridie, I know you've had dealings with Gideon Eames in the past—'

'It's not about that.'

'So what exactly are you accusing him of?'

Bridie puts her cup down too heavily and stands up too suddenly. She walks over to the window. 'I don't know yet.'

It has started to rain again. She traces the path of a droplet on the glass, wondering if she's the only one noticing them moving backwards.

Bridie presses her palm against the glass, then her forehead, for the coolness. She watches police officers swarm in the alleyway below.

'It's good to see you, Bridie,' says Rose, softly. 'Up and about.'

Bridie glances back at him. He's looking at her with a mixture of pity and concern. Neither of which she welcomes.

'Where is Sir Edmund being held? I want to speak with him, Rose.'

Rose gets up and goes to his desk. Ruby vacates the man's chair, taking a dramatic step back as the policeman passes. Rose sits down to write.

Bridie surveys the room, taking in the potted plants, the polished furniture and the glass-shaded lights. Rose has made his office comfortable, homely even; Bridie suspects he might live here. It's pleasant indeed, if you ignore the death casts smirking down at you. There's space, just over the window, for a few more. She would like to see Gideon Eames's face there, and the bastard who knocked out her teeth.

'Any news on my attacker?'

'A few leads, from your description. Leave it to us, you've enough to be getting on with.' Rose blots and folds the letter and hands it to her. 'You know the drill, give this to the guards.'

'Obliged, Rose. And I'll let you know if Mrs Bibby surfaces.'

'If she does, Bridie, for Christ's sake keep away from her.'

★

The Newgate turnkeys take their time reading Rose's letter. Then they think for a while. Then they read it again.

One guard is tall, with an egg-shaped head topped with buttery curls. The other is short, with a breadth to him and an exemplary set of jowls. They are suited entirely in black and affect gloomy expressions, as if to uphold the feeling of dread afforded the visitor by passing through the gates of the foreboding prison (and of hearing them close behind them). In the receiving room Bridie autographs the guest book under the death masks of Bishop and Williams in resentful repose. Rose ought to add them to his collection.

The tall guard fixes Bridie with wary eyes. 'And so a visitor arrives at the stone jug for—'

'Sir Edmund Athelstan Berwick, Esquire,' supplies the short guard.

The tall guard gives a dour bow. 'Thank you, Mr Scudder. Sir Edmund being a guest of ours in this depository of human misery.'

Mr Scudder laughs. 'Why, he's staying in our best chamber, Mr Hoy!'

'He is, of course!' Mr Hoy's face brightens with morose delight. 'He is receiving every comfort what can be afforded.'

'Three square a day and a clean nightie every Thursday.'

Mr Hoy nods. 'As befitting a baronet.'

'A peer of the realm.'

Mr Hoy frowns at Mr Scudder. 'You are mistaken, my friend, Berwick's a *baronet*. There's no peer about it.'

Mr Scudder looks confused. Then another thought crosses his mind and he cheers visibly. 'He's lively enough!'

'We've had some noise from him,' Mr Hoy concedes.

'When he's not weeping, he's griping, when he's not griping, he's calling for his lawyers.'

'His attorney.'

'His barrister.'

'His advisors.'

'Never still and never silent; always petitioning,' Mr Scudder crows.

'Protesting his innocence!'

'Night and bloody day, day and bloody night.'

'Or pacing,' suggests Mr Hoy.

'Up and down.'

'Down and up.'

'His confining yet well-appointed cell,' says Mr Scudder.

'Or chamber, really. More of a chamber.' Mr Hoy gives a coy smile. 'Where he receives every comfort, as befitting a baronet.'

'A peer of the realm.'

Mr Hoy looks at Mr Scudder with barely concealed frustration.

'Am I to be visiting the prisoner today, gentleman?' enquires Bridie, evenly.

Mr Hoy gives an officious nod. 'Admit the visitor, Mr Scudder. Conduct the visitor thence.'

'Right you are, Mr Hoy.'

'Follow the protocols, strictly and according to the multitudinous rules and myriad regulations laid down by our good governor in his infinite wisdom.'

'Meaning, Mr Hoy?'

'Get her to turn out her pockets and lock the doors behind you.'

'Aye, Mr Hoy.'

The tall guard narrows his eyes at Bridie. 'And check her bleeding boot heels.'

Bridie follows Mr Scudder down a labyrinth of passageways. Prisons, they will have you believe, are far nicer places these days. Clean-swept and whitewashed, and with spaces for health-giving exercise and sanitary quarters. The food is more than edible and the inmates are treated with gentle kindness. For example: the condemned man is no longer compelled to sit with his own coffin at chapel and the Salt Box (the last cell he'll see before he meets Jack Ketch!) boasts chairs with antimacassars.

Bridie reflects on none of this as she waits, wanting to be gone, watching Mr Scudder unlock and lock doors, bumbling with the loop of keys he wears at his waist. Ahead of them are many gates, which will require opening and closing. Ruby shuffles and picks at the bandages on his fists.

'What's wrong?' Bridie whispers.

'It's the confinement,' he says.

'You can walk through walls.'

Ruby shrugs.

'You did time, Ruby?' Bridie's tone is soft.

The mermaid on Ruby's shoulder turns her head away and buries her face in her hair. The anchor pulls up sharply.

Bridie nods. 'Wait outside for me.'

Ruby throws Bridie a look of relief and heads out into the courtyard.

Progress through the prison is slow. By the third gate, Mr Scudder, who has developed the demeanour of an expectant hen about to lay a blinder, starts to talk.

'The brutal murder of a local doctor, they're calling it. Cold-blooded, they're calling it. Horrific, they're calling it.'

They stride forward a few paces only to be stopped by another gate.

Mr Scudder starts the process again, examining his keys, testing them, discarding them and eventually finding the right one.

'Sir Edmund hasn't stood trial yet, guard. Innocent until proven guilty.'

'Oh, he's guilty all right. They both loved the waif, you see.' He unlocks the gate, smirking over his shoulder. 'The one that was found strangled in the chapel-yard near Maris House. Two gentlemen, both mad for her – imagine, a baronet and a doctor – and her no more than a tramp's daughter! She bewitched them, one after the other, when she was out selling clothes-pegs.'

'Now there's a yarn.'

'She chose the doctor. Overcome by grief and jealousy the baronet killed the happy lovers by means very violent.'

'A flight of fancy.'

'Then he lopped the doctor's head off with the doctor's own saw,' he recounts. 'And then – now here's a puzzle – he sent the doctor's noodle to the chef at Claridge's. He requested that it be set in *aspic*.'

'Extraordinary.'

'But then Mr Hoy and I realised: it's a *blue blood* thing. Sir Edmund's ancestors would have taken the heads of their foes on the battlefield and, really, what don't nobs put in aspic?'

'You have all this on authority?'

'Another guest staying with us at Her Majesty's Pleasure, he's quite the town crier.'

The corridor opens onto galleried tiers of walkways.

'Here we are then, ground floor, Hotel Newgate. I'd hold your nose if I were you, treacle.'

The ferocious smell of human misery takes a sideways swipe at Bridie Devine. She breathes shallow through her mouth. Other guards lead prisoners, fettered like yard-dogs, along the hall. Shells of men with haunted eyes. Dressed in prison clothes they offer a woeful picture. When they see Mr Scudder they throw him aggrieved looks and shuffle on.

Mr Scudder leads the way. Stopping only to clatter his truncheon between bars or shout encouragement.

'That bed sheet won't take your weight, Clements,' he calls out. 'Let me find you a sturdy piece of rope, sir.'

'Ain't you the artist, Minton. Would you like to go to the *snug*? You could decorate that for us, my love.'

Presently, Mr Scudder stops and turns to Bridie. 'This one, if you please, treacle.'

He unlatches a barred window, no more than a peek-hole at the top of the door.

'Visitor for you, Sir Edmund, Peer of the Realm, ain't that nice? You might want to pull down your nightie, sir, you don't want all your appurtenances on show.'

Mr Scudder gestures to a chair down the hall. 'Do you want me to come in or perch down there?'

'I think I can manage,' replies Bridie, coolly.

Mr Scudder nods. 'You've the face of a brawler. Don't hurt him now.'

Sir Edmund Athelstan Berwick is wearing no more than a nightshirt. He has the stubble of days on his chin and has lost his front teeth and found himself a black eye.

He's in no better condition than Bridie herself.

He rises quickly and climbs backwards over his cot. He holds his hands up over his face and cowers. If he was broken before, he's ruined now.

'Sir Edmund, it's Mrs Devine.'

He looks through his fingers and begins to cry.

Sir Edmund's suite at Hotel Newgate comprises a cell no bigger than his water closet at Maris House. He has been provided with the standard: bucket, window, bed-frame and mattress. He also has a blanket, a chair and a card table, as befitting a baronet. Other everyday essentials are sorely lacking. There are no sheets, inkpots, cigars or writing paper. Neither are there decanters of tawny port, seasoned cutlets, fruited jellies or clean linen shirts.

'I didn't do it,' the baronet sputters, an uncustomary lisp to his voice with the missing teeth.

Bridie could show him how to avoid that.

'Sir Edmund, we haven't much time. If someone is trying to fit you for this deed, you need to name your enemies.' She looks at him closely. 'Did you have any dealings with Gideon Eames?'

Sir Edmund shakes his head.

'What about a man called Kemp?'

Sir Edmund shakes his head again.

'So it was just you and the doctor, then, travelling to Bantry Bay to find a child and take her from her mother?'

Sir Edmund stares at her.

'Ellen Kelly, remember? The young woman found strangled in the chapel-yard near Maris House.'

Sir Edmund starts to slap his own head. 'No, no, no!'

Bridie moves over to him and grabs him by the wrist. There's an awful smell of piss rising from him; the front of his nightgown is sodden.

He begins to cry again but he stops hitting himself.

'You need to use your bucket, Sir Edmund,' Bridie says, gently. 'In the corner there.'

He calms a little and nods.

She lets go of his wrist.

'Then Dr Harbin took Christabel from you, very likely with Mrs Bibby's help. Only you didn't realise your trusted aide, friend even, had betrayed you until it was too late?'

Sir Edmund looks up at her, his eyes red-rimmed. Bubbles collect in the corner of his mouth.

'Is that how it went, Sir Edmund?'

Sir Edmund lowers his eyes.

'But you didn't kill him, did you?'

Nothing.

'And Ellen Kelly: you didn't kill her either, did you?'

Sir Edmund puts his hands over his face and sobs.

Bridie shuts the cell door behind her. Sir Edmund has crawled under his bed and is refusing to come out. He lies there now, sucking his thumb with all his appurtenances on show. Not a word of sense can be drawn from him.

There is no sign of the guard. Bridie steps back along the walkway.

'Miss!' A withered finger pokes through the peek-hole at the top of a cell door. 'Miss, from Maris House!'

Bridie draws nearer. An eye appears at the peek-hole, and the voice again, from inside.

'You gave alms to me.'

'I did. So you must be Mr Scudder's town crier? A sensational interpretation of the events at Maris House, featuring the doctor, the baronet and the tramp's daughter.'

There's a chuckle behind the door.

'What did you do to get yourself in here?' asks Bridie. 'It can't just be for tramping?'

'Croaked a man for his boots.' The eye at the peek-hole looks to see her reaction.

Bridie groans. 'I gave you money for boots.'

'His boots were nicer but he wouldn't sell 'em. Here, I want to tell you something.' The eye at the peek-hole is swapped for a mouth, the mouth whispers, 'About *what went on*.'

Bridie spies the guard coming back around the corner, swinging his ring of keys. 'You'd better be quick. Scudder's back.'

The eye returns. 'At first I thought it was a dream, a nightmare, what with me being on the beam end that evening. Oh, vain reasonings! Then I heard word of the finding of a body in the chapel-yard near Maris House. The body of a fair young maiden.'

'I found her, sir,' says Bridie.

The voice comes quivering. 'And I saw her light *extinguished*!'

'Are you saying that you saw her murdered?'

'O the fair young maiden: noble, skin curd-white in the

moonlight, walking among the graves! The very touch of her feet on the ground sweetening the cold soil for those who slumber gratefully in it.'

Scudder strolls down the corridor, giving each cell door a fierce rap with his truncheon as he goes.

The mouth is back. 'All of a sudden – a succubus foul, a hag, the very apparition of death, set upon the fair young maiden!' The mouth trembles. 'O the maiden did protest: giving scream and holding up her lovely young arms – to no avail.'

Mr Scudder stops to pry into a cell.

'The maiden fell.' The mouth shuts. The tongue runs over the lips. 'The spectre limped away.'

Mr Scudder approaches, pointing his truncheon at Bridie. 'That is not your bleeding prisoner.'

The eye is back at the door. 'Miss, I saw the grim reaper herself in the chapel-yard that night. That's what did for that sweet maiden.'

'Does the grim reaper have a name, Father Road?'

The eye closes. '*Bibby.*'

September 1843

Chapter 29

The document lay between them on his desk, the title rendered in Bridie's careful hand.

Pertaining to the grievous assault of Eliza Kempton

Bridie stood before him, her hands clenched and held behind of her and her heart belting in her chest. Standing in the same spot she'd stood over two years ago, dressed in a dead man's blood.

She waited, breath-stopped.

'And you used my microscope, for this?' asked Dr Eames.

'Yes, sir.' She willed herself to speak clearly and let the right words weigh in, the ones she had practised. 'The slides showed under magnification that threads from Eliza's shawl were present in the mud taken from Master Gideon's boots. There was blood in the groove of his ring and burrs in—'

Dr Eames held up his hand. 'There are witnesses, a clear account of events that day. A man has been arrested, Bridget.'

'Sir, the arrested man is innocent of the crime.'

'Then who is guilty: my son?'

Bridie lowered her eyes. Struck as she was by the bitterness in his voice.

'We have the testimony of Mrs Eames,' he continued. 'She saw the accused in the field around the estimated time of the attack. She clearly stated she had left Master Gideon in the library, where he was cataloguing books with Dorcas Chapman.'

Bridie frowned. She knew that Dorcas had no business in the library that day, nor on any other day.

'On Mrs Eames's return Gideon joined her in the drawing-room, and did not leave his mother's side for the rest of the evening. Gideon could not have attacked Eliza.'

'The evidence tells a different story, sir. It puts Master Gideon with Eliza in that field.'

'And what of the witnesses?'

'Witnesses can be mistaken, sir.'

'Are you saying that my wife is mistaken?'

'Yes, sir,' said Bridie, and the words were no more than an exhalation of breath.

Dr Eames got up from his desk and walked over to the window. He turned to Bridie. 'Have you considered, Bridget, that someone might have fabricated this evidence to place false blame on Gideon?'

'The threads were lodged deep, sir,' Bridie responded. 'And then the blood in the ring and the burrs found—'

'That is enough.' Dr Eames ran his hand across his forehead. 'Why didn't the police find this?'

Bridie answered, even though it didn't sound like he was asking her this question. 'They only searched where Eliza was found, sir. The ring was at the other end of the field.'

Dr Eames turns to her in amazement. 'You searched the entire field?'

'Yes, sir.'

'How long did that take you?'

'A week, sir.'

Dr Eames turned to the window and looked out over the

grounds, a new stoop to his shoulders. Bridie felt sad for him in his troubles.

'Gideon's past behaviour, I am aware, has not endeared him to people.' He turned to her with a bitter smile. 'But lately he's shown himself to be a model of compassion. Has he not made every effort to help Eliza and her boy?'

Bridie stayed silent. It was true that Gideon had made something of a pet of Edgar. Once or twice he had ridden into town with the child balanced on the saddle before him.

'Besides, Edgar demonstrates no fear towards Gideon,' Dr Eames reasoned. 'The child witnessed the incident – if Gideon was the assailant, surely the child would be frightened of him?'

Bridie had no answer for this. That Edgar was an unsound, contrary little boy was common knowledge: could his reactions be relied on? And besides, how could she argue that it was precisely Gideon's attentive behaviour that was suspicious: he was going to too-great lengths to show Edgar's tolerance of him.

'And Eliza is not disturbed at the sight of Gideon, is she?'

'No, sir.'

'Which means she does not recognise him as her attacker.'

Eliza didn't recognise her own son.

Bridie looked down at her written report, meticulously prepared and utterly useless.

Bridie was too old to cry and too proud to beg.

How old?

No older than twelve, no younger than ten.

She took her hands from behind her back. She'd pushed her nails into her palms without knowing it, as she'd stood in front of this man. Red crescents. If she looked at her palms long enough, would she divine some long-written fate?

In one palm: Della Webb, staring at a chalked cross on a wall.

In the other: Eliza Kempton as she was. Eliza: who had smiled at her in this room and taken her filthy hand without hesitation.

'Dr Eames,' said Bridie. 'Gideon assaulted Eliza: I saw him do it.'

There were questions, easily deflected. Fear had stopped Bridie from coming forward sooner. And without evidence, who would believe her? Bridie knew how to lie. Jesus, she'd been raised by Gan Murphy.

She had been out walking when she heard muffled cries and she had run into the field to see Gideon in the grass on his knees. As Bridie spoke the scene grew clearer and truer in her mind. She recounted, too, the exchange between Gideon and Eliza in the stables: as accurately as she could, from what she remembered.

Finally, there were no more questions. Just Dr Eames standing at the window for the longest time.

He turned to her. He had blue eyes, and a long face, like a sad horse. And he had bought Bridie for a guinea.

'Have you told anyone else about this? What you saw, what you have found?'

'No, sir.'

Dr Eames nodded. 'Then this matter stays between us, Bridget, do you understand?'

October 1863

Chapter 30

'If you could just angle his lordship's head into the light, Mr Scudder, that's the ticket.'

'Pliers, Mr Hoy?'

'I think so.'

'Hammer, Mr Hoy?'

'Not quite yet.'

Sir Edmund kneels before the two guards like a penitent. He holds his mouth obligingly wide and flinches, although the instrument Mr Hoy is wielding has yet to touch lip or tongue, tooth or gum.

'Hold still, Sir Edmund, and we'll have you out of here in a jiffy. Won't we, Mr Hoy?'

The egg-headed man nods stoically. 'And don't scream, my love.'

'Or bawl.'

'There's a good lad.'

Mr Scudder places two firm hands on Sir Edmund's shoulders.

Sir Edmund, eyes reddened, hair on end, holds a blood-sodden rag up to his jaw as he crosses an empty street near Newgate Prison. He could not tell you where he is, but he knows where he needs to be. He has lost five more teeth (gold this time) and a pocket-watch but gained his liberty and another man's smock. Part werewolf, part bumpkin: Sir Edmund Athelstan Berwick disappears into the night.

Chapter 31

Bridie is out early today. Her injuries are healing well, the bruising is less livid, her cut lip knitted and dry. But her face still startles passers-by, so Cora has pinned a veil to Bridie's bonnet. Bridie takes a walk to Bart's to enquire after Kemp at the mortuary, only to be told that he hasn't shown up for work in days. Next time she will don her gentleman's disguise before she visits. Would their answer be any different? Ruby, as always, is by her side. He must understand her mood, for he asks no questions and offers no talk. Bridie waits awhile at the hospital, outside the entrance, at the patients' gate. The clock at St Paul's speaks the hour. People pass and stop, gather and disperse. The luckless are stretchered in, roofers or run-overs, lolling and groaning, conveyed by friends or strangers. The doorbell is pulled and the porter answers at once and the crowds dissipate until the next show of human misfortune.

After Bart's, Bridie strays homeward: down alleys and lanes, along thoroughfares and streets. The rain still falls from time to time and the floods persist in some parts, mixed with London mud, a startling compound in its own right (name not the ingredients). Bridie's boots and hems, like everyone else's, stay sodden these days. Rich and poor alike are besmirched with wet dirt. But not to the same degree: there are some who must live in filth while others just visit it. And what's a mired petticoat or a caked boot to a maid with soapy preparations and stiff brushes?

Bridie, like many other Londoners, takes advice from omnibus conductors, street vendors and police constables in order to avoid the worst of it. She is less inclined to listen to the tales about the floods being traded in pubs, shops and street corners. With the resurgence of London's lost rivers and the biblical rainfall, forgotten nursery tales bubble up in many minds. The people start to remember the folk figures of old. Creatures that have long been asleep, in lakes and under bridges, in horse troughs and in ponds, awaken. They trickle and paddle, slip and sneak into London. It's as if they've been summoned. Names from nursery nightmares are remembered and spoken again: Peg Powler, Jenny Greenteeth, Nelly Longarms. Creatures with wild waterweed hair and long sinewy arms; all the better for reaching out and dragging you into the depths. A rash of children, it is said, have been drowned in buckets. Several more have been pulled into wells. A gentleman daren't walk alone by the Serpentine these days, else some wet-haired floundering beauty will do for him. Three little mud-larks, it is said, were found drowned beside the creek at Deptford, just down by the old ship-chandlery shop.

Bridie thinks on none of this as she reaches Denmark Street. All that's on her mind is a pot of coffee and perhaps another pipeful.

'Inspector Rose is waiting for you in the parlour. He's been here for some time.'

'What's his business, Cora?'

'Wouldn't say, but he's taken five cups of tea, a portion of mutton cobbler and the last of the cold collation. He's a decent appetite on him. I've knocked him up a quick fool. You know, for afters.'

Bridie passes her cape to Cora, who shakes it, wrings its neck and hangs it up. The two of them look in the parlour door, opening it just a crack. Rose stands deep in thought, in front of the instrument on the mantelpiece. He draws forward, as if to touch it, but thinks better of it and clasps both his hands behind his back.

Cora nudges Bridie. 'He's very distinguished in that coat, is he not?'

'Peacock,' mutters Ruby and struts past them into the room to stand against the mantelpiece with an air of the patriarch about him.

Bridie follows. 'Rose, I hear you've been fed.'

'I had no choice in the matter.' Rose takes Bridie's hand, his eyes warm on hers.

'Of course you didn't. Where do you get these flowers? Each one is a miracle.'

In the policeman's buttonhole is a rose of an exquisite colour: the palest peach.

Rose unpins it and hands it to her. 'Find it a drink and it's yours.'

Ruby looks to the heavens.

Cora brings the tea tray, tiny in her colossal hands. She puts it, just so, on the table beside the inspector. 'Afters, sir.'

Adjusting her mob cap, she takes a dusting rag the size of a bed-sheet out of her vast apron pocket and begins to run it slowly along the shelves of the bookcase. With an ear turned towards the proceedings.

Rose glances at Cora.

'I'll only tell her after,' says Bridie.

Rose nods. 'Sir Edmund has escaped from Newgate. I know you consider the man innocent of the charges against him—'

'Of course he's innocent.'

'That's as may be, Bridie, but if you see hide or hair of him I need to know.' Rose picks up the dish and the spoon.

Bridie looks on, mystified: over by the bookcase Cora has stopped dusting and is mouthing something emphatically and pointing at the door.

Rose turns and Cora stops abruptly.

'This is delicious, Cora,' he says, 'what is it?'

'Gooseberry,' she says.

Ruby curbs a smile.

'Is there any end to your talents, Cora?'

'No, Inspector Rose,' says Cora, with one eye on the door. 'There isn't.'

Sir Edmund sleeps next to the kitchen range on a couch Cora has made up for him. Blood from his most recent dental extractions is drying at the corners of his lips. Cora has dressed him in a knitted hat and stockings and acres of worn cotton that she has hitched up and tied about his waist.

'Is he wearing one of your gowns, Cora?'

'His own clothes are drying. I lent him my second-best sprigged.'

'Well, let's get him up and on his feet.'

'Couldn't we let him sleep on a bit? It wouldn't do any harm, would it?' says Cora, in a waspish tone, as if to offset her kind-heartedness.

'We need to give him a chance to tell his story, before we hand him over to Rose.'

The man moans in his sleep.

'Can't we keep him a while? I've never met a baronet.'

'He belongs to Newgate, Cora. But let him rest awhile.'

It is night when Sir Edmund wakes. He refuses food but will accept a cup of tea.

Cora puts the kettle on the hob, sets cups and saucers and takes the teapot from the dresser. The baronet sits at the kitchen table. He is a forsaken figure in Cora's old dress, with his face roughly wiped, like a slattern's infant, and a rag on his lap with which he stems his bleeding gums.

'I've killed no one, but my actions led to those people's deaths,' Sir Edmund discloses with grave dismay.

Cora, settled in the corner, tea in hand, glances at Bridie.

'Go on, sir,' says Bridie.

Sir Edmund nods, hardly able to meet her eyes. 'I wish to make a confession, Mrs Devine, pertaining to the wrongful acquisition of the child latterly known as Christabel Berwick.'

'Begin at the beginning, Sir Edmund.'

It took three visits. On the first visit they sat down with the Kelly family in a cottage in sight of the sea. Ellen was present, but not the child that the baronet and the doctor had heard tell of. The child who had brought them to the wilds of Ireland. Ellen's brother, the head of the family, listened. Ellen's brother's wife, the real head of the family, listened too. The visitors told the family it was fortunate they had arrived when they did, with the infant young yet, not even half a year. They showed the family scientific drawings and read them passages from the writings of Reverend Winter of Highgate Chapel. When the family remembered the rumours about their ancestor Margaret, the visitors steered them to sunnier waters. Namely: a new life for Ellen's child, one of security and comfort, specialists and medicine.

Ellen said she hadn't thought of her daughter as sick, thanked the strangers politely for their interest and declined their offer.

On the second visit, Ellen was encouraged by her brother to show Sir Edmund some local attraction – a holy well in a horse trough, a ring of magic stones in a freezing field, that sort of thing. Sir Edmund was tender with the girl and by degrees she told him what she knew of her family history and of the circumstances surrounding her confinement.

The Kelly women of Bantry Bay, she had told him, are famously lovely but every few generations a true beauty is born. The last being Margaret, who had hair the colour of sand and eyes the colour of sea shallows. Her skin was as smooth as a pebble, and her voice was like the waves moving over those pebbles. Margaret was on the beach one day when a wave came for her and she was lost to the sea. Until she walked back out of the water days later, barely wet. In a few months more she was delivered of a child and the child was said to have been remarkable.

Ellen had thought of Margaret the day she came round to herself, lying prone on the beach, a good way down from where she'd been collecting seaweed, and with no recollection of getting there.

Ellen thought of Margaret when her belly began to swell.

When she craved crab and ate it raw, shell and all. When she craved fish and ate it raw, bones and all. She drank sea-water by the bucketful.

Ellen thought of Margaret when she was delivered of a daughter. She called her Sibéal.

In the first days the baby roared down the rafters and would not feed. Ellen offered a world of things to the child but she would take nothing. Until, on a cold day, the cat went to sleep in the cradle, curling up with the baby for warmth. Ellen found the child covered in blood. Her panic abated when she saw that the child was unharmed. Ellen realised that the baby had killed and pulled the cat apart, eating only the bones and leaving the fur, flesh and sinew. Realising what her daughter needed, Ellen brought her cuttlefish and carcasses, kept to the cottage and prevented prying visitors. Few people saw the infant, the priest being one of them (he left as quickly as he arrived, for the mother, it was said, would not ask for forgiveness for a sin she'd never committed). Word spread wide and wider still. All the way to Polegate, to the baronet and the doctor.

On the third visit, with her brother's encouragement, Ellen walked out to the cliffs with Sir Edmund. The night fell and it was beautiful. Ellen sang a song about a merrow in land-locked love. Sir Edmund was enthralled, although he understood not a word.

While they were out walking, Ellen's brother (a practical man who, his wife told him, only wanted good for his family) and Dr Harbin concluded their negotiations. The doctor left with a small bundle, slipping along the track back to the hired cart. Sir Edmund cordially thanked Ellen for her song, and left her at her gate.

It took several months for Ellen to arrive at Maris House, but arrive she did. She was no longer the soft, delightful girl Sir Edmund remembered. He tried to reason with her but she cried and hectored, wailed and threatened. Her brother and his wife had spent the money and she had seen none of it. She wanted return of the child who she'd never agreed to give up. Sir Edmund refused and threatened her with the police and with the asylum if she persisted in asserting her claim. He warned her that no one would believe the word of a peasant over a baronet. Ellen left.

Thereafter, from time to time, she would slip back to Maris House, silently, covertly. Sir Edmund made sure that the child was kept secret and secure at all times, for he did not doubt the mother would snatch her if she could. Sometimes months would go by without Sir Edmund seeing Ellen Kelly, then, without warning, she would turn up: a shadow on the lawn, a pinched face at the window. For five years she haunted him: until the day she was found dead in the chapel-yard.

★

In the cold quiet that fills the kitchen, Sir Edmund, his attire incongruous, gathers acres of sprigged cotton around him with all the dignity of the condemned.

Cora speaks first. 'You wronged Ellen Kelly, sir, you wronged mother and child.'

The baronet nods numbly.

When Bridie retires she leaves the key in the latch. She can do no more for him and no less.

In the early hours a figure can be seen walking east towards the quondam Blackfriars Bridge. With the crossing point lately demolished there is no route across. This is the place where the Fleet deposits its tribute of dead dogs to the Thames. The figure descends the steps, dressed in worn cotton; the broken stonework of the bridge fills his pockets. He is a tall man, gaunt, with the look of a martyr of old; biblical, afflicted. Or he has the countenance for Old Father Thames; he has the expression of one who has known dark currents and noxious pollutions. A heron regards him with lofty disdain. The figure stops and stands still. Heron and figure stay motionless for the longest time. The figure is the first to move; when the world is a liquid wash of early morning grey, he steps into the water, his eyes raised to the lightening sky.

Chapter 32

The ancient mariner watches his wife carefully. Whenever she goes out she checks the lock on the repair-room door and hangs the key around her neck. Then she shouts through the door.

'Christabel, do your worst. Bill Tackett's head is an empty pond; the minnows have long swum away.'

Then she limps off with her leer and her rotten foot to spend the day drumming up buyers for her stolen child.

Bill tells his wife that this is no place to keep a small girl.

It is dank and dark and the rats that live in the old ship-chandlery shop are three-foot-long and as fat as well-made loaves. Clever and malevolent with yellow teeth and thick worm tails, the type that carry off infants. They are a torment, Bill should know, skittering up the moment you close your eyes. Felonious, they are, making off with a ball of hair, a nail or a tooth, to squabble over what they've thieved.

The ancient mariner stands outside the repair-room door with his heart in pieces. He tells the child, through the door, that he would kill his wife, if only he was brave. He tells the child he would set her free, if only he were sly. Plans form in Bill's mind, astounding him with their complexity and cunning. But in the time it takes him to assemble the requisite tools, being stiff of body and forgetful, his wife is back.

Bill Tackett tries, without success, to remonstrate with his wife. He pleads with her to return the child to her rightful home, no good will come of this.

His wife answers him. 'Husband, pray tell, what lives in your cash-box?'

Bill shakes his head in despair.

'I shall tell you, sir: pebbles and gull feathers.'

'It is wrong, wife. To sell an innocent for money.'

'She is no ways innocent, husband. Think of those children she drowned: them girls, them poor small girls. Three little mud-larks – dead outside our door!'

Bill narrows his eyes. 'How could she have drowned those poor little bleeders? She was locked in that room all the time.'

'Did those wee girls die a natural death?' asks his wife, with a gleam in her eye.

Bill is silent. He cannot deny the increasement of *unnatural* happenings around the shop since the child's arrival. What with the sea-birds circling and the great surging of snails up the walls and the bloody newts by the bucket-load.

'Those mud-larks, husband, were found with every stitch dry on them, and their lungs brim-full of water. And you asked me, "Wife, what kind of foul death has befallen these mites?" and I told you, "Death by Christabel."'

Soon enough, Bill's wife returns triumphant.

'The child has been sold, she'll be on her good way tomorrow.'

'Then you are finished, wife.'

She studies him. 'Come and meet her, why don't you, husband, before she goes?'

He snarls. 'Won't she do for me?'

'And you her friend and protector, always with her best interests at heart!' Bill's wife smiles. 'What are you thinking?'

Bill takes off his sou'wester and neatens the rope knot on his breeches. Then (because he is no old fool, whatever his wife says) he pockets a paring knife before following his wife into the repair-room.

★

Mrs Bibby rests with her leg up on the corner of Christabel's open casket. The child lies inside it. She's not worth tuppence, by the looks of her, although she's been sold for hundreds.

'You may not seem your best,' observes Mrs Bibby. 'But you are not dying. You are *sloughing*.'

Christabel looks at her blankly.

'According to the late Dr Harbin,' adds Mrs Bibby, 'and the even later Dr Winter, who was a written expert in whatever it is that you are.'

Christabel closes her eyes.

'Elsewise ain't you a flower in your pretty new dress?' says Mrs Bibby brightly.

Christabel is motionless.

They sit in silence, until Christabel opens her eyes again and taps the side of the casket with one cracked finger. She is gazing down the ridge of her cheekbone at Mrs Bibby, her eyes lightening from ink-black to the palest opalescent grey; maybe a trick of the candle-light.

Mrs Bibby nods, a little sadly, if truth be told. 'All right, so. On the occasion of our paths diverging, Kraken. In the old days . . .'

Two ladies there were, who lived in a shop by a creek and sold wonderful treasures, like rowlocks and monkeys' paws, pitch and storm lanterns. One lady was called Della and one was called Dorcas. The shop was quiet and cosy and they had all the things they needed and most of the things they wanted. Della had a parlour and Dorcas had a pocket-watch. It was Dorcas's wont at low tide to walk out along the foreshore to see what the water had left behind. A bottle-glass gem, a love knot of twine — gifts for her grey-eyed love, Della! Della sat waiting for her outside their shop, wrapped in the coat Dorcas had made for her. A patchworked coat of a thousand pelts with a silver-grey collar.

One day, when Dorcas was walking by the water, she came across something curled up in the pebbles and mud. Believing it to be a sleeping eel she picked it up and put it in a bucket and took it back to the shop. When she rinsed it off she found, of all things, a perfect little girl! With pale stony eyes and sharp little teeth and bright white curls. Della clapped her hands in delight and called her Christabel.

And so, the baby grew and was often to be seen in the shop window, rock-a-bye in her fishing net cradle, or busy with her story-books in her lobster-pot high chair. The child was everyone's friend and would wave and smile at every passer-by, showing her fierce fingerling's teeth. Sometimes a customer would come inside, taken by the sight of the odd little girl. Della and Dorcas refused to part with their bonny water baby, although they had offers from fine scientific gentlemen who heard about their precious find and came from miles around to meet her.

As the child grew the shop shrunk and Christabel became bored and listless watching out of the shop window. She was a miraculous fish in a dull creek. Which wasn't her purpose at all.

One day the circus came to town, and with it, the ring-master.

The ringmaster had a grand plan. He would make Christabel the most famous act in all the world. She would *travel, meet queens and kings and dignitaries, be feted and admired. She might even, one day, be persuaded to speak out loud to her legions of admirers, or at the very least publish her reminiscences. When she was ready to retire, she would leave the circus and return to her friends in the old ship-chandlery shop.*

Della gave Christabel her many-pelted coat and Dorcas gave Christabel her pocket-watch.

And so Christabel went off to make her fortune.

Mrs Bibby glances over at the child, who is, thankfully, asleep. She'll put the lid on now and then it will be done. She takes a quick swig from the bottle beside her and wipes her eyes with the hem of her shawl. Blame where blame's due; she holds the bottle up to the light, tilting it this way and that. Then she swallows the dregs.

Chapter 33

A little after dawn Bridie stirs from her bed. She taps the contents of last night's pipe into the fire and reaches for her pouch of Prudhoe's *Bronchial Balsam Blend*. It is empty. Then she searches for her other supplies, the twist in the parlour cupboard, the stash in the umbrella stand, the packet in her petticoat pocket. All smoked. She'll send out to Prudhoe directly, but it could be days before a delivery. And then it strikes her, how much she has come to rely on the continued presence of Ruby Doyle, boxer, deceased, who may or may not have known her. This is a tenuous basis indeed for a friendship. Yet here she is, unable to contemplate life without the man. A *dead* man, who appeared with a wisp of smoke in a chapel-yard, and who, in all likelihood, could just as soon disappear. Bridie inspects the empty bowl of her pipe. She could start smoking cigars, *Hussar Blend*, and see what sort of monstrosity that would throw up. With sudden joy she remembers the nugget under her pillow and hopes to God it will be enough.

Ruby is late joining Bridie at the breakfast table. She barely looks up from her newspaper nor does she show the rush of relief she feels. He's been sparring again; his bandages loosed, spectral sweat sheening his skin, his drawers hanging low. He nods at her, smoothing his beautiful black moustache.

'I need a disguise, Ruby, I need to get inside that house.'

'Ah, now—'

'His housekeeper has been taking delivery of crates. And a sack carried carefully from a late-night carriage.'

'And how do you know this?'

'Master Jem the crossing-sweeper: my new retainer. Gideon Eames is up to something.'

'You'll be donning your top hat, Bridie?'

'I have a better idea.'

Cora says it's best to work outside, where the light is better. She props her shaving mirror on the coal-bunker and mixes the stage-paint. The neighbourhood children hang over the wall, watching with fascination as Cora creates Mrs Devine a new face – twenty, no *thirty*, bloody years older! The tiny paintbrush handled with precision in the housemaid's huge fingers. Even close up it is convincing. When Bridie smiles, revealing her knocked-out teeth, it is even better. Bridie adds the massive spectacles Cora uses for the reading of penny-bloods. She knots her hair in a headscarf and throws an old shawl about her shoulders.

Bridie leaves her widow's cap, ugly bonnet and good cape at home. She stops the first ribbon seller she sees. For a heavy price Bridie buys the woman's bonnet, clogs and basket of wares. Then she tucks her own boots into the basket.

Now she walks differently: in too-tight, pinching clogs she patters. She carries the wide basket out in front and keeps the too-big bonnet from slipping down by keeping her head high and her chin stuck out. The whole effect is that of a purposeful owl.

She makes her way to Cavendish Square, slips into the

garden opposite Gideon Eames's house, and sits down on a bench and waits. The house gives nothing away. It is as elegant and respectable as its neighbours. Bridie knows better. And because she knows better she has her pepper-box pistol tucked in the bottom of her ribbon basket, under the organdies and velvets, satins and lace, printed and plain and top-notch jacquards. She turns her face up to the sun and waits.

Bridie wakes to a feeling of movement; a little hand rummaging in her ribbon basket. She opens her eyes and looks down at Myrtle Harbin.

Myrtle Harbin, her bonnet on crooked and chocolate pudding around her mouth, one-eyed Rosebud under her arm. The doctor's daughter slowly extracts her hand and grins widely.

Myrtle sits on the bench next to Bridie. She swings her legs and glances over her shoulder from time to time.

'So you slipped out, Myrtle?'

'The nurse has her sleep in the afternoon, after her gin.'

'And that's when you go on your wanders?'

'It is.'

'Your nurse is not Mrs Bibby, by any chance?'

Myrtle shakes her head. 'You look silly.' A laugh comes bubbling up. The child puts her hand over her mouth politely.

Bridie squints peevishly through her spectacles.

Myrtle laughs.

'You live with Gideon Eames now, why is that, Myrtle?'

'I am his *ward*.' She pronounces the last word slowly and with emphasis, the way it has been taught to her.

'Dr Eames must know your papa, then?'

Myrtle thinks about this then she wrinkles her nose. 'Mr Kemp came to get me.'

'I see,' says Bridie. 'Any sign of Christabel?'

Myrtle shakes her head.

'Would you like to come home with me? You can meet Cora Butter. She is seven feet tall and has mutton-chop whiskers.'

Myrtle's eyes widen. 'Might there be chocolate pudding? I'm very partial.'

'There might be.'

Myrtle ponders this for a moment. 'No, thank you, I have a job to do for Dr Eames.'

'What is it?'

'Never you mind.' She opens her hand and inspects the ribbons she's stolen and the ribbons Bridie has given to her.

Bridie points through the railings. 'See that boy over there, Myrtle? The crossing-sweeper.'

Myrtle nods.

'His name is Jem. If you ever need to get a message to me, he'll take it.'

'If I want to come and meet Cora Butter?'

'Exactly.'

'Or if I see Christabel?' she says, craftily.

'That too.'

Myrtle winds a blue satin ribbon around her finger and looks back at the house. 'Oh, mercy, it's awoke.'

The front door of Gideon Eames's house has opened. A bleak-faced omnibus of a woman is advancing down the steps.

'Your nurse?' says Bridie.

Myrtle groans.

The nurse rattles across the road and into the gardens with argument in her eye and a set to her jaw.

Myrtle bobs a clumsy curtsey and is gone, grabbing up Rosebud, hopping off into the shrubbery.

Chapter 34

Cremorne is reborn. The gardens are the new one-time-only-visit-while-it-lasts home of Lester Lufkin's famous circus. The big top is erected; Lufkin's colours fly on every flagpole. It's all acrobats and bunting, grottos and caves and gambolling seals and Arctic bears. The little circus king sails up and down the river daily on a golden barge. His oarsmen, a tribe of Greeks to rival Jason and his Argonauts, wear fins on their glistening naked brown backs. Lufkin waves regally at the populace, returning their shouts of affectionate abuse. Or else he rides up and down the Strand in a barouche, drawn by a team of zebras supplied by Mr Jamrach from Ratcliff Highway. Mr Jamrach is also the likely supplier of penguins; a large and bellicose male seal christened Wilberforce; and whole shoals of bright tank-able fish. The bear, lion and elephant are the showman's own.

Madam Cremorne has seen it all, of course; the pleasure garden is an expert in transformation. By day, she's rose-lipped and bright-eyed, wholesome and fun for the family. But at night, painted gaudy, lolling seedy, picking her remaining teeth, she entertains fops, pimps, artists and molls. But now here is ringmaster Lufkin with every honest chance of tripling revenue! Cremorne senses the quickening pulse of commerce and rejoices.

Lufkin, however, is not so sure. He stands, fur-trimmed and perplexed, outside his campaign tent. He's a spit away from the grand opening and without a headlining act. And his showman's intuition is telling him he isn't going to find one in the coffin-like box that his men are carrying towards him with trepidation. The hired boat-hands cast off with a look of relief.

The gathering of flocks of bickering sea-birds and the sudden choppiness of the Thames hardly reassure. Thankfully it's a murky day on the cusp of evening, with a sudden icy wind that sends sensible Londoners seeking shelter in snugs and by homely hearths. So perhaps Lufkin and his guard are the only witnesses to this delivery.

Lufkin calls for more lanterns. When these are brought he orders all entrances to his tent to be secured. He circles the casket, slowly, scratching his beard, noticing the drilled air holes. Not a sound can be heard from inside.

He gestures to his regal guard to open it.

The little circus king peers into the casket. 'Gentlemen, I have been taken for a plum. She looks like a plain girl to me. Where's her bleeding tail?'

'You have to put it in water first,' volunteers one of the guards.

'What's with the restraints?'

'It's violent, sir.'

Lufkin runs a caustic eye over the guard and returns his attention to the occupant of the casket. 'Who would keep an individual in this way?' he asks in disbelief.

One of the guards, nudged sharply by the other, steps forward, removing a folded piece of paper from the pocket of his gold liveried jacket.

'Begging your pardon, sir, but a note came too. Shall I read it to you?'

Lufkin holds his hand out for the note. Extracting a monocle from his embroidered tabard, he commences to read it, upside-down, with all the attendant noises that the effort of reading usually provokes.

'You have to wear gauntlets, sir,' suggests the guard. 'The note says.'

'Quite.'

'The note says that it bites,' adds the guard, clenching his teeth meaningfully.

Lufkin is indignant. 'My acts do not bite, sir. Nor are they kept in a bleeding box. They have contracts and country estates. They are amusing after-dinner speakers. They are received by high society and nobility.'

The guard drops his oculars to the carpeted ground.

'Bring my wife – she makes a great fist of anything slippery. She'll know what to do with her.'

'Yes, sir.'

'Tell Euryale to pretty her up a bit, get the hair off her face, a dab of rouge. See if she can hold a note, or bloody juggle. And for God's sake, do something about that smell.'

Night is all but past and the circus king is long abed by the time his errant queen is found and brought to his feasting tent.

The casket stands closed under heavy guard. It is studded with snails. Snails pool, too, on the floor all around, along with the newts.

Euryale, clad in cloak and python, draws nearer. As she does the python drops down and wraps itself in quick desperate loops around her legs, shackling her to the spot.

'He won't let me,' whispers Euryale. 'He's frightened.'

The guards look sympathetic, but there's no way they'll hold her snake.

Euryale makes soothing noises, untangling it and wrapping it instead around a tent pole. Then she nods to the guards, who open the lid.

The smell is unholy.

Euryale approaches with her sleeve over her mouth and nose.

The child lies at the bottom of the casket. White hair obscures her face. She wears a restraining jacket of thick canvas over a reach-me-down velvet dress that has seen better days. Her arms are crossed and secured to her chest with buckles and straps.

Euryale strokes the hair from the girl's face, for she is a girl, whatever else. She finds tight-closed eyes with matted lashes, a dainty nose and a white-lipped mouth. Her skin is flaking, sloughing strips of dying tissue, and her hair falls out in patches. It is wrapped around her fists, tangled around her fingernails.

There is movement, but it is not breathing. Creamy maggots burrow in the strands of her pale hair; they tumble in the folds of her clothes. Fighting back her revulsion and her pity, Euryale touches Christabel's face lightly, gently.

The child is cold stone.

When Euryale arrives on Bridie's doorstep in Denmark Street with the morning, her face is raw with tears.

October 1843

Chapter 35

Bridie stood before Dr Eames's desk as he signed the letter, blotted and sealed it.

'Are you certain that this is what you want, Bridget?'

'Yes, sir,' she replied.

Dr Eames nodded.

Between them lay a world of lies and truth, of Gideon's leaving and her part in it.

Dr Eames had aged since Eliza's attack, becoming very much thinner but walking as if he was very much heavier, moving his limbs slowly and with effort. This was a worry for Mrs Donsie, who rightly predicted that the doctor (being no longer hale and hearty) would be more easily carried off by a hospital fever. Oddly, it was the sending away, not of Gideon, but of Edgar, that was the breaking of him. Dr Eames had watched Gideon's carriage out of sight without a flicker of emotion, but when it came for him to hand over the small, surly bundle, he had cried. The butler saw and told no one. The footman saw and told the world. This was curious behaviour indeed for a commonly composed man. And besides, the household knew Edgar to be a joyless child who had latterly begun to show a troubling cruelty to helpless things. Everyone but Dr Eames, apparently, met the boy's removal to an appropriate institution with relief.

'I understand. This place, without her—' Dr Eames lowered his eyes. 'Was it peaceful?' he whispered.

'Eliza didn't suffer, sir.'

He sat a moment, at the desk, head bowed.

Then he pushed the envelope towards her. 'Your letter of introduction. You will learn with this man; he has *ideas* but he's a good doctor and an excellent chemist.'

Bridie picked up the letter. It was addressed to *Dr. R. F. Prudhoe.*

'You will have an annuity, enough for a simple but respectable life.'

'Thank you, sir.'

As she turned to go he called her back. He stood up and took her hand. Into her palm he put a guinea.

October 1863

Chapter 36

Blue walls, white sheets and outside it is raining again: big soft drops landing plash against the glass.

The child in the bed in the blue room, see her: she's a church-yard angel, a marble carving, with her pale curls and her stony, sealed-closed eyes.

Sleeping, perhaps.

Snug as a pearl in an oyster. But she is not a pearl, for she has lost her lustre.

She has a visitor. The child in the bed in the blue room. A girl comes creeping to the chair at the side of the bed.

The visitor climbs onto the chair with much clucking and the adjusting of petticoats. She taps the toes of her new shoes together. White satin, blush bows, O Lord! She wiggles her feet in their finery.

She glances at the child in the bed who has no shoes at all. Poor lamb.

She walks a one-eyed doll across the pillow.

Rosebud, a breakfast of porridge in her hair, looks down aghast (through her one working peeper) at the child in the bed, who doesn't move at all.

'Christabel,' Rosebud whispers softly, through her tiny china mouth. 'Wake up!'

Rosebud will not say the new name. *Sibéal.* For it's perfectly ugly and she doesn't believe in ugly names.

Rosebud taps the child's face with her little china hand. 'Chris-tah-bel.'

The child in the bed does not move.

Rosebud pirouettes back across the pillow.

The visitor, weary now (isn't it dull to be ever at a sickbed!), hops down from the chair.

Being a good visitor she extracts a token of her esteem from her pocket, to increase the comfort and cheer of the invalid. This time it is a prune. Before breakfast it was an interesting button. The time before that (after the patient had been bathed and was not stinking): a beautiful ribbon.

The child in the bed wears the ribbon now. Blue satin in her white hair.

The good visitor sculls to the mantelpiece where the given gifts are ranged. She pushes the prune into line with her fingertip. She strokes the button.

Rosebud whispers in her ear. 'What was that, Rosebud? Yes, you may kiss her *gently.*'

Doll and visitor stalk back across the room.

Rosebud very gently bends her face to the child in the bed. Kiss. The touch of cold, porridgey china.

'Don't die,' advises Rosebud, in a solemn whisper.

The good visitor closes her eyes and says a prayer to Jesus, who watches over all sickly children and creatures, that Christabel won't die.

Rosebud says, 'Amen.'

'We shall come again very soon,' says the good visitor brightly and pats the counterpane.

The child in the bed does not move.

★

She has a visitor, the child in the bed in the blue room. A man comes skulking to the chair at the side of the bed.

He sits down on the chair and runs his hand through his thin, light-brown hair. It cleaves thinly to an oddly-shaped head.

He eyes the girl in the bed who has not moved at all.

He sets about lighting a cigar, a pop of the flame and then the sweet reek of cat shit and straw.

He sits in the chair, watching the child. Smoking.

The child in the bed does not move.

She has a visitor, the child in the bed in the blue room. He moves the chair close to the side of the bed and sits down. Blue eyes, a golden beard threaded with grey.

He leans forward and strokes back her hair. He touches her cheek.

The incredible touch of her. She is like nothing in nature. Skin waxy and damp and cold, an unnatural coldness.

The child in the bed does not move.

He studies her face; the closed pods of her eyes. The ridge of her cheekbone, curved as a gill. Inside the pale lips parted, teeth just visible – small and sharp, pike-like.

'We lost you for a while,' says her visitor, 'and for that I'm very sorry.'

Behind the eyelids the inky shadows of the pupils flicker.

He bends down to her ear.

'Wake up, Sibéal,' he whispers. 'Don't you want to see the sea?'

Chapter 37

There is silence this luncheon-time in Lester Lufkin's great feasting tent. All eyes are fixed on the little circus king, whose eyes are locked on Bridie Devine, who is flanked by a giant housemaid and Euryale, *Queen of Snakes*. Lufkin's guards, sensing a threat towards their master's person, step back. Mrs Devine's scowl is primal. As if, given half a chance, she would leap over the table and shake Lufkin to death by his throat. Lufkin is in love.

He puts his fork down slowly and gets up from his swan pie. 'Now, Mrs Devine,' he coos. 'Let's not be too hasty.'

'You,' says Bridie Devine, pointing directly at him so that he's in no doubt, 'are a liar, sir.'

Her women agree; they nod their heads unanimously. The python around Euryale's neck nods too, rhythmically.

'How was I to know she was your child? She wasn't exactly the poppet you showed me in the picture.'

'She was the girl in Bridie's picture, Lester,' corrects Euryale. 'Although more grown, I'll give you that.'

'You'll give me that?' Lufkin reddens. 'You are a traitor, madam. I ought to divorce you.' He turns to his guards. 'Too Anne of Cleves: indifferent, thick ankles.'

The guards make consoling noises.

Cora nudges Bridie. 'Will I shake him now? See if the truth drops out?'

Lufkin startles. 'Mrs Devine, we have a difference of opinion. If I inadvertently bought your stolen girl, then I'm sorry.'

The guards mumble their support. How could he know?

'It's a calamity. Here I am, with the grand opening upon me, and my main bloody attraction is delivered *deceased*.' He shakes his head. 'And not only deceased, but rotten, with a smell that would lift off your head.'

A few courtiers grimace.

'He couldn't even trot her out as a stiff,' concurs Lufkin's guard. 'And then the snails were hardly pleasant.'

'That's why he sold her so quick,' appends the other guard, helpfully. 'Knock-down.'

'They don't need the bleeding ins and outs,' Lufkin flares. He addresses Bridie. 'Pity me, madam. I'm left with the rat-eating woman, the second-rate mind reader, or the boy with the extra toe as the headlining act.'

'We've still got the penguins, sir,' reminds the guard. 'They're very appealing.'

Lufkin looks up to the heavens.

'You're not off the hook, Lufkin,' says Bridie. 'I've been collecting some information about your *affairs*.'

Cora and Euryale smile at each other.

Lufkin nods, he quite understands. 'What do you want from me?'

'The name of the collector you sold the child's body to.'

'The deal was made with the utmost anonymity. No names were exchanged, Mrs Devine.'

'Then I'm off to visit Inspector Rose.'

'Large-headed cove, likes a sneer, not wonderfully tall,' Lufkin says.

'Kemp?'

'If you say so.' With an expression partway between a squint and a smoulder, he adds, 'Luncheon with me, Bridie Devine?'

Bridie Devine throws Lester Lufkin a look of distilled scorn and strides out of the tent.

The courtiers muzzle smiles.

Lufkin's heart is aflame.

Chapter 38

London has never seen rain like it. And now, all over the city the streets run with water, this foul, grey-foamed downpour. As if God has emptied his wash-tub after boiling Satan's inexpressibles in it.

A fell wind blows in from the coast, bringing news of the havoc it's caused: turbulent seas and shipwrecks. The Thames picks up pace, rising again; she sweeps along with such ferocity that mud-larks don't dare step off the bank and watermen suck air in through their teeth and shake their heads. The river has never been so angry. They will not set foot on water that lashes and boils in temper.

And above London, the sky keeps getting darker.

Bridie and Myrtle stand in the shrubbery in Cavendish Square. The branches keep some of the weather off. Bridie likes hearing the rain patter on the leaves and the rising earth smell. Myrtle likes the puddle mud; her stockings are speckled with it. Bridie has on her disguise, of course. An old ribbon seller, hen-stepping in her too-tight pinching clogs, blinking behind spectacles under the rim of her too-big bonnet.

She has a jar of toffee in her basket.

Myrtle takes a piece and another for Rosebud.

'Isn't Rosebud smart in her new veil?' says Bridie. 'Will we get her face fixed?'

Myrtle considers this. She adjusts the scrap of lace on Rosebud's bonnet and pushes an exploratory finger into the doll's broken eye. Then she tips her upside down and inspects her pantalettes.

'No, we'll keep her as she is,' she says.

'Grand, so.'

Myrtle cradles Rosebud in her arms. 'She's home,' she confides. 'But she's sick.'

Bridie's heart turns sideways. 'Who's home?'

'Christabel,' whispers Myrtle. 'Only that's not her name now.'

'What is her name?'

Myrtle rolls her eyes. 'Sibéal.'

Bridie looks up at the house.

'Would you like to come and say *how-do-you-do*?' asks Myrtle.

The small girl leads the old ribbon seller through the servants' door, past the kitchen and up the back stairs. It is a good time of day for an adventure like this. The nurse is having her nap, the butler is at the book-keepers and the cook is soaking her corns.

Dr Eames is at the hospital and it's not the day for Mr Kemp to visit.

Myrtle doesn't like Mr Kemp. He does card tricks that aren't funny and has silent footsteps and is good at sneaking up on people.

Myrtle walks Rosebud up and down the corridor. They play at sentries while Bridie tackles the lock. She is applying the skeleton key she found at Mrs Peach's.

By the time Rosebud has made two turns of the landing, Bridie has the lock picked.

There is a mineral sharpness to the air and the powerful smell of sun-heated seaweed. Myrtle, marching outside the door now, warned her about this, but Bridie doesn't find it unpleasant. The window is hung with blue gauze; through the gap in the curtain Bridie can see that the window is barred. Snails slick in thick clusters over the glass. The blue-painted walls run with moisture.

There is little in the room but a bed and a chair. A few collected objects are carefully ranged along the mantelpiece, a button and so forth. On the bed sits a child wearing a white dress. She has her back to the door and is propped up with bolsters and cushions, her legs covered with a blanket. She has healing sores on her ear and on her neck, a shallow bowl of water on her lap.

Bridie moves forward and the child looks round. Eyes grey-white marble and then the expanding black of darkening, widening, oddly flat pupils. A trick of the muted light?

She smiles, the child. An awkward, close-lipped affair, not unlike Bridie's own new smile. Her fine white hair has a marine cast from the blue at the window. Her face is lovely, an uncanny kind of loveliness, a strange flawless symmetry. Apart from the lopsided ribbon-bow over one ear, which Bridie recognises as Myrtle's handiwork. Here is the child in Bridie's photograph, only grown. Fragile of build, her prominent spine just visible beneath the thin stuff of her dress.

Bridie takes the chair next to the bed, moving slowly. Sibéal returns to her bowl. Dipping her fingertips, dabbling and splashing. Bridie watches, riveted. Sibéal hooks a drop with her finger, and another, and another. She cups them in her other palm.

Bridie loses herself, drop by drop; the memories ripple into clear view.

A woman rescues a daisy chain from a small boy's unthinking fingers and hangs it proudly on her cap, her hazel eyes warm with laughter.

A girl slips on wet wood, under a table, in a tavern, after a cat. Wet wood on the yawing deck of a steam-packet in a storm . . .

The child tips her palm and watches the drops roll away.

The past floods in and with it the urge to embrace this creature. And the pity of it stills Bridie; this little one, like her own young self, cast adrift.

Chapter 39

Bridie sits in her parlour in Denmark Street staring at the wall. There is nothing much to see, other than faded wallpaper of an indistinct design, likely urns or fountains, definitely wreaths. But that's not the point; Bridie's attention is not on the wall. Cora is in the parlour too, scattering spent tea-leaves on the rug and then going at them with haphazard stabs of her long-handled broom. When Cora scatters the tea-leaves she hums; when she sweeps, she whistles through her teeth. The rug looks no cleaner, but that's not the point; Cora's attention is not on the rug.

Bridie has been ruminating for hours, possibly all night. Cora found her at first light and she hasn't stirred since, for the pipe in her hand is unfilled and the coffee at her elbow is still untasted.

Cora edges nearer, catching sight of a book forgotten in the folds of Bridie's skirt: *On the Manifold Wonders of Fresh and Salt Water Creatures: A Scientific Observation by Rev. Thomas Winter.*

'A middling to interesting read,' says Cora. 'I must say the section on sandworms failed to entertain me.'

Cora imagines she sees a flicker of response on Bridie's face, the beginnings of a blink, the slightest dilation of a nostril.

Cora leans in closer. 'A thrilling history of the private lives of whelks, though.'

Bridie blinks, sighs, and is back in the room. 'How do I even begin to get her out?'

'From under his nose: difficult, I would say.'

'And if I do get her out, what in God's name do I do with her?'

'Take her to Mrs Prudhoe, she can stay with the other waifs.'

'She could be a killer.'

'Then release her into the sea.'

'Cora, she could be a killer.'

Cora points to the Reverend Winter's book. 'So you believe in this now. Merrow and suchlike?'

Bridie says nothing.

'Let her stay with a collector then. You know, an expert who can manage her.' Cora makes a few stabs with her broom, watching Bridie from the corner of her eye.

'Jesus, Cora, how do you think he'll manage her? A malignant bastard like Gideon Eames?' Bridie takes up her pipe with a frown. 'Just bloody let me get Sibéal out first, then I'll decide what to do with her.'

Cora grins and sweeps up with a deft clatter of broom and pan.

Bridie goes from staring at the walls to pacing between them.

Ruby stands in the fireplace out of her way, hatless and persevering. 'So, the drowning in air and burning bites, you'll be taking account of that in your plan?'

'She didn't drown or bite me, did she?'

Ruby lowers his voice. 'Is she still in your mind? Dredging memories?'

'It wasn't like that. Jesus, I regret telling you anything.'

'And you didn't remember me at all, even when she stirred up your recollections a bit?'

'Didn't I tell you—'

'She might be listening to us now.'

'And she would hear you, Ruby?'

He grins. 'She's a miraculous creature, is she not? Just like myself.'

Bridie groans and begins to pace the floor again.

'Would there be guards at the house, Bridie?'

'I don't know, but there'll be a rake of servants to get past. The nurse alone is a wardrobe of a woman.'

'What about Eames?' Ruby looks at her closely. 'Are you planning to get past him too?'

Bridie hesitates. 'I'll strike when he's out.'

Cora sails back into the room. 'Caller for you: would Mrs Devine be at home to Master Jem, crossing-sweeper?'

'She would.'

Cora exhales. 'He won't come in without his broom.'

'Then his broom is welcome too.'

Master Jem, wearing his bright neckerchief, modified wide-awake and an expression of great alertness, inspects the unfathomable instrument on the mantelpiece, tapping the gauge and peering at the rubber attachment.

'What is it?' he asks.

'No idea,' admits Bridie.

Cora brings in a tray with the requisite refreshments for a child of poverty: three meat pies and a half-pint of stout.

Jem props his broom carefully (being his livelihood and all) by the side of the fireplace, eyeing the giant housemaid with awe. Until, remembering his manners, he dips a bow.

'Much obliged, Your Highness.'

Cora gives him a stately nod.

'You have news for me, Jem?'

'The doctor is doing a flit, Mrs Devine. Leaving for Windsor, he is.'

'Albery Hall?'

'That's the one,' agrees Jem.

'Gideon Eames's childhood home?' asks Cora.

'The same,' says Bridie.

'Then we will give chase,' proposes Cora. 'Ambush them. If that doesn't work we break into the house and steal back Christabel—'

'Sibéal.'

'Exactly . . . and Myrtle Harbin,' adds Cora. 'We can't leave her in Eames's clutches either.'

'Cora, the dangers, I can't ask you to—'

'I want to help save those children.' Cora straightens her mob cap and draws herself up to her full stunning height. 'You might need a big hand.'

Jem's eyes widen.

'They'll likely have a few hard-headed men around, pistols even,' ventures Bridie.

'And you have your pepper-box and I have this . . .' Cora selects an implement from the fireside companion stand. 'Poker.'

Jem gazes at the giantess in admiration.

Cora tests the heft of her weapon. 'Now all we need are a few fast horses.'

Bridie checks her pistol as she waits in her parlour. She can hear the sound of hooves outside. It is Cora, riding down Denmark Street in a phaeton with a sprightly pair. Cora brings the carriage to a bumpy halt outside Mr Wilks's window. She taps on it with her crop. The old man puts down a clevis bolt and flutters to the window. He squints outside but sees naught, not even a seven-foot-tall housemaid.

'Jem,' says Bridie to the crossing-sweeper standing before

her. 'As much as I appreciate you volunteering for this affray, I have another job for you.'

Jem glances up from the pistol in her hand with a disappointed expression. 'Mrs Devine?'

'A job of utmost importance.'

His face brightens.

'If this should go wrong, Jem—'

Cora hollers up from the road below.

'—and something tells me that it might,' continues Bridie, stoutly, 'we will need reinforcements.'

She sits down at her bureau and dashes off a note. She hands it to Jem. 'Take this to Inspector Valentine Rose, Scotland Yard.'

Jem looks doubtful. 'A copper, ma'am?'

'A good one.' Bridie straightens the grubby flower in the boy's buttonhole. 'He'll bring you with him if he sees fit.'

The boy brightens. He bobs off with the note.

'Are you ready, Bridie?' asks Ruby.

'I am. It's just . . . him.'

'I'll be there with you. And you have that.' Ruby eyes the pistol. 'Use it if you need to.'

She nods and is out the door, dagger strapped to her thigh, pepper-box in her pocket and perhaps a little something in her boot heels.

Chapter 40

A raven lands next to you. She fixes you with her eye, an eye as black as pooled tar, and stalks nearer. She nudges you with her beak and lets out a soft chirrup. She wants you to follow her, to see what she sees. If you're ready – she pushes off into the air.

Maybe she's one of Prudhoe's flock, maybe not; either way, borrow the raven's sharp eye, which penetrates any fog, London or otherwise.

Hers is a world of roofs and chimney-stacks, steeples and trees, and the shining serpent of the river running through it all. The early bustle of London below. People are no more than punctuation from above! Hat tops . . . full stops. The dash – of a running dog.

And all around you: sky. The raven turns in her element and the world turns too, confirming what she already knew: she is the centre of everything.

She lands on a gutter and shakes out her feathers. Below, two broughams are being readied in Cavendish Square. The horses twitch their ears and the footmen check the doors. The coachmen are sombre, sinking into their cloaks, reins in hand. The carriages draw off, close by one another, as if for protection, blinds drawn down. Bridles jangling, more jittery than jaunty, the horses know something is afoot. The footmen pull up their mufflers and keep wary. They predict an ambush at every jolt.

The road from London to Windsor is good and the carriages are new and the horses strong and fresh. But if the footmen looked behind (on a straight road, with the aid of a field-glass) they would see a robbed phaeton following. In the driver's seat: a seven-foot-tall housemaid with a resolute expression. Beside her sits a small, handsome woman in a widow's cap and ugly bonnet. In the back of the phaeton stands a partially clad dead man, hatless and with eyes burning. The ride is thrilling; after all, the driver learnt her skills at the circus. But her living passenger pays no mind to this. She is watching the raven circling above, paying notice to every dip and tilt of the black flags of the bird's wings, as if reading some dark portent.

Today Windsor is laid out in all her perfection. The air is apple-sweet and clear, with not even a wisp of fog in sight. Here is the venerable old town, with its comfortable taverns and comfortable residents. The hilltop castle, the warm-stoned ancient churches and pleasant villages. The great park where Herne the Hunter trips in dappled shade, as the leaves, those bright jewels of autumn, tremble and fall in the cleanest of breezes. Old Father Thames winds through this favoured land-scape at his most stately and benign.

Albery Hall has an enviable aspect; located out past the town in a wooded part, it enjoys privacy and a sylvan surrounding, enclosed on three sides by a brick wall and on the fourth by the river. From the tree-lined approach it can instantly be seen that this is a glorious house. Its stone façade lit to honeyed cream on this autumn afternoon. This is the house of Bridie's memories, with its even-eyed windows and a well-proportioned portico.

The coaches sweep past the gates and along the driveway, the first stopping at the front door, the second continuing round to the coach-house. The gates are locked immediately behind them. A tall man steps from the carriage in the full flush of vital midlife, smiling beneficently. His hat in his hand, his hair thick and long and combed back from his crown. He wears the fine golden beard of an ancient god, shot through with grey now, which only lends distinction and an aura of wisdom. He has brief words with the butler, the housekeeper, nods to the servants collected outside the front door, and enters the house. An unfavourable-looking young man follows, large-headed, slight of stature and with a mouth made for sneering. He holds a child by the hand. The child, clasping a doll, breaks loose from his grip and skips up the steps and into the big house, the line of servants bobbing and bowing as she goes.

At the coach-house the driver reins in the horses and the carriage stops. A casket is unloaded and carried quickly inside, as if the light of day is a dangerous thing.

At first sight Bridie could be deceived into thinking Albery Hall hasn't changed at all. On closer inspection, it's evident that nowadays the dogs let loose in the grounds are of the kind wild to feel something pulsing between their teeth: every gate is locked and the walls are three feet higher.

Having left their carriage down the lane, tethered out of sight, our friends stand at the maze gate, the least frequented of the house's entrances. The gate is screened from the road by dense thickets, giving onto the grounds behind the hedge maze at the far edge of the property. Legend has it that Albery Hall's first owner created the gate to allow him, under the maze's cover, to slip out to the local tavern.

The dogs, such as were on patrol, are succumbing to the stupefying concoction Cora scattered through the gate, a powder they lapped up readily. They turn in circles, padding the ground, to sleep where they fall.

'We'd better make it quick, they won't stay like that for long.'

'Where did you even get that, Cora?'

'Dr Prudhoe. I keep it in the pantry for your more disagreeable clients.'

'You haven't . . .?'

'I was tempted to slip Dr Harbin a little.'

Ruby laughs.

Cora forces the lock and they're in, running across the grounds, scattering silently, using hand signals. Cora heads round to the front of the house, whilst Bridie skirts the side, towards the servants' entrance.

For Bridie, this is as strange as a dream, this garden with its stone urns and topiary and the sunlight on the lawn and the river there in the distance – all just as she remembered. Only the grounds are oddly empty. There's a tense feeling, a bated-breath feeling about the place. Bridie has the sensation of being watched, although she sees no one. She runs faster, cursing her petticoats. Keeping to the lawn at the edge of the gravel path, she reaches the door. It's propped open, as it always used to be in good weather. Ahead: a whitewashed corridor with a line of silent servants' bells. She listens. Hearing nothing but the blood belting in her ears, she proceeds, Ruby follows.

Making her way past the servants' hall and the housekeeper's office, she finds no sign of life.

Ruby stops by a closed door. 'There's someone in here.'

Bridie takes a breath and enters.

In the kitchen that belonged to Mrs Donsie, next to the cook's old range, in the cook's old chair, sits Bad Dorcas.

★

Dorcas Chapman sits in the patch of sunlight laid out by the kitchen windows. She wears her years heavily; the sunlight doesn't flatter. Even so, Bridie can still see the face Dorcas wore when she was a young housemaid and Bridie was an Irish street rat. Bridie recognises the wide-apart eyes, very blue, the strong bulk of her body and her nimble thief's hands. She can also see that this woman has a terrible infection, doubtlessly fatal. The leg in question is up on a stool and divested of shoe and stocking. The toes are without nails and suppurating, three of them no more than pus-filled stumps. Ulcers adorn her leg, which is hideously swollen. Next to her chair, a card table is set with a bottle, a box of matches, a cigar and a book, open face-down.

'Bridie Devine.' She selects the bottle and holds it up in a toast.

'Dorcas Chapman.'

'I haven't been called that for years.' She unstoppers the bottle. 'Mother Bibby's Quieting Syrup — assuages agony, soothes the fractious, grants cloudless serenity. Want some?'

'No, thank you.'

'So here we are, back at Albery Hall, dependent on the mercy of Dr Eames. Nothing changes.' She stoppers the bottle and puts it back on the card table.

'His mercy?'

'You are trespassing on his property and I rooked him sideways.' Dorcas looks Bridie full in the eyes. 'We are sunk.'

'You and Dr Harbin were to steal the child from the baronet for him?'

'Such a simple plan,' Dorcas admits. 'Only I'm treacherous, and so, it turned out, was Harbin. You'd expect a bit of perfidy from me. Harbin, on the other hand, was a disappointment.' She straightens her skirts.

'Careful, Bridie.' Ruby moves to her side. 'She has a revolver.'

'Keep your hands where I can see them, Dorcas.'

Dorcas turns her hands palm-upwards and puts them on her lap. 'Berwick, the old goose, had a golden egg he could keep neither secret nor safe. Gideon, knowing this, tried to strike a deal, through his agents of course.'

'Kemp?'

'If you like. Berwick refused but Harbin didn't. Gideon offered the doctor a partnership, touring the world, exhibiting the child. Not *publicly*, mind, to favoured gentlemen of scientific leanings.'

'But Harbin threw that up – why?'

Dorcas smiles. 'I encouraged the doctor towards an understanding that Gideon Eames takes no partners and splits no profit. Hard choice: deliver to Eames and be dead, thieve from Eames and likely be dead. Besides, there was a deal of money to be made. It was the money that swayed the doctor.'

'So Harbin took his chances.'

'Paris, a big show. He would try and outrun Eames's reach.'

'So you stirred all of this up?'

'Now, I was only a cog in the machinations of these gentlemen.' She glances down at her hands. 'Do I have to sit like this? I'd like a nip and a smoke. Time's fleeting and all that.'

'Slowly.'

Dorcas reaches for the bottle. 'But the doctor was a weak spoke.'

'So you killed him and sold the child to Lufkin?'

'That silly circus bastard thought she was rotten dead. She was *sloughing*.'

'Then Lufkin sold her to Kemp, who works for Gideon.'

'Full circle,' says Dorcas. 'And the wheel of fate rolls to crush me down. So, you've the whole story now.'

'You must have known Gideon would catch up with you. Why did you do it?'

'For the money.' Dorcas grimaces and takes another nip. She holds the bottle to her breast. 'What will you do with her?'

'Find her a home.'

'Oh, set her free, put her in the water,' says Dorcas. 'Then you'll all be frigged.' She laughs.

'She's only a child, Dorcas.'

'Tell yourself that.'

Ruby at the kitchen door, listens. Voices outside in the grounds. 'We need to move, Bridie.'

'She's a baby yet, full grown she'll drown the world.' Dorcas puts the bottle on the table and picks up her cigar. 'She will have her way with me first.'

'What do you mean?'

'My penance.' Dorcas strikes a match and waves it towards the card table. 'Last supper.' She lights her cigar with a few quick puffs; she closes her eyes as she inhales. 'Gideon wants to test her capabilities.' She blows out the match. 'I have volunteered.'

'Then you believe she kills – you've seen it?'

Dorcas looks at her cigar. 'I don't know why Kemp smokes dung when Eames has clutches of these.' She takes a deep draught and then: 'Do I believe she kills? I believe this leg will do for me sooner.'

Bridie draws nearer. 'An amputation—'

'No, ta.'

'I could clean it up. Dress it.'

'You'd do that for me?' Dorcas smiles and leans forward in her chair, biting her lip against the pain. 'I remember the first time I saw you: hopping with lice, the clothes stuck to your back with filth.' She points across the room. 'The old laundry, through there, I helped to bathe you, remember? No one understood a bloody word you said.'

Bridie keeps her eyes on Dorcas. 'I never asked to be here.'

'Eliza loved you, as much as she loved that little bastard.'

'Edgar?'

'*Kemp*,' says Dorcas, waiting.

Bridie speaks slowly. 'Edgar Kempton Jones. Kemp is Eliza's boy.'

'Dr John Eames's spot of trouble.' Dorcas turns back to her cigar. She takes another slow draw, as if to prolong the suspense. 'After his banishment, Gideon tracked down his half-brother and brought him to live abroad with him. It was a shrewd move.'

'Why?'

'Kemp inherited a good share of the estate and, of course, his inheritance wasn't dependent on him staying away.'

'Why did Gideon return?'

'I'm more surprised that he stayed away.' She fixes Bridie with a sharp eye. 'But then John Eames trussed his son up like a market fowl on your say-so. No annuity and the threat of arrest hanging over him should he return.'

Bridie frowns. 'How would you even know that?'

'Let's just say' – Dorcas pats the arm of the chair – 'that I'm the inheritor of old Mrs Donsie's wisdom.'

Raised voices come from the garden; Ruby walks out through the wall.

Dorcas takes a pull of her cigar. 'But now Gideon has his own money and his own powerful friends. The old master is gone, Bridget.' She breathes out, watching the smoke spread. 'You might not be popular with the new master of this house.'

'You told him my part in his being sent away?'

'You'd take me for a peach?' Her smile is strained, as if offended. 'I merely agreed with his theories. His main one being: you had it in for him.'

'He was guilty: I found the evidence. He attacked Eliza and left her for dead.'

Dorcas's smile fades. Bereft of it, her face is empty. 'You're sure of that, Bridget?'

'Everyone knew he did it.'

'Gideon was guilty of many things, of course, but not that particular crime.'

Bridie stares at her. 'What are you saying—'

'Here is my confession: forgive me, Bridie Devine, for I have sinned.'

'You attacked Eliza?' Bridie draws forward. 'But the evidence – his ring, his boots—'

'You went digging so I left you something to find.'

'If Gideon knows I was involved . . .' Bridie falters, understanding. 'He must believe I fabricated the evidence against him.'

'Bull's-eye.'

'Who did he think attacked Eliza?'

'Not me.'

Bridie thinks on this. 'You gave him an alibi.'

'He couldn't prove he wasn't there.' Dorcas crosses her arms high on her chest. 'And Gideon was grateful. Which is why I'm still here, with my leg up, supping tincture of opium and smoking a Havana.'

'Why did you do that, to Eliza and to him?'

'She was an upstart and he was a prick.' Dorcas shrugs.

'She was my friend.'

Dorcas studies her cigar. 'I had a friend once, lived out past Cranbourne, all on her own. Barmaid at the Fleur de Lys.' She puts the cigar to her mouth. 'Wheel of fate.'

'Della Webb,' Bridie says, quietly.

Dorcas flinches. She shifts her rotten leg. 'They say you live your whole life again, drowning. I am wondering if the noose would be better than letting Gideon's prodigy at me. I must say you have a capacity for survival too, judging by the face on you.'

'I was burgled.'

Dorcas smiles and taps her mouth. 'And you lost something other than your full set of dominos, didn't you?'

'You know: you sent him—'

'A snap job like that? I would have come in person.' Her expression brightens. 'Harbin in a hatbox, that was all my own work.'

Ruby passes back through the wall. 'No sign of Rose yet, but the footman and the head groom are searching the house. They know something's going on.'

Bridie nods. She turns to Dorcas. 'Inspector Rose is after you. He's on his way here.'

Dorcas exhales. 'He can have my bones.'

'Bridie—'

'All right, so.' Bridie turns to go.

And Dorcas's voice: muted, tired. 'The merrow is in the nursery,' she says. 'Kemp fights the dirtiest but neither brother will observe fair play. Nor will they finish you cleanly. They both know their way around the human body. Take from that what you will.'

Bridie pulls a twist of Prudhoe's *Bronchial Balsam Blend* from her pocket, steps over to Dorcas and puts it on the card table. 'Have you a pipe?'

Dorcas shakes her head.

Bridie takes out her pipe and leaves it next to the tobacco.

Dorcas looks amused. 'What's this?'

Bridie glances at Ruby, half in the hallway, waiting on her. He shoots her a harried smile.

'Something for the pain,' says Bridie, heading for the door.

'Under the counter,' calls out Dorcas. 'The old ship-chandlery shop, Deptford. Put Lufkin's money to good use; orphans, alms for the fucking merrow—'

But Bridie is gone.

Chapter 41

The servants of Albery Hall are having a trying day. Cora Butter has been rounding them up as and when they cross her path – the cook, assorted maids and a weeping valet have now joined the butler in the cellar. The butler has uncorked several bottles to treat the shock subsequent to being corralled into a windowless dungeon by a seven-foot-tall housemaid armed with a poker.

Bridie is aware of none of this, noting only the uncanniness of a big house deserted of servants. She passes through the baize door up into the house proper and along the passage, finding nothing. Ahead of her: the drawing-room. Having sent Ruby to look for Christabel, Bridie must rely on her mortal senses. She listens carefully and, hearing nothing, goes inside.

The room is exactly how she remembers it.

Here is the spot where Maria Eames dispensed judgement with her embroidery needle. There is the fireplace, where Eliza would laugh at a carving of a cupid; an imp among the cherubim who was the spit of Edgar. Bridie draws closer to see that the face is identical to the others, so that perhaps she is mistaken in her memory. And the wallpaper, although yellow still, seems to be of a paler shade than she recalls.

Bridie advances past the dining-room, the library and toward the study. Becoming aware of a dragging of her feet, a knotting of the stomach and a sense of inevitability.

Dr John Eames's study has hardly changed. Here is the window seat where Bridie sat, there are Dr Eames's bookcases. Bridie can almost feel his presence, obsolete now, shuffling in a corner, or drifting with the dust motes, a question forever forming on his lips.

Gideon, a sheet of paper in hand, walks into the room, closing the door to the laboratory behind him. He sits at his father's desk, picks up a pen and begins to make notes.

Bridie could run, pull out her pistol and shoot him, or shout to Cora for help. Instead she stands very still. Which surprises her. She waits with breath held. For one mad moment she imagines he hasn't seen her.

Gideon, eyes down, points to the spot in front of the desk.

Where she stood all those years ago, dressed in a dead man's blood.

Where she stood to deliver the lie that changed Gideon's life.

If she's not going to run or shoot or shout she will at least choose a different bloody spot to stand.

She walks slowly over to a window framing the lawn and the river in the distance and the sky clouding over. But Bridie is marking the man, not the view.

Gideon Eames puts down his pen, leans back in his chair and looks up at her.

'You, Bridget Devine, always were a fucking nuisance.'

★

Bridie tells herself to breathe, she tells her heart to beat, she tells her legs to hold, under the burden of his blue, blue, terrible eyes.

She isn't a child now, but she is shaking and her tongue is a stone in her mouth. And then, with relief, Bridie sees Ruby move across the room, so that he is standing beside Gideon's chair.

'Look at me, Bridie.'

She looks at him.

'Grand, so, you have a pistol,' says Ruby. 'He doesn't. The nearest doors are behind you. If you can, run.'

Bridie turns her eyes to Gideon Eames.

He is watching her face. 'Did you think I was dead?'

'Yes.'

'You hoped.' The chill of his smile.

Bridie doesn't answer. She hears someone come into the room behind her, the door opening and closing softly.

'Ah, no,' groans Ruby. 'Kemp.'

Kemp walks over to the desk holding Myrtle Harbin by the hand. She is dressed outlandishly, in a costume of blue spangles and sea-green netting, her light brown hair in ribbons and ringlets.

She smiles at Bridie, a small, polite smile, and extracting her hand from Kemp she runs to Gideon, clambering onto his lap with surprising familiarity. He strokes her cheek and she ignores him, picking at her bare toes.

Kemp crosses to the bookcase, takes out a cigar, lights it. Bridie catches the smell of *Hussar Blend*: cat shit and straw.

If she is going to run she ought to get on with it.

Bridie notes the exits and obstacles, the clear lines of flight. How would she manage to scoop up Myrtle? And would the running set off some predatory urge? If not in Gideon, then in Kemp it would. He is staring at her with feral enmity.

She studies the young man. There's more than a trace of the unwholesome boy she knew; it's plain, now that she knows. And she remembers him, playing at Mrs Donsie's kitchen range, wiggling his scrap of string, or after the attack on his mother, whinging and stumbling after Gideon and Bad Dorcas.

'What happened to you, Edgar?' she asks.

'My name is Kemp.' He glances at Gideon. 'We know the truth of what you did.'

Gideon smiles. 'Oh, the truth of what Bridget Devine did!'

He pushes Myrtle from his lap and stands, holding his hand out to the little girl, who immediately takes it.

He leans down to the child's ear. 'Shall we show Bridget Devine the refurbishments?'

Myrtle gives a shrug and a skip.

Gideon nods. 'Do the honours, Kemp.'

Kemp, his cigar clamped between his teeth, opens the double doors to the late Dr John Eames's laboratory.

Bridie is astounded. The old laboratory has been vastly extended. Floors and ceilings have been removed to give the space a stunning, echoing height. An abundance of windows rain-drummed now. White marble steps lead into a confusion of ladders and paint pots, wrapped objects and opened crates. A museum and a laboratory combined; empty tanks and display cases jostle with cabinets full of bottles and apparatus.

Gideon strolls down the steps, Myrtle cantering ahead. Bridie follows and Kemp slinks behind.

'We are still rather disordered,' Gideon remarks. 'But you get the impression.'

Bridie follows Gideon through a lacquered room divider, some kind of medieval hell scene, the rich colours all the more striking in the pale surroundings.

'This area is almost completed. You'll notice, Bridget, that some of our exhibits are already at home here.'

Bridie looks around at the specimens on stands or in jars: strange wonders. There are aquariums along the wall replicating a range of watery abodes, from fens to rock pools. There is an ornate glass casket containing the stolen bodies of Margaret Kelly and her offspring, still in their crypt wrappings. Margaret's merrow infant swaddled and no bigger than a turnip, its tiny teeth clamped around its mother's finger. To the left of the casket is an upright cabinet, glazed on all sides. Inside, a single specimen: the Winter Mermaid.

'You stole that from me – you sent that bastard—'

'And you stole it from Berwick,' says Gideon, his face impassive. 'Centrepiece, over there.'

At the middle of Gideon Eames's Great Exhibition is a tank surrounded by rows of bentwood-framed chairs. Pentagonal in shape, like the armour of a sea urchin, the tank is constructed from sizeable sheets of glass. Beside the tank there is a movable staircase with an extendable walkway to reach over the top. Nearby there is an operating table and a cabinet containing medical instruments. Bridie notices a glass bottle of chloroform and a mask, along with restraining garments with leather bands and loops.

Bridie feels a sudden revulsion. She turns to Gideon. 'What is all this equipment for?'

'Vivisection.'

'You're going to kill her.'

Gideon takes a seat on one of the bentwood chairs and Myrtle flutters down beside him.

'Any investigations will be made with the sole purpose of prolonging her life and understanding her species.'

'She's a child.'

Gideon rubs his forehead, his expression suddenly weary. 'No. She isn't.'

Bridie gestures to the chairs. 'And these . . . You'll have an audience for the carving up of a child?'

'We are a collective; men of science who wish to learn about a valuable new species.'

'And that's what you tell yourselves, is it?'

'Come, Myrtle.' Gideon stands. He leads the child to the tank and lifts her up onto the staircase. He stands back, surveying the structure.

'River water feeds it at a constant flow but there's no egress. The enclosure is made perfectly secure by the use of electrical currents.' He turns to Bridie. 'You are familiar with the work of Duchenne de Boulogne?'

Bridie looks puzzled.

'Electrical probes, facial grotesques, gateway to the soul?' Gideon pauses. 'No? No matter.'

'If she tries to escape,' Kemp skulks out from behind the tank, 'the electrical current will convulse her.'

'Just so.' Gideon turns to Myrtle and gestures up the stairs. 'Get in the tank.'

Myrtle widens her eyes and shakes her head.

'You are supposed to *demonstrate*, remember?' Gideon turns to Bridie. 'We had a time getting hold of the Bantry Bay mermaid. Dr Harbin dealt us a deal. But he wasn't the only traitor in our midst. Like father like daughter.'

Myrtle buries her head in her netting skirt.

Gideon retakes his chair, gesturing at Kemp.

Myrtle starts to cry as Kemp approaches. He grabs hold of her arm.

'Leave her alone,' says Bridie.

'She's a chattering bird, you know,' Gideon muses. 'Flitting around Cavendish Square, selling secrets for ribbons and toffees.'

Kemp climbs the steps, dragging Myrtle after, the child too alarmed to cry.

Bridie takes out her pistol and cocks it, aiming it at Kemp. 'Let her go.'

'Put Myrtle down, Kemp,' Gideon commands. 'Bridget has a gun.'

Kemp lets go of Myrtle's arm; she runs to Bridie.

'Put the gun away.' Gideon's voice is calm but his face is tells another tale. 'There's no need for that.'

Myrtle screams and pulls on Bridie's skirts. Kemp is edging nearer with a bayonet of sorts connected to a wire.

'No nearer,' warns Bridie.

Kemp keeps moving, his expression one of malevolent intent.

Bridie fires.

Gunshot and the spiralling echoes of it in Gideon's high-ceilinged hall. Then: nothing.

Then a bright ringing, as of a goblet hit with a spoon.

The clear panes of the tank begin to craze, a series of dull crackles, followed by a grand splintering.

Gideon frowns.

With an explosion of glass and water, the tank shatters.

Kemp crumples and slides across the floor, a baffled expression on his face. The floor is awash with river water. Chairs are bowled over. Gideon stumbles to his feet.

Bridie picks up the barefooted child next to her and runs.

Chapter 42

Cora listens at the closed door. She still has a fighting grip on her poker, although she has met with no real opposition as she's searched the house, only nervous servants.

She opens the door to a nursery, in a style decades out of date.

The child sits on a nest of cushions inside a slim-barred wrought-iron cage. She wears a pale blue dress and her hair is tied back with a blue ribbon. Ordinary clothes which only serve to heighten her difference: the unsettling perfection of her features, her white hair. Her eyes, palest grey, seem to rapidly darken. Likely a trick of the light, which is dim in the room as the day is made sullen with rain.

'You are Sibéal,' says Cora.

The child doesn't answer; she leans her head against the cage and runs her teeth along the bars.

'You want to get out, of course.'

The child looks at Cora blankly.

Cora examines the lock. It's beyond her skill. She assesses the fabrication of the cage, judging where to bend. She cannot move the bars with her hands; they may be thin but they are strong. Using her poker, Cora levers them apart but soon they will widen no more.

'Can you slither out? You have just enough room, being a little thing.'

Sibéal tries to edge forward. Cora sees with a rush of pity how thin her legs are, and her arms, and how weak the child is.

'Oh, the bastards.' Cora shakes her head. 'They have kept you in a cage.'

Sibéal regards her, unblinking.

'Come to the edge and I will lift you out. Do you understand?'

The child begins to move towards the gap.

'Right so, Sibéal. I am going to reach in and pull you out, gently, gently. No biting.'

And then the child is through and in her arms and no weight at all; there is nothing of her. Cora feels the ridges of her spine and sees the cut of her cheekbone and she fights against tears of pity. This child is dying.

'Shall we take you to the river?'

Sibéal presses her face against Cora's arm.

'That's the ticket, isn't it?' says Cora.

Bridie pushes Myrtle behind a wall of stacked crates. She stands listening, hearing nothing but her own held breath and her own heartbeat. They have run out of the exhibition space, down a flight of steps and into what looks to be a storeroom. Soaked from the tank, they leave footprints, that can't be helped.

Bridie tries to think and tries to breathe. Myrtle glances up at her with a small, brave smile. The child is shaking with the cold and the wet and the shock.

Ruby emerges from a bank of boxes; his face grave and his tattoos skeeting about his body.

'There's a locked door behind the crates there, Bridie, and

· 380 ·

a passageway to the garden. You're below ground here, but if you can open that you'll be up and out.'

Bridie holds a finger up to her mouth and Myrtle nods. They edge round the crates to the door. In her pocket Bridie finds, with relief, the skeleton key. When she applies it to the lock she sees that her hands are trembling.

Cora steals through the house with Sibéal in her arms. Down the main staircase and through the drawing-room and out onto the terrace, moving as quickly and quietly as she can.

Through the door, into the passageway, they run. Myrtle lagging, the sound of her bare feet slapping stone, Bridie pulling her onwards. Up the steps and to the lawn will be ahead of them.

Bridie, slowed by more than her wet petticoats. He has a grip of the back of her, now his arm goes across her breast. The shock of his touch.

She tells Myrtle to run. But Myrtle, sobbing with fear, hangs from her.

She cannot see what is coming next.

Bridie screams at her and the child does run.

It's an ignoble tussle. Bridie has one thought: getting up the stairs and out onto the lawn where Gideon Eames is less likely to kill her. And she does reach the lawn, but when she does he has her pinned entirely, the bulk of him upon her. His hand on her skull pushing her face into the grass. Her, biting soil. And the rain pelting on the pair of them.

Then all at once he lets go and is gone.

Leaving Bridie on the ground as slack as a snapped-necked rabbit.

She looks up and sees nothing but Cora running with a bundle in her arms in the direction of the river.

★

Cora sees the river through the rain. The downward slope of the lawn speeds her on her way. With the first blow, aimed low to her back, her face crumples, but still she holds on to the child. With the second and third blows she realises that these aren't blows with just a fist.

Shielding Sibéal with her colossal body, Cora pounds her attacker to the ground, but he has hold of her waist. He stabs at her skirts again and again. Cora barely believes all the blood.

Cora drops the child. Her right arm is shredded but she lays a downer on Gideon Eames with her left that sends him skidding. And here is Bridie, running over the lawn.

Gideon Eames is a man like any other, Bridie tells herself, as her fist makes contact with the underside of his jaw. Then he's on her, his hands on her neck and he will kill her.

Cora, bleeding heavily, crawls towards them and, with the last of her strength, holds Gideon by the neck in the crook of her great arm.

'Take her.' Cora nods to the river. 'There.'

There is a wooden landing-stage, just down from a willow tree, which spreads over the water. A sheltered spot, with a rowing boat moored there. One craft alone with no craft to follow, Bridie sees that.

Sibéal lies on her side eyes closed, white hair, blue dress. Bridie puts her arms under her, lifting her awkwardly. Sibéal, slippery with rain, is not heavy but Bridie is spent. The child is rigid, as an animal stunned: not resisting quite, but not helping. And so cold to the touch, her breath chill on Bridie's cheek.

Bridie half carries, half drags Sibéal. Behind them, the grounds are full of running, shouting men. Above them, the sky is all cloudburst and reeling, screaming gulls.

Bridie steadies herself at the river's edge: she will lower

the child into the boat, the boat filling with rainwater, and get in after. There are oars. She leans out.

Sibéal thrashes and twists in her arms with sudden, startling strength.

The child falls between landing stage and boat.

She sinks in an instant.

With one breath between them, Bridie follows.

February 1837

Chapter 43

Gan Murphy wrapped her in a blanket, gave her a carrot and carried her onto the ship. The ship dipped and rocked and strained, her funnel sent great sooty belches into the sky. As Bridie crossed the walkway in Gan's arms she peered down at the water below, sure she would never see land again.

The weather was savage and the sea should not be crossed – everyone said it. But sail the boat would, because the weather could hardly get worse and may be a long time getting better. Gan said they would take their chances. High peril on the open sea would be safer than Dublin Port.

They had waited for a steam-packet for weeks. There were others to go before them and the ship could only hold so many, although it was three times as many as a ship like that should hold. Gan would spend the fare on the drink, disappearing for days to earn it again. Coming back smelling of earth and whiskey, or sweat and brimstone. They lodged in a place of low inns and hovels, puddled cobbles and freezing winds. But Gan lived in the snug at Maguire's, a squat, frowning place at the end of a blind lane. There he smoked with his hat pulled down over his eyes. Bridie ran about the lanes with the other children. They were a bedraggled tribe made of rags and snot. They would chase one another, calling godless curses across the courtyard and tenements, until they were slapped and thrown out to roam the streets again.

Bridie had no real friends and nor did she want for them, until the day she came across a fight in the courtyard. All of them were going on the one boy, hanging off him, biting lumps out of him, beating the hell out of him. The boy, outnumbered, was falling under.

Without thinking, Bridie picked up a bucket of water and threw it over them, to scatter them like fighting dogs. A few left off but the others paid no mind, so she picked up a piece of wood and waded in.

This set them laughing. At the tiny, grim-faced girl waving a bedpost the same height as herself. The boy on the ground took his chance and was off without a second glance, climbing up over the roof of the privy.

'That's Ronan,' they had said. 'He's a little bastard.'

And he was.

Ronan would hit you as soon as look at you. He was no more than eight, fought like a man and was made for trouble.

He was strong; he could lift Bridie easily. He showed her, later, when he crept back into the courtyard. And, Jesus, he was fast: she watched him run and climb and punch the air. After that they spent every day together and when it was time to sail they were loaded up together, Ronan close at Gan's heels as he carried Bridie on board, but nowhere to be seen when the officials came around.

Gan paid deck fare and found a corner. When the storm worsened he was still asleep with his hat over his face. He couldn't be woken even though the ship bucked and swung and the waves rinsed the deck. Gan slept on, while all around the people wailed and retched and prayed.

At each tip Bridie screamed, at every plough she sobbed, until she felt a hand in hers and saw his face. Long-lashed liquid brown eyes, bright black hair.

'If we live we'll get married,' he said. 'Will we?'

Bridie nodded. 'We will, Ronan.'

'Grand, so.'

The ship lurched, an impossible angle, and the whole expanse of the sea rose up to claim them.

'Can you swim, Bridie?' he asked.

'I can't, can you, Ronan?'

'Like a bloody rock.'

And they had laughed.

They were counted off the steam-packet at Liverpool Dock, like a delivery of sheep. Only they were filthier than sheep, the feckless Irish. Reeking of peat-smoke and firewater, loaded with lice. Bridie looked around for Ronan. She began to despair of ever seeing him again when she did see him: being dragged down the gangplank by a port official who had caught himself a stowaway.

Bridie let go of Gan's hand and ran towards Ronan. A man grabbed her and she bit his arm, so that he dropped her and she fell.

The shock of the water – her eyes opened wider than wide and she bobbed like a bottle.

Ronan saw her, rushed to her, jumped into the water for her.

She saw that. And then she was under.

She was landed on the dock vomiting salt water, Gan or someone crouching, rubbing her back, sitting her up, her skirts heavy and one boot gone, trying to crawl between the legs of onlookers to where she could see him.

'He can't bloody swim,' she screamed, only the words came out as a sobbing croak.

'He can't bloody swim.'

'I was no more than a girl,' whispers Bridie into the darkness.

'I was no more than a boy,' the darkness whispers back.

She can feel his breath on her face.

October 1863

Chapter 44

Bridie is drowning with her eyes open. She sees nothing but rushing river. She hears nothing but rushing river. The noise and the ferocity under – you would never know it from above.

Nearby, Sibéal wakes in the water.

She watches a figure sink past her, strange fish.

Sibéal follows, nudging this curiosity with her shoulder and with her forehead. But still she sinks; the small woman, with her skirts swelling and her hair spiralling and the bubbles popping from her nose and mouth.

Sibéal swims down alongside; she touches the woman's face with her fingers and looks into her eyes.

★

Bridie is born coughing onto the bank, downriver from the mooring. She sees the rowing boat along from her, hardly rocking, not even at a bob now, as if nothing at all has just happened. And the rain ceased and the sunlight, weak, through the willow. She crawls forward, stopping to untie with numb fingers the cords on her petticoats. They slump back into the river like glean. At the sound of shouting she looks up. Gideon

· 393 ·

is coming down the lawn. He limps to the mooring, then up and down it. He scrutinises the water near the boat. And then he sees Bridie.

He comes slewing to where she lies in churned mud. He drags her up the bank as if he's saving her. Turning her on her back, he knocks her head on the ground. His hand on her jaw and chin, her still coughing from the river. The expression on his face familiar: certainty and contempt.

He wore it the day he killed Della and whenever he saw Eliza.

Up close, she remembers the colour of his eyes – a blue eye, seen through a crack in the stable wall.

His hands on her neck now, her throat, for he's in earnest. As she chokes, she raises her hand and touches his cheek, his beard, with gentle fingers.

Gideon loosens his grip in surprise, as if hit with a stinging blow.

Her eyes on his, Bridie runs her hand over his hair, behind his head, under his collar, to his neck. Between them: close as they are, their breath, fast and hot. And the smell of his sweat and pomade and her pipe-smoke and river-water.

At her touch, his expression changes: revulsion and interest, or somewhere between. Bridie motions that she wants to say something, to whisper; he's broken her voice.

He hesitates.

Look closely: Bridie's fingers, so light on his neck his nape hairs rise beneath. Her other hand, stealthy, pulls up her skirts, moves to her bent leg, feels round her thigh, finds what is strapped there.

Gideon Eames puts his ear to her mouth; Bridie grits her teeth against it, as she stabs him.

He grunts in answer and turns his face away. Bridie drives deeply; she will jag him neck to nethers and never stop.

Hands pull him off her, hands restrain her and hands

wrestle the dagger from her. Arms hold her while she cries and curses.

In the river a splash stops proceedings.

It reaches up over the bank and sends the rowing boat hopping.

Gideon sees, everyone does. He slips the constable restraining him, punching him down, and is up on his knees, his feet, down to the river's edge.

It happens in a moment: a splash and a whipped arc described by something sleek, fast-moving.

And Gideon is gone.

On the surface of the river bubbles form and break.

Chapter 45

In Albery Hall's yellow drawing-room Bridie downs another glass of Gideon Eames's fine whiskey. She ought to be on her knees but she's straight-up sober. She watches from the French window as Rose's men search the river-bank in the dying light. Rose moves among them, calm and authoritative. Cora has been taken to hospital, Bridie having made a good fist at patching her friend up. Edgar Kempton Jones was admitted alongside her with severe blood loss from multiple lacerations and a gunshot wound. He was lucky on that score: the bullet glanced him.

Rose's master criminal is nowhere to be found. Rose, as angry as Bridie has ever seen him, has sent half his men out combing the surroundings. But he holds no hope. Dorcas Chapman is long gone.

Bridie sat for the longest while in Mrs Donsie's kitchen, in the cook's old chair, by the cook's old range. On the card table next to her: a half-smoked cigar, a half-empty medicine bottle and a half-read volume (overdue) from Mudie's library. After reading the title, not without surprise, Bridie turned to the first pages and read them.

She has the book with her now. Where else but lodged

in her thief's stuff-pocket? And will she show it to Rose? Another time, perhaps. She crosses the room and pours another glass for herself.

Ruby watches her. She feels his eyes on her. He hasn't left her side since the river. She can't look at his face for the concern on it.

'I lost another child, Ruby.'

'But you saved that one.' Ruby points at Myrtle, asleep on a chaise longue, Bridie's cape thrown over her spangles.

Bridie walks back to the window.

Chapter 46

Mr Wilks, bell hanger, is delighted, as always, to see Bridie home. He perches by his window fashioning his gudgeons and watching out for her. But he is disappointed of further sightings in the days that follow. Bridie keeps to her rooms. She sits for long hours, smoking and thinking of the past, of Eliza and Edgar, Dorcas and Della, Gideon and Dr John Eames. But most of all she thinks of Sibéal. In her mind she sees her, drawing near, under the water; she feels her little hands on her face again, the twisting of her body, the strength of her in her own element.

Sibéal's are the only eyes Bridie sees in her dreams now, pearl darkening to jet, and they are not frightening at all.

Cora doesn't bother Bridie with corsets and hairbrushes and London news. On that score there's not much to tell, for the floods have subsided and the rainfall is commensurate with the season (although there are omens that the winter will be direful harsh). Otherwise there's news Bridie doesn't need to hear. That the bodies of the two people recently drowned in Windsor – a man and a small girl – have not been recovered. When Cora remembers the events that day her wounds hurt, but really they are healing well, for Bridie dresses them diligently. Cora is confident she could still give a good clatter, although her days of man-throwing may be numbered. Besides, Cora has her large hands full with more peaceable activities – what with Bridie's new young charge in the rooms above Wilks's of Denmark Street. Myrtle Harbin, chocolate pudding around her mouth, dancing her one-eyed doll between the parlour and the kitchen. When Jem can be spared from his new job, tea-boy at Scotland Yard, he visits. He looks dapper these days, now that the flower in his buttonhole is real. And then Cora and the children sit down for another instalment of *Wagner the Wehr-Wolf* with Myrtle feigning fear, safe in the housemaid's capacious lap and always a slice of something on the kitchen table.

Sometimes Cora is distracted, gazing off in the direction of Chelsea and the Cremorne Gardens. Perhaps the *Queen of Snakes* spares a thought for her, as she stands wrapped in a python watching the carpenters strike the stage and the clowns muster the penguins. The circus will be leaving soon and Euryale with it – could there have been any other ending? Lester Lufkin, with the buoyancy of Old Coppernose himself, remains undefeated by his Cremorne fiasco. He has his sights set high, *Royal* high. He is planning a show fit for a queen – bigger, stranger and more marvellous!

But for some, life continues in a quieter fashion. Gale and Widmerpole welcome new worshippers daily, it seems. Only this week an elderly pipistrelle and a drabble-coated vixen joined the congregation at Highgate Chapel. And below them, the crypt has been sealed and the lost mother and her merrow-child forgotten. In his Brixton windmill, Prudhoe tends flasks and test-tubes, books and corvids, dreaming up ever-wilder smokable concoctions. His latest broadside is a cautionary tale about collecting, with thinly disguised characters you would almost certainly recognise.

While life goes on, Bridie sits and thinks.

Ruby stays by her side. They hardly talk: but this is not contentment and Ruby knows it.

As he knows it can't last.

He yearns to lie down and close his eyes. He wonders if a dead man can be exhausted. He wonders if Bridie has noticed.

She has, of course. She keeps the curtains drawn and the gas-lights dim, for he is fading daily. Today she can barely see him as he stands by the window, peering out at the visitor below.

'It's the inspector,' says Ruby. 'He has roses.'

Bridie draws on her pipe. 'Good for him.'

Ruby listens. 'There's the sound of Cora hobbling down the stairs to answer the door. Will you be indisposed again?'

'I will.'

'He's a good man, Bridget.'

Bridie glances up at him. He holds his hat in his hand with the air of a man taking his leave.

And all at once Bridie's heart turns in her. 'What are you even saying?'

Bridie notices the tattoos on his body. They are no longer moving.

The anchor has taken itself up, its rope coiled neatly, the skull's teeth meet in a rictus grin and the mermaid gazes fixedly far into the horizon, shielding her eyes with her inked hand. The heart on Ruby's chest is complete now, still and whole. Bridie reads her name on it, etched in blue, where it has always been.

Bridget

'I think you should live a bit, Bridie.'

And she is crying, sobbing, with the heart floored in her, but not looking away, not now, not ever.

He holds her with his eyes for the longest time.

For this is their parting: as sudden and slow, surprising and foreseen as any parting. Between together and apart: an eye-blink and all of eternity.

'What do I have to do?' she asks.

But he is already gone.

★

Cora opens the door to the parlour a fraction and they look inside. Inspector Valentine Rose paces from the fireplace to the window and back again. Stopping briefly only to examine the large unfathomable mechanism on the mantelpiece.

Bridie runs a reckoning eye over him. 'He is different, somehow.'

'It's the frock coat, it's new.'

'What's his business?'

'He wouldn't say, but it'll be *personal* business,' Cora says slyly. She nudges Bridie. 'Will I give him a clatter? I could try holding him upside down—'

'With your injuries? I'd rather he admitted to nothing.'

Cora snorts and sails, a-lop, into the kitchen.

When Bridie opens the door of the parlour, Rose turns and smiles.

Bridie returns his smile, a little stiffly, perhaps. 'You're here on business, Rose?'

'On a matter of great importance and even greater delicacy, Bridie.'

'Do you represent yourself in this matter, Rose?'

'I do.'

'Let me guess: you've a case, something strange and unsolvable.'

Rose glances at the bouquet in his hand. 'Not quite.'

Bridie ignores the flowers. A spark, devilish, kindles in her eyes. 'Does it involve Dorcas Chapman?'

· 401 ·

Rose frowns.

'Before we proceed, Rose, would you care to join me in a drop of Madeira?' Bridie smiles, a little wider now, perhaps. 'It can only help matters.'

She goes to the door and picks up the bell; Cora is in the room before she can ring it.

'Would you bring the Madeira, Cora? The special vintage.'

Cora winks at Bridie and grins at the guest.

Bridie has a plan.

Acknowledgements

With huge gratitude to Susan Armstrong (C+W), the very best of agents, for your wisdom, creativity and encouragement – and for the fun of developing ideas with you from start to finish. To my editor, the ever-brilliant Francis Bickmore, and to Megan Reid, thank you both for your editorial magic. A massive thank you goes to Luke Speed (Curtis Brown) and to Emma Finn, Jake Smith-Bosanquet, Alexander Cochran, Clare Conville and all the supportive people at C+W. To the talented crowd at Canongate, particularly Becca Nice, Vicki Watson, Jenny Fry, Jamie Byng, Jamie Norman, Anna Frame, Pete Adlington, Leila Cruickshank and Vicki Rutherford – thank you for all you do for my books and for me. To my fellow writers, friends and the people and places who have championed my work from the start – thank you. To my fellow writers, friends and the people and places who have championed my work from the start – thank you. Special thanks go to Rick O'Shea and his magnificent book club, Simon Mayo and the Radio 2 Book Club, the Reading Agency and all the brilliant Indie bookshops getting my books into the hands of readers. Your support means the world to me, everyone.

To all the people who have read, advised, listened to my

ideas and answered my questions with patience and good-humour, I thank you. Special thanks to Eva Farenden (my *favourite* reader), Gavin Clarke, Dr Mary Shannon, Michelle Birkby, Ken Titmuss (map man and walk finder), Edmund 'Aspic' White, Lucinda Hawksley, Christopher Skaife 'The Ravenmaster', Helen Barrell (for her wonderful book on Professor Alfred Swaine Taylor – Prudhoe's role model), Alex Arlango, Rob 'Jim' Briggs for the window debates, Dr Ailsa Grant-Turton and Dr Matt Lodder. Any deviation from the realm of historical fact (accidental or deliberate) is entirely my own fault.

To my family, thank you for always supporting me.

Finally, to Travis McBride, I owe you a debt of gratitude for your belief at the very earliest stage, when this was a small, little acorn of an idea.